R. J. Eliason

The Mage Chronicles

R. J. Eliason

Editor: Janet Fix

Cover Art: Aidana Willowraven

DEDICATION

This book is dedicated to the thousands of fantasy fans I have met at conventions and elsewhere. I have had many hours of great conversation with you. Thank you.

CONTENTS

ACKNOWLEDGMENTS

A novel is the work of many people. It's hard to even know where to begin with acknowledgments. This work is built upon ideas given to me by hundreds of fellow fans, honed by a legion of beta readers and perfected by my editor, Janet Fix. The cover is courtesy of Aidana Willowraven.

Thanks to all who made this novel possible.

1 ASHLEY LA'MARGIN THE FOURTH

Mary stood on the brown cobblestone of Muted Lane and waited while the oxen cart rumbled by. As it passed her, she caught a glimpse of Muted Market. She wondered, as always, how such a noisy place came by the name "Muted." She crossed the lane, feeling the warmth of the stones underneath her sandals as she left the shade of the apartments behind her.

To her right was the market itself. It was a single-story building the size of a small park and without walls. Arched pillars of granite stood every fifteen feet, and the roof rose over them in billowing waves, like a giant pavilion frozen in stone. That such heavy stone could be shaped into such a delicate structure made the market one of Tomlin City's marvels.

Not that those inside were paying much attention to the architecture above them. The market was crowded. *Then again, it was always crowded.* Merchants hawked their wares in loud voices, haggled with customers, and complained to each other of the day's business. The market's assault on the senses did not stop at sound. Jewelers flashed bits of gold and silver. A tailor threw a bright brocade of silk around a woman's form with a practiced flourish. Small, contained fires heated an incredible variety of pots, pans, and skillets, which in turned contained an even more incredible variety of foods and spices. The aroma mixed with the sweat of the many patrons and hung thick in the air.

Mary ignored the market, and for the moment, it returned the favor. Mary was a slight figure, almost a head shorter than the nearest man in front of her. She was thin and had long, coppery-red hair pulled back into a long braid. She wore a simple dress of burnt orange held fast around the waist with a silk scarf. A pentacle, embroidered into the sleeve of the dress, marked her as a healer.

To the left of the market was the Tower of Ashley La'Margin. If the market was one of the marvels of the city of Tomlin, the mage's tower was *the* marvel. Set about two hundred feet back from the lane, the building was maybe a hundred feet across at its base and rose to nearly five hundred feet high. It literally towered over the market and every building nearby. It was composed of white stone that appeared to be seamless.

The land around the base of the tower was entirely covered in a hedgerow maze. Where the maze opened onto the lane, there stood twin sandstone sphinxes, eighteen feet tall. There was an almost imperceptible sound of stone grinding on stone as one of the sphinxes turned its head to look at Mary as she drew near. Though slight, the sound cut through the din of the marketplace. There was a collective rolling gasp as the people in the crowd turned their attention toward the tower.

A hand reached out and pulled Mary from the lane.

"Careful, young maid," the merchant said. "Wouldn't want to see you crushed under the heels of that beast."

"What devilry is the mage up to now?" a nearby woman wondered out loud.

"Appearances can sometimes be deceiving," Mary said.

"Aye," the man agreed, misreading her completely. "I thought they were mere statues. They've never moved an inch as long as I've been at the market."

Mary smiled. "Be not afraid; they mean no harm." As she stepped back into the lane she chuckled to herself. *Young maid indeed. The fool doesn't realize I could well be the one who delivered him.*

All of the collective eyes of the market were on Mary as she crossed the lane and approached the sphinx. It dropped its head, and its mouth gaped wide.

In her mind, Mary felt its excitement. "Yes, Azroth," she said aloud, for the benefit of those in the market. "I have brought you a gift."

As she reached into her small purse, a raspy sandstone tongue extended from the sphinx's mouth. It cupped its tongue delicately, and she placed a small river stone onto the tongue.

In a single swift movement the tongue was gone and the sphinx returned to its former, immobile state.

A sense of contentment and the memories of other stones, other places, rolled off the sphinx.

"I have one for you too, Shemazai," Mary said to the second sphinx. Slowly, and with a much greater sense of dignity, the second sphinx bent and accepted its gift.

This will be the talk of the market for weeks to come, she thought.

They are all fools anyway, Azroth said in her mind, settling itself into its usual stony, watchful silence.

Without a backward glance, Mary entered the maze. There was a brief pause, then the noise of the market rose again. Inside, most of the merchants broke into loud, speculative conversations—about discovering the sphinxes were real and about the young girl who seemed to know them. A few merchants stayed quiet; wondering, no doubt, how many of their misdeeds had been observed by the statutes and to whom they had been reported.

Mary's feet took her within the maze. She stopped briefly at the imposing main entrance. She had brought another, more mundane gift for the doorman, a pastry from the bakery near Cornall Hospital, where Mary both lived and worked. She did not ask for entrance. He understood.

She passed the much smaller and simpler servant's door just within the maze as well. Her feet sought the student's entrance, hidden deep within the hedge. More than a decade had passed since she was a student of the mage, but she felt intuitively that this was the best approach. She could only surmise she had guessed correctly when she found Ashe himself was waiting for her at the student's entrance.

"I am delighted to see you, Mary," he said as she approached. He looked as he always did, a tall, graying man, who could be described, depending on his mood, as either imposing or fatherly. He was wearing brown leggings and a light tan shirt with an embroidered edging. The shirt was simple in design but of high-quality construction. The hair on his head, though graying, was full and worn short. His movements, as he stepped forward to give Mary a hug, were strong and graceful, belying the age of his appearance.

"Indeed it's been too long," she replied, returning the hug with warmth. "But I suspect you did not call me back simply because you missed seeing me."

"Indeed not," he replied. "Though I have missed you. Still we need not sit on the doorstep and talk." He ushered her inside.

As they walked along the gently curving corridor, Mary said, "So for whom was that display outside?"

"The sphinxes?" he replied. "A trifling matter."

"It will be the talk of the market for months, if not years, to come."

"Indeed." Sensing her curiosity he went on, "Some of the merchants wish to have entertainment in the market at night."

"I can recall when they had minstrels and dances," Mary said, "and for a while there was the theater group."

"These are far more illicit and unpleasant entertainments, I regret," Ashe continued. "I thought it would do well to remind them the market is watched."

"Very civic of you," she said.

Ashe was fond of the number three, and just as he had three entrances to the tower, there were three rooms that he used for greeting visitors. Near the main entrance, he had a throne room of sorts, where he could sit high above his visitor, to impress or intimidate. He used it often with petitioners who came to request magic from him. He had a business office where he would sit behind a large desk. It was there he took his peers, men of power from the city council, and court officials who sought his advice. Then he had a small sitting room for more personal visits, lessons with a rare apprentice (Mary was the first apprentice he had taken in anyone's memory), a visit from a fellow mage, and the occasional individual graced with status of friend.

Today he passed all three rooms without a second glance. He ushered her instead into his private study. It was an interesting choice, and Mary could not help but wonder what it portended. Here was a singular room in a tower built around the number three. Most mages had a number they were obsessed with and for Ashe, it was three. Everything about this tower, from its dimensions to the number of rooms, was some multiple of three. The man even had three bedrooms, which Mary knew because she had shared all three rooms for a short time after her apprenticeship had ended and they had been lovers. But he had only one study. It held two simple, wooden chairs, a low table, a bookcase, which held a very select portion of Ashe's library and a window that overlooked a seaside beach — nowhere near Tomlin City, if indeed it was even in this world.

They sat, and Ashe gestured at a steaming teapot

and a selection of tea canisters on the low table. Smiling slightly, Mary pulled out her final gift, a tightly bundled Chrysanthemum flower.

"My favorite," Ashe said. "You always think of the little things, Mary. It's one of the things I love about you."

He placed the bundle in the teapot and left the lid off so they could watch the flower unfold while the tea steeped.

After a long time, Mary spoke. "You have an assignment for me, I take it?"

"I do," he replied. "Though you are no longer my apprentice and I can hardly compel you."

"Still, you may speak."

"It's an unusual request, I must warn," he said. "There is a situation in a distant province. Someone needs to look into it. A mage."

She thought about other assignments she had taken from Ashe. Mostly they were humanitarian missions, as befitted her main gift, healing. Once she had fought a demon for him. Two or three times, she had sought out other mages for rituals, herbs, or other magical lore. These last assignments had been more for her own benefit, to increase her own knowledge. None of these assignments prepared her for what Ashe said next.

"It's war, Mary. In the Barony of Cordona, a far distant corner of the empire, war is again threatening the land."

She almost laughed but caught the serious expression on her former mentor's face. "But surely there hasn't been a war in the empire for several—" She stopped abruptly before she said the word *millennia.* She knew enough history to know that was a pleasant fiction. Still . . . "For several hundred years at least."

"Three hundred forty-two years this March," Ashe said. A troubled look crossed his face. Then he laughed. "No, even that is a polite fiction. The empire lives by the sword. War is a constant companion."

He stared out the window for a long time before going on. "The emperor's peace is merely a controlled war, Mary. You must understand this. The border legions and the army fight and conquer distant worlds, all in the name of keeping war far from our borders. But this is not the war of which I speak.

"Despite the emperor's peace, or perhaps even because of it, small internal wars erupt frequently. For small nobles, hemmed in by each other, there are few ways to grow or increase their holding or power. Some play at court intrigue, some play at love—or marriages of convenience, rather. A few play at war."

"Nobles, playing at war?" Mary said. "I don't understand."

"They fight border disputes, often over trivial trumped up offenses," he said with some distaste.

"And the emperor allows this?"

"Of course not," Ashe said. "These things are stopped as soon as they come to someone's attention. But if a noble moves quickly enough, takes a village here, a town there, it's fait accompli. When the dispute is ended one lord has another village in his domain, and the other is that much smaller."

"But we are talking fighting here, right? With soldiers and spears and stuff?" she said.

"Yes."

"Don't people get hurt?"

"They get killed, Mary."

"But—"

"Mary," he interrupted, "you need to understand the kind of people we are talking about: power-hungry nobles. If it increases their holding, even a couple of acres, a hundred deaths is worth it to them."

She shuddered.

"In the Barony of Cordona, such a border dispute is currently underway," Ashe went on. "And I fear it has the potential to spiral into a much larger conflict."

"You said the emperor puts a stop to these sorts of things," she said.

"Usually," he replied and fell silent for a long time. "You must go and put a stop to this, Mary."

"Me?" she protested. "Surely there is somebody more suitable. Who usually puts a stop to these things?"

He shrugged. "The emperor cannot be everywhere, obviously. The bureaucrats usually send a simple ultimatum and that's that. Or the courts intervene; some noble house large enough to command the respect of both parties. Neither of these things has happened."

Mary watched him, trying to understand what he was saying. She took a different tack. "But the soldiers, they are part of the military, no? Do they really fight each other? Can't they just be commanded to stop?"

"Each lord must raise a certain number of soldiers for the imperial army, this is true. But they have a local militia as well, which is not beholden to the military. These are the soldiers who fight and die in these border disputes. The military can't command them. However the military certainly could intervene, and has in such situations in the past."

"Are there not war mages?" Mary asked.

"There are."

She stared out the window at the seashore, trying to put the pieces of the puzzle together. "So the bureaucrats could end this, the courts could end this, the military, the war mages, all could end this. Why haven't they?"

"That is an interesting question." He turned toward Mary, a serious look on his face. "The council of mages, the *civilian* council of mages," he clarified, "are deeply troubled by this entire situation. But we must not be seen as interfering. There are larger forces at work here. Why? I cannot say.

"However, if a healer were to show up, offering humanitarian aid, and then find some way to get both sides to sue for peace, the pretext is gone. The forces must then reveal themselves or retreat."

"And the Council of Mages wishes me to go?" She did not believe even half the council knew of her existence. She was too young, too small a mage for them to notice.

"I wish you to go," Ashe said.

After a pause, she replied, "I have always trusted you. If you ask, I will go."

***

After Mary left, another man entered the study. He appeared much younger than Ashe, little more than a boy, but when it came to mages, appearances were not be trusted. He had wavy, black hair worn loose and down to his shoulders. He was dressed in a fine tunic with brightly colored and slightly puffed sleeves, with green tights underneath. He wore an ornate belt and a blade that was too long to properly be called a dagger but too short to be called a sword. His fine leather boots made a gentle slapping noise as he walked, and his knee-length tunic swished as he sat in the now vacant chair next to Ashe.

"She will go," Ashe told the younger-looking man.

"She trusts you," he said.

"I wonder if she still will when all this is done," Ashe said.

"You did what you must."

***

Mary paused, the six-story red brick edifice of Cornall Hospital rising up on her right. She had walked the entire way home on autopilot, wrapped up in thoughts about the talk she had with Ashe and the strangest assignment he had ever given her. She looked around, trying to figure out what brought her out of her reverie. The wide lane in front of her dipped down toward the river.

On this side of the river, Tomlin City was made green by a huge network of irrigation, water pumps, and caring gardeners. The far side of the river was a patchwork of yellow and brown. Draadustin, "dry and dusty," the local slang called it, Tomlin's poor twin. It was maybe half the size of Tomlin, but it sprawled much larger. There was not a building higher than two stories to be found there.

Though she could not make out any of the buildings from here, her eyes sought to the east, toward the orphanage that had once been her home, so many years ago. The empty lot where the boy, Martin, had drawn his pictures in the sand and told his stories, Dryad watching over him. Mary shook her head. It had been years since she had thought of Martin.

"Mary!" Eli's deep voice called her name just as his arm went around her shoulder. "Impeccable timing as always. You must come to the cafeteria at once. We are having a feast in your honor."

Eli was a broad, handsome man despite a slight gut. An athletic man, once upon a time, now gone slightly to seed. He had wavy, dark hair with patches of gray. "You are worlds away," he commented as he ushered her into the shade of the hospital. His leather boots thumped on the polished wooden floors, making the attendant healers look up from their card game. Mary's sandaled feet made no more sound than they had on the lane

"Not yet," she replied.

"Oh, so the old rascal has another assignment for you?" he said. "I figured. Why else would he send for you?"

She scowled but did not respond. Eli was jealous, of course. They had known each other for some forty years and had shared so much in that time. He had many things that she did not, like a family. Two in fact: a birth family with mother, father and two brothers and a second family with his wife, Melony, and two kids of their own. Despite this, he was jealous of the one thing Mary had that he did not: magic. Eli was a great healer, but his magic potential ended there.

"So he's stealing you away yet again," he went on.

"Is it as important as saving lives here in Tomlin City?"

War. It was a vague notion to Mary. She had gone, on her days off, to see the ceremonial guard in the town center do their drills. Their spears were topped with wicked looking blades. Their scimitars flashed in the sun as they moved in precise rhythm, then banged menacingly on their opponents' shields and slid off each other. But that was merely a ceremonial display, an elaborate dance to impress visitors. War had not visited Tomlin in many ages. Mary had no idea what real war would be like.

"People die outside Tomlin City," she replied.

"I am only teasing," Eli chided her.

She saw Shanti coming down the hallway toward them. Shanti looked to be eighteen, her blonde hair and flushed face radiant. She would have been beautiful, and some would say she was still, but she was too thin, small breasted and bony, with a sharp face and prominent nose. For that, Mary was grateful. If not for these flaws someone would have wooed Shanti away from the healer's life long ago . . . and out of Mary's life, like so many others before her. Shanti was too good of a healer to waste her life as a wife to some thankful patient.

Mary knew many would say much the same about both her appearance and her talents. She too was thin, a lifelong scar of a childhood spent malnourished. She too looked to be young. Often, newcomers mistook the two of them for fellow students. Shanti found this funny and would often tell the new students horror stories about how strict and mean the teachers were. The looks on their faces when they discovered Mary was master of healers and Shanti her senior instructor were priceless.

"I've a letter from Judith Ringold," Shanti said, waving a piece of parchment.

"No letters from that woman today," Eli joked, snatching it away. He held it up high, out of the two women's reach. "If Ashe has an assignment so important he must drag our master healer from us, she certainly doesn't have time for charity cases from across the river."

Mary normally enjoyed Eli's teasing, but today she was out of sorts, her equilibrium thrown off. She reached out with her mind and flicked the parchment away.

"Hey, no fair," Eli protested as the parchment landed gently in Mary's hand. He caught her look and dropped his protest quickly.

The aroma of roasting fish caught Mary's attention as the three turned the corner into the hospital cafeteria.

"Did Eli tell you?" Shanti asked.

Mary looked up. The cafeteria was more crowded than usual. "He said something about a feast in my honor, but I assumed he was joking."

"I don't *always* kid," Eli replied in mock outrage.

"Remember the fisherman last week?" Shanti asked.

The man's hand had been caught in a net as it went over the boat's side. He was sucked deep under the water, and his hand was nearly ripped off. To make matters worse, he was dragged into a school of spiny cuttlefish. As the cuttlefish struggled against the net, their sharp poisonous spines repeatedly stabbed the helpless fisherman. He was, to anyone other than Mary, as good as dead when they carried him through the front doors. It had taken the better part of a day and the help of several senior healers for Mary to save him.

"The fisherman, yes," Mary said.

"He was poor," Eli said, "but popular. The fisher guild has donated an entire day's worth of catch to the hospital. A huge feast tonight and plenty of smoked fish for the future."

"Ashe gave you an assignment?" Shanti asked.

Mary nodded.

"Saving a village from a rampaging demon?" Shanti's eyes sparkled. "Or stopping a rare disease from destroying a town?"

Mary smiled and shook her head.

"Oh, oh, I know! You have to seduce one of his old mage friends to discover some secret magic," Shanti joked.

Sometimes Mary wished she had not shared so much about prior trips she had taken at Ashe's behest. "You treat it like it's an adventure novel," she chided.

"To a simple gal like me, it is," Shanti protested. "Mary to the rescue!"

"And this request?" Eli asked, standing at her other side.

Mary frowned. "Unusual. Let's get our dinner first and find a quiet corner."

∗∗∗

"War?" Shanti asked. "In the empire? What about the thousand years peace?"

"It is more like three hundred years," Eli replied. "They exaggerate a bit. It may well be close to a thousand years since a war has touched the inner worlds, though."

"It's not a full-blown war," Mary said. "Just," she searched for the words that Ashe had used, "a border dispute or something. Apparently these things crop up all the time amongst the petty nobles in the more distant corners of the empire. They are technically illegal, but the emperor can't be everywhere at once. Besides it is the only way for the nobility to increase their holdings in some regions, so they fight little battles and quit before someone notices.

"As for the emperor—well, the bureaucracy anyway—they don't want to be seen as interfering. So they don't do anything official unless it is really bad, like a full-blown war. Instead, the court will intervene, usually indirectly."

Eli interrupted. "But this doesn't make any sense. Surely a combat mage or a hard magician would be sent. I've read somewhere about crack military units designed for that sort of thing. But you? Why?"

Mary shrugged. This was the point she did not understand either, and why she needed to talk about it. "Ashe was . . ." she paused, and then decided honesty was the best, "uncharacteristically vague and evasive. He said he didn't know why the military was not intervening, or the combat mages. The mage council felt they should do it, but delicately. And they want me."

"But you're a healer," Shanti said. "Even your magic, it's mostly healing stuff. You don't do war. Why would Ashe put you up to it?"

"That's the strangest part," Mary said. "I got the impression that it wasn't Ashe at all, but someone else on the council." She stopped. Who on the council even knew of her existence? Aside from Ashe and his friend Larsa, she didn't know any mages. She had met one or two others of Ashe's level, but they were few and far between. Her meetings had been brief, and while memorable to her, would they be to the mage?

"So this place?" Eli raised his brows.

"Sohen," Mary said. "I have directions, but it is nowhere I have heard of, or should have. It is tiny and remote, so remote I can't get there directly. It'll take me weeks at best. I have never been so far."

"Sohen, huh?" Eli mused taking the written directions that Mary proffered. "Never heard of it either, but it's a big empire. Damn these directions are complicated. Can't you just jump there?"

"I am jumping there," Mary pointed out, "but there aren't any direct gates. None of the gates in Tomlin even connect with that quadrant. I have to fly by airship over the Jinten Mountains to the city of Bezra to find a gate that will take me to the edge of the quadrant, and then take about half dozen different gates to cross the quadrant."

"I didn't know the empire was that big," Shanti said, awed.

"Or that anywhere was that remote," Eli added.

"At least I will get to see a lot of the empire this way," Mary said with a smile.

"The back ass end of it anyway," Eli said. "I doubt there are any tourist destinations along this route."

"I don't have time for sightseeing anyway. People are dying out there." Mary waved vaguely outside the hospital.

"Mary to the rescue!" Shanti laughed.

"So that's it?" Eli said. "You go there and negotiate a peace between these two lords, get them to agree to behave like good little children?"

"Something of the sort." Mary shrugged. She assumed that was her assignment. She knew little to nothing about war and less about how they started or how to end one. Why had Ashe given her such an assignment?

She took a deep breath and sighed. It was just another of Ashe's tests, she decided. She had been sent to deal with a demon once. She had not known anything about that either, and told Ashe as much. He sent her anyway and to her own surprise she did it—and discovered a lot about magic on the way.

"You aren't going have to do any fighting?" Shanti asked.

Mary felt a chill go through her. "I should hope not." This was something that was bothering her. She was being sent into a war. She knew nothing of fighting. She had seen plenty of violence as a healer, but that was after the fact. She tended the injured, staunched the wounds, and healed them. Not since her youth had she faced violence directly. That was a world away from who she was now. Then she had run. How would she handle it now?

"Well, I should get to work," Mary said. "There is much I need to do before I can leave. I need to find someone to fill in as master healer for me."

"A volunteer," Eli said, indicating himself.

"Thank you," Mary said. To Shanti, she added, "You will take my classes for me?"

"Of course," Shanti replied.

"Then that takes care of the lion's share. I don't

know how to repay you, or what I would do without the two of you," Mary said.

"I expect you would completely fall apart," Eli assured her.

"You can repay us by coming home safe and sound," Shanti said.

"And with some good stories," Eli added.

2 THE HERETIC'S BOX

Half an hour later Mary was sitting on a pillow in the middle of the floor of her small dorm room staring at a box. It was a simple rectangular box without any adornment, maybe two hand widths long and slightly more than one wide. For as simple as it was, it was beautiful. It was hard wood, dark, smooth, and covered with a varnish that brought out the natural grain patterns of the wood.

She would have to get rid of it. She hadn't technically needed the box for some years now and keeping it was foolish and sentimental. It was a dangerous thing to have. Still, she loved it.

She reached over and flipped the box open. It opened at the top and on the sides, revealing a small platform. On the back of the top was a mirror. The platform had a small carved basin to hold an offering and a metal candle holder.

Neatly wrapped in brown paper were a handful of

small candles, a box of matches, and several little cones of incense. She set a tiny, violet flower she had found outside in the basin and lit a candle. She bowed three times to the mirror.

"I recognize the divinity within," she began, "and through my own divinity, I reach out to the divinity of all things . . ."

Mary had practiced Oomutoo for many years. She had mastered the highest levels of practice where no box or ritual was needed. However, she liked using the mirror and candle. It reminded her of the peace she had found during what she thought of as the troubling times.

The problem was that Oomutoo was a heresy. It was forbidden by the Reformed Church of the Empire. In Tomlin, it was common enough. Peddlers could be found in almost any market who, with careful asking, would sell "from under the cart" short pamphlets explaining the beliefs and practices of those who sought the spirit in all things.

When caught, which was infrequent, they got a slap on the wrist. The pamphlets were destroyed and the peddler paid a small fine or, at worst, lost their license to peddle. That was nothing compared to what could happen in other, stricter parts of the empire. There were places where the harshest punishment, torture and death, were routinely given out.

For the followers, it was much the same. She had never in all her years heard of anyone in Tomlin being imprisoned for the practice. Many people more or less openly followed the beliefs. But it could cost you. Just a few years ago, someone in administration got wind of an Oomutoo group informally meeting in the hospital. Several junior healers lost their jobs and one senior healer was censured. Mary hadn't been involved in that group, though she had been tempted to join. She shuddered to think what would have happened. She had not had a life outside this hospital in more years than she cared to remember. She did not know how she would be able to start a new life at her age.

Finishing her invocation Mary settled herself into the wisdom pose, her legs curled under her and her head down, resting on the floor. *How? How will I face war? Violence?*

Immediately she felt her body slip into the trance and the spirits rush upon her. She felt herself floating then tumbling like a leaf in the wind. A sense of peace stole over her. She relaxed and went with the flow, a feeling of great power coursing through her body.

When Mary came to, her body was stiff. She had no idea how long she had been laying there, but judging from her joints, it had been a long while. The vision had been glorious, the most potent she had experienced in a long time. But it made no sense to her. It had been the same throughout, always flowing and floating through lines of energy. What did that have to do with violence? She closed the box and put it back under her bed, still wondering about her vision.

***

Mary could hear Markus Strengelm's voice coming from the auditorium well before she opened the door. Markus was at the podium, lecturing as she entered. The entire classroom turned to take her in.

"Why, it's the master healer," Markus said. "To what do we owe this honor?"

The flash in his eyes showed that he did not see any interruption to his class as an honor, and he would certainly have let anyone of lesser rank know this. Mary schooled herself not to react. She didn't like Markus. He was arrogant and opinionated. The student healers, mostly young girls, adored the handsome, well-dressed Markus, and he in turn loved the attention. Joseph, the administrator, had reminded Mary on numerous occasions that Markus's family was incredibly wealthy and his presence greatly increased the hospital's standing. But Mary tolerated Markus because underneath it all, he was a very talented healer—and, thinking of Judith's letter, because he could be easily manipulated.

"I am terribly sorry to interrupt like this," Mary said. "But I have a rather urgent request to make. I have been called away and am likely to be gone some time." There was a brief tittering of conversation as the students took in this news. "There is unfortunately another rather urgent matter closer to home which I cannot attend to. A friend who runs an orphanage in Draadustin has written, saying that several of her charges are suffering from some new intestinal disease."

Markus tisked at her pronouncement. As a student, he had made no secret of his disdain for the poor "charity cases" across the river, but as a teacher he knew he must appear more caring. Which is why Mary choose to interrupt his class for this request instead of asking him in private.

"I was hoping you could maybe take a few choice

healers and look into this?" Mary finished.

Markus tisked again. "The poverty, the malnutrition, and the filth that so many on that side of the river live in, it's half their problem right there. It makes the perfect breeding ground for such diseases."

She almost laughed. It was meant as a snide comment, but he had boxed himself into the corner now. "Maybe while you are there, you could look into that as well. A better irrigation system at the orphanage could go a long way . . ."

Markus nodded, his eyes were dark. "Of course, consider it done. And blessing on your trip. I hope that goes well."

As she left the auditorium, the gnome Kendran slid from the shadows and paced her. "I would look into this for you, if you wish," he said.

"I know you would," Mary said with a smile. The first time she had taken Kendran with her to Draadustin, he had been terrified. A ranger and a veteran of the border legions, he was used to the woods and wild places. The sheer press of humanity had unnerved him.

But the people of Draadustin were poor. Kendran may have known nothing of cities or humans, but he understood poverty all too well. He had grown up on a reservation, with too many gnomes and too little land for them to maintain their traditional hunting lifestyle. The only escape from the bone-crushing poverty was military service; gnomes were prized trackers and rangers. Once he got used to the city, Kendran had been Mary's right hand on many errands of mercy.

"If Markus goes," Mary continued, "then half his class will go too. Besides, the kids will need followup visits and care. The border legions could call you up at any time."

"True," he agreed. "And your other errand? Will it keep you away that long?"

"Perhaps I should ask you to do that one for me," she remarked. Kendran had no doubt seen plenty of war with the border legions. He seemed to sense her reluctance to talk further and did not ask more.

***

Joseph, the hospital administrator, didn't even look up from his ledger as Mary entered. She found herself talking to his bald head, his ears and a few stray tufts of hair at either side.

"I know," he said without introduction. "I've heard already. You've got to go on some sort of trip for your old teacher." He sighed. "I could say how much I need you, but I know it won't do any good. Besides I owe you far too many favors."

"That's true," Mary said.

"You are going to have to cover your own classes though. I can replace most of your shifts at the hospital, but I can't compel the senior healers to teach."

"Shanti and Eli will share those duties. Kendran will teach first aid as long as he's here. He's really better at that anyway."

Still not looking up, Joseph slid a sheet of parchment across his desk. "Of course, of course. Here's the sabbatical slip. We'll do our best." Just as she was leaving he looked up, his gray eyes and tight lips pursed. "And Mary? Good luck."

***

"You're up late," the young woman said as Mary joined her in the line. "Anything going on?"

It was late, and Mary was exhausted. It took her several minutes to place the woman. Sherle was her name. She was a midlevel healer, journeyman class. She had passed her training and was working toward independent practice. They were not particularly close, but close enough for casual conversation.

"Just checking in on a few last minute details," Mary replied. "Seeing a few patients one last time."

"One last time?" Sherle asked as a bored halfling woman spooned stew into their respective bowls. "Are they going somewhere, or you?"

They left the lunch line and took an empty seat in the cafeteria. There were plenty to be had. This was the midnight meal, served for the benefit of those healers who must work through the night. If all who were awake in the hospital at that hour took their break at once, they would have barely filled one table.

"It's me," Mary said as they sat down. "I have to take a leave of absence. I don't know how long I will be gone."

"Is it family?" Sherle asked. "Someone sick?"

"No," she replied. "It's business."

Sherle did not question this answer, but began to eat. Mary felt a sudden tug, an instinctual tingle. Trusting her intuition, she leaned closer to the young woman.

"I have something I would like to give away before I go, a box. Are you interested in such a thing?"

"A box?" Sherle asked. She hesitated. Mary knew that she understood what sort of box. After a pause, she said, "Yeah, I'd like that."

3 THE AIRSHIP

Mary's small pack bounced against her back and shoulders. She shivered slightly in the chilly air. The earliest rays of dawn were creeping over Tomlin City and soon, she knew, she would be warm enough.

Around her were signs that the city was beginning to stir. A few bums still slept off last night's debauchery in alleyways or under doorways, but already the bakers were feeding logs into ovens, hoping to finish their day's work before the afternoon sun made it unbearable to tend the baking. Merchants sleepily unpacked their wares in various markets as she passed.

She looked up the hill, away from the morning sun, and wondered briefly whether she should feel happy or sad about how easily her life had been put into order and on hold.

Sherle had been delighted when she saw the box. She had learned the rudiments of Oomutoo from an aunt who was also a healer. The teachings mirrored the life of a healer in so many ways, but Sherle had been scared to pursue things openly. This was her first real initiation.

Mary worried slightly that the initiation itself and one time through the ritual was hardly enough training for a devotee of the box. She had recommended a peddler who, the last she knew, sold the appropriate pamphlet. She could only hope that would be enough. Sherle seemed genuine in her desire to know the spirit, and Mary was content to see the box in her hands.

The other healers either respected Mary, owed her favors, or both. In one short day, almost every teaching assignment and work shift had been covered. And these were mostly the extent of Mary's life. She had no apartment or house to sublet. She had no current lover to say a tearful goodbye to. She had no family to inform.

An elderly baker waved her over. He held out a small pastry for her to sample. It was filled with a spicy lentil filling. She tried to offer him a coin from her purse. He waved it away, showing a long pale scar across his arm. "I owe you," he said. She paused and decided, on the whole, she was content with her life as it had been.

The far end of Tomlin, opposite Draadustin in so many ways, rose to a tall bluff. Here the houses were shorter but more elaborate and set back from the lane by low walls and gardens. Most housed only one family, and perhaps four or five servants.

The commercial district that nestled directly under the bluff had no booths or stalls, no hawkers in the street. Instead, the entire lane was made of permanent shops. A finely dressed merchant with a book under one arm was unlocking the front door of one of the shops.

Mary was engulfed suddenly in shadow and looked up to watch the airship slide gently into the dock. If it had fallen, it would have filled the entire lane and crushed shops on either side. Ships such as these had once plied the rivers and oceans (and in places they still did). It had a smooth, long keel for cutting through air or water. Even from underneath, she could see the wide, round shapes of the brightly colored silk balloons that floated above the ship.

Mary found the long staircase that led up to the dock at the top of the bluff.

"Do the balloons really hold it aloft?" a small girl asked an older man, her father presumably, as they mounted the steps beside Mary.

"Well, see it up there," the man replied.

"What if the balloons popped?" the girl asked.

Mary smiled. "There is high magic involved as well." The girl gave her a sharp look. Mary went on. "The military craft and the dragon hunting vessels do without any balloons. But the civilian lines learned long ago that most people have trouble trusting their lives to magic and are more comfortable if there is something that gives them the sense of being held up."

The girl looked at her father as if to see if he would contradict Mary. He rubbed his chin. The girl regarded Mary, her eyes scanning her up and down. Mary's simple dress, her shrug, and her small bag did not, apparently, equal "world traveler" in the girl's mind. "Have you ever flown on one?" she challenged.

"Yes," Mary replied, "twice now. This will be my

third such trip."

The girl's eyes went wide, and she looked to her father. He spied the pentacle on Mary's sleeve. "A healer, yes," he said to his daughter. "They must travel to help people, no?"

Mary nodded.

"We are going to pick up my Uncle Enzo," the girl said. "He's an engineer. He had to spend four whole months in Shep, helping to build a bridge. He's coming home now."

They had reached the platform. Mary turned back and looked down on Tomlin City. To the right, Ashe's tower stood out, an easy landmark. Far to the left, she spied the squat pile of buildings that were the university—*perhaps where Uncle Enzo had earned his engineering degree.* Somewhere down the middle and over the final swell of hills before the river lay Cornall Hospital. The river itself was a vague blue snake. On the far side, Draadustin was a mere brown and yellow stain.

"Will you be gone for long?" the man asked.

Mary shrugged. "As long as it takes."

Dock hands bustled around the edge of the platform. Already they had the ship tied to the dock in a number of places. Long planks were brought out and laid side by side, spanning the gap from the dock to the ship.

Workers walked carelessly across the planks, but it was not until they had lashed several together side by side and erected a rope railing on either side that they let any passengers cross.

While they worked, Mary went to a small covered pavilion and purchased her ticket. As she turned, she saw the young girl again, this time between two men, exiting the platform and talking excitedly.

At the gangplank, Mary joined a small throng of passengers-to-be. She showed her ticket to a harried looking sailor, who pointed across the deck. The ship swayed slightly in the wind as she crossed. She shifted her balance, but noticed several of the passengers were having trouble, grabbing for the nearest solid object or walking with a slow deliberate sort of gait.

"They'll get their air-legs by tomorrow," a sailor on the far side of the deck assured her. Glancing at her ticket he added, "Bottom of the stairs, fourth on the left."

Her cabin was tiny and sparse. It contained a bunk, built into the wall, with a drawer underneath. The back wall had a bench and a small desk, also attached to the wall. There was little room for other furnishing. *More than adequate*, she thought as she deposited her bag in the drawer. Having nothing else to do, she returned to the deck.

The passengers had been loaded, and now dock hands were carrying crates of dried goods and merchandise across the gangplank and stowing them in the large forward compartments under the deck. The sailors were already making ready for their departure. Four men climbed spider-like up a web of thick ropes to tie a huge canvas sail fast to the wooden beams above. Another walked cat-like on top of the ship's outer rail, hanging on to a rope that swung the beam so the sail could catch the wind.

The ship had three masts, each with two large lower sails and two smaller higher sails. Each of the three masts ended in a hub of sorts, from which sprang a clockwork of ropes leading to three silk balloons.

The man on the railing caught Mary's look and returned it brazenly, a leer on his face. She blushed and looked away. Not wanting him to mistake her interest, she turned her attention outward toward the distant mountains.

Mary felt a presence beside her. She looked and found a large man in a rich purple shirt bound about the waist by a large, golden belt. He had on brown tights and knee-high leather boots. He was heavy, his belly protruding over the belt. A few wispy gray hairs stood under a purple beret with a long feather in it. His face was lined and jowly.

He too stared at the distant mountains, though Mary knew a moment ago he had been staring at her. He tisked loudly. "Will not do, will not do."

"What will not do?" she asked.

He gave an exaggerated startle, like he was just now noticing her. "Oh," he waved dismissively, "those clouds. They bode ill for the journey."

She turned again toward the mountains. Clouds indeed swirled around their base.

"It'll take five, six days at least to reach our next port," he sighed.

"I understood this was to be a four-day journey," Mary said.

"So they say, so they say," he replied. "But these craft have only rudimentary propulsion. They must use the wind for most of their power. With that line of storms, we will be tacking this way and that."

He turned his attention back to her. "You are a healer, I see. How long have you studied?"

He thinks I am an apprentice, Mary thought. *Well, so be it. Ashe did say this was to be a discreet mission.*

"A while," she answered evasively, "at Cornall."

"Fine program," he said. "I hear some of their teachers have enough potential to be real magicians, if they chose." Mary snorted at the "real magicians" comment. He continued, "I tried to get my daughter in, she's about your age I'd say." Mary snorted again. "Alas she's got little magic potential." He sighed.

He went on, oblivious to the fact that Mary was only half paying attention, about the failings of his daughter, his son, and his wife. She could sense the arrogance and vanity in the man and found it distasteful. He did not know what he'd do if he didn't have his business, it was the only bit of fortune he'd been handed. He managed to let it slip that half the cargo they were hauling was his.

Finally he returned to obsessing on the impending clouds and the length of their journey. With yet another dramatic sigh and a slight leer, he said, "Oh well, I guess you and I will have to make the best of it, no?"

The image of his corpulent flesh pressing down on her flashed in her mind. She shuddered, the sailor's crude invitation suddenly more appealing. "I am confident we will make the journey on time."

"I'll make you a wager then," he said playfully. "Dinner on the fifth night, if there is a fifth night."

"There will be no fifth night," she said as much to herself as to the man.

"Not with the help of a mage can we make this flight in four days," he replied.

Not with the help of a mage? We will see about that.

***

That night a breeze ruffled the fur of a rat sniffing around a trash heap in Draadustin. The rat lifted its nose and sniffed the air once and then quickly returned its attention to the trash, the breeze forgotten. The breeze shot across the river, growing to a full-blown wind. It raced past the city of Tomlin and shot, arrow straight, toward the distant mountains. It cut the oncoming clouds like a knife, raising wild thunderstorms on either side, lightning streaking the sky. A single airship caught in the middle of the wind was pulled swiftly and dry through the storms.

I should not have raised the wind for my own selfish ends. Mary watched the lightning through the open door of her cabin. Most mages would have never given such concerns a second thought, but she was also an Oomutoo practitioner. The spirits of nature are wise and powerful, Oomutoo taught, and they should be allowed to do what they would. *You are part of the spirit too,* a voice answered in her head, *wise and powerful.*

***

Mary still felt guilty the next morning as she ate her breakfast with the other coach passengers in the small lower galley. She climbed the stairs to sit in the sun on the deck and watch the day pass. The sailors scrambled frantically up and down the sails, trying to keep the lines tight and the sails true. The ship heaved under the force of the winds.

A shout brought her attention upward. She watched in horror as one of the sailors lost his grip and plummeted downward. The ship heaved to one side, and she feared he would fall past them. The ground was hundreds of feet below. Then the ship heaved back. The beam of the lower sail rushed up to greet him. There was a sickening smack as it caught him on the thigh and the sound of bone breaking. He fell the remaining fifteen feet and hit the deck with another loud smack.

Three sailors had been sliding down ropes after the man and landed only seconds later. They rushed for the body. There were cries of "Get the skipper! Get the swainson!" Both men would be educated and have some basic first aid training, but likely there was no doctor or healer on a ship this size.

Mary was already rushing forward, pulling energy from the wind around her. She pushed through the growing crowd of sailors. They grunted in surprise.

The man's thigh bone had not only been broken, it was sticking out of his inner thigh. He groaned, and his breathing was labored. She scanned his body quickly, taking in broken ribs, a ruptured spleen but thankfully no other internal injuries. She turned her attention to the leg.

"Grab him by the shoulders," she commanded two sailors. Wordless, they obeyed. She grabbed the leg and pulled, setting the bone. The healing trance fell over her. Later she could not recall everything she had done or even how long she had worked. It was often like that with deep healing; the trance was too deep, too different from waking life. She came to, sitting on her knees with one hand on the man's chest. He was breathing lightly, and his eyes were closed.

She looked up into a pair of gorgeous brown eyes. The man squatting next to her had curly dark hair and a slender build. He was maybe all of twenty years old, dressed in a white shirt and brown leather pants. He had one hand on the man's neck, feeling his pulse.

"No healer has such power," he said, awe in his voice. "You are?"

She blushed, looking away. "I am Mary," she replied.

"A mage?"

She nodded.

"A mage-level healer!" he said. "I've heard of such a thing, but never seen anything like this."

"Her, a mage?" It was the merchant. "But she's just a girl."

Mary looked at the young man again. His face crinkled into a smile, his eyes bright. "A mage can be anything he or she wants," he said. "Young, old, rich, poor. I heard a story once of a mage that got so sick of being pestered to do magic for others that he shape-shifted into the form of a dog and went to live with some poor family that had no idea their family pet was once a powerful magic user."

The sailors chuckled at the man's story, and for a moment, it took the attention away from Mary.

"I am Jerome," the young man said, extending his hand to Mary and helping her to her feet. "The Swainson for this voyage." The Swainson was a mid-level magician who specialized in the magic that kept these ships afloat.

"Take the man to his quarters," Mary told one of the sailors. "He will need to rest for a few days, but he will be quite sound."

"Captain!" a voice from somewhere shouted, and the crowd parted.

The captain strode up and shook Mary's hand, praising her in a long-winded manner about how her "heroic deed" had saved the company a "valuable asset in the form of one of its employees." She got the distinct impression that it was the value of the sailor's work, rather than his life, that mattered to this man.

"Are you working, master Swainson?" the captain

commented snidely toward Jerome, who had not left Mary's side.

"Is the ship afloat, sir?" Jerome replied.

Several sailors scowled and looked about.

"We are," the captain affirmed.

"Then I must be working," Jerome said. He gave Mary a slight bow, "Perhaps we will meet again."

4 JEROME

The petty officer bowed deeply at the door to the private mess. After healing the sailor, Mary had barely been able to convince the captain that she did not require a cabin upgrade to first class. She could not, however, refuse an invitation to the captain's table.

It was just as well; she could not remain an ordinary passenger anyway. The sailors treated her with a respect that bordered on awe, and the other passengers were either ingratiatingly pleasant or slightly afraid to be in her presence. *This is why so many mages lock themselves up in tall towers and avoid most people,* she thought wearily. In her case, it was why she didn't reveal her status often.

Captain Terrance Manley rose and bowed as Mary was led to him. So did the others at the table. On his left was the merchant, now introduced as Klaus Von Stubern. Mary was to be seated to the captain's right, the place of honor. On her right was Jerome Stanchion, the Swainson. Two petty officers and a noble lady filled the opposite side of the table.

As they sat down, Klaus's eyes slid over her and then uncomfortably away. *Is he afraid that his earlier words gave offense?* she wondered. *Or is he upset to find that I might not be the 'young maiden' he perceived?* She knew from past experience it could easily go either way.

Jerome alone seemed comfortable with her presence at the table. She wondered at this. The Swainson's job was to renew the incantations and spells that kept the ship afloat. Such low-level magic users were typically even less comfortable with mage-level practitioners.

As if guessing Mary's mind, the captain said, "Master Stanchion is on loan to us from Galldet University in Syrano. When he graduates, he will be able enchant these ships from the start. Right now, he's just learning the ropes, but the boy's got real promise."

Jerome looked at Mary. "Have you a title?"

"Just Mary, please."

He seemed pleased at this. "Mary, what school did you go to?"

She paused, knowing this would further distance herself from the other passengers, though hopefully not from Jerome. "I was apprenticed by Ashley La'Margin."

There a quiet gasp around the table. "*The* Ashley La'Margin?" the woman asked.

"Can there be two Ashley La'Margins?" Jerome joked. "Master Harkins says the old coot hasn't taken an apprentice since the Han dynasty fell."

Mary looked at Jerome and had the sudden sense that he must be the teacher's pet at the university—

not a mage certainly, but on easy terms with the teachers. Perhaps they expected him to join their small ranks one day.

She returned his playful smile. "Indeed. I was, he would say, an exception."

He raised his glass of wine. "You are indeed exceptional."

"I am curious," she asked after the toast, "about this mage who turned himself into a dog." There was a titter of nervous laughter around the table.

Jerome waved his hands dismissively. "Master Cid at the university, but it's only a joke he makes when students screw up or make stupid comments."

"How many mages are there at the university?"

"Three full mages. Several high-level magicians, almost a dozen. It's truly an elite school," Jerome said with some pride.

***

Mary stepped into the cool night air. Lightning again lit the sky. The wind was still with them, cutting a path through the wide front. It had slowed, perhaps from the energy she had tapped when she healed the sailor, or perhaps in response to her mood. The ship swayed less and held a steady course.

Unaccustomed to wine, Mary's head was swimming. Still, the meal had gone far better than she had feared. Jerome carried the conversation for the most part, talking about life at the university. Under his easy grace, the others soon lost their worry of Mary and began asking questions of her life.

"It's not so exciting or glamorous as one might think," she told them. "I was and am a simple healer. The healers at the hospital saw my potential early on, but they were just healers themselves; how could they know its limit? Later I started to learn that I could bend many of the supposed limits or rules of healing. I myself didn't think much of that.

"Then there was a building collapse in one of the poorer sections of town. I went, as a healer. Ashe came to assist. He saw my healing and recognized I had untapped potential. A few days later, I received an invitation to his tower. He asked me if I would 'do him the honor' of becoming his apprentice."

The door behind her opened, and Jerome slid out onto the deck. He stopped beside Mary and stared into the night. After a while he said, "Maybe tomorrow you will do me the honor of letting me show you the sigil room."

"I would be delighted," she replied. "I have only been trained in, or done, soft magic. Such spells intrigue me."

"I am glad you feel that way," he said. Then he leaned in conspiratorially, "Soft magic scares the pants off me." With that, he was gone.

***

"Right this way, m'lady," Jerome said as he ushered Mary down a narrow hall. He carried a wine carafe in one hand and a loaf of heavy bread in the crook of his elbow. The opposite hand reached for the door. He paused, his hand on the doorknob. "I should perhaps warn you," he began, "My sigil room, I keep spotless." Indeed, it was with richly-drawn, white magic symbols elaborately decorating the floor of the otherwise bare room underneath the main deck. "My incantations are particular and precise. My personal quarters . . . not so much."

Mary held her free hand to her face to stifle a laugh. Jerome's room was no bigger than hers. Instead of a bunk, a canvas hammock hung across the length of the room. There was an open foot locker beneath it, and clothes were strewn in, on, and around the locker and across the floor. A desk and a bench seat took up the backside of the room, and the desk was cluttered with papers and three open books piled on top of each other. "I see," she said.

He looked around for somewhere for them to sit. "I fear neither the food nor accommodations can quite match the captain's table . . . "

She sat in the hammock, her feet leaving the ground. The hammock rocked slightly. She had a bowl full of roasted vegetables in one hand, which she transferred to her lap. "Do not worry yourself, the food *and the company* are both far more to my liking."

He blushed as he cleared a small shelf. It was big enough to set either the bread or the wine carafe on, but not both. He set the wine down and tore a chunk off the bread as he sat next to Mary on the hammock. It gave under his weight, sliding the two of them together in the middle. Mary shifted herself but made no effort to pull away.

"Now you must tell me something of yourself," she chided him.

"I have done nothing but talk all afternoon," he teased. "My throat is parched from all the talking I have done."

"No, no," she said waving her finger. "You do not get off that easy. You have talked certainly. You have told me about the sigils and the magic that holds the ships afloat. You have even talked about the university. But you have not told me about yourself."

"There is little to tell. Like you said of yourself last

evening, it's not that exciting of a story."

"I do not believe you," she replied. "For one thing, you are cocky, but you lack the ingrained arrogance of the upper class."

"I am not upper class," he shot back. "As to cocky," he went on more lighthearted, "cocky is about all I got."

"So if you are not upper class, how can your parents afford to send you to one of the most prestigious magic universities in the empire?"

"A scholarship," he replied. "I am quite easily the poorest wretch at the university. My studies are heavily underwritten, partly by the university itself, but mostly by a couple of rich merchants. I will have many years of indentured labor ahead of me when I graduate, I fear. I can only hope to excel well enough to get a good job to pass that time."

"And what does Master Stanchion describe as a good job? Something like this?"

He groaned theatrically. "Swainson on a civilian ship? By the emperor, kill me now. I don't know, but not this. Certainly something where I pilot as well as hold the ship aloft."

"And those jobs?"

"Military craft run that way—no balloons, no sails, just magic. I doubt my principals will farm me out to the military though, and I have no desire for a soldier's life. A few of the faster courier ships are like that. That would be okay. It would get boring doing the same routes over and over, though."

He shrugged. "I don't know." He sat the bread down on the shelf and looked around for cups. Mary took the carafe from him and drank from it, handing it back when she was done. He took the hint and drank from it as well, lying back on the bunk as he did so. "I suppose I will apply for a research ship. That will make both the university and the principals happy. I'll get to test fly new designs, and they'll get to profit from them."

"Why be an air pilot at all?"

"When I was little, what I wanted more than anything else was to be a dragon hunter," he said. "I grew up in Formforst, a dock town on the edge of broken space."

Mary had heard of broken space. Even by imperial standards it was an unusual world. It was a universe of small planetoids and asteroids, featuring low gravity and uniform atmosphere. Dragons bred on the small asteroids and hunted the wide-open spaces between. Men, in turn, used fast, light airships to hunt the dragons.

"We were poor, my family. We lived in a tiny, three-bedroom brownstone apartment just off the docks. My dad was a day laborer, loading dry goods for the hunters. He and mom shared one bedroom, my two sisters had the second, and I had to share the third with three brothers."

"Every day after school, I would climb to the roof of our apartment building. All of three stories mind you, but overlooking the docks. I would watch the dragon-hunting ships and imagine I was on one of them, getting ready for a big hunt, swooping amongst the asteroids in hot pursuit, dodging fire." He laughed at the memories.

"My brothers used to tease me about it. Said I was daft. I was scrawny." He shrugged again. "Still am. There was no way I could ever be one of the heavily-muscled harpooners, sailors, or even a simple deckhand."

"But you could be a pilot," Mary said.

"Exactly. You don't have to be big or strong. You just have to magic." He sighed. "But of course, nobody tests kids like me for magic. My parents could never afford even the cheapest school of magic, even if anyone had seen my potential. It was just a stupid kid's dream."

"Still, I watched and I dreamed. I memorized the sigils they used. Dragon ships don't put them below, like here. They scrawl them out on the foredeck. I watched the pilots drawing and renewing the sigils over and over from my perch."

"Then I would go downstairs to our apartment. To escape my brothers, I would hide in the washroom. I would sit in the big copper tub we had and pretend it was an airship. I would duck and dive like I was flying." He ducked and dove on the hammock, swaying them both. Mary laughed.

"One day, I took it in my head to use a nail to scratch the sigils I had seen. I got really into it, until I heard mom calling for me. I was terrified that she would be pissed I had scratched up her good tub; we had so few good things. Then the whole tub starts shaking. I grabbed the sides of it, even more terrified. I thought we were having an earthquake or something. I wanted to get out of there fast."

Mary laughed again. "Oh, that was a mistake," she said.

"Tell me about it," Jerome replied. "The tub did it's best to follow my command. It started slamming against the walls. It smashed the window and broke through a big section of wall, and we were off."

"Flying?"

"Not exactly," he said. "More like skipping a stone, *thunk, thunk, thunk*, down the busy lane."

"What stopped you?"

"Only the biggest, most expensive-looking coach I had ever seen. I smashed into the rear wheels and wrecked it up."

"Oh, poor little Jerome." Mary was giggling almost uncontrollably. "What happened?"

"The man, a rich merchant on the way to see about one of his hunting crews, got out. He had a strange, inscrutable look, and I was so terrified I almost peed my pants. He asked what had happened, and in a shaky voice, I told him. He said something to one of his servants and then marched me home."

"My dad had just got off work, and the landlord was berating him about how expensive it would be to fix that hole. I felt so small, but Dad just kept standing up for me, saying he'd pay for the hole and the merchant's coach. I knew he didn't have that much money and that he and Mom would both have to work extra for the rest of their lives to pay for my stupid mistake.

"The merchant just told everyone, in a polite but firm way, to shut up. We sat in the living room of our little apartment, no one speaking, for a long time. Then one of his pilots came. He asked me a ton of questions. Who taught you that sigil? How did you know the proper order of construction? What incantation did you use?

"I told him I had no idea what I did, I just did it. He stared at me a long time and then said to my parents, 'The boy has high-magic potential. Let us hope he doesn't waste it in a slum.'"

"Then the merchant slapped his thigh and said,

'He will not,' as if answering his own question. To me he said, 'I will pay for the hole in the wall. I forgive the damage to my coach. I will even pay for your parents to move out of this hovel. Finally, I will pay your way to university. In return, you will do your best, fulfill your potential, and give me thirty years indentureship. I will return tomorrow with the contract and bank notes.'"

"And that's how you managed to end up at the most prestigious university?" Mary finished.

"More or less," Jerome said. "I went with him the next day. He had me enrolled in a private boarding school until I was of age."

"He treats you well?"

Jerome shrugged. "He is indifferent. I am an investment and nothing more. We meet a half dozen times a year and talk. But for all that, he's been generous. When my family spurned 'charity,' he underwrote the cost of a villa on the edge of town and made sure both my parents had jobs that would make the payments. He has given me ample stipends, and when I got top marks at boarding school and earned entrance to Galldet, he gave me dowry money for both of my sisters. He's hired all three of my brothers on his ships. I can't complain."

Mary sat the now empty bowl on the shelf and leaned back against Jerome. He rolled toward her, their faces only inches apart. She could feel his breath on her cheek. He reached up and stroked her hair. "I have no right to ask anything of you, but if you wished to stay, I would not object."

Mary smiled, "I am old enough to be your mother. No, grandmother."

"What is age to a magic user?" he replied.

"Indeed," she said, "but there's something else." She knew somehow, as she said it, that this too would not matter to him.

R. J. Eliason

5 A LONG-SHORT JOURNEY

Mary sat basking in the dying sunlight. The stone bench beneath her felt warm and solid. After four days of constant swaying, it was disconcerting to be so still.

In Bezra, the airships docked to large towers constructed on a hill deep within the city. Underneath the docks was a busy lane, with merchants loudly hawking their wares and hundreds of people pressing through. The smell of food from a merchant's stall was drifting up, rolling Mary's stomach, but she was not hungry yet.

She had been to Bezra only once before. That time, she had been heading to one of the beach resorts not far from the city. She knew the jump gates were on the opposite edge of town from the dock, wedged into a lee in the Jinto Mountains behind the city. By the time she could get there, it would be too late in the day and the station would be closed. However, an inn or hostel should be easy enough to find, and Mary was not in a hurry.

Her ship, the *Mother Queen*, was getting ready to leave dock. She watched as Jerome climbed the webbing, easily outpacing the sailors and making for one of the balloons. He seemed so graceful and natural, she had no doubt he would someday fulfill his dream of piloting the top craft. She could see him sailing through a maze of canyons, chasing a dragon in flight. She smiled at the thought.

Nearby a young woman sang an old folk ballad while a man played a guitar. "Lovers come and lovers go," the song went, "but in my heart I am so alone."

It was a bittersweet feeling as she looked again at Jerome's back. He had neither time nor attention for her, but they had said their goodbyes earlier. She did not regret their short tryst. He had proven a competent and gentle lover. It was foolish for her to want more.

Money, material possessions, desire, and lust: these are not barriers to true happiness, Oomutoo taught, *but the expectation of these things is.* When we come to expect that each day will be filled with these things, we cannot enjoy the moment that is before us.

True happiness, Mary thought, *comes in accepting the compromises that life presents to us.* She had no fear their time together would quicken her. Mary would never have a family, but she would always have her freedom. She was content with that.

A movement brought her attention back to the moment. A creature was moving slowly underneath the bench toward her bag. At first she thought it looked like a giant squirrel or a small dog, but as it came out from under the bench it rose up on two legs. The face, dog-like and furry, had a sentient, if shifty, look. The creature was wearing pants made of coarse, woven flax and a simple leather vest.

"Can I help you?" she asked.

The creature started and then looked up. "No, sorry, just passing through," it said in a high, scratchy voice.

It was a dogboy. Mary had never seen one in life before, but nothing else could fit the description. They were short, maybe knee-high to a human, furry with short tails. Their hands were claw-like. They could drop onto all fours to run or stand on two legs to walk. They were one of many defeated peoples, once wild tribes that had fought against imperial control. Now they lived in tiny reservations that were a fraction of their original homeland, or in crowded cities. They had little native technology or skills. They took the most menial jobs or, when nothing was offered, turned to petty theft to survive. Mary assumed this one had been about to make off with her bag.

Now it turned and moved off, limping painfully as it went.

"Have you a name?" she asked the retreating back.

The dogboy turned and bowed slightly. "It's Gimpy, ma'am."

"Others have named you this," Mary said. "Have you a name among your own kind?"

The dogboy pulled himself erect. "I am Kariff of the Fett Clan."

"I am just arrived," she said. "I need lodging and food. Would you be able to direct me to an inn?"

"Of course," he replied. "I know a wonderful place, simple, rundown even, but the owners are clean and the food is good."

Mary stood. "Then if you are ready, please lead on."

As they walked down the stairs and into the busy lane, she slowed her pace to match Kariff's. It was one of the things healers learned. Kariff took the stairs slowly and his lame leg must have pained him, but he didn't show it.

"Your clan, they can't take care of you?" she asked.

"All who eat must earn their keep," he said, indignant. Then with no small pride, "I bring home more than any other in my clan. Some humans feel pity for me because of my infirmity, which works well for a beggar. Others—" He broke off.

"Others ignore you," Mary finished for him. "Not bad for a petty thief," she said without judgment, another knack healers pick up.

He didn't deny it. "Food is food, no matter how it's come by."

The inn was as billed. It was run by a middle-aged halfling couple. The outside was run down, the chairs in the dining room were all mismatched, and the curtains were threadbare. But it was clean, comfortable, and the odors coming from the kitchen were pleasant.

"The dogboy who brought me here," she said to the innkeeper, "he'll get something for his trouble?"

The man shrugged. It was a common enough arrangement, but one no one ever wanted to admit to it. Mary pressed an extra coin into his hand. "He'll get a full meal tonight," she said. He nodded and pocketed the coin.

The next morning, Mary stepped outside the inn's door to find most of the Fett Clan there. The innkeeper had been true to Mary's request. Bread, soup, and a flagon of ale was a meal for a human or halfling, but it was a feast for the clan. Respect from a human was perhaps no less remarkable. At any rate, Mary's walk to the gate station was with an honor guard of sorts.

***

Looking back on her trip later, Mary would often remark on how the longest portions of it were the shortest, and vice versa. After a four-day voyage to get to Bezra, she crossed two whole worlds in the span of a couple of hours. The Bezra gate station was a long, low building. It housed seven archways, each enchanted to pass to a different world. She had given Kariff a small coin, paid a larger coin to the attendant, passed within, found the gate for Tyryst, and walked through.

The gate station at Tyryst was bigger than any in Bezra. It was the size of a stadium with a carousel in the center where tickets were sold. All along the edges, there were gates. A few at the far back were permanent open gates, with people wandering freely in and out of them. She knew from her last trip through here that these gates mostly led to other parts of this world, or nearby worlds.

The rest of the gates were blank. Two pillars rose on either side of a small recess in the station wall. An attendant in a purple robe stood beside each gate.

She went to the carousel and purchased a ticket for Mombay, the next world on her itinerary. The ticket woman gave her a slip of parchment and pointed her toward gate 256. It was still early and there was no line.

The attendant was a bored-looking, middle-aged man with a receding hairline. He took the ticket without so much as a glance at her. She thought briefly of Jerome, but this second encounter with a fellow magician bore no resemblance to the last. He turned from her and began to chant softly, as though speaking to himself. A fog filled the gate, so she could no longer see the wall, even though logic told her the recess was only inches deep. The fog quickly cleared, and she could see a second station on the other side. She passed into Mombay.

She stopped and stared in awe until the next traveler coughed irritably behind her. She moved deeper into the station and out of his way. She had thought the Tyryst station was big, but it wasn't even half as large as Mombay. She had known, theoretically at least, that the Mombay station was one of the key portals into and out of the central empire. It was mentioned in numerous travel books. But one could not fully grasp just how big it was without seeing it for oneself, nor how busy.

Even at this early hour, the place was crawling with people and other humanoids. It was as crowded as beggar's row in Draadustin, but these people were no beggars. (There were plenty of beggars, mostly dogboys, dashing underfoot or lurking in the empty corners.) She watched as a group of dwarves, dressed in silk shirts with dragon hide vests and boots and wearing plenty of gold jewelry, walked by. They spoke to each other in their own tongue, deep, rolling, and guttural, as they passed.

A drax, a tall, thin humanoid, glided past, heading the other direction. Its large head was misshapen, giving it the appearance of having a brain twice the size of a human. Its eyes had an almost insect-like appearance, and its bearing was regal and disdainful.

She spotted a small group of gnomes moving toward the distant wall. They were dressed in tunics and brown leggings; leather aprons across their front marked them as smiths. Two of their group were hauling an expensive-looking chest between them. The fronts of their aprons were embossed with a familiar crest. They were Bezra Clan. Mary knew they were the top tinkerers in the empire because the hospital's herbal scales were all of Bezra make.

Overwhelmingly, however, there were humans— of every stripe, color and size. Humans were certainly the most numerous and most diverse of all the empire's races.

There were tall, fat merchants in richly spun silks. There were trim soldiers, carrying, rather than wearing, their armor. A group of tall, black men in pillbox hats and long, flowing robes were engaged in deep conversation near the ticket carousel. Mary was pushed coldly aside by a circle of olive-hued men in robes with long, curved swords on their backs. In the center walked a woman with thick, black hair tied in a high bun, her face painted the purest white, with bright red lips. Her robes were metallic emerald green.

Mary was surprised when she reached the carousel and discovered that the stadium was only one of ten that comprised the whole of the station. She gratefully accepted the parchment map that was offered and made her way toward the distant hub that held her next gate.

It took her over an hour to find the gate, in part because she was not looking very hard. These two jumps comprised the lion's share of her journey, yet would only take minutes to pass. She wanted to linger, to watch all the strange people and creatures pass by.

She took a break at a stand selling some sort of seafood on flatbread. She loved exotic food; besides, she couldn't pass up the chance to linger and chat with the seller about the people who passed. But in the end, she had a mission ahead of her.

The first thing to strike Mary as she passed through the next gate was the stench, followed almost immediately by the noise. She had never seen, smelled, or heard anything to compare to the din she found around her.

She knew from her research that this station was only about half the size of the one on her own world, even though this was the central hub for this world and several others in the quadrant. Few travelers went this way, and Mary had been under the mistaken impression that the station would be mostly empty. But she had never traveled to the remote agricultural worlds that filled the empire's bellies.

All about her were cattle, goats, sheep, and oxen. At first she was frightened, fearing that a stampede had broken its way into the station. Then she spotted a bored-looking shepherd standing nearby. He seemed unimpressed by the herds of cattle that pushed close to both of them.

Mary made her way cautiously into the station, being careful of where she stepped. The smell of barnyard was almost stifling. She had been into the countryside around Tomlin City a few times, taking rotations as a traveling healer. She had a wonderful romantic notion of farms—quiet little places filled with neatly dressed halfling women feeding a few chickens. A few of the human farms raised cows, and Mary had watched them grazing in the pasture.

She had never been this close to a cow. They

seemed much bigger and stronger than they did from farther away. She could see no way around the herd, and she was fearful of trying to push her way through. They stood tightly pressed together. They wouldn't even notice the poor little healer crushed between them, suffocating.

I am being silly; they're just cows. Whoever heard of cows crushing people?

The locals did not share her concern. A young boy, who couldn't have been more than eight, forced the herd forward, wielding a long cane of bamboo and shouting. The cows mooed disconsolately but showed no sign of turning on the boy. They shuffled slowly off, and the way was mostly cleared for Mary.

She was left to wade through a waist-high mixture of sheep and goats that followed in the wake of the cows. As she looked around, it was the same everywhere. The entire inside of the rather small station was packed with animals of one kind or another. The gates here were different. There were only a half dozen door-sized gates. The rest were much larger arches, designed for the passage of livestock.

As she watched, one gate opened to let in a long line of wagons pulled by oxen. She paused, forgetting the scent for a moment, and watched in awe. She had heard about settlers, heading out to distant worlds to build new homes, but had never seen them before. These were simple folk mostly, dressed in flax and cotton clothes, walking in thick leather boots alongside their wagons. The men were broad and walked with a confident swagger—men used to hard work. The women, too, were sturdy, thick, and strong like the men, but no less feminine for it. Mary longed to be among them, to have such purpose and quiet strength, to go out knowing you were making a better life for yourself, for your children.

She was brought back to her senses by the approach of another herd of cows. She forced her way through the remaining sheep and out of the flow of traffic. It took her several minutes to make her way to the carousel here, and she lost sight of the settlers in the crush.

The name of the world she was traveling to was Sohen. It took the ticket seller only a moment to point out her gate. She was a bit unnerved to find that it was one of the large, permanent gates that had a rather large volume of livestock issuing almost continually from it. One attendant, a non-magician by the look of it, was standing beside the gate.

She held out her ticket, but he merely nodded her through. She looked at the large herd of cattle currently entering, then back to the attendant, wondering how she was supposed to get through the gate. He merely shrugged as if to say, "How would I know?"

In the end she had to wait until a gap appeared between a herd of cows and an oxen train of dry goods and force her way through. The lead teamster scowled at her.

The air on the far side of the gate was still ripe with the odor of farm animals mixed with sewage, but it was almost fresh compared with the station she had left behind. Mary moved quickly away from the gate, which was not in a station proper, but merely part of one wall in a large outdoor courtyard. The courtyard was crowded to overflowing with livestock and baggage trains. She could see now why the teamster had been so irate. They must have been in line for hours already.

Mary pushed on and didn't stop until she was outside the courtyard and well down one of the side streets, away from the din and the odor. The side street narrowed briefly, then opened onto another lane. She stopped and took stock of her situation.

She had come to a different world. *Physically I have come to a different world several times already*, she reminded herself. She had passed through three different worlds in one day. She had magically passed over, through, under, or in between countless more. (Despite being a mage, Mary had only a vague notion of how world jumping actually occurred, or what sort of geography it entailed. That was the realm of the most advance theoretical magic.)

Each of these worlds was unique. They all had different climates, different landscapes. Many had different sizes and configurations. Some were flat, some were round. Some were infinite in size, at least as far as anyone could tell, and others quite limited. She had read an article in one of her favorite travel magazines about a world that measured a mere two square acres. It contained a single farmer and his wife, with one gate off the world.

The central worlds were, if anything, more distinct. On the outer areas, worlds were chosen for their suitability for the empire's primary cash crops: grains and wheat. Worlds that were too different were left uninhabited. In the central worlds, beauty and uniqueness made those worlds valued.

However different the landscape and climate of the central worlds might be, they were still all imperial worlds. There was a distinct style—tall, imposing stone architecture, wide lanes, open parks, and crowds. There was a distinct feel to them.

Here it wasn't the weather that startled Mary, nor the landscape around her, though it was cooler than her home and much wetter. The town looked nothing like Tomlin or Draadustin. To be honest, she had expected something like Draadustin, but on a smaller scale. She knew they were poor in the remote part of the empire, and she thought she knew poverty well.

But this was something totally new to her. The buildings were short and squat, mostly one or two stories. They were made of wood, with small heavily-glassed windows and shutters. They had high, thatched roofs and stone chimneys. The lane was narrow, and it stunk. Rough board planks lay in the middle, and the few people she saw out on the streets walked carefully on the planks. On either side, up close to the houses, was refuse. Everything from bones and vegetable cuttings to human feces was left to rot in the streets. Mary covered her face with a loose shawl and made her way forward.

The buildings on either side had little by the way of decoration. She had to read the tattered and faded signs to decipher which were businesses and what sort of business they were.

The only one that was obvious was the whorehouse. A half dozen women of various ages and levels of undress lounged on the porch, shouting provocatively at men as they passed. As Mary passed one cried out, "Look, a *lady*!" She and two of her fellow whores held dirty scarves over their faces and strutted comically along the porch.

Mary found their display quite humorous, though probably not for the reasons they did. She was rarely, if ever, accused of being "a lady." Her simple, floor-length, silk dress, her complete lack of adornment—none of this spoke of gentry, at least not in Tomlin City.

She found a slightly less run-down building, whose sign stated that it was an inn. *As good as any,* she thought, turning in at the door.

6 HOGSLEG INN

Immediately she wondered if she had made a mistake by entering the inn. The patronage here seemed to be entirely dwarves and halflings. They were what in Tomlin City would be described as a rough crowd. The dwarves wore thick leather jerkins over coarse wool. The halflings just wore wool. Most of the dwarves had axes and long daggers. The halflings had stout sticks.

Mary knew that outside of her relatively liberal friends, race relations were not the best in the empire. She was about to turn around and leave when the owner emerged to greet her. He was human. Or at least she thought so. He was big and beefy, with a wide round middle, like a halfling giant. His face was red, what little could be seen under the thick, gray beard. His eyes were tiny, black spots in his head, but his crude mouth opened in a wide smile, and his manner seemed friendly.

"You'll be looking for lodging, I expect," he said.

Mary nodded.

"Havlin will take your stuff. Havlin!"

Mary barely had time to wonder who or what a Havlin was, or how to explain that she had no stuff, when the wood floor echoed with the sound of hooves.

"Your things, ma'am," said a dull voice.

Standing in front of her was the first faun Mary had ever seen. He had the body of a man and the legs of a goat. His head sprouted the smallest buds of goat horns. She'd heard fairy stories about wild fauns, but this one seemed a different sort altogether. He was not naked. He wore a leather tunic and short kilt. His face was placid and dull. "Your things?" he repeated.

He's not right in the head, Mary decided as she handed over her one small bag. *A little slow maybe?* She followed him down a narrow hall and up a short flight of stairs.

She was shown into a large room, larger than she expected at least. There was a low bed, straw sticking precariously out of the bolster. It appeared none too clean, and she did not relish lying down on it. There was a nightstand next to the bed, and a dresser and wardrobe just opposite. The wardrobe had a cracked mirror attached to the front of it. The room also contained a small table and two chairs. One wall had a fireplace.

The owner, who introduced himself as Lagoon, appeared. "I took the liberty of bringing up a bite of supper. An off-worlder such as yourself wouldn't want to mingle with . . ." He gave a nod toward the common room.

Mary started to protest but was brought short by

the sight of the innkeeper's "bite of supper." On a long wooden tray, he carried a large bowl filled with an enormous chunk of meat swimming in a greasy soup along with a few root vegetables. Next to it were half a loaf of bread, a thick slab of butter, and half a round of cheese. There was also a large mug of milk. It was no wonder the innkeeper looked like an overgrown halfling. There was enough food here to easily feed six people. Tomlin was not an agricultural center. There were farms, a few at least a few at the outskirts. Mostly they produced green groceries, which supplemented the locals' diet of grains that were shipped in from elsewhere. Only the rich ate meat, and then only rarely.

The innkeeper stood by, awkwardly waiting for her approval. She sat at the table and started to fish out one of the vegetables. Taking it all in, the best she could do was to say, "This is more than adequate." He looked relieved.

She didn't know how to ask if there was anything lighter to eat, so instead she turned her attention to her next chore: attiring herself appropriately for this new world.

It took a surprisingly long time to convey what she needed. She asked for the nearest retailer. He stared blankly at her. Tailor, she offered next? Another blank stare. Finally, she said, pulling at her dress, "These will not do in this weather. Where can I find more suitable clothing?"

His face lit up. "No, begging your pardon, ma'am," he agreed. "No, they won't. You will freeze to death, my lady. I'll send Havlin for one of the halfling womenfolk. They'll fix you up right."

She tried to protest. She wanted to go to a shop,

but apparently this wasn't how things worked here. Instead, about an hour later, an older halfling woman showed up at her door with her pack bulging with two bolts of cloth and assorted pieces of fabric.

The fabric turned out to be partly sewn outfits. Within a half an hour, the woman had pinned and hemmed them to fit. She chatted deferentially as she worked.

"What brings m'lady to Sohen?"

"Just Mary," she corrected, for the third time. "Business."

"What sort of business?"

"I'm a healer."

"I've a sister who's a midwife, and a cousin who's a wise woman. In the blood you might say." The halfling began talking about healing herbs and home remedies for this and that. It was clear to Mary that neither the woman's sister nor her cousin were anywhere on the caliber of what Cornall Hospital offered or taught.

Looking in the dusty mirror at the end result, Mary had to laugh. The woman looked so anxious that Mary at once felt sorry. "It's beautiful, really it is." She explained about the whores, how they had mistaken her for a lady. "Now I feel more like a lady than I ever have," she ended.

The halfling blushed and looked away. Mary wasn't joking. She had been outfitted in a long peasant dress, and over it was a leather corset and thick belt. A richly knitted and brightly colored shrug kept her upper body warm. She had long, black leather boots that came to the knee. Finally, for outdoors there was a thick, wool cap and wide-brimmed Cordova hat.

As she was gathering up her things, the halfling

woman bent over as a coughing fit took her. Mary grabbed her arm and led her to the bedside. The coughing subsided, but the woman was still short of breath. Without thinking, Mary reached out with her mind, her hand resting on the woman's back. The woman had consumption, an advanced case.

The woman's eyes went wide with awe as her breath became freer and easier. "M'lady," she gasped, "when you said you were a healer . . ."

"It is nothing," Mary told her.

***

Amidst all the other strangeness of this world, it had managed to escape her notice that there were none of the tall graceful aqueducts that were in evidence throughout Tomlin city. Nor were there any public fountains, bath houses, or for that matter, toilets. She had been given a chamber pot by Havlin before he retired for the night. Apparently, running water simply did not exist in this part of the universe. Sanitation on a whole was a secondary concern, as she was soon to learn.

As for the temperature, Havlin had come in that night bearing wood and a clay pot of glowing embers. He made a roaring fire that lasted most of the night. However, the boards in the walls were roughly chinked, and the wind blew through them. Despite her earlier concern for cleanliness, Mary had hunkered down between the heavy bolster and the thick quilts that had been left for her.

When she woke up, she looked around for some way to clean herself, but the room was equipped with nothing more than a simple basin and ewer of cold water. She removed her clothes, her nipples standing out in the cold and goose bumps erupting on her back. She used a rag to quickly sponge down. She stood in front of the remains of the fire until she was mostly dry, then decided on the warmer dress the halfling had made for her.

Downstairs the main dining hall was all but empty. Three halflings were up early and eating at one table. The innkeeper called to her to sit, then he disappeared into the kitchen. He was back in a matter of moments with a tray of porridge and a fried egg. There was also a cup of something that might have been a strong tea or a weak coffee.

"If I could impose on a minute of your time," she said as he sat the tray in front of her.

"Of course m'lady," he responded. He stood back a step, wiping his hands on a dirty apron.

"I need to travel to the Barony of Cordona," she said.

"Where is that?" he asked.

Mary stared at him, flummoxed. "Here? On this world."

"Hmm. Never heard of it. Oh well, it's a big world, m'lady." He didn't seem deterred by his own lack of knowledge. "I will have Havlin show you around to the nearest stagecoach. If they can't help you, well, you can have him the whole day if need be. I am sure one of the coaches will know of it."

Mary bit back her reply. She was not use to accepting help, but she was lost here. "Yes, that would be wonderful. I will eat and then pack what few things I have."

"I shall let Havlin know. When you are ready, just let me know, and I will show you the stables," he said.

When she had finished eating, settled her bill and packed her few things away, she headed to the stables.

There she found Havlin waiting beside a rickshaw. He gestured her in. Once she got used to the bumping, she found the ride was certainly more comfortable than trying to walk through the mud of the streets. It had rained most of the night, and she saw numerous people emptying the night's chamber pots straight into the puddles alongside the street, often dumping them unceremoniously from second-story windows. She wrinkled her nose and again covered her face with a shawl.

This was the new shawl, a thick woolen one given to her by the halfling woman. It served not only to block out the odor, but also the wind. Her face felt raw in the cold, damp weather.

She was glad she had accepted Havlin's help. Not only were the buildings infrequently marked, the streets were no better. None of the streets had names, though Mary wasn't sure if this was the result of Havlin's lack of wit or if they indeed had no names.

"Where are we now?" she would ask.

"A couple of streets over from where Wilson's granary is," he would reply, or "near where my cousin Millie lives."

He was no more forthcoming about his own life, but after just a short attempt at conversation, Mary felt that was probably for the best. She had heard enough.

"How long have you worked at the inn?" she asked.

"I've been there since I was a foal," he replied.

"Do you like the work?"

"Like?" He seemed perplexed by the question. "I do my best."

Taking another tack, she asked, "Does it pay well?"

"Pay?"

"You work for the innkeeper, right? You get paid?"

"Mister Jarm is my master. I work for him. He keeps me. I work as hard as I can for Mister Jarm."

"But he doesn't pay you?" she asked not fully believing what she was hearing. "Are you a slave?"

"No," he replied without a trace of guile, "I am not a slave; he just owns me, that's all."

Mary was appalled and bewildered. The empire outlawed slavery years ago, generations ago. There were no slaves. All were equal in the eyes of the empire (*Just not the market place*, Eli's voice intruded in her thoughts). And yet here was an obviously sentient being saying quite calmly and clearly that he was owned by another. Did the empire know of this? And yet how could it not? It knew of a war going on in a barony that turned out to be so distant even the locals couldn't find it. Why would this be tolerated?

Riding in the rickshaw, she could only see the back of Havlin's head. She couldn't tell his expression. How did he feel about his enslavement? Was he happy? Sad? In all their interactions so far he hadn't betrayed any real emotion.

Soon her own mission and its latest obstacle took her mind away from this uncomfortable subject. The first two stagecoach services had never heard of the Barony of Cordona either. Finally they broke free of the city proper and rode across a long, grassy field down to the river, where wooden docks stretched out into the water. One of the barge people thought he might have heard of such a place, but it was far off their river route.

He did have some useful information though. He told them to ask at the Riven brothers. Their coach went along the river for a ways and then turned toward the far off Cargill Mountains. That was where he thought the barony lay.

At first the Riven brothers drew a blank as well, until one older driver said, "The Lingleton Line goes out there, just past the Duchy of Shulfa."

Mary's heart jumped. *Shulfa!* That was the name of the duchy they were fighting. She had found not one, both places at once. She asked immediately where she might find the Lingleton Line.

"In Lingleton," the Riven brothers both answered together, as though it were obvious.

Lingleton, it turned out, was the end of their line, almost twelve days' ride out, and the barony at least another twelve days from there.

She booked her place immediately, dismissed Havlin, and then settled down on the porch of the station to wait for the next coach later that day

7 THE LINGLETON LINE

"They're little more than beasts really," Beorn explained in his deep drawl. "They are not slaves since technically they are animals. A cow isn't a slave surely, or a goat."

Mary was already regretting her curiosity. She had three fellow passengers on the coach with her: a poor mousy woman who had barely spoken other than to utter the name "Mary Lynn" in response to a direct question; Beorn, a rich rancher who had just been in town to supervise the delivery of a large herd of cattle; and Beorn's wife, Judith.

Mary had taken an almost instant dislike to Beorn. He was ostentatious about his wealth. He spoke loudly and forcefully about anything and everything. Like so many rich men everywhere, he seemed to think he had a valuable opinion about everything. She had resolved to busy herself somehow and to talk as little as possible.

Curiosity had gotten the better of her. Staring out

the coach window, which was moving only marginally faster than she could have walked, she had been watching Beorn's three fauns marching alongside. She had asked about their status, saying she had gotten the impression they were slaves.

"Sure, they have some basic intelligence. They can speak and follow directions." Beorn continued, "But some of them ain't no smarter than my cows, I tell you."

He continued in this vein for some time. At the first break, Mary turned on the mousy woman, desperate for any change in conversation. It was a false hope; the woman answered in painfully short bursts, stating that her boyfriend had bought a farm and managed somehow to raise enough dowry to send for her. Neither family was rich, but she seemed, in her own resigned way, happy enough with the arrangement. However, she would not, or could not, keep a conversation going, and soon Beorn was on again in his drawl, now giving the poor woman "sage advice" for her husband on the subject of ranching.

Worse still, that evening Beorn broached the subject again, over a dinner of heavily-salted pork in a stew. He pointed out one of his fauns, Hershel. Hershel was as different from Havlin or the other two as night and day. The other two were quiet and placid like Havlin. Hershel was far more like the fauns Mary had read about. He was always smiling, and frequently went into fits of giggles. He would laugh and then caper around the coach like a young child.

Beorn began telling how he had instructed Hershel to take some cows out to one particular pasture, but the cows had wanted to go to another, greener pasture. The cows had led Hershel on a chase through the woods, and in the end, they found the pasture they wanted.

"They tricked me good, them cows," Hershel agreed, laughing. He seemed unaware or unconcerned about being the butt of the story.

"Hershel himself has given me plenty of trouble," Beorn said as though the faun wasn't there. "They're always more trouble, the ones like him, running off to play with the wild faunesses, if you know what I mean." He sighed, "But hey, if you fix them all, where are you going to get new fauns?"

Then it dawned on Mary why the others were so placid. Her groin ached in sympathy, and her face flushed. She looked down into the greasy wooden bowl, her stew still uneaten.

She thought of the boy, Martin—the one she left back in Draadustin all those years ago. But that had been different, so very different. She could remember him so clearly, more clearly than she had in years. She could see him staggering across the bridge in agony after that desperate act, lying on the steps of Cornall Hospital.

I'm dying, he had said when the healers found him.

No, you are being born, she had replied.

Mary forced herself back to the present. She looked at the two fauns eating their steaming bowls of oats, their faces vacant. They had not had a choice in this. It had simply been done to them, with an indifference that was worse than any cruelty.

But what about what Beorn had said? Was it any different than the cows, pigs or goats? Were they given any choice? She stared off into the gathering twilight and saw a whole world made dull and placid by the loss of sex. She shivered.

"Cold, ma'am?" the driver asked, missing the mark.

"I am not used to such fine fare," she lied, handing over the stew, her stomach turning. She wanted nothing more to do with this world. "Could I beg some bread and maybe a potato or two from the pot?"

They camped three nights in all, the women sleeping in the coach and the men under a canvas lean-to against the side. Mary Lynn and Judith pulled out their knitting to help pass the time and expressed great amazement that Mary had never learned the skill.

Mary Lynn gave Mary two long needles and proved a better teacher than Mary a student. She struggled, but in the end managed to start a small scarf. She admired how the other two women's hands flew. The socks they were knitting grew at a surprising rate.

On the fourth day, they pulled into the first real town along their route. Here they picked up another couple. It made the coach very crowded, but it proved worth it. The couple knew Beorn and his wife reasonably well, and the two men thereafter talked only to each other.

The new rancher had with him three ranch hands who rode alongside the coach on tall horses. The weather had begun to clear, and for the next two days, Mary rode on top of the coach next to the driver, chatting with the men.

Toward the end of the first day after the newcomers had joined the line, one of the men asked Mary, "What is a young maid such as yourself doing making such a long journey by yourself?"

"I'm a healer." Mary went to gesture at her sleeve, but of course the pentacle was not embroidered on this outfit. The driver made a sharp low sound that might have been a word, and the conversation was quickly dropped. Later that night, she overheard them talking. She couldn't understand what the driver was saying except for the word "lady," and in an almost reverent whisper, the words "off-worlder" and "imperial." The next day, the ranch hands were cooler, more deferential.

As the days passed, a routine set in. One day, about midday, they found a young man in a tram waiting by the side of the road. Mary Lynn hurried down from the coach. Without a backward glance or a token goodbye, she climbed into her husband's tram, and they were gone. A day later, the pulled into a small town and spent the night in an inn. The next morning, with much fanfare and well-intentioned advice, Beorn and his wife were gone.

Two more passengers were picked up, a traveling button maker and a boot maker. None of the towns in these parts were large enough to support either craft, so they traveled instead, bartering their wares for lodging and pay.

The button maker had traveled extensively and was as much a storyteller as a craftsman. He was also the first person Mary had yet encountered who had personally visited the barony. He told her many stories about the place. She wasn't sure how much she would remember or how much use it would be, but at least it gave her the feeling that she knew what she was getting into.

The land about them grew wilder as they went along, wilder than she had ever seen. There were patches of dense forest, but mostly it was a land of rolling hills and plains. Over the plains, large herds of cattle roamed. It frightened her at first, when she realized they were not fenced in. Small gangs of men on horses, accompanied by the occasional faun, herded the cattle through the plains and guarded them at night.

Two signs told her the land was getting wilder. More of the cattle still had their horns. "Better able to defend themselves," the driver said. And the men were better armed as well. Short bows and utility knives gave way to long bows, swords, and even armor.

Lingleton, Mary's halfway mark, proved little more than a bump in the road. It was a town of a mere dozen buildings or so, and the businesses were all devoted to the rancher's life. There was a depot that sold dry goods and horse tack, an inn, a smithy that shoed horses and did small work, a tiny one-room bank, and a whorehouse.

The coach dropped her, the final passenger, off and picked up a few parcels for delivery back home. Then with a tip of his hat and a polite "Nice to have you on board" from the driver, her final line back to the empire was gone.

It was three days before the next coach was expected. Mary got to know the little town well in those days. She let it be known she was a healer and ended up seeing a dozen or more patients, from the arthritic shopkeeper of the dry goods shop to several of the women from the whorehouse with a variety of ailments. She did it in part to replenish her rapidly dwindling stash of coins, but mostly from sheer boredom. She had done no real healing in weeks, and she didn't want to get rusty.

She need not have worried. Whether it was the land, the people, or herself, she was growing in power by the day. The magic rushed on her, hard to control but potent. As she practiced her Oomutoo, she felt it too, the restless nature of the land about her. She still asked every day how she was to handle violence should it come upon her, and every day she got the same vision: the peaceful floating that was no answer.

8 MEN AT ARMS

One morning, Mary was awakened by a timid knock at her door. It was James, a scrawny boy who worked at the inn. He had been mothered by one of the whores and fathered by any one of a dozen or more ranch hands who frequented the whorehouse. He stared resolutely at the wooden floorboards as he stuck his head into Mary's room and announced that the coach had arrived late last night and they were hoping to leave early this morning. He left without raising his head. She found his modesty around her amusing, given that he had been raised in a whorehouse.

She rose, sponged herself off with water from a small ewer that had been left the night before, and dressed quickly. She had no idea how early they intended to leave, but she dared not miss it. She didn't know when the next coach would be.

"Morning, ma'am," the innkeeper's wife greeted her as she entered the main room. "You be wanting a bite of breakfast before you go, I reckon. Be a long ride before your next hot meal."

"Do I have time?" she asked.

"Well, the drivers ain't finished theirs yet," she said with a nod.

Mary turned. Two men-at-arms were sitting at a table with a huge breakfast piled between them. A large slab of ham, fried eggs, coarse ground grits and a half round of cheese lay on a serving platter, and they each had a plate in front of them. They helped themselves to ham with thick wood-handled forks with two tines.

They were a rough-looking pair. The one on the right had black hair and a thick black beard. A scar traced its way under his left eye and above the beard. He was heavyset with broad, powerful shoulders. The man on the left had long, sandy-blond hair pulled in a ponytail and a thick, sandy-blond beard.

Both men wore hauberks of chainmail and heavy leather belts with broadswords hanging off them. The blond looked like he could be friendly enough in the right circumstances, but both men's eyes had a wary caution about them, and the dark-haired man could only be described as a rough character. Mary wondered how many days she would have to spend in their company, and what those days might hold. Not that she had any choice now.

The innkeeper's wife presented her with a bowl of porridge and a fried egg on one side. "Where do I purchase my ticket?" Mary asked.

"Settle up with them lot directly. Here, I'll introduce you."

Mary followed the lady to the table. "This here is the lady I told you about," the innkeeper's wife said.

"The one needing to go to the Barony of Cordona."

"Hmm, yes." the black-haired one said.

"The one with the . . ." the blond waggled his fingers in the air. Mary gave him a quizzical look. "Magic."

"I am a healer, yes." Mary said. "And I need passage to Cordona."

The dark-haired man nodded thoughtfully.

"Is it true you're an off-worlder?" The blond asked.

The dark-haired man scowled and rolled his eyes. "I have threatened more than once to sew his mouth shut," he growled.

"And I," the blond replied with a hint of smile playing at his lips, "won't shut my mouth for fear that he will make good on his threat." Underneath their weary caution was a twinkling in both men's eyes. Mary smiled.

"I am Joe," the blond said, "and my companion here is Kenneth. We would stand and bow, but I fear my leg is game and my companion's gut is so large that it might upset the table if he rose too quickly."

"Why, I never," Kenneth muttered.

"Please, I need no formality," Mary said and took a seat opposite them, "merely passage."

"The Barony of Cordona is the end of our line. That's a week's journey. Standard fare is five gold pieces, up front. That's passage, food, and lodging each night."

"On the last line, we camped most nights," Mary said.

"We do not camp on this one," Kenneth said.

"The Marquis and the Count," Joe waved a hand negligently in the direction Mary had come from, "keep their peace. Knights keep court. Militias do patrols. Bailiffs make inquiries. Out there . . ." he waved back the way they had come.

Kenneth tapped his sword and finished, "Out there, men must keep their own peace. We sleep indoors."

Mary was glad she had worked the week and had some extra coins. She still had no idea whether she would be expected to support herself in Cordona, how long she would be there, or what she would be called upon to do. For now, her purse was sufficient. She withdrew five coins.

"No matter," she said. "However you wish it is fine with me." She handed the coins over.

"Local mint," Joe said. "I was hoping for some real imperial gold."

"I did some healing for some of the ladies next door," Mary said.

Joe spun one of the coins in his hand speculatively. "Next door, eh?" He turned to his partner with a wicked grin. "Say, think I have time to put a few of these back?"

"I think," Kenneth said with a scowl, "that if you could watch your tongue around a lady, you wouldn't be needing a whore." Mary bit back a laugh. To her, Kenneth said, "We do not, I am afraid, have much time. The next town is Hurran, and it's slightly more than a full day's ride. We will leave as soon as we can get your things packed. We will carry bread, ale, water, and," he paused for effect, "a chamber pot. We will not stop until we are there."

"I have only one bag," Mary told them, setting her empty bowl down. "I can be ready immediately, if you wish it."

Kenneth nodded and pushed his plate away. "That would be for the best."

Joe pushed himself up, wincing slightly as he did so. "Do not fear, my companion exaggerates slightly. Today will be a hard ride, but tomorrow we will be in civilized lands again."

The day's ride was long, as predicted, but uneventful. The men rode up top to keep a sharp look out, but one or the other, whichever was not currently driving, would lean down and check on Mary occasionally. They kept the horses at a steady pace but not so fast as to tire them. Miles of rolling plains went by. Finally toward nightfall, the plains became clumps of trees and eventually forest.

The path they were following became more established as well. They would periodically hit a crossroads or fork, and the road would be that much more established and traveled thereafter. Just as evening was giving way to full dark, two pale lanterns appeared on either side of the road. They were passing through a wooden gate into Hurran.

An old man sitting upon a tall wooden platform gave the two men-at-arms a genial nod as they passed. He turned and gave a shout. The gates began to shut behind them.

Hurran was a small village, less than two acres, all told. It was surrounded on all four sides, as far as Mary could tell, by a ten-foot-tall wall of thick pine timbers standing on end. The tops of these timbers were crudely carved spikes. The inn was the only business in the village other than a blacksmith, and it sold dry goods and served as a communal space in addition to lodging for the occasional visitor.

"The usual poor bunk that our skinflint of a boss

pays for," Kenneth said to the wizened man at the front door of the inn, "and the best room you have for the lady." The man raised an eyebrow at Mary then nodded.

Joe limped past, and Mary followed him inside. "May I ask how you received your injuries?"

"An accident, no more," he said. "Many years ago now. I was in the Baron's service. We were guarding a group of workers, clearing a path into a remote area so we could better keep out bandits. A tree fell on me, shattered my leg. My arm," he held up his right hand to demonstrate, "can still bear a sword, but the Baron has no need to of men who can't march."

"So you went to work for the coach service," Mary finished. "And you?" She directed this at Kenneth who had just come in bearing the mail bag.

"I've no stomach for war," he said. "I'm too big and clumsy to be a hunter, and I've no desire to herd cows." He shrugged. "So here I am."

"I am a healer," she said to Joe. "I could help with your leg."

"I would not wish to impose."

"It would not be an imposition," she said. "I can help with the pain at the least. To make it so you can walk correctly, I would first have to re-break the leg and then heal it."

"I would be quite happy to help," Kenneth put in from behind. "I've been wanting to break his bones for years now."

"With all due respect, I think I would have to decline the offer," Joe said.

"Seriously," she said, putting a hand on Kenneth's shoulder to quiet him. "Is tomorrow so far?"

"No, it's an easy ride from here on out," Kenneth

replied.

"Then tomorrow night, let me at least see what I can do."

Joe nodded.

The next day, they wound through wooded hills. The two men were at ease, taking turns riding in the cab with Mary to keep her company. The coach bounced and jumped on the rough road, but they did not set a hard pace. Toward midday, they broke into a clearing. A small logging camp had been erected at the far end, and they stopped and ate lunch with the loggers.

They rolled into the next village well before dark, and Mary had time before supper to perform a deep healing on Joe's leg. He expressed amazement that she was able to rid him of the pain he'd endured for so many years, yet his faith in magic was not so great that he would let Mary re-break the leg to permanently heal it. She shrugged and let it go.

He tried to press on her two gold coins in appreciation. She knew this was his entire month's salary and refused it repeatedly. Finally she was able to convince him that four pieces of silver was the going rate for the work she had done.

In the common room at the evening meal, both men jumped the innkeeper over their seating arrangement, demanding a better table for "the lady," as they kept referring to her. At first she felt a little put out. During the ride, she'd enjoyed an easy informality with both men. She wanted no titles or pretense.

After a certain amount of haggling, the innkeeper sat them at a corner table, toward the edge of the common room. The two men sat on either side, flanking her. As the room began to fill up with men—exclusively men, broad men in leather shirts, rough-looking men in coarse flax, and more than a few men in chainmail or leather armor—Mary began to understand. It was not pretense but protection. This was a rough crowd, and the men wanted to make it clear that Mary was not some maid to be trifled with. She was a woman of importance, best left alone.

The serving woman had no such protection and endured many lewd comments and more than one less-than-playful grab. As she brought a tray to their table, Joe remarked, "Last we passed this way, there was no garrison here. Is there a patrol?"

"Mercenaries. I'll be glad to see the back of that lot. Though no doubt more are on their heels."

"Mercenaries?" Mary asked, astonished.

"There are rumors of war between the baron and the duke," the woman said. "These carrion are going to feed on that war."

"Carrion?" a man at the next table jeered. "Is that any way to talk to the Baron's next protectorate?"

"Yeah," his partner chimed in. "Men who are soon to have huge," he made a crude gesture, "purses." He laughed at his own joke.

"Protectorate?" A man farther down laughed. "If you go to serve the baron, 'corpse' might be a more fitting title. I hear the war goes ill for him."

"He is a strong man," the first man said. "He'll crush the duke."

The second man was on his feet, hand on his sword. "Maybe I should save the baron your first wages, and you the walk," he growled.

The innkeeper came out from behind the bar, armed with a heavy cudgel. He used it to bang on a thick iron cauldron in the far fire space. He yelled for attention. When everyone had stopped still and was watching him, he brandished his cudgel. "Listen up, every one of you. Neither the duke nor the baron has paid you to spill blood in my inn. Is that understood?"

There was some quiet grumbling but the men took their hands from their weapons and sat at the tables again.

"What sort of fool mercenary fights before he gets paid?" a voice said somewhere off to Joe's left. "To whom are you bound? I figure I'll get a little closer, maybe get some fresher information before I decide."

"I serve the coach," Joe said. "No more."

"What if the war were to end?" Mary asked.

The man made a disparaging noise to show what he thought of Mary's suggestion. His friend leaned in to the conversation. "Always a danger," the friend replied. "Get there late and miss the spoils." He shrugged. "What are you going to do, huh? I heard the countess of Shinten was raising a force to deal with some robber barons, but it was nowhere near the pay."

When the men had turned their attention back to their own dinner, Kenneth leaned in and said, "It would be best, for you at least, to make an early night of it. Food will settle the men for a while, but once they start on the ale, it could be a rough night."

Mary nodded her assent. Her eyes scanned the room. Here was another side of the empire she would have never expected: mercenaries. How many were there? Was there steady work?

***

Luckily for Mary and her two guards, the

mercenaries were mostly making for one of two forts on the southern spur of the Cargill Mountains and the baron's home was farther north. The parting of ways came at an unmarked crossroads around midday, and that night the inn where they stayed was empty of all but a few locals.

This stretch of forest belonged by tradition to a clan of woodsmen, mostly loggers, carpenters, and huntsmen. They all swore fealty to someone who bore the title "Lord of the Mountain." The lord was on easy terms with the baron but had no part in the current war.

This land seemed both wilder and more civilized at the same time. The woods were deep, dark, and definitely wild. The villages were mostly small and protected by high walls. At night, the woods were alive with sounds: the howling of wolves and the scuffling of other larger beasts that Mary never saw. Once while they driving, she was overcome by a powerful, earthy odor. The horses neighed, and when she asked, Joe told her in a quiet voice that they were in the territory of a large bear. She did not see the bear that day or any other, but villagers showed her skins of bears many times the size of anything Mary had ever seen.

In other respects, the land was growing more civilized. Villages were closer to together and growing to be small towns. Local craftsmen worked in leather and wood. The markets overflowed with goods, and while they did not match the markets of Tomlin City, they were of surprisingly high quality. Villages and towns began to feature public buildings, churches and small imperial schools.

A few things remained constant, as they had since

she arrived on this world. Buildings were mostly wood, constructed low to the ground with thatch roofs. These people lived close to nature and close to the animals they raised. Often the barn would be directly attached to the house. One morning, she arrived in the inn's common room to find a Dutch door at the back and a cow regarding the morning proceedings with a detached air from over the open top. Another time, Mary had requested milk to go with her tea, and the placid faun who served her returned with milk still steaming from the cow's udder.

More distressing was the lack of concern about hygiene. She made due with sponge baths since arriving. More than once, she had tried to take a bath, but locals would just look at her quizzically. "A bath?" one innkeeper had said. "This time of year?" Another informed her that the inn didn't have a bathhouse.

Perhaps it was for the best. "This time of year" meant that it was wet, rainy, and cold. Several times, there were thick, heavy snows. She had experienced snow only once before, on a trip with Ashe. It had been a memorable and romantic encounter. These snows were wet, cold, clammy, and far less romantic. Couple that with the rough wood construction and poorly mudded planks of the buildings and the wind and wet spray would often blow through the walls. It would be easy to catch a chill and get sick in this climate. Even so, Mary felt grimy and wished to soak and forget her troubles for a while.

***

"Halt."

Joe slowed the coach. Mary leaned out the window to see what was going on. Kenneth waved her back inside as he dropped onto the running board beside the door, loosening his sword as he did. His face was lined with worry, which did nothing to lessen the feeling of ill ease that coursed through Mary. She shared a glance with the other two passengers in the coach.

"We are collecting a toll on this road," the voice continued.

"For whom?" Joe answered. "There has never been a toll on this road before. Whom do you serve?"

"Say," the voice paused, "say it's for the Veterans of the War Fund."

There was a smattering of laughter at this. Mary tried to count, but she was not able to place how many there were. With only two men on the coach, however, they were outnumbered.

"How much is this toll?" Joe continued.

"Oh, what do you got?" the man laughed again. She could see men encircling the coach.

"There's a girl in there," someone said, spotting her. "We want her."

A feeling of restless energy and rising power gripped Mary. She felt angry at the man's presumption. Ignoring the other two passengers and the warning look from Kenneth, she stepped out of the coach and walked directly toward the leader of brigands.

"Yeah, she'll do for a starter," the man drawled as he watched her. Beside him were three burly figures with crossbows. She understood Kenneth's concern; all told, there were about a dozen of them. Even without the crossbows, Joe and Kenneth were hopelessly outnumbered.

"What's your name little girl?"

Now was the moment in any storybook that Mary should have shouted something like "I am Mary de Castellena, mage of the Tenth Circle of…" But Mary was just Mary. An orphan. She had no family name she knew of. A personal apprentice, she had never inquired or been told whether there was an order, lodge, or school to which she belonged.

But she was a mage, and that counted for more than something. The energy was rushing upon her, though she had no clue what to do with it. Behind the man, a large, knotted rowan tree swayed, though there was no wind. She felt its spirit, restless and angry that men had disturbed its patch of forest. *Use me,* its voice said in her head.

So she did. She bent her will to the tree and called upon it to move. It did so slowly at first, with a lot of creaking. Then the entire trunk flowed and bent like greenwood. One long branch with four smaller branches, like fingers, reached out for the lead bandit. She meant to grab him but instead swatted him heavily and knocked him from his horse. The horse bolted in fear.

The man was dumped unceremoniously at Mary's feet. "You will leave this road," she told him. "You will leave these woods. And you will leave these people in peace. Or I shall waken every tree in the forest. Do you understand?"

He nodded, carefully pulling himself to his feet. He looked around to motion for his men to go, but they were already gone, one crossbow laying on the road.

"Go!" Mary commanded, and the bandit fled, chasing after his men.

Joe retrieved the crossbow as Kenneth helped the

now shaky Mary back into the coach.

"Waken the trees?" One of the passengers said in a shaky voice. "Can you do that?" His name was Marlin, and he was a lumberjack. Both he and his young wife were looking at her with a mixture of awe and fear.

"I am not sure," Mary said, accepting the wineskin that Kenneth passed as the coach creaked forward. "I am a healer," she added, trying to calm their fears. "I have mage-caliber magic, but I haven't had much use for any magic other than healing, until now. What I did was just to scare them."

Now that she thought about it, she had scared herself. She did not realized she had such power in her, to command trees. Yet when she had spoken the words, she was certain she was capable of raising the entire forest. The image of an army of trees, with her at its head, went through her mind. She shook her head and took a long drink before passing the skin on.

9 THE BARON OF CORDONA

The current baron of Cordona was Aldrith Von
Helfen de Cordona, and he lived in his ancestral
home in Grenwich City. The city was nestled in the
foothills of the Cargill Mountains. Mary was surprised
to discover, as they crested a steep hill on the twelfth
day of their journey, that Grenwich was indeed a city.
It was not as big or grand as any imperial city, but it
certainly dwarfed any of the villages she had passed
along the way. It was perhaps twice the size of the
gate city that led off-world.

Looking down from the high valley walls, Mary
was even more surprised to see that it was ringed on
all four sides with a stout wooden wall. Tall wooden
towers stood at intervals of a hundred yards or so,
and she could see ant-like men-at-arms walking along
the top of the wall between the towers.

Before the coach turned and began its descent,
Mary leaned far out of the window and called up to

Kenneth, "May I come up?"

"Be my guest," he replied. Joe slowed the coach as she pulled herself up using the handrails on the side of the coach. Kenneth slid over to make room for her on the bench beside them.

"Thank you," she said as the coach lurched forward and began to turn sharply to the right. The road they were on snaked back and forth across the valley wall in an effort to smooth the otherwise steep descent.

Mary took a deep breath. The air was cool and wet but not unpleasantly so. The sky above was a light gray; the sun did not show, but it was light and free of rain. She could smell the musty soil and the heather that grew along the road. Down below them, as the valley began to level out, farms were terraced high up the valley walls, and the smell of farmyards greeted her.

She looked again at the city. It stretched more than a mile in either direction from the gate. From what she could see, the city seemed to be a rough square. She could count a dozen and a half towers on the side they were facing.

"They have fortifications all around the city?" she asked.

"Yes," Joe replied. "The entire city can function within a siege. Under the baron's great-grandfather's reign, it did. The dwarves of Cargill Mountains made an alliance—all the dwarfish clans under one banner and aided by the Lord of the Mountain. They wanted to force the baron to give fealty to them rather than the other way around. They came out of the mountains in numbers and set siege for nearly two years."

"In the end," Kenneth said, finishing the story, "they couldn't break his spirit. His son was away when the siege was started and trapped outside. He managed to raise a mercenary army and to rally the villages about. He led a force to break the siege."

"But to keep a whole city fortified like this," Mary said, "it must take a lot of men and resources." She thought of her home. There were two forts in Tomlin. The original fortification was in the center of town, now a bustling commercial district. It was little more than a historical site and tourist attraction. The fifty-member town guard was a ceremonial unit that marched or performed drills for spectators.

The imperial fort on the edge of town had some five hundred garrison troops. It was little more than a way station; the recruitment office by far was the busiest part of the fort. All of the soldiers within Tomlin would barely be able to man a couple of towers or length of wall here. Yet the cost of maintaining those troops was a constant source of irritation for the burghers, the guild masters who collectively ran Tomlin's governing council. Mary recalled an editorial in a local paper not many weeks before she left. *Who is going to heal all those people stabbed with all the swords they are buying?*

"The expense," Mary said, "of housing and equipping that many soldiers must be great."

Kenneth laughed. "I suppose in the central worlds you can rely on magic to protect you. Out here we must make due."

They coasted down through a couple of small agricultural villages before breaking free into the valley itself. As they rolled up to the gates of Grenwich, Mary was struck not only by the relative size of the city, but by the amount of traffic flowing into and out of the gate. Grenwich was a merchant city.

The city planning was only marginally better than it had been in the gate city, Hartnel. The road they were on became a wide cobblestone lane. It intersected other wide cobblestone lanes at intervals, obviously meant for coach and cart traffic. In between, however, houses were clumped without any thought for size, wealth, or purpose. Large houses for the wealthy stood next to hovels. Businesses were wedged in at random. Smaller lanes branched off into various ghettos, but the lanes were of inconsistent size and construction.

The markets they rode past were active and showed a rich diversity of people. There were mostly humans of the same basic stock as Joe and Kenneth, light-skinned people with blond hair and sandy beards or dark hair and thick beards. halflings were fairly common as well, somewhat taller and more muscular than the ones back home. She saw a dwarf dressed in nothing but a short kilt using a bellow to heat a fire in an open-air smithy. There were several more dwarves in rich wool garments at one of the markets. The occasional faun made its way through the crowd, and Mary spotted an odd humanoid with a greenish cast to its skin and long, pointed ears.

Out of the corner of her eye, Mary caught sight of a tall, blond form that seemed to glide through the crowd as though above it all. It appeared to be male, dressed in a long, green tunic and tight, brown leggings, but the graceful lines of the elfish face were ambiguous. Mary turned as far as she dared in her seat to watch the elf pass. They were a race that was rarely seen in the large cities of the central world, and Mary had never seen one in real life before.

There were also plenty of indications that war was no stranger to this part of the empire. Many of the houses, even within the city proper, had tall narrow windows meant for archers. Merchants often carried long daggers or short swords. In one of the markets, she saw a military recruitment stand and an incredible variety of mercenaries gathered around. Many did not seem to be local stock. There were a couple of men with straight black hair and yellowish skin and a tall man with bluish-black skin and strange tribal scarring on his face.

As they neared the far end of the town, the ghettos and mixed buildings gave way to public buildings, a courthouse, a barracks, and a large cathedral.

"Where does the baron live?" Mary asked.

"His manor is on the far edge of town, with its own walls," Joe said.

"It is said to be three stories in places and have over a hundred rooms," Kenneth said. "Not that we've been invited, mind."

"A hundred rooms?" Mary asked.

"It houses most of his extended family," Joe explained. "Many of the minor officials, fifty armed guards, and probably twice as many servants.

The road branched off to the right, but Joe kept the coach going straight on, rolling around a wide fountain and up to a stone wall, some ten feet high.

"There it is," Kenneth said, nodding at the wall, "behind that wall is the baron's manor." Directly in front of them were a gatehouse and an iron portcullis. The coach came to a creaking halt in front of the gatehouse.

"The end of the line," Joe said, "for you at least. I wish you luck with whatever you are here to do." For Joe, it was as eloquent as he got.

Mary patted his cheek affectionately. "Thank you," she said.

"I wish you luck as well," Kenneth said, "and my deepest thanks for the most memorable trip we've had. Joe's leg. The bandits. We owe you a deep debt."

"Nonsense," she replied.

"We do," he insisted. "And if you should need a ride back, we would be greatly honored to bear you on our coach again."

"I would like that as well," she said. She gave him a warm hug goodbye and climbed down from the coach, retrieving her lone bag. With a final wave from the men, the coach completed its circuit of the fountain and was on the road, heading back the way it came. Mary turned back to the gatehouse.

The large iron portcullis was down, closing off the road and denying entrance to the manor grounds. There was a small side door in the right tower, with two guards standing outside. They were covered in chainmail and carried long swords at their sides and crossbows in their hands.

She felt apprehensive. This was it. The moment of truth had arrived. How should she begin? "I am here to broker a peace between . . ." or perhaps, "The Emperor demands peace be made between . . ." She did not know if she had that much authority.

In the end, she reached the men before coming up with an answer to that question, so merely said, "I am Mary, and I am here to see the baron."

The men looked at her skeptically. One smirked. "Here to see the baron? What is your business, little lady? Perhaps we can be of help."

"I doubt it," she said, angry and embarrassed. "My business is with the baron."

The second guard laughed outright at that. Jokingly, he called within the guard house, "We have a lass named Mary, who says she has business with the baron."

This was answered with another laugh. Mary stood stock still, bewildered, her face red. Now what? She wished again she had some name or title that sounded impressive. Was she to blast down the gates with magic and storm the manor herself?

She almost laughed out loud at the image of her smashing her way through, and at the image she must present now: a dirty little redheaded girl demanding entrance to see the most powerful man in the region.

After what seemed to be a very long time, she saw a young maiden running across the manor lawn at full speed, holding her dress up as she came. She made it to the opposite side of the guard house and disappeared. There was a murmur of surprise from within, and then the maiden burst forth. She took one look at Mary, and her face fell. She caught herself and dropped into a low curtsy.

"The baron bids you welcome, m'lady," she said breathlessly, "and would bid you patience. He has sent a coach worthy of your rank, and his apologies that it

105

was not kept ready. We are afraid, m'lady that we had no idea of the time or manner of your arrival."

"It's okay," she replied. "I don't need a coach. Just lead me to him."

The maid would not hear of it. Within a few minutes, and to the surprise of the guards, who were now trying their best to act obsequious, a coach arrived. It was several times the size of the one she had just ridden in for two weeks. It was pulled by a team of six large draft horses, bigger than any she had ever seen. The portcullis groaned as the men, sweating with more than exertion, pulled it to.

A guard, this one in full ceremonial regalia, stepped quickly down from the coach's passenger seat and opened the door. "My lady," he said, ushering her inside. The maid followed after.

They rode slowly down the wide, hedge-lined boulevard toward the distant manor building. Mary felt small, dirty, and poor as she sat on the cushioned, red-velvet seat. The seat was too high for her, and at every bump her feet left the floor. This only accentuated her feelings of being small. She was, she knew, in over her head. Still, she had a mission to do, and she was not known for backing down. All the way up the road, she rehearsed what she would say.

"You were expecting me?" she asked.

"Yes, m'lady. You were sent for, no?" the maid answered.

Sent for her? Had they asked for her?

"Well, not you personally," the maid went on answering her unspoken question, "but someone. We wrote to the mage's council to send a mage. You are a mage, right?" The maid looked her up and down.

"I am," Mary replied, taken aback.

"I'm sorry," the maid blushed. "I hope I haven't offended. I have never seen a magic user before. I thought—"

"I'd be grander," Mary finished. "All pretty robes and hocus pocus."

"What?"

"Something my teacher used to say," Mary explained, "about those who pretend to magic. They must look the part; real mages have no such need. Besides, I am here to broker a peace settlement, no more."

As soon as the coach door opened, Mary stepped out and strode up the carpeted steps of the manor house. *I always thought the red carpet was an allusion, a figure of speech.* At the top of the steps stood a tall man in a richly-embroidered jacket and black tights.

"I am Mary, my good sir," she began, "mage from the emperor's council and here to assist you and the duke to achieve the emperor's peace. If we may—"

He stopped her with a worried gesture and bowed deeply. "No offense, my lady, but I am not the baron. I am Jerald, the castellan. You are no doubt tired from your journey, and the baron is momentarily indisposed. He sends his cordial greetings and offers the hospitality of his humble home. He further says that he is looking forward to meeting you in person at the feast tonight in your honor."

Tonight? It wasn't even lunch time yet. She sighed. It had been a long trip, and while urgent, would one more afternoon make a difference? For the men out there fighting and dying, yes. But apparently this was beyond her power right now. Trying not to appear too submissive, she followed the castellan into the manor.

She was quickly lost in the maze of hallways. After some time, the castellan stopped in front of a large set of double doors and announced, "Your quarters, my lady."

She was shown into a huge room, one of four that had been assigned to her. The room was dominated by a four-poster bed, but still had room for a large wardrobe, a dresser, a desk, a dining table, a full-length mirror, and a changing screen. Her bag fit into one drawer of the dresser, and she wondered if anyone really needed that much space for clothes.

The castellan excused himself, and a maid led her to the next room, where a steaming bath was waiting. A young girl of nine or ten tended a fire and kept kettles of water heating atop a grill. After over a month of sponge baths in cool or cold water, this was too much to resist. Mary stripped, heedless of the women, and stepped into the large copper tub. She soaked a long time, spurning the occasional attempts by the maids to assist her. She washed her hair more thoroughly than she had done since the journey's start. Finally the water began to cool, and she felt guilty about letting so much time elapse.

The maid handed her a thick towel. She dried herself slowly and then looked around for her clothes. She could not see them anywhere. The maid had disappeared as well, back into the main chamber. She thanked the young girl tending the fire. The girl dropped a quick curtsy but did not respond.

Wrapped in the towel, Mary made her way back into the main room. She was confronted not by the maid alone, but by about a half dozen women. The oldest of these, looking like a drill sergeant in a long dress with a cloth bolt for a spear and a thin cigar of needles between her teeth, looked her over appraisingly.

Mary sighed. "And I am to be?"

"Suited for the ball," the old woman said in a business like tone. "Come on, girls. We have work to do."

Wondering if that was a swipe at her looks, Mary climbed onto a pedestal. The women surrounded her quickly, stripping her of the towel and throwing a loose-fitting dress over her head.

And there she stood for what seemed like hours. Layer after layer of cloth, item after item of clothing went first on, then off. One of the young maids ran a powder-blue cloth of fine cotton around her waist, pulling it tight. The old woman tisked and said, "Won't do at all, makes her look like a little boy in a dress." Mary bit back a reply as the cloth was tossed to one side.

Then a dark brown, woolen cloth went around, and light green silk. Finally a length of burnt-orange silk seemed to satisfy the older woman. "Sets her hair off nicely."

When the whole process was done, Mary was surprised at how simple the end product looked. They settled, without consulting Mary, on a loose-fitting dress in a classical style, with gathered shoulders and no sleeves. The back dipped dangerously low, as did the cleavage. There was a light brown shawl of the softest wool Mary had ever touched to cover her back and keep off the chill. It was pulled together with a small, silver belt. They finally parted so she could reach the full-length mirror. It was not a style she would have ever chosen for herself, but she had to admit, it looked good.

As the women gathered up the unused pieces of cloth, the first maid whispered to the older woman and gestured at the dresser where Mary's bag had been stored. The older woman nodded and turned to Mary. "We have your size," she said holding up a tape measure, "and your color. We'll have some suitable things put together before tomorrow." With that the old lady was gone, along with two of the younger woman.

Now perhaps some peace, Mary thought . . . *or maybe not,* as the remaining three girls pulled a chair over and bade her to sit. Another couple of hours passed while they combed and styled her hair and did her makeup. Mary had only the tiniest kit of makeup at home, having few opportunities to wear any coloring. These women seemed to have an unending collection and were quite content to spend endless minutes trying one thing after another.

After that was a visit from the concierge. Mary didn't know what a concierge was and had to ask. She had never thought that anyone would need somebody just to arrange things for them to do. Who was that busy or that important? But it was gratifying nonetheless. They discussed the menu for the evening, and she was given the rundown on what to expect. She felt for the first time like she had some idea what was going on.

The concierge brought a light snack of cheese and crackers. Breakfast was long since gone, and lunch too had come and gone. On previous assignments, Mary had fasted for days at a time and felt no hunger. However, she had not prepared herself for such hardships here and was starving.

As the evening progressed, she was more and more thankful for the snack. She had never been to a fine ball. First, she had to wait for what seemed like ages in the foyer until she was announced. A young knight named Harold escorted her in. "A grave honor," he called it as he took her hand. "And no hard chore either," he added more genially after looking her over briefly.

The castellan announced her as Mary, "a visitor of great distinction from the central worlds." She was led down a long staircase and into a wide, long hall. The walls were covered in rich tapestries showing various scenes. The wood floors gleamed by the light of a large fire that was blazing in a fireplace big enough for Mary to stand in. There were a number of small tables and chairs along the edge of the room and a four-person orchestra played in one corner. The middle of the floor was open.

Harold led Mary along the edge and a beautiful young maiden, who introduced herself as Shurya, joined her on the other side. Shurya had long, black hair, rich, brown eyes, and a graceful poise. She wore a simple, black dress but managed to make it look more stunning than the more elaborate dresses the noble women wore.

They walked at a slow pace, Shurya stopping and introducing Mary to the guests one by one. Occasionally, Mary heard the castellan announce another late arrival, and they, too, made the rounds behind her. She had been accorded a place of honor,

Shurya assured her, far enough toward the end so that everyone was waiting on her.

She soon lost count of the names and titles of all the people she was introduced to. It seemed, she commented to Shurya, that half the barony was nobility of some sort or another. There were counts, squires, lords, and other titles she had never heard before. Shurya chuckled appreciatively, then she questioned Mary about the nobility on her home world.

"I don't know," Mary said with a shrug. "Tomlin City is traditionally under the Caliph of Emerait, I believe."

"You believe?" Shurya asked after pausing to introduce her to a portly older man who was an "esquire of the fifth precinct in Horva."

"The caliph has never been to our city, as far as I know," Mary replied, "but someone told me once he was our liege."

"Then who runs the city?"

"The burghers do, of course." To Shurya's confused look, she explained, "The guilds run the city collectively, the tradesmen's guilds, the builders' guild, the craftsmen's guild, and the healers', etc. They each select one elder of their guild to serve as burgher. The burghers have a council that makes all the major decisions. The burghers, in turn, elect a burghermeister."

Shurya frowned, "But do you swear fealty to the burghermeister?"

"No, we swear only to the emperor."

"You have seen the emperor?" Shurya asked in an awed whisper.

Mary chuckled. "Of course not. We swear upon his name in court. Nobody sees the emperor. Nobody normal anyway."

"But you are a mage," Shurya continued, "and mages are very powerful, some almost as powerful as the emperor himself."

"Some more so," Mary replied, "at least at a personal level. But they serve the emperor. Yes, some mages see the emperor regularly, I am sure. I am a mage but not *that* powerful. My teacher, Ashe, has never even seen one of the Harcourt dynasty, though he was heavily involved with the Han emperors, serving one personally."

"Impossible," Shurya replied a little too loudly, and several people turned towards them. More softly she went on, "You think me a country fool, to tell such stories. The Hans haven't ruled in three centuries. No one is so old."

"A mage of Ashe's caliber can prevent aging," Mary said, "and most live for centuries, if they so desire."

"Who wouldn't desire that?" Harold said at her other side. His comment made her pause. It was a common enough attitude. And yet few realized what it was like emotionally. Mary was a mere baby of some eighty years compared with Ashe's several centuries. Yet she knew already what it was to feel so old, like you had lived too much, seen too much. It was hard being old, even if your body did not age. She didn't know how the older mages did it, truth told.

Ashe had laughed at her when she told him this. "Few mages are as introspective as you," he said.

"They experience so little of their own lives."

They had made a complete circle of the room when the castellan's voiced boomed again. "I give you your grace, the Baron Aldrith von Helson of Cordona, lord of the all the reaches of Cordona, Shurfa, Holdith . . ." the place names and the titles rolled on. Mary quickly lost track as she turned her attention instead to the holder of these titles.

The baron was a big, beefy man—one who was muscular as well as fat. He looked, if she had to describe him, like a giant dwarf. He had thick, reddish hair and a bristly beard. He was dressed in a leather vest, a reddish-orange silk shirt, thick brown tights, and a long leather belt, richly adorned in silver and gold. He had a sword hanging at his waist, and the leather vest was thick with medals.

He stood with his feet spread wide apart. It was a commanding stance, but one that also spoke of wary caution. He stood as though ready for an onslaught. His eyes too moved back and forth as though on the lookout for any enemies.

It must be hard to be a baron in wartime, Mary thought as she eyed him. His gaze swept over her, brimming with arrogance. *On the other hand,* she amended, *he is probably always mistrustful.* She felt an immediate dislike for the baron. She pushed it down. If she was to negotiate peace between the lands, she must deal with the baron.

The castellan's introduction finished, and the baron waved down a smattering of polite applause. He then launched into a speech dedicated to Mary— to her own surprise—their "esteemed visitor." He spoke in glowing and vague terms about how he was overjoyed at her visit and looked forward to showing her the grandeur of the barony. He managed to speak a long time, considering that he never mentioned who Mary was or why she was visiting. Mary found the speech odd, but knowing nothing of polite society, she let it pass.

After the baron's speech, which he finished with a slight bow to Mary, the doors on the left side of the hall opened. Another large hall was visible within, this one filled with a long, square table with the entire middle empty so that servers could carry trays and food within.

Mary was led in towards the front of a procession, only feet behind the baron. He did not turn to see her, nor did he give any sort of personal greeting. She was placed at the seat of honor across from the baron.

In the middle of the room, to Mary's disgust, was an entire ox, skinned and roasted with an apple in its mouth. Unused to as much meat as these people ate, or how close they were to the actual animals, Mary lost her appetite. Luckily, she had discussed her own menu with the concierge and was not served off the big ox in the center.

To her right sat Shurya. To her left was a man named Shane. At least she thought he was a man. He was short enough to be a halfling almost, except he was thin and pointy. He reminded her unpleasantly of a rat. He had dark hair, neatly combed, and a tiny slip of a black mustache.

"What an incredible and polite snubbing you are getting," he commented casually to her as she ate.

"Come again?"

"The baron is nothing if not thorough. He throws a fine banquet."

"I am not sure I follow you"

"It is nothing, no worse than the snubbing I receive daily."

"Shane is Duke Leto's ambassador," Shurya said from the other side. "Pay him no mind."

"The handmaiden does her job well. I mean no offense. Surely the baron honors the visitor Mary with the grandest feast of the year, and the ball after will no doubt be as good. But has he greeted you himself? Or has he used the excuse of courtesy to avoid you?"

"The baron is a busy man," Shurya snapped, "and the war is no help."

Still, Shane had hit a nerve. Mary had expected to be brought directly to the baron and to speak at once about her mission. Instead she had been shunted from one servant to the next, each with their own perfectly reasonable explanation. When would she meet the baron directly?

Shane said no more about the subject, instead turning to small talk, about which he seemed to have no end. Yet his comments soured the whole evening. Not particularly hungry, and having neither the experience nor the desire for small talk, Mary was bored.

The feast went on for several hours. What did they do with all that food, she thought? She had eaten her fill with the first course, and without seconds. Yet these minor nobles shoveled in helping after helping.

Finally the feast finished, and they were ushered back into the other room. The band now played a livelier tune, and a few people danced. Most circulated the edges. Servants shuffled through the crowd, bearing trays laden with drinks and yet more food. Mary took a drink to be polite. It was bitter and far too alcoholic for her taste, but she held on to it as a defense against servants trying to force yet another drink upon her.

Shurya stayed at her side throughout the ball and provided a continual commentary about the people who tried to engage Mary in banter.

As with all things, the banquet eventually ended. The castellan announced the baron's retirement for the night. Guests were encouraged to stay as late as they wish, and a few seemed likely to do so, but most began to shuffle towards the door almost on the baron's heels.

"You seem tired," Shurya offered, to Mary's relief. "Shall I escort you back to your room?"

She stared down the passage where the baron had gone. She needed to speak to him, but that clearly wasn't going to happen tonight. She sighed and let it go. "Yes, thank you."

10 SHURYA DE LA LENSA

Once they got back to her quarters, Mary expected Shurya to depart, but instead she followed Mary inside. A metal brazier had been placed in the center of the room, and a dark coal fire smoldered inside. Heat radiated from the brazier, but to Mary, it made the room feel colder by comparison. She found a cushion and settled down in front of the fire.

Shurya found a cushion and sank down beside Mary. She said, "I am Shurya de la Lensa, Lady in waiting of the court Cordona. My mother was the Lady Raven, of court Ramone, in the eastern province. My grandmother was the famed courtesan Sophia de la Lensa, concubine to Grand Duke Garvin on the world of Hartlin in the imperial central quadrant."

Damn, even the servants have more prestigious names than I. I must talk to Ashe about that when I get home.

"Do you know of my grandmother?" Shurya asked.

Mary shook her head. "The central worlds are

huge, Shurya. I have heard of Hartlin, though I didn't know it had a grand duke. Who his concubines were . . . "

"In her youth, my grandmother was a rare beauty," Shurya interrupted, "but she was involved in a scandal. Her paramour was a mighty mage, Larsa Upisilon of the imperial council of mages."

"Larsa!" Mary said in a gasp. Suddenly a lot of pieces were falling into place.

Shurya smiled. It was probably the first genuine display of emotion Mary had seen that evening. Mary liked it much better than Shurya's other smile. "So we have at last hit on something we both know. I was getting worried."

"Yes, I know Larsa." Mary replied. *A bit too well*, she added to herself. One of her assignments for Ashe had been to con his old partner and friend out of a secret ritual.

She hated that assignment at first. It had seemed dishonest and artificial. She had expected a bitter old man, given to plots and intrigue, for that was Larsa's reputation. Instead she had found him lively, engaging, and most importantly, genuine. He had been forthright with her, so she returned the favor, telling him directly of her assignment and asking for the ritual.

He had relented, perhaps a bit too readily. The rite had been advanced sex magic. She should have been angry, at Ashe and Larsa both. They had manipulated her into sex (sex magic is still sex). But she wasn't. They had opened her eyes to the ways that sex, like any energy, can be shared and used. They helped free her from societal constraints about with whom she should or should not share this kind of intimacy.

"Larsa and my grandmother were lovers once, long ago," Shurya was saying, bringing Mary's attention back to the present. "I wrote to him, asking for help."

Larsa's involvement solved one puzzle anyway. He had maintained for a long time that Mary was capable of more, magically, than she realized. "You are going to waste your life as a healer," he had said more than once. *Being a healer is nobler than what most mages do with their power,* Mary maintained.

"The baron does not want you here," Shurya said, "but he dares not send you away."

"Why doesn't he want me here? I thought the war was going badly for him. Surely if it can be ended—"

"If it ends now, he loses much. He will not willingly stop this war until he is at an advantage, no matter what the cost to his own people.

"Gregory has appealed to the court of the empire and to the overseer's office, both to no avail. He even took several cases to the criminal courts, under charges of murder, in hopes of getting one of the high courts to intervene here. But they have all refused, claiming they don't have jurisdiction until the baron's court tries the case. He has even appealed to members of the military. They will not intervene, or so they say. There seemed nothing left to do. When he confided all this to me, I thought that I must act. I wrote to Larsa and reminded him of my grandmother and their love. I begged him to send help, to come himself if possible or send another in his place. It was a wild hope. I was surprised to find a reply, but all it said was 'Mary is coming.' And now here you are." Shurya ended in a rush.

"Here I am," Mary agreed. "Now let's start from the top. Who is Gregory?"

Gregory, it turned out, was a paladin and one of the baron's top military advisers. He had been leading the campaign against the duke. It had not gone well. In fact, the baron had removed him from the campaign twice, only to put him back in charge when the other commanders failed even worse.

"The forces of both the baron and the duke are pretty evenly matched and the war should not be going so badly. However, the duke has something new, an elite team of soldiers they call the Juggernauts. They are fearsome in battle. Some say they are devils disguised as men. Others say they are invulnerable. Whatever the truth, wherever they go, we invariably lose," Shurya said. "This is what Gregory fears. He served in the military for many years before coming to this post. He has spoken to many old friends. Some have come as observers or mercenaries, but their superiors refuse to get involved. Gregory worries that they have already committed themselves, to the other side. These Juggernauts—what if they are some new type of soldier? What if the military is testing them here?"

"Testing them?" Mary asked. "Against our own people? The emperor would never."

"The emperor, maybe not," Shurya responded, "but many things happen without the emperor's knowledge."

"The mages would know, surely," Mary said.

"The intelligence bureau, the combat mages—yes, certainly they would know, but they work for the military," Shurya said. "What of the civilian mages? They would know, yes? But would they interfere? Would they go against the military?"

Mary stopped, considering. Yes, they would know.

Would they interfere? They would not be afraid, as was Shurya's implication. She knew little of the power of true mages if she thought they held the military in awe. But would they make an open conflict of it? Or intervene more carefully . . .

Ashe's words when he gave her this assignment came back to her: *"We must act delicately, Mary. We do not desire to be seen as taking sides in this matter."*

Delicately, she thought ruefully, *understatement of the year.* What did this mean for her assignment? Was she really here to investigate what the military was doing? If so, why not tell her directly? Or did they merely hope that if she could bring peace, it would end the military's excuse to experiment?

No, she decided, she had no evidence the military, or anyone, was involved. This was all speculation. She would not decide without more solid evidence. She liked Shurya, and Mary considered herself a good judge of character—but this was too important. For all she knew, Shurya, or this Gregory, might have some ulterior motive for telling her this. She would have to wait and see.

"Well, you have told me much. It will help me greatly," She said. "But really I am here to work toward peace, nothing more. Tomorrow I must speak to the baron. For now, though, it is late."

Shurya looked disappointed, but she covered it gracefully. Mary expected her to excuse herself, but instead she settled herself on a small divan. "As you wish, my lady. I am at your service."

Mary sat on her knees on the cold floor in front of the fire. She bowed low, her head resting on the floor in the wisdom pose. As always, she thought, *how am I going to face violence?* As always, the waves of peace swept over her, providing no answers.

***

"This is some sort of magic?" Shurya asked when Mary at last rose and moved toward the large bed. A blanket around her body, she lay awake on the divan, watching Mary.

"Yes, a sort," Mary answered. "You are spending the night?" She slid out of her dress and then under the heavy quilts.

"I am to serve you, my lady, as long as you grace us with your presence," Shurya replied a bit coldly. "And yes, I will be available whenever you need me."

"I meant no offense. I am not used to people serving me," she said as she blew out the oil lamp at the bedside. "It is cold here on your world. Will you be warm enough with just that blanket?"

"I will, my lady."

"There is room in this bed for ten, and plenty of quilts to go around," Mary said.

Shurya rose and came obediently, sliding gracefully next to Mary, wrapping her arms around her and pulling her into a kiss.

Mary pulled back, but not out of her embrace. "I do not require this service." She could feel Shurya blush, so she quickly added, "I am not offended, and if you were to offer again . . . from the heart, that would be different. But I don't require you to do this."

Shurya nodded. "I am sorry, my lady. When others have said such—"

"It was not your well-being they were concerned about," Mary finished. They lay quiet for some time, then Mary asked. "Does this happen often?"

Shurya shrugged. "It's the life of a lady in waiting."

"Even women?"

"Men mostly, but women sometimes as well."

Mary frowned, "But I thought . . . well, isn't it a sin?"

"You did not seem too averse a moment ago," Shurya replied. "*If you were to offer again . . .*" she mimicked.

Mary laughed. "Sex is just part of the spectrum of life. I meant doesn't the church preach against this particular act? I always thought the outer regions were more conservative?"

It was Shurya's turn to laugh. "Indeed, that's what makes it so exciting, isn't it? The priests say sex between married couples is okay, so it almost never happens. Sex with a man other than your husband? That's dirty, so of course they can't wait to try it." But corrupting the heart of a young maiden? That's truly evil, as far the priests say. So that's the real trick, isn't it? I play the innocent and let the old ladies have their thrill."

"And do you enjoy this game?"

She shrugged. "They are not as rough as the men, and there is no fear of being dishonored. It can be enjoyable, in its own way."

***

When Mary woke, she was alone. She usually slept lightly, yet she had been exhausted and was not use to the cold. Even now her body wanted nothing more than to wriggle down deeper into the covers, seek warmth, and sleep. Instead, she peered out, looking for what had disturbed her.

The old lady was back, looking less like a drill sergeant without her mouthful of needles. She was carrying a pile of fabric in her hands.

"Your clothes," the woman began, seeing that

Mary was awake.

"You may set them on the divan," Shurya's voice said. "I will attend to them shortly. And tell Farim to bring breakfast in twenty minutes."

Shurya turned her attention back to the brazier. She was using long metal tongs to add coal to the fire, blowing on it to bring the fire up. Mary wrapped herself in a quilt and went to the divan. She chose the thickest and heaviest of the newly-delivered clothes and pulled them on: a heavy, red wool sweater with a long, matching skirt.

"Today I must speak to the baron," Mary said as she sat down by the fire.

"I have spoken to the concierge and to the castellan," Shurya said. "As I have said, the baron is unwilling to speak with you." Before Mary could protest, she went on. "He is also unwilling to deny you directly. He begs off. He is too busy. He has court all day." She paused and smirked. "So I told him we would be there as well."

Court didn't start until late morning. It had almost as much ceremony as the ball the night before. Each person was led in and announced according to rank. For each ranking person introduced, there were at least half a dozen more following behind them: servants, family, knights, all of whom were non-ranking, and therefore, unannounced. Shurya explained the proceedings to Mary. She seemed to have an inexhaustible knowledge, and told Mary names, relationships (both open and illicit), and histories for each person.

As a guest of honor, Mary again waited in the wings until almost every other person was seated. Once again, she was announced merely as "Mary, guest of honor to the baron."

The castellan seemed embarrassed by Mary's lack of title or rank. Mary realized, as she was sure Ashe had from the beginning, her lack of title worked to her advantage. She was unique. She was just Mary. These petty nobles stood on rank. Their entire world was subdivided by increasingly smaller divisions of people. They looked up to those above them; they looked down on everyone else.

But what about Mary? They had no idea how to treat her. She was an enigma, not part of their ordered universe.

After she was ushered in and given a seat, the next individual announced was, "Johm, son of Aldrith, heir apparent to the Barony of Cordona." Mary craned her neck to see the baron's son. He was a big man, much like his father. He was thinner, but by no means thin. He carried himself with an even greater sense of arrogance.

Shane came in at the end. He was not announced. Shortly after this, they were all told to rise as the baron swept into the room. He was much as he had been last night. His dress was somewhat simpler, but he still wore the sword at his side. He took his seat on the top of a small dais and without preamble said, "So what business does this day bring?"

There was a murmur through the crowd, and a few people moved as if to speak, but they were silenced by the rap of the castellan's rod. "The first case of the day is the matter of Harold the Sheriff of Arong."

Several cases later, Mary wriggled uncomfortably in her seat and sighed. She was not cut out for the life of nobility. She didn't see the point of the court. Surely these were all simple matters. The sheriff wanted a detachment of men to hunt out some bandits in the woods in his precinct. Having no knowledge of local geography, she wondered briefly if it was the same forest, and possibly the same bandits, she had already encountered. The baron complained about the war and about how many men were already committed. Then one of his advisors pointed out that the bandits were in all likelihood mercenaries, possibly in the hire of the duke. Wearily, the baron agreed to send a detachment.

The next several cases were just as inane. A small group of dwarves were brought forward to discuss their annual tariff. Again there was polite grumbling, the baron complaining of the war and the dwarves of the fees and tariffs they had already paid. In the end, a compromise was reached about exactly how much gold, silver, iron, and coal was to be given the baron that quarter.

And so forth. Just when Mary thought the whole day would pass without any chance to talk about the war, or make any move toward her ends, the door at the back burst open and tall, thin man marched through. He was gray haired and his face was weathered, but his stride was strong and he showed no sign of age. Mary guessed him to be in his fifties at the oldest. He wore a chainmail jerkin that went to his knees, with a red shirt over it, bearing the imperial griffin. A wide, leather belt was at his side, with a long sword. His head was bare and his gray hair was short and thinning slightly. He drew his sword as he marched resolutely towards the baron, handle first held high before him like a cross.

"The paladin, Gregory Falfnir the third, master of arms and chief steward of the defense, general of the

. . ." the castellan was saying breathlessly, trying to keep up with the paladin's relentless march.

"Enough!" the baron roared. "We all know who Gregory is."

The paladin stopped directly in front of the baron and bent low, laying his sword at the baron's feet. "Your Grace, I am here to beg an audience with your majesty—"

"Come to beg more troops, no doubt," the baron interrupted. "Which you already know is impossible. I have given you men again and again. For what? Have you come back in front of a victorious column of fighting men? Do you bring us booty and tokens of victory? Well, do you?"

"You majesty," Gregory said, his face still down, "you know the answer to this."

"I have had your messages, yes," the baron complained. "You come with a column of refugees and the ragtag remnants of your army, mostly injured."

Mary could see Gregory blushing, but he did not look up. "It is as you say, my lord," he answered. "Though the desperation of my journey led to me to leave them, as is not my wont, to reach here more quickly. They are about a week behind."

"And to you I should give more men? More men to go off and get killed by your incompetence? What of the defense of Grenwich? Who will be left?"

"To fight them elsewhere, that was the plan," one of the advisors said.

"And look where it's gotten us," the baron roared. "The campaign is in shambles, and our defense is weakened. All because of this man." The baron pointed angrily at the paladin.

"Leave him alone!" Shurya yelled from Mary's side, causing her to jump. "It is not his fault." The baron's gaze swung blazing in her direction, but Shurya stood her ground. "Have any of your other commanders done better? Why blame your own men that the enemy cannot be defeated?"

"Bah! There is no truth to these rumors. They are just excuses for failure!" the baron replied. There was a moment while the two glared at each other. The moment was broken by Gregory.

"Your Lordship, be at peace. The girl forgets herself. In times like this, it is easy enough. We must remember ourselves." Then changing the subject he went on. "I faced these rumors directly; the Juggernauts I fought." This served to pull the baron's gaze away from Shurya, and his expression changed to one of interest.

"They are tough, and my men suffered a great defeat," Gregory said quickly, trying to get the bad news over with. "I myself suffered several injuries in the intense fighting. However, they are not invincible. One we killed in the battle. Knowing now the full strength and limits of our foes, I am sure they can be defeated. But it will take more men—"

"It is as I have said!" the baron declared triumphantly to the court. "They can be defeated! Now who among my military commanders will take this assignment?" He looked to his left, where the lieutenants of his army sat.

They all kept their eyes down; none would meet his gaze. He glared at them and asked again, "Who will take this assignment?"

When it became obvious that none were about to look up or speak, he spat out, "Bah!"

Mary, who only shortly before had been astounded by Shurya's audacity, saw her moment and stood. "Why not sue for peace?" she called out.

The baron turned his gaze to her. She flinched at the anger and defiance she saw there. "Sue for peace?" he laughed bitterly. "Mary, my dear, I regret to inform you that you have come to the wrong place. If you wish to sue for peace, you must speak to the duke. He is the aggressor here. I merely defend myself."

"The duke is no aggressor," Shane interjected. "The land is his by right."

"Bah!" the baron yelled, "It is mine. It was my father's land and his father's before him. How dare you spread such malicious lies in my court! I could have you arrested for treason."

"I have diplomatic immunity," Shane said, not looking too sure of himself. Then he rallied, "And the land of which you speak—your grandfather stole that land from the duke's great-grandfather. The land is the duke's by heritage and tradition. The fact that it has been held illegally for nearly two generations does not change that fact."

"One more word from you, and you and your whole entourage will find itself in my dungeon," the baron roared. Shane bowed and sat down quickly.

Mary persisted. "Perhaps there is a compromise . . ."

"There can be no compromise!"

"Sir, the lady speaks wisely," Gregory said slowly, cautiously.

"If the mage wishes to help us," the baron replied. "she can fight for us. Raise an army of demons. Wake the trees. Lead our people to victory. Then we will have peace."

Mary was shaken by the reference to trees. Had the baron heard of her exploits with the bandits? "Your Lordship," she replied, trying to marshal her limited knowledge of etiquette, "begging your pardon, I am not a combat mage, nor am I here to fight or to take sides. I am here to assist in bringing peace to this land, no more, no less."

"As I thought," he barked. "You are worthless to us, Mary. Go back to the empire and tell them to send someone who can really help us."

With that, he turned away. Mary's face burned with humiliation. He gave her no further thought. Instead, he lambasted his military advisors again. "Not one of you is brave enough to go fight for your baron?" Again the lieutenants looked down.

"I will go," a voice boomed out across the court. "I will go and slay these Juggernauts that others say are unstoppable."

It was Johm, the baron's son. He stood as he spoke. He raised one leg up on a small dais, and struck a gallant pose, his hand on the hilt of his sword.

The baron's voice instantly softened. "You see, there is one brave enough. But no, my son, you cannot. I will not risk my only heir like that. You must learn the hardships of being a ruler. In life, as in chess, if the ruler is caught, all hope is ended."

What a pathetic act, Mary thought as Johm sat down with a smug look. *He knew damn well from the start his father wouldn't really send him. He just wanted to look big and important.*

The baron sighed heavily. "Gregory?" he asked in a resigned voice.

"As ever I am your humble servant," Gregory replied. Through all of this, he had not risen. "See to my wounded and give me as many men as you can spare. I will face this threat yet again."

"So be it," the baron said. "Court is adjourned."

There was a low, angry murmur from those with cases waiting to be heard. But everyone else seemed to understand: after what had just transpired, it was only right to stop there.

11 A ROWAN IN THE APPLE ORCHARD

Shurya led Mary back to her quarters. They found Shane already there waiting for them.

"I wanted to speak with you alone," Shane said as Mary entered.

"You wanted to snoop through her things, I'll wager," Shurya replied.

"Mostly alone," Shane amended.

"He has been through your things," Shurya continued. "Look this drawer is ajar."

"I have come to speak with Mary," Shane insisted. "Now that you have seen how the baron is, you will understand that you cannot simply sue for peace. Peace is only possible if he is stopped. He and his men are the true aggressors."

"What about what he said?" Mary countered. "That they have held this land for two generations. Is that not true?"

"That doesn't make it legal."

"No, but it does make the duke an aggressor in

this," Mary pointed out. "But I am not here to find fault. Surely the land can be divided somehow, or compensation arranged."

"No!" Shane said more forcefully than Mary would have expected, "it cannot be." Then, more restrained, he went on, "To divide the land would only deepen the scar. The people would be separated from kith and kin. The people themselves would cry out for war, to reunite their homes." Mary doubted the peasants would do any such thing, but she understood that Shane was just as committed to the war as the baron.

"You must choose sides, Mary," Shane continued. "There is no compromise. I have come to see if there is any way to convince you of this and of my half-brother's right in this matter. You have considerable power at your disposal, that much we know. Will you not use it for good? Help us to end this war and bring peace?"

"You have come," Shurya interrupted, "to steal her wand and make her do your bidding."

To Mary's great surprise, Shane merely shrugged, making no effort to deny this accusation. "Need drives," he said. "We would have her aid, willing or no. However it seems your charge here conceals her possessions well."

"You think if you steal my wand, you can force me to work for you?" Mary asked.

"Do not play coy with me, Mary. I am not a simple bumpkin. I know something of the ways of wizards. Your wand is your source of power," Shane replied. Mary almost laughed but then saw that he was serious.

She sat back and weighed her options. Did she

reveal to him the full extent of her power? Or did she let him continue to believe this utter foolishness? The latter was perhaps to her best advantage.

"You have a strange notion of peace," she snarled, "and loose ethics as well. I will not aid you in any way."

"But you will not aid the baron either?" Shane pressed.

"I will not fight for him, if that is what you mean. Other aid I will give or not, in order to bring peace. Now be gone with you."

After he was gone, she turned to Shurya. "You have perhaps looked for my wand as well?"

Shurya blushed and looked down. "I do not want to compel you to do that which you do not wish. But need, as he says, drives. Only ours is true need. You have no idea what is going on out in the field. Here, the war barely touches us; there are shortages of some goods, no more. But in the outer provinces, things are dire. We must stop this invasion."

Mary sat back and thought. Every day she asked the spirits for guidance, and every day she got the same vision. It was making her head ache. What should she do?

What would Ashe suggest? *Expect nothing.* She could almost hear the words in his voice: *Wait, expect nothing; a way will open.*

She sighed and looked into Shurya's open, waiting face. She raised her right hand, palm open, calling the power to her. "First," she said as a cool, blue flame burst into life on her open palm, "understand this: I don't have a wand, I don't need a wand, and I won't be compelled. Secondly, I speak truly. I do not have, nor do I desire, any combat magic or magic that would hurt. Any aid I give will be humanitarian. And I think perhaps I should see this war."

***

That night was another feast, though not as big or as fancy as the last one. Mary was not seated across from the baron in a place of honor, nor was she close enough to engage the baron in any personal conversation. Instead she was seated next to Johm.

Despite the initial similarities she had noted between the baron and his son, he proved a decent dinner companion. He was arrogant at times, especially on the subject of his own prowess and achievement. But he was also quick witted and jovial. To Mary's surprise, he turned out to be a good listener.

He had been to the inner worlds once. He had brought back numerous ideas for improving the barony when he took control from his father. His father had given him a small province of his own, which was thriving in part because of agricultural reforms, thanks to a master farmer Johm had hired from one of the big agricultural worlds.

As much as Johm had seen, still it was only a glimpse. He was intensely curious about the races he had seen, and magic. Mary was a bit ashamed to discover she was not able to answer many of his questions.

"I am afraid that I have not studied the magic that keeps the airships afloat," she said, "but I know of someone who ran such a ship . . ."

She had not thought of Jerome since they had parted ways. Nor had she thought of . . . well, sex had never been a big part of her life, romance less so. Not that she was thinking of any such thing now. Johm was handsome, broad, and strongly built. In spite of his arrogance, he was nice enough.

"I would continue this conversation," Johm said as the evening drew to a close. Other guests were already making their way to the door of the hall as Johm ushered her into a small side room, and added, "Just a little longer."

Mary had no objection. The heavy food that the people of this world consumed made her feel sluggish and tired the day prior. Since she had made her dietary preference clear to the concierge, she felt much more herself. She was not tired and had planned on spending the next few hours in meditation. She could easily spare a few more minutes for the baron's son.

She felt the air in the room change as he sat down, a little too close to her, on the low couch. "You are a pretty girl," he said.

She blushed but did not respond.

"I like you," he continued. "You are so elegant, so simple. Other women, the women around here anyway, they waste too much time trying to look good. They cover themselves in makeup and artifice. You don't have to work at it. You just are."

"Johm," she began, trying to move away from him.

He didn't give her a chance to finish. Instead, he leaned in and kissed her, pulling her to him.

She tried to pull back, but he held her tight. Gathering her strength, she pushed him off. He was a strong man; she was surprised she managed to move him. She stood.

He also stood, towering over her. His eyes were filled with need and rage. It was a frightening combination. He looked as if he was about to say something, and then he grabbed her again.

She was alert now and danced quickly out of his arms. "Johm," she started again.

"I am the baron's son," he said huskily, "be not quick to spurn me." He reached for her again.

Anger flared inside her. With her mind, she reached for the coat of arms hanging behind him. The shield pulled itself free of the wall. It swung clumsily and struck him hard on the back.

He staggered, caught off guard, but he recovered faster than she would have guessed. He spun around, pulling his sword as he went. "Who's there?" he demanded. There was no trace of the drunkenness that had been in his voice a moment before. This fact hardened Mary against him. He was a snake, she decided, preying on women.

"You may be the baron's son," she said with more confidence than she felt, "but I am a mage. You had best not forget that."

She watched as he glanced from the shield, still floating in the air in front of him, to Mary and back. Comprehension dawned in his face, but there was arrogance there too, and Mary knew he was not one to give up so easily.

Shurya appeared in the doorway. "M'lady," she said, with a hint of being out of breath, "I have found you at last. I am to escort you to your room at once. It is not seemly for us to be out so late."

Without another word, Mary followed Shurya from the room. She resolved to be more careful in the future and to make sure the baron's son never had any excuse to be alone with her again.

***

"You really are quite beautiful," Shurya whispered

as Mary rose from her meditation. Her encounter with Johm had left a bad taste in her mouth, and it had taken Mary a long time to settle herself. She was surprised that Shurya was still awake.

The younger woman rose and knelt beside Mary. "When you do that," she paused looking for the right words, "is it magic?"

It was hard. They spoke the same language, came from the same empire. Yet her life was different from Shurya's in so many ways. "It is a meditation exercise. It is like magic, yes. It uses the same sort of energy."

Shurya shrugged to show her ignorance. "When you do it, you glow like some beautiful painting."

Mary blushed as Shurya brushed a hair from her face. Playfully, she said. "Twice in one night. A girl could get used to this much attention."

Shurya looked hurt at the comparison. Mary reached for her before she could pull away. "I tease," she said. "I am sorry."

"I am not like him. I don't . . . it's not like . . ." she stopped. Blushing, she added, "I've never felt like this."

Mary chuckled. "I regret to inform you, it's not me. These exercises, they use energy. Call it magic, call it healing, or call it life energy. It doesn't matter; it's all the same. One energy, with one source. Larsa once told me, there is one source and the source is sex."

Shurya giggled. "Sex makes the world go round?"

"No, he meant it the other way around. Sex is just creation: creation between two people. All acts of creation are the source. Anytime you reach the source of anything, it is an act of sex. So building this life energy, this magic, is analogous to sex. Just as sex makes one feel good, more alive, so does this. You are sensing these things intuitively." She touched Shurya's cheek. "You haven't worked with these energies before, so you don't know how else to describe the feeling."

Shurya blushed deeper, her eyes downcast. "You must think me such a fool."

"Of course not. I feel it too."

"But it's not . . ."

"It can be, if you want."

"You were Larsa's lover?" Shurya asked.

"Yes, for a time. When he raised his energy," Mary paused, lost in the recollection, "it was magnificent."

***

"Yes, thank you, ma'am," Shurya said to the woman as she took the proffered envelope and closed the door. She was clad in a heavy robe against the morning's chill. "It is a request for an audience with Gregory," she said as she read. "After the church service today. You will meet with him?"

"Of course."

Shurya went to the fire and began to rebuild it.

"How long is the service here?" Mary asked.

"It will not end until near noon," Shurya answered without looking up. "We will meet him in the garden after."

Mary shivered. She wished the younger woman would come back and lay next to her; she longed for her warmth and her closeness. It had been a long time since she had shared intimacy with a woman. Last night, she realized that she missed it.

"Then we have until noon," Mary called softly. "Why not come here and sleep a little more?"

"Do not tease me," Shurya said. "We must make ready. The service will be soon."

"You are going?" Mary was surprised. She did not think Shurya the devoted type.

Shurya approached, looking puzzled. "*W e* are going. Surely there is service on your world? You are not a heretic?" She eyed Mary.

"Well, no," Mary said. She was frightened by this turn. She had come close, in the conversations that flowed within and between their lovemaking, to revealing her spiritual path to Shurya last night. She had felt so safe. "I am faithful," she said. Oomutoo valued honesty above all things, with one exception. *Don't die a martyr's death.*

Mary crawled out of bed. Shurya had already turned away, as if dismissing any suspicion. Mary went to the chest of drawers and found a loose, flowing dress. It was a soft-brown, woolen affair with a low-cut neckline and warm shrug. It was a style she was rapidly learning to love.

"You are not wearing that to service," Shurya said in exasperation. "Honestly, Mary! Don't they honor the Sabbath back home?"

"I'm a healer, Shurya," Mary protested. "The sick and dying don't wait for the service to end. I go when I can but . . ." It wasn't true. Mary couldn't recall the last time she had gone, if ever.

"Better the body dies with the soul safe, then the other way round," Shurya countered. "Besides, is it not mandatory?"

Comprehension dawned. "It is mandatory here?"

"Of course. I thought it was so everywhere."

Mary discarded the dress for the thicker, dowdier one that Shurya offered. *At least this one will be plenty warm,* she thought sourly as she pulled it on. She looked out the window. It couldn't be much past dawn. If the service ran almost to noon . . .

"We should eat well," she said, "if services here are so long."

Shurya laughed. "You are a heretic!" she said. She didn't sound angry or suspicious. "Your world must be very different. You do not eat before church. You must fast."

Mary stomach growled in protest. She quelled the hunger angrily. She had fasted so many times, as a healer in training, as an Oomutoo practitioner, and as a mage. Was she to be a slave to hunger now?

But those times she had been prepared. She knew she would have to fast, from this time until this time. She knew why, how, and when. To be expecting food and then be told no was irritating. *Don't expect, not even food, not even that you be alive in the next moment,* Ashe's voice said inside her head.

***

The service dragged on for Mary. The cathedral was huge and magnificent. The ceiling gleamed with gold and brass and stained glass images depicting scenes of the empire's triumphant past. At the front, behind the main altar, reared two life-sized griffons in bronze, flanking a statue of a man with sword held aloft. Mary stared at the face but couldn't recall which emperor it was.

The artwork and architecture of the place held her rapt for maybe a half an hour, which was good, since they sat at least that long waiting for the service to begin. First, people of various ranks were led in and seated accordingly. Then the acolytes busied themselves at the altar, doing spirits knew what, while the crowd sat. Murmurs of quiet conversation rippled through the crowd at intervals. The life of nobility was not for her, Mary thought not for the first time.

Finally the bishop came in, and the service began. Not that it relieved Mary's boredom any. She didn't understand old imperial. Few outside the priesthood still bothered with it, but here about half the service was read out of giant-sized books in old imperial.

The other half, though in common tongue, was so old that it sounded stilted and cryptic to Mary. Looking around the room, she had a startling revelation. The imagery and symbolism was largely agricultural. To Mary, it was old, antiquated, and had little bearing on her life, or the life of anyone in Tomlin or Draasdustin. But here, and over much of the empire, life was still very much as the holy books described.

These people got it. This wasn't Mary's religion. It wasn't even the emperor's religion anymore. It was the religion of these people. They understood the bits about the wheat and chaff. They knew they were each no more than a kernel of wheat in the emperor's field.

The main reading and the sermon had a clear political message as well. The bishop preached the value of obedience, particularly in trying times. "Fulfill your purpose, keep to your station, and discharge your duty." That was for millions of citizens the primary message of the Reformed Church of the Emperor.

***

The cathedral was adjacent to the baron's manor. As lunch with Gregory was to be in the gardens behind the manor proper, they returned not by the main entrance but by a smaller side entrance. Two bored-looking men-at-arms watched the steady stream of servants and the occasional minor noble who passed that gate.

Off to their right as they entered the manor's walls was a small apple orchard. A gardener was standing amongst the apples, watching Mary and Shurya as they passed. Something about the man caught Mary's attention.

He was thin, tall, and wore brown robes. He had brown hair and a long, brown beard. He was holding a rake. His eyes were dark and piercing.

A ripple passed through her consciousness, and she paused. He was not holding a rake; he was holding a staff. Why had she thought it was rake? Did gardeners often wear such robes?

Mary turned and made for the orchard. She walked up to the man and stopped.

"One wonders what brings a mage to so distant a corner of the empire," the man said.

"Indeed," Mary answered, "and one could have the same question of a druid."

The man nodded, "I am Harold of the Rowan Grove." Mary glanced at the apple grove around them, and the man smirked at the shared joke.

"I am Mary," she said.

"Mary . . .?" he inquired.

"Just Mary," she replied, relishing her new understanding and his discomposure about her lack of rank or title. *What was a druid doing here?* Mary knew a little of the druid order, and she felt a certain respect for them, but the presence of one of that order, here in the given situation, was too suspicious. She was not about to offer Harold her trust blindly.

He must have sensed her distrust. He looked away. "Lots of off-worlders around here suddenly," he said slowly. He watched her through the corner of his eye.

"For such a distant place."

She wondered if he was referring to the mercenaries, many who were clearly not locals, or to something else. More to the point, she wondered if he was part of what was going on, or like her, an observer. Did she dare ask?

She opted for the blunt approach. "Are you part of this war, druid?"

"I have no aptitude nor desire for military service," he replied evasively. "And you?"

"I would see the emperor's peace brought to this land," she replied. "I would think the druids would feel the same."

He laughed. "Druids serve balance, Mary, not peace. Order gives way to chaos, chaos to a new order. Peace is stagnation."

Mary was tired of the mental game of cat-and-mouse. "So you would have these two petty nobles fight and men die for your precious balance?"

He held a hand up in supplication. "I am not involved in this war, Mary. I can assure of you of that. Nor do I believe are you, now that we meet. I would speak more plainly, but there are too many things I do not understand. I must take my leave of you, Mary. I suspect that we will meet again before all is said and done, and I suspect the emperor may not wish his peace be kept." With that, he turned and was gone.

12 TRAPPED IN THE BARON'S ESTATE

As seemed to be the case so often these days, Mary's idea of lunch in the garden turned out about as wrong as it could be. She had imagined a storybook garden of high hedges and manicured lawns, with the players being well-dressed nobles eating dainty foods and making small talk.

The garden, it turned out, had, until very recently, been a vegetable garden. The spring produce had been harvested and the mid-summer crop not yet planted. With all the extra troops the baron had hired for the war, the barracks were already overfull. The paladin and his small escort had chosen to camp here instead. They erected one small pavilion on the cold barren dirt and placed heavy rugs within. Each soldier had a small wooden chest and a sleeping roll.

Outside the open pavilion doors, Gregory placed a long, wooden table, roughhewn. Mary and Shurya sat on a low bench on one side of the table, Gregory and his senior knight on the other. A young squire served roast rabbit, a thick stew of roots, and heavy brown bread.

Gregory was as down to earth and straightforward as the meal he served. "I wished to talk you about your desire to bring peace and to tell you what I can of this war," he said after a brief introduction.

Mary nodded. "Go ahead."

"I won't pretend the baron is a saint," he said, "as you have already met the man. But perhaps I can convince you that the cause is just."

"Peace is the only just cause," Mary responded, "and the baron seems hell bent on avoiding it."

"You will find the duke no better," the knight at Gregory's side growled.

"No matter," Gregory said hastily. "It is as you say. I too began wishing only for peace. I fought many wars for the empire once, as a paladin. Since retiring, I desire only peace."

"When this war began, I stayed out of it. I trained many of the baron's men, and I have served his defense as well. But I refused an active command. I thought, as you do, that the baron should sue the duke for peace."

"Then rumors began to circulate that the duke had demons working for him; men that could not be killed. I discounted these rumors at first. But more and more causalities were coming back from the front. Many were men I had myself trained. I knew their worth and their reliability. When they, too, spoke of these Juggernauts, these super warriors, I took notice."

"I resolved to learn the truth. So I accepted a command and led an army. I was defeated for the first time in my life."

"He saved more than half of his men," the knight

interjected, "and led them home despite incredible odds. He did better than any lesser man."

"No one here denies the paladin's worth," Shurya said.

"It doesn't matter," Gregory said. "I was defeated. When I got back, the baron removed me of my command and sent another."

"They, too, were defeated. I was again put in command. Again, I was defeated. And again another was sent. This is the third time I have faced the Juggernauts."

"You were at court yesterday. I need not repeat myself. I was defeated, but we injured two of them. Even killed one. They are not invincible."

"I don't see what this has to do with peace," Mary said when the man paused.

"I wanted peace too. I strove for it. Now I have seen these Juggernauts for myself. I have seen what they are capable of. There is only one path to peace, and that is to destroy them. They will not parlay, nor will they surrender. As long as the duke has them at his disposal, he will not agree to peace on any terms."

He sighed. "I do not expect to sway you with words alone. What I want to talk to you about is this: will you at least lend us humanitarian aid? Once you have seen the refugees from this war and heard their stories, then you can decide if peace is possible."

Mary sat quiet for a long moment, choosing her words carefully. "I will provide humanitarian aid wherever it is needed. My first task is healing. But you must understand that my aid is for anyone who needs it. I will not deny anyone because they are *your* enemy."

Gregory held his hands up in surrender. "Of

course, I am a paladin. I would never stand in the way of a healer and their duty."

Mary had never dealt with a paladin firsthand before. Their reputation, however, was legendary. They took binding oaths to uphold the ideals of the empire. They were truthful, honorable, and good. Humanitarian aid was part of that creed. He wouldn't interfere.

***

"Am I a prisoner then?" Mary asked in exasperation. Three days ago she had pledged humanitarian aid to Gregory. His recruitment was nearly done. His newly-reinforced regiments were ready to disembark. The train of refugees was nearly at the city gates. And still Mary sat in the baron's manor.

"Nobody can move freely in the baron's domain without the baron's permission," Shurya answered.

So far, the baron had consistently denied Mary permission. She had managed to speak him directly once in all that time, only to face the same list of excuses that the castellan had given her.

"I cannot guarantee your safety. Civilians are not allowed to move about in a war zone. They are a danger to themselves and to the military. You will simply have to do your observing from here," he insisted. "Don't you have a crystal ball or something?"

He ended the interview abruptly, stating that the castellan already discussed this issue with her and he had nothing new to add.

"There must be a way," Mary insisted. "These refugees move freely. Who sees to their safety?"

"The baron does not want you out of his sight," Shurya said. "He still is not sure about you. Part of him thinks that you are harmless." Mary scowled, but had to agree with the baron's assessment. "And part of him isn't so sure. You could be a valuable ally or a dangerous enemy."

"I must be allowed to see this war for myself," Mary went on. Somehow the idea had come to possess her. If only she could get out into the war-torn region, something would happen, and she would know what to do next. The more she meditated on it, the more certain she was.

"The baron will never allow it," Shurya said, and then after a pause, "but perhaps . . ."

Mary leaned forward, "Yes?" She was ready to try anything. She had thought more than once of simply declaring her intention and leaving. How far would the baron go to stop her? Guards had been discretely placed at the nearest two corners outside her room.

She did not think they would resort to using force, but she feared to push it. She still hadn't gotten a satisfactory answer to the question of how she would handle violence.

"A short trip he might allow," Shurya was saying. "In fact, it would be rude to deny it. With the refugees arriving, the hospital is short staffed. We have wise women and herbalists, but no true healers, not like you. I could have the head mistresses put in a plea on your behalf."

"I would be delighted to see what facilities you have," Mary answered. "I have done no healing in too long. I must practice as with anything. But I do not see how this helps."

"With so many refugees and the military ready to march, it would be easy for someone to get lost in the shuffle," Shurya said, grinning. "The baron won't realize we are gone until we are far from the city gates. Then what can he do? Send men after us?"

"Can he? Send men after us? I just need to know. What's the worse he can do?"

"He could," Shurya answered. "It is certainly within his rights, sort of."

"Certainly or sort of?"

"He has the emperor's full authority with his own people. But you are not one of his people." Shurya explained. "If he issued the order, the men would obey. But it wouldn't be legal. He won't risk it. You are a neutral observer. If it got back to the courts that you were being held against your will, it would look bad."

Looking bad didn't sound like a huge disincentive to Mary, not to someone like the baron. "How bad?"

"It could tip them toward the duke. Legally, he has a better claim anyway, since the baron's grandfather's takeover was never legalized. He won't risk that."

That made Mary feel a little bit easier. Not much, granted; as far as they were from the central worlds, it would be easy to say that Mary had just "disappeared." The alternative was to stay as a guest to the baron for the duration of the war, which had already lasted several years from what she could tell.

"You said *we* . . ." Mary said. She paused not sure how to proceed.

"I have sworn to serve you as long as you need," Shurya replied. "I will not back out now."

"I did not mean to imply any such thing," Mary said. "I would be glad to have you, but this is not a simple outing. There is a war going on; people are dying out there."

"I know," Shurya said. "All the more reason why

we must go."

"Then, we will give your plan a try."

***

Mary laughed at the magician's show. He was juggling four apples. With a sudden flourish, he threw all of the apples in the air. He held his hands out, grinning broadly. After a moment, he gave an exaggerated look of bewilderment and stared at the empty sky.

It was sleight of hand, Mary knew, but it was good sleight of hand. She heard several onlookers murmur to each other, each wondering where the apples had gone. One halfling youth was still staring at the sky, trying to spot the apples. This made Mary laugh even harder.

She felt a hand on her shoulder and turned. Shurya was standing behind her smiling. "It is a very good show," Mary said. "If I had any coins . . ."

This was, as far as the baron was concerned, a simple day outing. Mary had left everything behind to keep the illusion. She was going to inspect the local hospital and see what she could do to help the refugees who had just arrived this morning. The matron had done her job well. She had pleaded with the baron, the desperation in her voice more than an act. They were overwhelmed with injured. Worse still, diseases had plagued the refugees long after the duke's men had called off the chase.

"I have some coins," Shurya said, her eyes dancing. She passed a small coin from her purse.

"What is so funny?" Mary asked.

"You," Shurya replied, "great mage of empire, amused by this."

"I wish I could do that," she said.

"You can do so much more," Shurya said. "You can do real magic."

"Real magic?" The magician had overheard their conversation. "Why, girl, don't you believe your own eyes?" He deftly spun the coin that Mary had given him, and it disappeared. He reached over and pulled it out of an old lady's ear, to general applause.

"Mary is a mage," Shurya proclaimed. "She can do so much more than this."

"Hush," Mary told her.

"Real magic?" the man challenged. "This I got to see."

Mary reached out to the old lady. One eye was yellowed with an old black eye. Gently she touched the eye. With a small wiping motion, the yellow was gone. The crowd gasped. This was turning out to be a better show than any anticipated.

Mary got in return a short flash of memories; an old man half drunk but not nearly drunk enough, raging, a fist coming. She shook it off. Healing was often like that. It was a small depressing glimpse into the life of a peasant.

"We are needed at the hospital, m'lady," Shurya declared. "We dare not dwell here longer."

The oohs and aahs of the crowd was nothing compared to the reception Mary received at the hospital, but then again, the healing she had performed in the market place paled to her task there.

She felt it over two blocks away, the combination of chaos and need. Her own magic, held back too long, responded instantly. Before they rounded the corner and saw the front of the hospital, her power was already building.

Mary had been on many humanitarian missions

and recognized the chaos instantly. The grounds of the small hospital were overflowing. The refugees had far outnumbered the beds available. The extra had been laid out on cots or on the ground outside. Healers, or what passed for healers in this place, assisted by many helpers with more heart than training, moved slowly and helplessly through the living mass.

Mary's senses instantly centered in on a pair of soldiers at the edge of the crowd. One was holding his comrade propped up on the ground. An old lady was inspecting the fallen man's right leg. Even from a distance, Mary could see it was a mess.

It had been broken badly. The foot hung at an odd angle. The break was not new and three of the toes were black. The whole foot was dusky. The leg was dying. The man groaned. He seemed close to following his foot.

"It was broken three weeks ago," the other soldier told Mary as she came up. "They say the foot is dying beyond any healing. They will have to take it off, but he won't survive it. The paladin's healing has brought him this far. He can't die now. If only the paladin or the hospital surgeon would see him right away."

"They are with others," the old lady complained. Her voice softened, "Ones with a better chance to live."

"There shall be no death here today," Mary said. It was a statement. Her hands curled in a mudra, a magic hand sign. "Peace," she whispered. The man fell back.

"Is he?" the lady whispered.

"Sleeping only," Mary said. To the man's companion, she said, "Hold him about the chest, tightly. His leg has been broken and partly healed. To save it, I must first re-break it."

"A lass of barely nineteen . . ." he muttered, but grasped his partner as instructed.

Mary didn't answer. There wasn't time. How to explain anyway? This is what had brought her to Ashe's attention in the first place. Healing energy cannot be used to cause harm. This was the first rule of healing that she had been taught. But she had learned later, intuitively, that if the harm was in the service of a greater healing, as now, even this rule could be bent.

The chaos surrounding them stopped abruptly and several dozen faces turned at the crack of breaking bone. They watched in awe as Mary deftly snapped the soldier's leg and pulled it quickly straight. With a sense that could only be described as somewhere between hearing and feeling, Mary set the leg. Color flushed through the foot. It was not immediate health, but it was clear that the circulation had been restored.

For the crowd's benefit, Shurya spoke loudly to the old woman, "Go get the matron of the hospital at once. Tell her Mary, the mage from the empire, is here." To a nearby soldier, she added, "You, good sire, find the paladin as well. He will be expecting her. We will start—"

Mary stood and placed her hand on Shurya's shoulder. "We will start with that cask of wine over there," she said. "Bring it to me." Without hesitation, the cask was brought. By the time the matron arrived, Mary had enchanted the wine, turning it into a healing draught. She instructed the soldier to distribute the draught in small glasses to each of the sick or injured that were waiting outside. She turned to the matron. "We must begin work at once," she said. "Lead me to the sickest and we will go from there."

R. J. Eliason

13 A HEALER, AGAIN

"I apologize," the hospital matron, Laura, said. She seemed sincere. "I would give you my own quarters, but I fear they aren't much better. Even our best rooms aren't much after the palace."

"It is more than satisfactory," Mary said.

"Of course, it is fine," Shurya added. Mary could sense how much of her court training it took to make that sound sincere.

Mary would miss things about the baron's manor. The clothes more than anything. They had made her look and feel more beautiful than she ever had before. Now all she had left was the orange dress she wore today.

The quarters on the other hand . . . Mary had insisted they be housed only as healers, no more. The quarters were small and bare. The room was less than ten paces square, with two low beds, one small closet, and neither chair nor table. "It is no smaller than my quarters back home," she told the matron.

That was true. She found it safe, almost homey. She could pretend she was back in Tomlin City, waiting for her next shift. Then the shutters rattled. A cold wind forced itself through the cracks in the wooden wall. She shivered. *The stove. I will miss that as well*, she decided.

Wealth, fine foods, sex, none of these are barriers to true happiness, Oomutoo taught. It is *the expectation of these things. One cannot enjoy the present if one is constantly comparing it to the past, or the future.* "It is only for sleeping and only for the night," she told Shurya as the matron retreated.

"Yes," Shurya agreed, "and I am exhausted." She flopped onto one of the low beds.

Mary pulled a heavy quilt off the other bed and arranged it on the floor. She knelt on it.

"You are going to meditate?" Shurya asked. "Aren't you tired?"

"I am . . ." *How to explain how long sessions of healing left her feeling?* "Empty," she decided. "I will likely meditate all night. Feel free to sleep."

"Today was amazing. At the court, I thought . . ." Shurya stopped and blushed. "Well, you seemed so . . . inelegant, but healing today you were so . . ." She waved her hand in the air, mimicking one of the mudras Mary had used. She had a natural grace that Mary both loved and envied.

Mary laughed. The leftover energy made her giddy. "You have a natural aptitude, you know that? If only I could teach you the meanings and how to put some energy behind that, you'd make a decent healer."

Shurya flushed and lay back on the bed. "But it's so exhausting, twelve hours today and you seem fine. I could never have such endurance."

"You must learn to draw the energy. Use your own energy, and each healing drains you. Use energy you've drawn from the earth or sky and it will energize you instead."

This hospital, indeed this whole world, seemed to run with little or no true magic. The healers here were simple wise women or midwives, conversant in a few herbs and a lot of folklore and superstition.

They had one healer. She was a folk healer who threw large amounts of her own life energy at whatever seemed to be the problem. Sometimes this sustained the sick individual long enough for his or her own healing to kick in, but often it did more harm than good. Not to mention that it took an enormous toll on the woman herself. Mary suspected that such healings could be done once a month safely, no more. The woman had done several a day, for days on end. When Mary arrived, the woman was on death's door. It had taken a great deal of Mary's skill and time to bring her back.

Mary glanced up once she had settled herself into the meditative position. Shurya was already fast asleep on the bed. Mary smiled softly as she closed her eyes.

***

From deep within her trance, Mary sensed movement. She began to stir her body. Light was streaming through a crack in the shutters and Shurya was moving about the tiny room.

"Did you meditate all night?" Shurya asked.

Mary nodded.

"Won't you be tired?"

Mary shook her head no. "It is more restful than sleeping sometimes." A deep and abiding peace had settled over her, and she stayed in that state all through the night. Now she was starting to worry again. The flowing lines of energy were good, comforting, but none of it had brought her any closer to an answer. She still didn't know how she was supposed to deal with this war.

She rose and shed her dress. Her nipples hardened against the cold, and goose bumps threatened to erupt on her back. She acknowledged the cold, but wasn't bothered by it. The long healing session yesterday and deep meditation had brought her back to herself and her old training. Cold was just another sensation, one to be experienced but not concerned about.

The closet held five robes, all the same material, color, and cut. The healers here did not dress for fashion. A minor sort of religious order, they were directed to be modest. The robes were floor length and black, with a long hood.

Mary looked at the orange dress and allowed herself one moment of disappointment. "I hope the next woman enjoys this as much as I have," she said.

Shurya laughed. "How can you be so sentimental over a dress? Surely you have many more at home?"

"None so beautiful," she replied. She promised herself, when she got home, to indulge this one weakness. Spirits knew she deserved it.

The plan was simple, so simple Mary had a hard time believing it would work. Her dress and Shurya's were to be gifted to one of the healer apprentices, who weren't bound by the dress codes.

The healers planned to send a small detachment with the army as it disembarked that morning. Mary and Shurya would go with them. The two assistants would create the image, in the minds of those who didn't know better at least, that they were still among the healers. It wouldn't be until the baron sent someone who knew either of them personally that he would know they had left.

What he would do then was anybody's guess. They would hopefully be several days gone from the city, and the baron wouldn't have the time or men to spare to fetch her back. If, by some off chance, men did come after her, Mary decided she would refuse and dare the baron to use force against her. She only hoped Shurya and Gregory were right, and he would be scared of the imperial courts.

***

"Hold your hands farther apart, like this," Mary instructed the five women. "Now close your eyes and feel the trees around you. Feel how they draw energy from the earth."

The women did as they were told. Mary walked among them, checking their posture. "Good," she told one woman. Another she stood behind and then slid her foot against the woman's, moving it a few inches, "Better."

It was their fifth day out of the city, and no word had come to them. Perhaps the baron still bought the excuse of an extended visit to help train the healers. Perhaps the baron didn't want to publicly acknowledge that he had been duped. Either way, the plan came off as easily as the planning. Mary and Shurya left the city with four other women. They walked with their hoods up and only the leader spoke.

There had been no need. They were waved through the gates by a bored guard without a second glance. At the army encampment, Gregory, who was in on the plan, greeted them cordially and invited them into his own column. They rode in on, or often walked beside, the lead baggage train. The army moved at the pace of the slowest wagon, which was little more than a crawl.

Mary had taken to leading the women, in small groups with an armed escort, on long side trips. When they could, they would seek out coves and glades in the woods and spend much of the day in training. She was teaching them to draw energy from the world around them, and to send it back and forth.

The women worked hard, Shurya no less than the others. They were honored to be learning "real magic" and strove to do their best. For Mary, there was both pride and frustration. At home, healers were selected from a large pool of candidates. Only those with strong natural talent were allowed to enter training. Here she had to work with what she had.

On the other hand, back home it was often children from rich families who were chosen, spoiled brats who had little regard for the incredible gift they were receiving. Here, the women all were hard workers who had an intense pride in what they were being taught. They were progressing well, even though most would never make more than fair healers.

Shurya, however, had real aptitude. Mary had thought more than once, when this mission was over, she should invite the younger woman home with her, for real training. It was a shame to waste such talent.

Mary saw a rustling of brown out of the corner of her eye. "Please continue this exercise," she told the girls, and she turned toward the woods. The guards, uncharacteristically, did not follow her.

Harold was leaning against an oak tree as she approached.

"Mary rides to war," he said by way of introduction. "I thought you had no desire for military service."

"I will provide only humanitarian aid," she replied.

"And you hope by doing this you will learn what is going on here?" he said.

She nodded.

"I do not think you will find it pleasant."

"What have you found?" she asked.

He shrugged. "No answers, I am afraid, only more questions." He paused. "And a sudden liking for the emperor's peace, if it can be achieved."

"Tell me what you know then," Mary said.

"It's little enough. I know that for all the baron's faults, the duke, or at least his representative in the area, is much worse. The people suffer from this war, and they'll suffer from his rule as well. I have seen these Juggernauts briefly and from a distance. They are human, at least mostly. Though if we judge from their behavior, they do not paint a pretty picture of what it means to be human." He paused and then went on.

"The Juggernauts are off-worlders. From what little I can tell, they aren't from the central empire, but they aren't local either. There are two people traveling with them. They are rich and certainly from one of the central worlds. I am not sure exactly what they are doing. They have sharp eyes and are ever watchful. I dare not approach them, or the Juggernauts, too closely. I would not reveal myself to them."

Mary was feeling safer with the druid, but she was still not sure how far she could trust him. "This is news certainly, but you still haven't said why you are here, or what your part is in all of this."

"I am not sure I can tell you," he replied. Something in his voice made Mary think that it wasn't a matter of permission, but rather a matter of explaining. "There is something brewing in this world. I have come to find a peaceful corner of the world to meditate, to see if I could decipher what is disturbing my visions. Instead I find the same disturbance here." He paused and thought. "Something is happening, Mary. You are part of it. I cannot tell what part, but it will have consequences far beyond this region. There are hundreds of strands of possibility erupting all over the empire. This is but one, but it's a particularly nasty one."

"Strands?" Mary said. "You are talking about the future, strands of possibility?"

"You will be a great mage someday, Mary," he said, "or you will die . . ." he pointed in the direction the army was marching, "in that valley below us."

Mary started, her blood running cold.

The druid turned and walked off into the woods. "All I know," he called back, "is that neither the baron, the duke, nor the Juggernauts are the way to peace."

***

"Ooh a dragon, as a pet!" Johana crowed.

Mary shook her head. "Not a dragon, a flower dragon. They aren't real dragons at all. They are lizards, about this big." She held up two fingers to show how small the creatures were.

"Still, a lizard," Johanna said. "That would be so neat."

The women, particularly the younger ones, had been prying Mary for every detail of her life in the central core of the empire. *They are amazed and astounded over the oddest things.* Her description of her early home in Draadustin got barely a murmur of appreciation. The numbers were perhaps too abstract. The mountains far to the east struck them too much like home to be interesting, as did her attempt to tell them about the halfling villages on the intervening plains.

Then she let slip that the hospital was six stories tall. The baron's manor had three stories in places. The siege towers that stood along the walls were a full four. Anything beyond that struck them as magical. One wide-eyed girl, the daughter of a camp follower, asked if she could touch the clouds from "way up there."

And now Mary was certain she would have to spend most of the afternoon explaining everything she could remember about the tiny lizards that kept the aphids at bay in the herb garden.

Then they crested the ridge, and a long wide plain stretched out below them. Mary stopped, her breath gone.

"The plains of Tir-Na," a soldier named Roman announced from the driver's seat of the wagon.

Mary began to laugh.

"This is funny?" Shurya asked.

"No," Mary replied, "this is amazing. I would have never dreamed that one tiny out-of-the-way barony could possibly be so big. It takes my breath away thinking about how big the entire empire must be."

"The barony isn't tiny," one of the women muttered, but Shurya hushed her.

"The plains of Tir-Na are the northern edge of the war now. On the far side," Roman pointed at a distant mountain, "is the Castle of Hogsleg Pass. We lost that pass together two months ago, Gregory and I."

Mary liked Roman. He was an older man, like Gregory. In other regards, they were as different as possible. Roman was a small, unimposing man, but he carried himself with an ease and confidence that immediately brought him respect from the men. It was a respect that Mary had already learned was well deserved. He was Gregory's master at arms. He was a fourth generation disciple of the empire's most feared swordman, Eric Hammish.

"The best sword trainer money can buy," Gregory declared with obvious pride.

"The best the baron can afford," Roman corrected in his usual self-deprecating manner. He was, he assured Mary, a minor figure in the world of sword fighting, the student of the student of the student of a great swordman. Mary had seen him in practice sessions with Gregory's men, and if this was a minor player, she wondered what the real thing must look like.

Despite his relaxed demeanor and slow walk, with a sword he was devastatingly quick. His moves were so smooth and graceful that he appeared to be putting forth no effort, even though the students half his age were sweating freely. He had an unnerving tendency to be in the right place at the right time to topple his opponents easily. Gregory assured Mary this was not chance at all, but the highest level of skill.

Mary stared across at the distant mountain. "That is where the war is?" she asked.

"Down in the plain," Roman replied. "We lost the pass. For the last two months, the enemy has had free reign of this land. Our scouts put them somewhere over there," he pointed southward, "in the vicinity of the village Halden. But the last report was three weeks old. Who knows where they are now?"

Mary grasped Shurya's shoulder. "What I find funny," though nothing seemed funny to her suddenly, "was how amazed you all are of the simplest things from my world, and I am amazed by the simple things here."

"How will we beat this army, Roman?" Shurya asked, following the swordman's gaze.

Roman shrugged. "Gregory feels, and I agree, that facing the Juggernauts in close quarters was a mistake last time. This time we will chase them down on the plains. In an open battle, on open terrain, we can bring our cavalry to bear. Overpowering a man-at-arms on a castle wall is one thing, several hundred pounds of war horse and armor is another."

Mary tried in vain to see even the smallest detail of the plain, but it was too distant. They had been on the road for nearly two weeks already, and it would be several more, from the look of it, before they got down out of the mountains.

How long would she be stuck here? How were her friends back in Tomlin City? Did they think of her as she thought of them?

14 THE PLAINS OF TIR-NA

"Alms," the refugees called as the wagon train went by. "Alms." They were dressed in little more than rags; several had bare feet. Some held out wooden bowls hoping for food. Others held bare hands outstretched.

They were an increasingly common sight. As the military began to dip down toward the plains, they were greeted by refugees heading toward the barony. A few had their possessions with them in ox-drawn carts or heavy backpacks. A few had destinations, distant cousins who lived in more peaceful areas. Most had neither—fleeing their homes with only what they could carry, hoping the baron would have some place for them.

Judging from what she had seen and heard about the baron, Mary found it a slim hope. The thing that bothered her the most was how such a man had won the loyalty of the likes of Shurya, Gregory, and Roman. She tried to ask each in her own way, but the closest she got to a satisfactory answer was from Roman. He'd shrugged and said, "Well he's no better or worse than most nobility."

They marched only a short portion of the day. The men would set out early, leaving only a small contingent of guards and the teamsters behind with the women. The guards seemed superfluous—*who would want to mess with the teamsters?* They were built like the oxen they drove, thick and heavyset.

The teamsters loaded the tents and supplies. Though the oxen seemed slow at times, they went faster than men in armor. By midday they would pass the long line of soldiers, plodding wearily along. A few hours after noon, they would come to where the cavalry and other fast-moving units had already bivouacked. They would immediately begin unloading the tents and cranking out the chuckwagon for the evening meal.

There were many ways to move an army faster, Roman informed them, with a laid-out supply train or with a strong enough need. However they had no idea when they might be facing the enemy. Gregory moved slowly to keep his army rested and ready to fight at any time. He meanwhile deployed many scouts along the way, seeking eagerly for news of the Juggernauts.

There was a restless murmur from somewhere down the line ahead of them. Mary leaned out of the wagon to see what was going on. The refugees trudged past in silence.

The murmur rippled through the line again, and to her disbelief, Mary saw one teamster spit at one of the passing refugees. She swung herself off the cart to get a better look. She had seen the teamsters get short with refugees when they demanded food. She chalked it up to the teamsters' own sense of powerlessness. She had never witnessed them being mean, especially without provocation.

Something about the refugee woman pulled her attention. She was tall and thin, with the stooped shoulders that so many tall women seem to affect, as though they could somehow shrink themselves down. She wore a long peasant dress and kept her shawl wrapped around her head and face, despite the fact that sun was out and the weather warm.

As she passed the cart directly in front of Mary, another teamster pushed the woman out of the line roughly. The shawl fell partly off, and Mary caught a glimpse of days-old stubble on the face. This was no woman.

The teamster shoved again harder, knocking the woman, *no . . . man*, Mary corrected herself, to the ground. He shouted curses at the fallen man.

Mary pushed through the line of refugees with Shurya just behind her.

The teamster was livid, shouting curses at the man and waving his short crop in the air threateningly. Mary felt a rush of fear; the teamster easily outweighed her by three times. But she knew, through the fear, that if she could not protect one person, she could not stop this war either. She had to act.

She moved herself into the teamster's line of sight, holding her hand up in a gesture of peace. The teamster backed down, to Mary's surprise, but continued to rant.

"It's his fault. This whole damn stinking war, the lives lost, the homes destroyed," the teamster raged, pointing at the fallen man.

Mary was taken aback. She looked to Shurya's face, which had hardened. "I don't understand," Mary said.

"Shanron." Shurya muttered.

"Filth, degradation, perversion," the teamster said, still eying the man. "It sickens me."

Looking at Mary, who was still confused and shaken by the whole incident, Shurya said, "There is a man, a street preacher named Reverend Joseph Shanron. He claims the war is God's punishment, sent because people have grown too tolerant of sins, like homosexuality."

Another of the young trainees in healing joined them. She looked at the man with disgust. "Kick them all out of the damn barony then," she said.

"We," Mary lectured, "are healers. We will treat everyone, including this man," she gestured at the fallen refugee, "as human beings worthy of our care and respect. Regardless of what some street preacher says. Go and get some bread."

"Bah!" the teamster spat, "get us all killed." He turned and stomped angrily back toward the wagon train, still muttering curses.

Mary turned to the man, unsure what she could say or do that would undo this incident. Nothing, perhaps. "Are you hurt?" she asked.

"No," he replied. He rose to his feet shakily and pulled the shawl tightly around his face.

"We will give you a half loaf of bread and a canteen. I cannot protect you from everyone here. I suggest you stay off the main roads. With this preacher in the area perhaps a different destination might be advisable."

The woman returned with the bread, and Mary handed it over to the man. He looked at her with a curious mixture of despair and defiance. "You think I will be any safer elsewhere?" He turned away, disappearing into the refugees.

***

It was late afternoon, and the heat had settled over Draadustin like a shroud. In the relative cool and dark of the inner courtyard of the orphanage, some forty boys were straggling out of knee-deep water. It was bath day for young Martin—the worst day of the week by far. He endured enough teasing on an average day. He hated to expose himself to anyone, let alone the boys here, who hated him and called him names.

Thankfully, the ordeal was almost over. Coming out of the water and into the room where they were to dress, he spied it. In the next room, the girls were already disrobing and waiting for their turn in the bath water. Martin pushed the door, which was already ajar, and dashed in.

Misreading his intent entirely, the girls shoved him back, squealing. The door slammed. Martin was already gone.

A ten-year-old boy with shaggy, red hair and a penchant for trouble, Martin raced through the empty halls of the orphanage clutching his prize tightly. Already there was a rise of surprised voices and the sounds of the other boys pursuing him.

Somehow, between the long hallway, the kitchen area, and the main door, Martin managed to pull the one-piece dress over his head and down his tiny form, all without breaking his stride. As his bare feet hit the hot sand of the street, his spirit began to soar. A sense of freedom that he dreamed of but never felt while awake stole over him.

He raced through the crowded streets, running like he had never run before. He was a fool, Mary swore, as she always did at the memory. Always it was the same: he ran toward the river. They knew exactly where he was going. It did not occur to him even once to go another direction.

But this day it did not matter; he was outpacing them. The shouts and catcalls fell away. He reached the main thoroughfare, breathing hard but feeling better than he ever had. The bridge was just up ahead, the bridge and freedom.

A rough hand caught the edge of the dress and brought him to a halt, panting.

"No little urchin girls on the bridge," said a deep male voice in a paternal tone, without rancor or irritation.

Martin turned and looked into the dark face of the bridge guard. He saw reflected back not a trace of anger, no discomfort, no dawning recognition, just calm, gentle humor. "Little girls must stay on their side of the river," the man joked, reaching in his pouch for a sweet.

Martin smiled, his face breaking broadly. He was floating.

Then a voice from the crowd, raspy and out of breath from the run, called out, "That's not a girl, sir. That's a boy."

There were other boys from the orphanage now, jeering and pointing. Martin's world was collapsing about him again, forcing him back into himself.

Then Dryad was there. Dryad was one of the older girls, near to adulthood, and one of the few who seemed to like Martin. She grasped his arm firmly, her voice exasperated, "Come on, you, back to the orphanage."

His world shrinking as fast as it had grown, he took one last look at the opposite side of the river, at Tomlin City. It was as green as Draadustin was dry. Knowing nothing of irrigation, Martin thought it a magical place. There, dreams came true. There, he would be free.

I'll make it someday, he told himself fiercely as Dryad led him away.

Mary shook her head to clear the vision. She hadn't thought of Martin in such a long time. Now he seemed to haunt her, that lonely boy in the grave at the back of hospital cemetery. She shivered, remembering the night he died, the night Mary had come to the healers.

***

They set a semi-permanent camp in the village of Paxton. It was on the main road leading onto the plains and had enormous tactical value for Gregory. Just ten miles away, the city of Germain was held by a garrison of the duke's men. It was Gregory's intention to take the town and use it as the base for his campaign.

The garrison holding the town was large but did not contain the Juggernauts. Mary saw and sensed a deep relief spread with that news, in everyone except Gregory. He did not want to make any clear move until he knew where they were.

The incident with the cross dresser had passed through everyone else's conscious without leaving much more than a brief memory, but it still stood stark in Mary's mind. She had known, theoretically at least, what most people in the empire thought of such things. She had frankly been surprised to see one at all.

Her initial reaction, when she had time to think about it, had been a vague disgust. He had been so big, so coarse. He could never pass as a woman. Why try? It was ridiculous. He was nothing like Martin. Martin had passed.

Her own disgust sickened her. She couldn't deny it. She couldn't deny the similarities. It shook her core. Martin's ghost walked in her mind and dreams, restless.

Luckily, she had little time for dreams these days. In Paxton, she came into her own. The war was barely ten miles away now, and the devastation was obvious. Rumors had flown that the baron's army was back on the field, and the refugees flocked to it.

The young, the healthy, all those able, were fleeing the region. They had mostly passed by the army already. Now it was the sick, the injured, and elderly they increasingly saw.

The refugee camp had become both Mary's task and her domain. Shurya was her second in command, a bold and talented leader. The other young women they had brought had surprised Mary as well, maturing almost overnight. The camp was running with an efficiency that had Roman and Gregory looking on with open jealousy.

There was still plenty to do and plenty of room for improvement. While there were aspects of this that were similar to natural-disaster relief, there were shocking differences.

The hardest for Mary, an orphan herself, was the number of children. Fathers had died in the defense of their villages, or had been killed afterward to prevent revolt. Mothers had been beaten, raped, and killed—prizes of war. That left elderly grandparents to flee with the children. Many of the elderly died of illness before reaching the camp. It was not uncommon for a couple of elderly women, aided perhaps by twelve- or thirteen-year-old girls not yet in puberty, to bring in the children of an entire village.

Mary's experience as an orphan proved valuable. She had fled, making her escape before she reached the age where she would have been expected to take her share of the responsibilities. She knew what those responsibilities were.

The spirits show us the light and dark at once. It was an Oomutoo proverb, one that Mary was experiencing firsthand. Not long after, she managed to commandeer an old barn for the orphans, and they were assigned a permanent cook and quartermaster. To Mary's angst, it was the same teamster who had struck the cross-dresser.

Jeb, or father Jeb as he quickly became known, proved as gentle with the children as he had been angry with that man. The more time she spent among these people, the more it shook her sense of human nature. She had always seen people not as good or bad (a mage's training had beaten those limited concepts out of her head) but at least for or against. There were open-minded liberals and narrow-minded conservatives, with little in between.

And yet Shurya went to church regularly, listened to services condemning homosexuality (a topic that seemed totally out of proportion to the amount of said behavior that Mary observed) and yet she came quickly and eagerly to Mary's bed whenever the situation allowed. Loose women were condemned, but camp followers were praised for helping the men cope. She heard Jeb talk about the "good reverend" Shanron and his "compassionate work" of rooting out deviancy, but also lecture several of the youngsters about how their differences made them special. She did not know how to judge such people. To hate them for their small mindedness seemed unfair; to forgive them for it seemed to minimize their victims

The decision to wait on further information provided a relief to both men and animals. It allowed the army to establish something of a semi-permanent camp. It certainly made Mary's relief effort easier. But it had more than a few drawbacks as well.

The enemy knew they were here. The size of the army had so far prevented any attacks. Taking the town of Germain was going to be that much harder now that the enemy had time to prepare, or so Roman grumbled. The commander of the forces in Germain had sent runners out, and reinforcements were arriving rapidly, according to Gregory's scouts.

The scouts amazed Mary for their courage. Dressed in drab clothes and carrying little except a bow and arrow and long dagger, they went far behind enemy lines alone. They hid out in whatever cover presented itself, a small copse or an abandoned farm, and watched the roads. Whenever they spied activity, they would come running back.

They also presented Mary with her first serious ethical dilemma. She had taken to making healing draughts in large batches. They stored several of these in the camp against the day when they would need them. They also sent small flasks out with the scouts. It had been Mary's idea; it was dangerous work, and they were often injured far from any help.

However, several had learned that they could take the draughts even when well. This gave them tremendous energy. A man could run twelve hours straight if needed, crossing long distances.

Mary questioned if this crossed the line into active aid. She had made it clear that she was here to provide humanitarian aid, not military, and these draughts certainly gave the baron's men an advantage.

She also knew what happened to scouts who were caught. They were not just simply killed, which might be kinder, but beaten and tortured first. So she understood the scout's eagerness to get away, and she held her tongue.

As word of reinforcements heading for Germain mounted, Gregory clearly started worrying as well about taking the town. Still, he was unwilling to move without a better indication of where the enemy's main army was located.

The day came when scouts reported cavalry on the move toward Germain. The thought that the enemy would soon be able to field swift-moving forces to feint was too much. Though he was still unwilling to commit his full force, he began to use his own cavalry.

They rode out before dawn and before anyone else knew, meeting the opposing cavalry before it got to Germain, and Gregory decimated it. It was a good thing, too, Gregory told them later. The enemy's cavalry was mostly light horse, men armed with chainmail, swords, and shields. On an open field, they would have been more maneuverable and faster than Gregory's heavy cavalry. But caught on the road, and flat footed, they were no match.

It had not, however, been a win without losses. He had taken some six hundred men into battle, but came back with fewer than five hundred, and many of those injured. Shurya and the women set up triage lines, doing basic first aid and referring the more serious cases back to Mary. They worked well into the night. When dawn came the next morning, Mary was glad for the healer's plain robes. She felt no sorrow in commending her bloodstained robe to the fire and taking on a new one.

The battle seemed to galvanize Gregory. He gave up, for the time at least, his obsession with the Juggernauts and decided to take the city of Germain. The duke's forces were slowly gathering around the city. If they did not take it soon, they would have a serious battle on their hands. Gregory had hoped that the duke's men might abandon the town, but this clearly was not going to happen.

There was a new rumor in the camp, one even Gregory found worrisome. He had approached Mary about it one night at supper. "Scouts have reported seeing an individual entering Germain," he said, "a mage—a combat mage." He went on to describe the individual in great detail. He was an older man with long, gray hair tied back in a ponytail. He wore faded blue robes with gold embroidery. He had a tall, blue wizard's hat and a staff of black wood. He had sharp, blue eyes and a piercing gaze. He wore a goatee, well-trimmed.

With each detail, he paused and looked hard at Mary. *He thinks I might know the mage.* "It is unlikely I would know the identity of this individual," she said. "There are simply too many mages, if indeed this is one."

Gregory sat back, appearing relieved. "It is as I thought then, a ruse to scare us?"

Mary shrugged. "It is hard to tell. I certainly can't confirm that. But my teacher used to say that only those with little power feel the need to look like a mage."

"Refugees have told us the duke has hired a powerful wizard to fight on his behalf," Roman said. "One I interviewed had seen this man do . . . things. Possibly tricks, possibly real magic. Hard to say. Peasant are gullible."

"The problem," Mary added, "is that there are so many types of magic, so many schools. There are many levels as well. This man could be nothing more than a stage-show magician, or a simple hedge wizard with a few powers, or a true mage. The only thing I can say with any certainty is that he cannot be a true combat mage."

"No?" Roman asked.

"No," Mary said. "Such training is a closely-guarded secret. The military alone trains combat mages. However civilian mages can have many powers, some equally as dangerous."

"Can you find out somehow?" another soldier asked from Gregory's left. He was a petty officer. Mary had seen him numerous times before but did not know his name; Justin or something like.

"Not without meeting him personally," Mary replied. "And then I am not sure how much that would tell me."

"I know that you are here only to observe and provide humanitarian aid," Gregory said. "But if we are attacked magically, is there anything you can or will do?"

Mary just shrugged. How could she answer? How to explain to these people the difference between hard and soft magic? She wasn't even sure herself what she could do against a hard magician, if she chose to go against one at all. Hard magic relied on incantations, ritual activities, and special devices. They had books detailing spells they could cast.

Mary was a soft magician. She manipulated energy directly, without any ritual or incantation. She didn't control it; she merely bent it this way or that. While she had enormous power theoretically, what she could or could not do with it depended on so many variables.

"We will have to wait and see," she said.

The answer did not satisfy the men, but Gregory did not push. There was some grumbling up and down the table, but the men followed their leader's example.

The next day, the rumor was all over the camp. By the day's end, the tales had grown, died and grown back several times. Everywhere Mary went, she heard her name in whispers. She knew a huge debate was going on, and she was at the center.

Who was this so-called mage? And who was more powerful? Mary or this man?

Shurya had become her strongest champion, and by midafternoon, she was in a foul mood. She spent much of the morning retelling the story of every magical exploit she had observed since meeting Mary. Now she simply scowled at anyone who suggested this unknown mage was a match.

Mary herself didn't know, and it was making her anxious. The mage had his supporters. One or two reports had suddenly grown to dozens. People swore he had been seen turning people into pigs, and he went about accompanied by a huge demon that did his bidding.

Mary tended to agree with Gregory. It was unlikely that the duke could even afford to hire a real mage. It was far more likely a hooligan, a trick to scare the peasants into submission. It could just as easily be some hedge wizard with minor powers. That posed a vexing question for Mary: what could a mage with great power but no combat training do against a wizard with even one good spell?

It made her jumpy and irritable. When a small group of orphans broke from Father Jeb's care to tell her, awe in their voices, that she must run and hide from the "evil wizard with the demon," she replied, a little too sharply, "I have faced demons, I am not afraid." That mollified the kids, but the soldiers were another story.

"A healer is a great thing," she overheard one man say, "but if a real wizard gets hold of you, there won't be anything left to heal." She rankled at the "real wizard" comment but let it pass.

Around suppertime, Roman stopped by the barn that had become the healers' base. "Turn in early," he told them cryptically. "Morning could come quickly." He said no more than that, leaving shortly after.

Mary chose deep meditation over sleep that night. She was too strung out.

Lost in the dream world, she found herself face to face with an old tree spirit. "Is this man a true mage? Will I face him?" she asked.

"Your day comes soon," the spirit replied. The tone was unreadable, and the spirit spoke no further.

R. J. Eliason

15 THE BATTLE FOR GERMAIN

Morning did indeed come early. Mary sensed the rising energy within the camp before Roman came to rouse them. It was still the darkest part of the night when Mary, Shurya, and the other healers were brought to Gregory's tent.

"The attack commences today," Gregory said. His officers were already gathered. Without preamble, he began to lay out the plan.

It was as simple and straightforward as possible. The cavalry and the hobblers would leave as soon as the meeting was over. The men were already roused and dressing in their armor. The infantry would set out shortly after.

Hobblers, Mary had learned from Roman, rode to battle on horseback but fought as infantry. The cavalry and the hobblers combined would arrive just after daybreak. They would not likely be numerous enough to take the city. Their job was to surround the enemy and keep them pinned down until the bulk of the army arrived, sometime in the early afternoon.

Gregory and Roman planned to use the hobblers to test the city's defenses while the cavalry blocked the roads leading in and out. If things went well, they would find a weakness and storm the town. More likely the real assault would wait until the infantry got there. They would use the knowledge the hobblers had gained to take the city. If they failed, the wagon train would arrive by nightfall, and they would go into a siege.

It was likely to be a bloody battle, especially for the hobblers. So Mary and the healers were going with them. They had a small team of soldiers assigned to them. They would stay back, out of the battle, but close enough to help with the wounded.

Mary's stomach felt queasy. She had eaten nothing, nor did she wish too. Her nerves were shot. She still didn't know how she would deal with the violence she was likely to see this day. She had no idea if she would see another mage in action, if she would be compelled to face him, or what she would do.

The ten-mile ride to Germain, in the cold and the dark, both lasted forever and was done too soon. She heard, rather than saw, the first clash of the battle. Her horse was stopped at the back of a long column of hobblers. Ahead somewhere, there was the sound of galloping horses, heavy thuds, metallic clashes, and the occasional scream.

Then there was silence. After what seemed like an eternity, the line started moving again. In the brightening dawn she could see the fallen forms of dead horses and men to her right. None of that squadron would need her help today.

Ahead, the horses were galloping. She crested a

low ridge and saw the city of Germain in the early dawn light. The cavalry was already at full gallop, circling the city's wide fields. Her own column sped to a canter, moving toward the main road.

As they neared the road, the column spread out, turning into a phalanx of sorts. Gregory and a small detachment were sitting still on the road, facing the city gates. The hobblers moved forward in a line behind him and came to a halt.

The energy was intense. The horses shuffled and neighed. The men struggled vainly to control them. A few people broke and fled back away from the city.

It struck Mary as odd. Many men wore expressions of stark fear. *How is it that I am calm, and these men, veteran soldiers, so anxious?* She nudged her horse forward, trying to see what was going on. The line opened before her, and she found herself riding forward next to Gregory.

"Be warned!" a deep male voice boomed out loudly. "Your presence and plans are known, and have been all along. Continue this attack at the wrath of Kardon Shaldur, combat mage of the fourth lodge, master of war, controller of the demon Azreal."

On the road in front of them was a small group of enemy soldiers. They were honor guard to a tall, gray-haired man in a deep, blue robe with gold embroidery. With his tall, blue hat and his deep, booming voice, he looked the part of the wizard far more than Mary did. A dispassionate part of her mind thought, *This group looks to have set up in a hurry. How long had they really known of the attack?*

As he spoke, the wizard kept making queer gestures with his hands. Mary frowned, trying to understand what was going on. She felt a prickle and turned to find Gregory watching her shrewdly. Gregory and Mary alone acted somewhat normally. His cavalry, men she knew had fought with valor only days before, quivered with fear and fought their horses for control.

"Mary," Gregory said loudly, loud enough for everyone to hear. "What do you see before you?"

Mary turned towards the wizard again. After a short pause, she said as loudly as she could, "Only an old man making some odd gestures."

The men behind her gasped and then relaxed. Mary realized what they saw was an illusion. The men saw Azreal, a twenty-foot-tall demon with a flaming tail and giant sword. Trained in soft magic, Mary saw what was real, nothing more.

Her proclamation broke the spell, as Gregory no doubt guessed it would. The men chuckled, their fear gone. Gregory's horse snorted and stamped its hooves. "I would suggest," Gregory called in a low drawl to the wizard and his guard, "that you flee."

They did. The honor guard ran so fast that they very nearly left the wizard behind. Gregory and his men thundered after them. Mary's stomach rolled as the first man went down beneath a cavalry lance. She felt sick. She had forgotten momentarily that this was war, and people were going to die today. She did not have the stomach for soldiering, and she felt only guilt at her part in these men's death.

Mary turned her horse around. The hobblers had dismounted and were assembling in formation. At a nod from Roman, they parted to let Mary pass. A look passed between her and the master swordsman, and he seemed to understand. He did not question her leaving and stopped only to bark a quick order to her guards, who rode after her.

They joined the other healers and found a somewhat secluded spot in a nearby field. Here they could see what was going on and treat the injured quickly, hopefully out of range of the fighting.

Mary didn't have long to feel guilty. No sooner had she dismounted and started to pace off the area that would be their triage center than Gregory came galloping up. Across the front of his saddle was an inert form in heavy armor. Quickly he shoved the body down. The knight landed on his feet and wobbled precariously. He would have fallen except for two soldiers who rushed over and grabbed him.

The heavy plate armor was too much for even the two men to hold up, and they did little more than slow his fall. Without a word or backward glance, Gregory was gone again.

Mary went to the knight. The soldiers were already removing his arm bracers and knee bracers. Several arrows were sticking out of the man at odd angles. One had pierce between the side plates and was sticking into his ribs. Mary knelt and began to draw energy.

The morning passed quickly. As close as they were to the city gates, Mary barely noticed the battle. When she stopped working long enough, she could hear the clash of swords and the screaming. Mostly she worked. There was much to do.

A peacetime healer, Mary had never seen carnage on this scale before. Men were brought by knights on horseback or dragged in by comrades. Anyone fit enough to walk was fit enough to fight. Even with a mage-level healer, many of the cases were hopeless.

Particularly hard for Mary was leaving those who

could be saved but would take too much time or energy. There were too many people with too many needs to waste time. Repairing large sections of intestines was possible, but when there were seventeen cases of disemboweling waiting, she just couldn't do them all.

Mary barely noticed when the bulk of the army arrived. The tromping of that many boots caused her to glance up as they passed, but the needs of the wounded immediately drove the sound out of her mind until infantrymen began to appear among them.

A shout brought her to her feet. It was instinct more than anything; the shout hadn't been louder than any of the other noises around her. She looked around anxiously for what had pulled her so abruptly from the healing trance.

It took her mind a moment to register what was happening. Men had broken from the battlefield and were running toward their camp. They were strangely dressed; their metal hats had wide brims and points. Over their chainmail, some had cloth shirts with a strange insignia.

When they were only a few feet away, it finally dawned on her that these were enemy soldiers. She didn't know until later, but the city defenders had massed here, near the main road, to try to break out and flee.

She froze. It was too late to run, not that she could have. The wounded were here, and she couldn't leave them. But she had never figured out how she was going to deal with violence. Now it was too late.

As the first man approached her, the strange, calm feeling from meditation stole over her. His sword was raised over his head. His face was frozen. Too much stress and fear had filled his mind. He couldn't process that Mary was no threat. He could have so easily run right past her. Instead he brought the sword down on her. Without fear, she felt her body move slightly to the side. The sword missed by a mere fraction of an inch. Unbalanced, the man fell head over heels.

The second man held a spear in front of himself as he ran up. Mary relaxed, letting her body respond intuitively. One hand caught the spear just below the tip and pushed it down. She felt herself dip and then rise. The spear did a wide circle around the man, and he too was sent spinning.

Mary at last began to understand her vision. This was just another form of magic, another form of Oomuuto. They were all based on the same principles. Every attack came along a line of force. Mary sensed the lines and moved with them, rather than trying to stop them. Not meeting the resistance they expected, the strength and weight of the men alone toppled them. Clothed in heavy armor, they rose slowly and were easy prey for Mary's guards, who were rushing to keep up with her as she flowed through the line of attackers.

Mary spun around one assailant, sending him through the air and found herself face to face with Roman. The swordman was covered in blood but appeared unharmed. He stared at her, his eyes wide.

"You move like Eric," he said.

She wrinkled her brow, trying to place who Eric was.

"Eric Hammish," he explained. "You move like he does. I thought you didn't know how to fight. Where did you learn this?"

Mary paused considering. "I don't know," she answered. "I didn't learn it, I just . . . did it."

Behind the swordman, Roman's men were swarming over the field, closing the hole in the line. The enemy was in full retreat, back into the city. Mary noticed the battle for the first time in several hours.

Not built as a fort, the town had no proper wall. The defenders had erected a low wall from whatever material they had on hand. Even an inexpert eye like Mary's could tell it was quickly made and of poor quality. It changed material every few hundred yards or so, sometimes being a firm wooden picket, other times a loose stone wall, and yet other times little more than a pile of brush.

The town entrance had been part of one of the more substantial walls. Now Mary could see large gaps where the men had battered it down. A large section had fallen outward, as the defenders beat out the supports and pushed it down in their aborted attempt to flee. Now Gregory's men were pouring through the same gap and into the city.

There were a few pockets of fighting to be seen, but the real fighting was now inside the city streets. Mary could hear this, but not see it, which was just as well. She felt sick enough by what she did see. Most of the men were covered in blood, both their own and others.

She turned back toward the healer's area. She felt suddenly woozy and stumbled. Roman caught her. She leaned against him, appalled at his stickiness and comforted by his strength.

"It's like that the first few times," he said. "During the fighting, your adrenaline keeps you calm, but once there is some sign of safety, you get weak."

Sure enough she felt her strength ebbing. Her body shook. With each step, she felt less steady.

She couldn't stop. There was still too much to do, too many lives depending on her. She had been healing nonstop since early morning, without rest or food. Her brain told her she needed to stop and eat at least. Her heart told her people would die for this one human weakness.

She felt herself slowly crumble. She heard the concerned voices of her guards as though from a distance. She was fading, the ground rushing up to meet her.

She fell into the wisdom pose, her knees under her and her forehead pressed into the cool ground. She felt a huge pulse of the life force beneath her. "Be at peace," it said.

"Be at peace," she whispered back to the dirt.

16 THE PEOPLE'S ARMY

When she awoke, Mary felt refreshed. The shadows stretched far across the field and the light was fading around her. *It is twilight already?*

She sat up. There was a great deal of bustling around her, but she could neither hear nor feel any sign of battle. Guards, not her original guards, were posted in a loose circle around her, a respectful distance away. Their purpose, it appeared, was to keep the bustling men and horses from running her over.

Indeed, it appeared the entire army was camped right here around her—the army and then some. Not far off, to the left of the healers' area, there was a large group of men in the dress of town guards.

"They are prisoners," Shurya said. Mary turned to find Shurya beside her. The younger woman glowed with a calm energy that Mary had never seen in her before. She seemed to have grown greatly in magic in one short day.

Short day? It had been the longest day she

remembered.

"You have learned to draw from the earth," she said smiling.

"I wish I could take such credit," Shurya replied. "It came over me, it came over all of us healers, when you . . ."

There was an awkward pause.

"What did you do?" Shurya asked.

Mary looked at her blankly. "What do you mean?"

"When you . . ." Shurya nodded toward the ground. "When you fell, something happened." She paused, reflecting. "For us healers, it was like an upwelling of life energy. We were renewed. The healing went faster, better.

"For the others . . . it was like the spirit laid its hand on them and said, "*Enough*." The fighting just stopped. The defenders saw their position was hopeless and surrendered. Our men, their blood lust fell from them. They took the enemy's weapons and rounded them up, but there was no more killing. Gregory is calling it a miracle. Roman said it was magic of the highest sort."

As they walked towards the healers' area, an awed murmur followed in their wake. Whether miracle or magic, the men agreed on the source, and she was now walking among them.

"We organized the camp as we thought you would want," Shurya explained. "We treated our own critically injured first, then their most critical. We did not treat our lesser injuries until we had seen to worst of theirs."

"Thank you," Mary replied.

Shurya led her first to a tent where two healers assisted her with washing herself. They used water they had heated over fires in copper kettles and poured into ewers. They poured the warm water over Mary while she scrubbed herself. When she was done and mostly dry, they handed her a new robe from their stock. Elsewhere throughout the camp, the same scene was being repeated almost endlessly, without the benefit of a tent for privacy. The locals' disregard for sanitation had to make some compromise for the bloody reality of war.

Lanterns were being lit at Gregory's tent as Mary was led in. Roman was there, his hair still wet from the bath. Both he and Gregory had bandages on their arms, but neither appeared to have been seriously hurt. A meal was in progress, and Mary was quietly seated in place.

The battle had been a rousing victory for Gregory and his men. To Mary's amazement, both men assured her the number of casualties were far less than they expected. Her healers had saved many.

The battle had been going well and would have soon turned into a rout if Mary's magic hadn't intervened. This ending, however, had saved countless lives on both sides.

They ate quietly with little small talk. Occasionally an aide would come in with a report written on parchment for Gregory. Mary caught snatches of the reports, but they meant little to her.

After supper, Mary walked rounds through the healers' area. They had erected a pavilion just a few meters from their original triage area and moved the worst of the wounded under it. Those able to walk had already moved into the city proper with the rest of the army, which had taken over the enemy's barracks. Nobody was in critical condition, and there was little for her to do. Having spent the entire afternoon and evening in deep trance, Mary felt far from sleep. The other healers were mostly wandering through the healers' pavilion as well and seemed no closer to sleep, though most were frazzled and uncentered. Mary led them to an open area outside the pavilion and had them sit in a circle. She sat in the circle as well and led them through a basic meditation exercise, sharing healing energy until they were settled and ready for bed.

***

"The city of Germain numbered some ten thousand before the war," the elderly man told Gregory as they—Mary, and several of Gregory's aides—walked down the narrow lane. The town was still in the morning sun, but signs of yesterday's bloodshed were everywhere. The bodies had been removed from most of the major streets, but soldiers were still busy clearing side streets. The clapboards on the sides of several houses had dark blood stains on them, and the occasional arrow jutted out of them. "What with the war," he went on, "I doubt we have a full three thousand now." He sighed wearily.

The man was the city scribe. Of the entire nobility and governance of the city, he alone had been left alive. Women and children had mostly fled and would hopefully be able to return when peace came to the land, but the men had largely been killed, either in the fighting or by execution by the duke's men.

"The town seems so empty: houses vacant, families gone, the inn full of strange soldiers." He stopped and regarded a brick building set so low to the ground that they had to go down a short flight of steps to reach the small, narrow door. He pulled a large iron key from his pouch. "Of course, there is one exception." He went down to the door and unlocked it.

Mary was the third one through the door, after the scribe and Gregory. The stench was incredible—human feces and sweat predominating, but with the sickly sweet scent of rot as well.

The interior of the town jail was set low enough that the barred windows were up out of reach. They provided enough light to see, once Mary's eyes adjusted, but deep shadows hung.

The long communal cell to her right writhed with bodies. They sat huddled together, so crowded that no one could stretch out. They were ragged, beaten-down men. Their coarsely-woven shirts and threadbare pants betrayed lifelong poverty, but now the men were dirty and emaciated as well. Tired, hopeless faces regarded her.

A rattling brought her attention to the left side. Here a smaller cell contained only four occupants. They, too, were emaciated and dirty, but their clothes appeared to have once been finer quality, a battered fringe showing what had once been embroidery work.

One of the four men, barely more than a boy with dark hair and haunted eyes, was staring hard at one of the aides. "The baron's men!" he exclaimed. "They've retaken the city."

At this there was a stirring on both sides of the room, and the men looked with more interest, though with little hope.

Gregory turned to the young man, "And you would be?"

"Jerald," the boy said, "Son of Harim the Castellan of North Tir-Na."

"Your father?" Gregory asked without hope.

"Dead," the boy replied. "Killed by that lot." There was a murmur across the way.

"It would appear so," the scribe said. "These four were resistance fighters, captured a few weeks ago. As to the boy's claim, I can only say that I have no reason to doubt his parentage. I met Harim once, and there is a resemblance, but I never laid eyes on the boy before."

Gregory sent an aide with a message for one of his knights and turned his attention back to the scribe.

"These men," the scribe went on, looking toward the larger cell, "were captured in a battle on the north marches. They were part of a band of rabble describing themselves as the 'People's Army.' These peasants . . ." he spat the word out. The men remained passive. They seemed aware that their fate was being decided, but they did not utter a word in their own defense. "These peasants conspired with the duke's men to overthrow the castellan. However, once the deed was done, and the duke's new governor turned out to be worse, they revolted again. They have been wreaking havoc throughout the marches for the better part of the year."

Gregory sent an aide for Roman and then sat himself on a three-legged stool to wait. A petty officer arrived, and Gregory commanded that the four prisoners to the left be released and taken by the petty officer, who would care for them. Then he sat quietly, not looking at the men in the far cell. His face betrayed nothing. Mary found a relatively clean spot on the floor and sank down, waiting.

When Roman arrived, Gregory turned to the scribe and said, "You may leave us." The man nodded and left. With a look from the paladin, the aides left as well, leaving only Roman and Mary with Gregory. He waited until everyone else was gone before speaking.

"The baron no doubt would wish vengeance," he said.

"Paladin's don't execute in cold blood," Roman said simply. "And you wouldn't have brought Mary if that was your intention."

"Of course, compassion dictates we let these prisoners live." There was a stirring. "I will have them freed and given waybread." He paused a long time, then added, "A long fast, and a long time in the cold. Perhaps this People's Army is ready to parlay?" He raised an eyebrow as he said it. Mary saw Roman nod, and out of the corner of her eye, she thought she saw one of the men nod as well. With that, Gregory rose and walked out of the room without a backward glance.

***

"Do you have the reins?" the man asked Mary for what seemed to be the hundredth time. The horse shifted its weight as it sought footing on the slippery stones. The man gripped tight to Mary's waist.

"I have them," Mary answered automatically. "Do not fear." She held her left hand up to show the reins. The horse shifted its weight a couple of more times, causing the man to almost shake with fear as he clung to Mary.

Mary found it funny in a dry sort of way. The man's name was Alaster. He was one of the People's Army. He was tall enough that when he pulled her tight, his chin bumped the top of her head. At full weight, he would easily be double her size. Even as emaciated as he was, he was heavier than she.

For all that he had seen and done with People's Army, he was a peasant from a very poor region. He had never ridden a horse. At the beginning of their journey, he had been alternately terrified to be on the horse at all, and equally appalled to be riding behind "a lady." He sat as far back as he could, trying to keep both physical distance and formality between them. As soon as the horse began to move—or worse, to shift its weight around to descend or climb a hill—he would become fearful of falling and cling to her like a child. As soon as they reached a level spot, he would slide back away from her and mumble apologies.

And yet, for all she had seen and done, Mary had not ridden before a few weeks ago either. Tomlin was too large a city to support more than a few horses for the rich, and too crowded to make them necessary or feasible for the average citizen. But after only one session of training with Shurya, Mary had proven a natural in the saddle.

Alaster clutched her even tighter as the horse climbed the far bank. Roman, sitting astride his horse, waited patiently at the top for them.

"Do you herd cows?" Mary asked as they crested the bank. Roman began to move on ahead of them.

"Did," was the awkward reply.

"Before I came to this world, I had little experience with cows," she said. She told the story mostly to abort yet another wave of apologies for getting too close to "m'lady." She added, "The city where I am from is large and farms are far away. The first time I had a herd of cows come up to me, I was terrified too."

Alaster snorted but said nothing. Roman however said, "It is hard to believe that you would be afraid of anything. I've seen you perfectly calm in the midst of a battle, and you've taken to riding like an old pro."

"Most riders do not have an empathic bond with the horse. It makes things easier."

"I knew it!" Alaster exclaimed. "You have been holding the reins all day but haven't moved them once." Mary held the reins up again to show him, but he was right, she hadn't used them yet. "You can control its mind," he said, "like a witch."

"No," she retorted. "I would not do that."

"And I would not call Mary a witch either," Roman said, a dangerous edge in his voice. "She is a mage of great power. Accuse her of peasant sorcery at your peril."

Mary bit back a response. He was protecting her in his own way. She knew enough of the peasant culture to know that if they suspected a woman of witchcraft, they would soon be blaming her for all manners of bad luck.

Mary's horse tensed as the wind changed. *Men,* it said in her mind. *Four. Smelling of stress and fear.*

Before she could say anything, Roman froze. His eyes narrowed and then relaxed. "Alaster, I think it would be wise if you announced your presence," he said.

"I swore by Helm's Creek three moons ago," he called out loudly. It was apparently some sort of password or code.

"We come in peace," Roman added, holding up his hands to show they were empty.

Mary raised her hand as well, though why anyone would be afraid of her she did not know. Alaster jerked in fear, and Mary quickly retrieved the reins she had dropped.

Two heads appeared out of a clump of tall grass. "Who says they swore with us by Helm's Creek?"

"Alaster," the man replied.

The men forgot caution, coming out to look at the man behind Mary.

"By the emperor's balls," one said, "it is. It's Alaster. Damn you look near dead."

"I was near dead," he replied swinging himself down from the horse cautiously. Once he was on the ground, his gait was surprisingly steady and sure. "Even two days ago, I thought I'd die any moment."

"Are we at peace?" Roman inquired from where he sat.

"The baron's man," Alaster said. The two men started. "He comes to parlay," Alaster added. "Be at peace."

The men nodded, and Roman casually unhooked his sword and handed it, still sheathed, to one of the men. Then he slung himself out of the saddle. "I will be wanting that back," he told the man mildly and handed the reins to the other man.

Mary too climbed out of the saddle. They were led within a copse of trees. The other two men were perched in a tree and armed with bows. One of them jumped down and ran off. Mary sat in the shade while Alaster filled the other three in on the events of the last couple of days—Gregory's retaking of Germain and the release of the men. At Alaster's description of the healing draught he had taken, the men regarded Mary with a wary respect.

Soon the archer was back with a small crowd of men in tow. Though certainly in better shape than

Alaster and his men had been, they were malnourished. Their clothes were tattered and worn. They were armed with an irregular assortment of weapons; a few had swords or spears, but most simply carried a variety of farm implements, from flails to crescent scythes.

The leader of the band, a thin, hard-looking man with black hair and a thin, scratchy beard, talked with Roman for the better part of the afternoon. Gregory had hoped that the men would be disillusioned with fighting and rebellion and agree to come in peaceably. Then he hoped to recruit the better and more disciplined for his own ranks and send the rest home to become peasants again.

It would not be that simple, Roman soon discovered. Neither the old castellan nor the former sheriff were remembered fondly. Jerald and his "resistance force" had been more bent on vengeance then on retaking anything in the baron's name. The argument that they could return to the way things were wasn't an attractive option for any of them.

They knew of Gregory. The paladin, they allowed, was an honorable man. If he granted them forgiveness and new land contracts, they believed it would be honored, as long as he was in the valley. On his chances against the duke's army and the Juggernauts, they were not quite so generous.

"But surely," Roman protested, "as long as the duke and the Juggernauts remain in power, you must remain outlaws. Is it not better to remove them and then take up honorable jobs again?"

"We've survived this long," one of the peasants pointed out.

"But if we fail, the Juggernauts will have free rein

and all the time in the world to come looking for you," Roman replied.

"So we should join the paladin and go look for them?" was the sarcastic reply. "Better them looking for us. We can hide."

The leader revealed that they had the sheriff's youngest son. They assured Roman he was safe and well treated. They had planned on holding him hostage if need be, but they would arrange to have him given over to Gregory as a show of good faith.

Beyond this, they achieved little. The best deal Roman could convince them on was a simple nonaggression pact. The People's Army promised to stay in the northern marches and not create problems for Gregory and his army. Roman promised to return in person and parlay again if and when they had defeated the Juggernauts. Until his return, there would be no effort to root them out as bandits or to move against them.

It was already dusk when Mary and Roman remounted their horses. They left Alaster with his former comrades. Roman followed Alaster's trail only a short way. It was clear that they would not make it back to Germain before nightfall. Roman spied a farmhouse, a low, brick building with a thatched roof that had smoke emanating from the chimney. They made for it.

It was dark when they arrived. Roman dismounted and removed a large loaf of bread from his saddlebag before going up and banging on the door. The door opened the tiniest crack, and an old, tired-looking eye regarded them.

"We seek lodging for the night," Roman told the eye.

"We've nothing here, go away," the eye said.

"All we seek is lodging, for two horses and two people," he repeated.

"We barely have enough for our own supper. We can't feed even two more," the eye said.

"Then let us provide," Roman replied, holding out the loaf. The eye went wide. The door shut and a chain was slid. The door opened, revealing a deep-red firelight.

Roman handed the bread to Mary. "You go in, and I'll see to the horses," he said.

The door was so low that Mary had to duck to enter. The house was set two feet or so into the ground, making it less a building then a depression in the ground covered with a roof. The walls were lined in field stones and the floor covered in a thick layer of straw. There was a crude wooden table in the center of the one-room house and a low, wooden bench to the right. At the back was a large open fireplace with a roaring fire and heavy cast iron cauldron hanging over it. The left-hand side of the room had a sleeping loft and storage underneath.

The man who stood aside to let her enter was worn and haggard looking. He was old, but exactly how old was hard to place. A heavy-boned woman with gray hair tended the fire and the cauldron. Three small, dirty children eyed the loaf of bread hungrily as she laid it on the wooden table.

The old woman looked Mary over appraisingly and then barked something at the oldest of the children, who might have been named Adam. He obediently went to the woman, and she handed him a chipped ceramic ewer and gestured toward a barrel in the storage area.

"We have nothing fine to offer you, m'lady," the woman said.

"Please, it's Mary."

"Of course, m'lady."

The boy returned, the ewer filled with a frothy liquid that smelled of both yeast and pine needles—some sort of homemade ale. They all watched her expectantly. She held the ewer and concentrated, bringing her energy to her.

Roman came in while Mary was still holding the ewer. The man shut and barred the door behind him, and the woman attempted to bow to Roman, who said shortly, "We are not nobility." He unbuckled his sword, set it next to the wall, and sat down by Mary. One of the children, the youngest girl, had taken a seat on the other side of Mary, quiet as a mouse. The old lady spooned a thin gruel into several bowls and brought them to the table.

Mary looked around. Seeing no cups being offered, she took a drink directly from the ewer of the healing draught she had just made. Then she handed it to the girl. "May you never thirst," she said.

The girl drank hesitantly at first and then broke into a wide smile. "It tastes like happiness, Grandma," she said handing the ewer to the old lady.

17 MARTIN'S PASSING

Mary and Roman arrived back in Germain the following day to find the city all but empty. Gregory had established a small detachment, mostly soldiers who were too injured to march but hopefully not to fight if needed, for the town's defense. The majority of the army had marched out that morning, heading for Hogsleg Pass on the far side of the valley.

Gregory had no intention of taking the pass, Roman explained as they rode out after the army. But in Germain, they had uncovered enough information to make solid plans. The duke's main force was on the southern edge of the valley, where a wide river crossed the region. By controlling the trading towns and, therefore, the river trade, they hoped to strangle the baron into submission. The small force loyal to the baron had been quickly squelched, but there was apparently another peasant army in revolt, wreaking havoc up and down the front and proving hard to control.

Gregory hoped to send a small contingent of men to set siege to the pass. Then he would park his main force along the road south and wait. Their supply line cut, the duke's forces would have to send soldiers back to re-secure it. With the bulk of Gregory's forces between them and the pass, the duke's general would have to bring the Juggernauts. On the open plains, Gregory could affect his plan, bringing his heavy cavalry to bear on the Juggernauts.

They rode until dusk and found the army already encamped and waiting. Gregory was in a jovial mood. Two battles they had fought and won that day, he told them, without the help of his master swordman or healer mage.

Over supper they traded reports. Gregory's "battles" barely even counted as skirmishes. One village had surrendered to his heavy cavalry without so much as a sword drawn. The hobblers had chased a contingent of the duke's men out of another village and decimated it a couple miles away. His plan was to continue to march his army directly toward the main road and to use his cavalry and hobblers to liberate villages and towns on either side of their route as he went.

At Roman's report regarding his parlay with the People's Army, Gregory nodded gravely and said, "I expected no better. To know there is no enemy coming from that quarter is enough for now."

***

For three weeks, they marched. Twice the forces loyal to the duke massed in this town or that and tried to resist Gregory's advance. Twice they failed. For the most part, the small forces fled without a fight, or they surrendered. Time and again, Gregory sent small groups on horseback out to liberate villages and try to reestablish some order in the land.

Mary's reputation was growing rapidly. Word had spread far across the valley of her incredible healing gifts, and people were coming with longer and longer lists of ailments. She did what she could, often taking long side trips away from the army to visit farms and villages in need. What she could do, increasingly, was a lot. The power of this earth, so long untapped, flowed freely through her. Her power was growing by leaps and bounds.

Even without the war, the life of the peasant was hard and simple. Frequently, Mary found herself giving advice as well as healing. The peasant began to see her as something of a spiritual leader. This turn of events frightened her. She feared that she would say the wrong thing and be revealed as the heretic she was. She tried to keep her advice simple and bland.

Neither her new respect nor her increasing powers satisfied her. She was restless. She had come to hate this war, to hate all war. The soldiers quickly became inured to the violence and bloodshed. Healing depended on openness and sensitivity. She could not become inured. Every battle was as bad, or worse, than that first one.

Healing involved sharing of energy. Often she had glimpses into the brutish lives of the soldiers. She found it distasteful. They got glimpses into her as well. Memories kept dredging themselves up from within her, hungry ghosts of the past. Her sleep was broken by bits of her past, once well buried. None appeared more often than Martin, the boy from Draadustin. Why this land, so unlike the dry and dusty streets they once shared, brought him back so forcefully she couldn't say. She thought of him daily.

One day they were camped outside a small village that had been relatively untouched by the war. She and Shurya walked along a lane into town. A small boy ran by, and Mary had to look back, he reminded her so painfully of Martin. Another boy ran past as she watched, a stick raised over his head. "Run, sissy, run," the second boy shouted gleefully. Two more boys followed close behind him, laughing as well.

Mary started after them, reaching for the stick, but the boys were running too fast. Shurya stopped her.

"You cannot save them all." Then with a strange prescience, she said, "Tell me about Martin."

Mary turned and stared at her.

"Martin," Shurya repeated. "You and I have shared so much. We share energy, and I get pieces, flashes, of people I don't know. We share a bed, and I hear you call in your sleep."

Mary looked away. It was true. She had seen many pieces of Shurya's life as well. It was also true that she dreamed of Martin often now and woke calling his name. She should have realized that Shurya would notice.

"Most of the things I see . . . I don't know the people but they seem to fit somehow. I can guess who or what they are," Shurya was saying. "Shanti is . . . a friend? The old woman, the one named Justina, was your teacher once."

Mary nodded.

"But Martin, the boy," Shurya groped. "Your memories of him aren't like anything else. Who was he? Why does he haunt you so?"

So Mary began, slowly at first, to tell of Martin's death.

***

After the incident with the dress, life for young Martin had gone from bad to worse. The other boys teased him relentlessly, with the mocking cruelty only children are capable of. He hid whenever he could. At night, he'd crawl under his bunk and lay curled up, shaking with tears and rage that he couldn't express.

Puberty was a rough time for all the orphans, between mood swings, barely understood impulses, desire, and juvenile affections. For Martin, it was an agony. He hated what he was rapidly becoming. He hated all the other children. He found solace with a few of the older girls. But they were rapidly reaching an age where they could be married off and were leaving him.

Then one day several of the boys surprised him. They beat him, worse than they had ever before. Motivated by gods only knew what impulse, the boys held him down and raped him repeatedly. "That's what a sissy wants, isn't it?" one crowed in his ear as they did it.

Knowing the futility of justice in the orphanage, he hid what had happened. That night, he lay awake until all the other boys were snoring noisily. Quietly he crept from the dormitory and out into the hall. He stole a small kitchen knife and, because it made the thought of dying alone more bearable, a dress that had once belonged to his friend, Dryad.

It took him a surprisingly long time to work up the courage for the act. He thought of many ways he could cut or stab himself. In the end he decided, with the strange logic of the tormented, that if he was going to end his life, he might as well take the source of his pain. At least in the moment of death, he could have his greatest wish.

So stripping his pants off, he knelt in the dusty alleyway, just a few blocks from the orphanage. He put the knife down between his legs and with one last act of will, he cut.

When he woke up, it was the deep, dark hours before dawn. He lay passed out in a pool of his own blood. It still ran from between his legs in a slow drizzle. He felt cold, and he wondered vaguely why he was not dead.

He rose shakily to his feet, shivering. He pulled Dryad's dress over his gaunt form. His feet, moving on instinct, carried him toward the river.

It was a quiet night, and peace had reigned in the land for a long time. The Tomlin City guards dozed, leaning their chairs up against the bridge abutments. They took no notice as a ghost-white form slipped past. Their slumber would be broken in the first light of dawn, when their replacements would find a line of bloody footprints heading into Tomlin City. By that time, the healers would have already found him.

***

"It was Justina who found him," Mary said, looking up from her narrative. "She was coming home from a house call to a sick child. When she saw the wound, something passed over her, something akin to understanding.

"No slight woman, she lifted him easily and ran for the hospital.

"When the city guards came, the healers told them that Martin had died. He was even given a grave at the back of the hospital.

"Three days later, they put out the story that they had taken in an orphan girl, one that would require much care. It seemed a routine matter, and the city burghers approved it at once."

"The girl was called Mary," Shurya said.

"I have been called that ever since," Mary replied. "And I lived there from that time on. My body healed quickly, my heart and my soul took much longer. The healers were patient, however, and kind. I proved adept at healing. Justina began to teach me herself."

"You told me once that the healers had to undergo rigorous tests, to show they have the necessary talent," Shurya said.

"Justina said my surviving that ordeal was my test," Mary said. "It showed an enormous will and deep reserves."

"I wondered," Shurya said. In answer to Mary's questioning look, she went on. "I have seen both women and men, Mary. I know what women are like. Outside you look like any woman, but there's nothing inside, no depth, no organs. In all the time I've known you, not one menses. You are no man, but you are not exactly a woman either.

"Forgive me being so ignorant, but I thought that in the inner worlds, there was magic. Magic that could change a man's appearance and form readily. Would this not have served?"

Mary was slow in answering. "Do you think such magic was available to an orphan?"

"But, now you are a mage. If you wished it, you could have anybody you want." Shurya smiled suddenly and shook her finger at Mary. "Don't bother denying it. I have seen you rebuild a disfigured face. You could turn some of that skill on yourself and have," she gestured with her hands, "big old gazoombas, or thick breeder hips, or, whatever . . ."

"That," Mary said, pointing down where Shurya's hand had ended, "isn't possible, I am afraid. The damage I did to myself was too great."

She knew as she said it . . . it wasn't true. It had been true once, or she had thought it was true. The healers were sure of it. Ashe knew better. But she had never pursued it. The fact was that her own imperfection was too much a part of her. To magically alter herself in that way would change who she was, cut her final ties to Martin and her past. She could not let go. Not yet anyway.

"As far as gazoombaas," Mary laughed, "or hips, who says I want great big ones? You find me beautiful enough."

"I do," Shurya replied. "And knowing what you've been through, I admire you all the more."***

They marched for close to a month. They faced no serious opposition in all that time. Gregory's cavalry, aided by the hobblers, defeated such small forces as they encountered far from the main body. This suited Mary. The healers could not go along if the fighting was to be on horseback. Cavalry battles were too fast; positions were won and overrun repeatedly. Gregory was not about to risk something as valuable as his healers.

They were valuable. Under Mary's guidance, and with the constant practice they received, the women healers were growing far more powerful than she would have dreamed. A small band of men volunteered to become permanent guards for the women. This allowed them to train these men in basic first aid and triage, which freed the women to do magic exclusively.

By the end of the month, they reached the main

road leading into the far mountains. A small team was sent to set siege to the castle at the base of Hogsleg Pass. The rest of the army camped and waited.

Already they had cut the enemy's supply lines. Word would have most certainly passed back to the main part of the duke's army. They would have to come back and fight them. For now, Gregory's strategy was to wait. They had to time their departure just right to catch the enemy on the wide plains, with no major cities or fortification to hide in.

They waited the better part of the summer. The enemy was not eager to give up the cities along the river. They first sent a light force of horsemen. Gregory's heavy knights decimated them. Again, they waited, while news of the defeat was carried back. Finally, word came from spies farther south: the bulk of army was on the move, and the Juggernauts were with them.

***

Walking back toward her tent one afternoon, Mary spied three men making for Gregory's command tent. The lead man, who walked side by side with Roman, wore the dark robes of a cleric. He had rich, gold vestments over his robe and carried a long staff. He walked with a stiff arrogance. The man walking directly behind Roman was thin but broad. He wore a plain, brown shirt, dark leggings, and a sword strapped to his back. It was the third man who had drawn her attention and caused her to follow the group—Harrod the druid.

The druid paused almost imperceptibly, but Mary knew he sensed her presence. At the entrance to Gregory's tent, the druid paused and the other men entered.

"Let us walk," he said without preamble. She nodded and the two turned back into the camp.

"Who was that?" she asked when they had walked a few paces into the camp and when the din of activity hid their conversation as effectively as the private glade where they had last spoken.

"That was Shanron, the cleric," Harrod answered. "You know him?"

"By reputation only," Mary said scowling.

"You do not approve," Harrod commented. "I would expect as much."

"And you?" She asked.

He opened his outer robe enough to reveal the scimitar that hung discreetly at his waist. He tapped the circular symbol on the hilt. "We druids do not serve good, or evil. We serve balance," he said. "I would think a soft mage would understand this."

"I do," she replied a bit more harshly than intended. "But isn't humanity a higher good? This Shanron seems to have little respect for what his words do to others."

Harrod nodded. "Aye, I do not relish that man's company," he admitted. "But druids don't serve humanity either. We serve the balance of all things. We serve the woods and glades, the wild places. This empire would tame all wilderness, bring order to all chaos." He paused and looked at Mary. "I came here to escape the enforced order of the imperial worlds. I came to find freedom and peace, but I found instead an even worse imprisonment. These peasants . . . their own cattle have more rights and are better treated. Even without the war and the Juggernauts, the peasants have little and no hope to ever have more. It's degrading that men are allowed to live like this."

Mary shuddered. She couldn't help but agree. "But what does this have to do with that man and why you are traveling with him?" she asked.

"Shanron is the spiritual and de facto leader of an armed group of peasants. They call themselves The Righteous Hand. They have been leading an armed rebellion to the duke's rule for the better part of year. There are three such uprisings now. In the north,"

"The People's Army," Mary supplied.

Harrod nodded. "And the Freedom Brigade in the south."

"And you are helping them?"

"I am trying." He sighed.

"Is there hope for them?"

Harrod shrugged. "They have nothing else. Whoever wins control of the valley doesn't matter much. Any peasant suspected of fighting in any of these rebellions will be executed. The rest will return to their dreary, poverty-filled lives, without the tiny benefits of the land and animals they once had."

"Tell me what you know of these three groups," she asked.

"The People's Army is hopeless," he said. "Which is too bad, because at least their hearts are in the right place. They are all peasants to a man. They have been beaten down too long. They haven't the organization, size, or training to last even a short battle. They run and hide and stay alive."

He gestured back toward the command center. "Shanron is a snake. He doesn't trust me. Men like him never trust, but in this case it's probably the wisest thing." Mary wondered at the druid's easy admission that he wasn't trustworthy, but the man went on. "He seeks power, the basest of motives. He leads the men under him competently, but he'll sell them out at the first opportunity. He's here to negotiate with Gregory. For the small price of a Bishopric, he'll sell out his men."

"Gregory's a paladin," Mary said. "He'll never agree."

"I tried to tell him that," Harrod said. "But like I said, he doesn't trust my counsel."

"And the Freedom Brigade?" Mary asked. "What of them?"

"Robber barons," Harrod spat, "financed by a group of merchants who see a chance to negotiate a new, better trade agreement with the baron when all is said and done. They are run by mercenaries, though most of the men, like most of Shanron's, are simply peasants who want a better life."

"And what is your role in all this?"

Mary was surprised by his prompt answer. "Their only hope, slim as it is, lies in unity. And the only hope the peasants of this valley have is if the influence of power-hungry men like Shanron is kept in check by other forces."

"So that is why you accompanied him here, to help parlay with Gregory?"

He looked back at the command center. "We have just established that is a pointless gesture; Gregory will never agree. I came to see you."

Mary was startled by this proclamation.

"I am troubled," the druid said. "There is something about to happen. It goes beyond this little valley, and it involves you."

"Me?"

"There are great events, great changes, coming in our lifetime. Perhaps not the lifetime of these people, but certainly within our lifetimes, yours and mine. And you may have a part to play in them."

"*May?*"

He stepped in close and looked at her sharply. "Your destiny will be great, Mary, or short. It will be decided here, and soon."

"Harrod?" It was the man in the brown shirt with the sword strapped to his back, "Shanron is leaving."

Harrod nodded once. To Mary he said, "We may be on opposite sides from time to time, but I am not your enemy, Mary. I will have an eye on you. Know that." With that, he was gone.

R. J. Eliason

18 THE JUGGERNAUTS

By the time the two armies met upon the plains, almost three months had passed without a major battle. The men were keyed up. They were excited about the prospect of beating the Juggernauts; at the same time, they were fearful of meeting them. They argued repeatedly about the value of Gregory's plan. The notion that the Juggernauts were invincible was hard to shake.

The armies had marched to within sight of each other, and then they stopped and made camp. To Mary, unfamiliar with war, this was inexplicable. After coming all this way to fight, why drag it out so? Why give your enemy a chance to prepare? Yet this was apparently how things were done.

The second day, they parlayed. Again, Mary found this behavior odd. Neither side wished for peace, nor did they have the authority to grant it if they had wished it. It seemed a pointless gesture.

Mary watched as Gregory, Roman, and several aides rode out to meet the enemy's general. The general seemed unremarkable to Mary. He was a relatively short man in military dress uniform. He wore a long, thin sword at his belt and numerous medals on his chest. Alongside him rode three squires or aides. (Mary couldn't keep track of all the ranks and positions of these soldiers.) Just behind him rode two other men.

They were as different from each other as they were from the men around them. The first was finely dressed in a red silk shirt and a fine leather vest. He wore woolen tights and thick leather boots. At his side was a thin, light, short sword. He stood high in saddle, looking around with mild disinterest. There was something about the way the man moved that spoke of arrogance.

It took Mary a moment to put everything together and to see what was out of place. The vest was more than fine quality: it had a greenish sheen to it that spoke of dragon hide. This man was incredibly wealthy, she decided, and from the inner worlds.

The man riding next him sat relaxed but alert in the saddle. Though sitting back, he was easily as tall as his companion. On the ground, he must tower over him. He was dressed very plainly, in a light brown shirt and long pants. He was unarmed. Even at this distance, Mary could tell he was muscular.

Gregory was grim as he rode back. "Tomorrow we fight!" he exclaimed loudly to the men who waited in formation.

The men cried triumphantly and Mary sighed. Another tense and restless night, for what? Why so much pomp around killing each other? It seemed to Mary that you shouldn't go to war unless you had a very good reason for wanting to kill someone. Then you should do it in the most efficient manner possible and be done with it.

When she shared this view with Roman, he laughed. "That's why I wouldn't want a woman in charge," he said. "If women were in charge, there'd be precious few wars, but they would be damn vicious."

Mary could be affronted, but she knew Roman was only joking, blowing off steam like all the soldiers. She let it slide.

The next morning, she was roused early. Roused, not woke. She had chosen to spend the night in meditation. She wouldn't have gotten much sleep anyway. She felt disturbed, on edge. She couldn't say what it was. She desperately wanted to lay herself down and call for peace, as she had in the first big battle. Aside from Gregory's disapproval, she knew somehow that it wouldn't work this time. The energy of land felt chaotic. It seethed beneath her feet.

The earliest ray of dawn was barely lighting the sky, but already most of the camp was up. Knights were hurriedly suiting up, aided by their squires. Infantrymen were pulling chainmail hauberks over their heads and tying on sword belts. Everyone looked grim and nervous. The chuckwagon was serving an early breakfast, but had few takers.

Mary and the healers were camped on a low knoll in front of the field of battle. When the action started they would have a bird's eye view and easy access to the wounded. Mary had no doubt there would be plenty today.

A purple haze of clouds hung on the horizon. As Mary watched the sun rise, a crow called sharply. It was, she felt, a bad omen. Every hair on her head stood on end. She put it down as nerves and turned back toward their camp. This would, in ways, be much better than any previous battle they had witnessed. They had tents and supplies ready at hand. They would not go to the wounded; the wounded would come to them.

She had spent the better part of the last two days preparing her area. Now there was little to do. Still, she began to roll bandages, as something to do to calm her nerves.

Shurya joined her quietly. "Do you think Gregory can beat the Juggernauts?" she asked.

Mary shrugged. She had no idea. She had never seen them in action and probably wouldn't be a good judge anyway.

She looked at Roman's back as he stood on a small podium a few yards away. He was busy directing aides, who were sent running in various directions. He had been appointed general for this battle. The men had taken the news in stride. Roman was experienced enough, and they all understood Gregory needed to stay with his heavy cavalry.

Roman glanced back, as if he felt Mary's stare. He gave her and Shurya a silent nod and turned his attention back to the battlefield, which was laid out below him. The men had gathered now in rank and file along the hillside. Visible over the next rise of land, the enemy soldiers had assembled as well. There they stood, mute.

Mary turned away from the battlefield. She wanted desperately to call for peace, as she had before. It was not even the thought of Gregory's anger that kept her from doing it—the land itself felt wild and chaotic. She tried to draw enough peace for herself, but couldn't grasp it. She felt as if the energy of the land was distant from her, across a deep divide. Peace, if it came at all, would come at a price.

The divide frightened her. There was a chasm between her and her source. To cross it would require a leap of faith, but she could not see what that leap would be, only that it would be big. It felt, in some unfathomable way, like another initiation. She had been through many in her life, and the feelings were familiar. Something was coming: something that would change her forever. It felt wilder and rougher than her previous initiations, however—more akin to Martin's crossing.

She heard the horns blow and both heard and felt the horses' hooves as the first charge began. She did not turn back toward the battle, not even when Shurya cried out that it was starting. She didn't have the heart to turn when she heard the distant twanging as archers loosed their first volley. She knew the sounds of war well enough and knew her first patients would soon be here.

She drew the healing energy from the earth and the sky. It sputtered in her palm, and for a moment, she feared that she would not be able to find the energy to make it through the day.

As soon as the first knight was dropped unceremoniously in the triage area with numerous arrow wounds on his chest, neck, and back, the power flowed freely, and for a time, Mary forgot her concerns. They had plenty of wounded, but it seemed that the battle was going well for the baron's men.

Roman came down into the medical area from time to time, when the battle was in a lull or when his direction was not required. Mary only half-listened to his eager reports of their progress. It seemed that

Gregory's strategy would work.

The Juggernauts were proving as good as their reputation. They fought in chainmail, on foot with sword and shield. Swift, deadly and powerful, they broke Gregory's line four times over the course of the morning.

Each time, Gregory was able to bring his heavy cavalry down on them. Good though the Juggernauts were, they couldn't stop several hundred pounds of charging horse. They had been repelled all four times. Better still, several of Juggernauts soldiers had gone down under the lances and hooves of Gregory's elite unit, and three had not risen again. Since the entire unit numbered less than twenty, and they had been rumored to be invincible, these were huge losses. Roman hoped by nightfall the Juggernauts would be disabled as a fighting unit.

But as the morning gave way to afternoon, the tide began to turn. For Mary, it was a literally a tidal increase in the number of wounded and the severity of the wounds that first told her of the change. Roman's visits grew less frequent, shorter, and more cautious.

The duke's general had grown wary of Gregory's cavalry. The Juggernauts were being kept closer to the main action. Here, amidst the sea of infantry, they could decimate Gregory's numbers while avoiding the horsemen.

The next time Roman came to the healing center, he grabbed Mary roughly with one hand, pulling her forcefully from the healing trance. She felt dazed, angry, and confused. He had never handled her roughly before. Then she saw the sword in his free hand, thickening blood on the blade.

"We are leaving," he said.

She gestured mutely toward her current patient.

"Leave him," Roman said sharply. "Now!"

She turned and saw masses of armed men moving past them. The entire army was in retreat.

"Gregory and his men are trying to establish a rear guard, to prevent this from becoming a rout," he said in answer to her unspoken question. The men around her were shouting, their voices rising in pitch as fear gripped them.

"The Juggernauts," Roman said.

Mary saw them. There were more than a dozen, dressed in chainmail, bracers on their arms and knees. She knew that much armor weighed close to a hundred pounds, yet these men moved quickly and deftly. Despite having fought since sun up, they didn't appear tired.

At their lead was the muscular man whom Mary had seen the day before during the parlay, the one who had ridden beside the rich man. She could identify him from his stature and posture despite the heavy armor. She could also see, from his stance, that this must be the leader of the Juggernauts.

"Run, Mary, run!" Roman commanded loudly, letting go of her. He ran toward the Juggernauts, sword raised.

Mary did not run. She felt no fear. The memory of earlier battles, the flowing energy surrounding her, was there. She felt no fear of violence now; it was just another form of energy to flow with or control as the situation demanded. Curiosity held her as well. Something about the Juggernauts mesmerized her. This was what she had come all this way for: to understand them. Now was her chance.

Roman had told Mary on numerous occasions that the stories had it wrong. The long, drawn-out sword fights between heroes was a fallacy. "When two skilled swordmen meet," he said, "the result is decided in the first instant, and happens in the second."

So it was. Roman approached the Juggernaut with his usual grace and confident. Moving deftly along the lines of energy that Mary was learning to sense, his sword rose and fell in a smooth motion. He sidestepped and then dipped to his knees, the Juggernaut withdrawing his sword from Roman's chest. Roman fell face first on the ground and didn't rise.

She rushed forward toward the Juggernaut, not sure what she was going to do when she got there. A horse leaped between her and Roman's murderer. It reared and kicked out. Gregory, atop the horse, held a long spear in one hand. It came down swift and sure.

The horse screamed and fell to the ground, throwing Gregory wide. As the horse thrashed, its chest split open, Mary could see the Juggernauts' leader on the far side of it. Gregory's spear had hit true. The leader's chest heaved ineffectually, and he, too, dipped to his knees.

The other Juggernauts were surrounding her. Out of the corner of her eye, she could see Gregory rising, only to be swept away amongst a knot of fighting men.

The men surrounding her threw their swords at her feet. For one wild moment, she imagined they were surrendering. With the same fluid motion, they drew short leather cudgels. It was the last thing she remembered.

Epilogue for Part One

Two men stood on a knoll some distance away and watched the battle. The fleeing soldiers ran past them as though they were invisible. The older of the two stood still and calm; the younger bounced with impatience and repressed energy.

"By all the gods!" Larsa exclaimed loudly.

"Careful, that's a blasphemy," Ashe replied mildly. "The emperor has replaced the gods, now."

"Do you not wish sometimes that we were hard magicians?" Larsa went on, ignoring Ashe's comments. "That we could perform silly rituals in big warm towers and call *that* an initiation?"

"These are the only initiations that matter," Ashe replied. "The ones that life brings us, the ones that strip us of everything but ourselves, force us to grow, bend, change or die." He looked over at Larsa with a look of mild amusement. "You are the one who told me that. And you are the one who watched on as the Han dynasty fell in a bloody civil war, and every ambition I ever had, along with most my friends, died."

"And I assure you, my old friend," Larsa replied without malice, "that I was just as much a nervous wreck that day. I would undergo my own initiation a hundred times over if I could save another."

"But you cannot," Ashe replied. "Any more than a parent can forever protect his child. Eventually, we all must stand or fall on our own." After a while he went on. "I wonder though . . . Mary has no ambition. What is she to lose?"

"It's not always about losing," Larsa replied. "Her empathy is her weakness. She feels the suffering of others too acutely. She must master it."

"And the Juggernauts?" Ashe asked. "What do you make of them?"

"To defeat them," Larsa said, "would only encourage the hands behind them. They must be unraveled. Mary is indeed the best suited to the task at hand."

The End
(of Part One)

THE MAGE CHRONICLES
PART TWO:
THE JOURNEY BACK

R. J. Eliason

1 IN THE DUKE'S CAMP

Mary was ripped out of the blackness as a bitter liquid flowed down her throat. She gasped. Light clawed at her eyes, and she shut them quickly. Hands were on her, something was being placed around her throat. It was tight, not quite choking, but close. She tried to reach for it, but hands held her.

"Oh, no you don't," a voice chided, "not yet."

She blinked and opened her eyes. Three men were bent over her. She was lying on the ground, the afternoon sun shining in her eyes.

"Now, that should do it," one of the men said casually, and two of them stood. They were impeccably dressed, the pair who stood. The first was thin and dark haired, dressed in black trousers and a white shirt with rich embroidery on the cuffs. He had a greenish leather vest: dragonhide. His partner was heavy, dressed in brown tights and a rich red shirt. His hair was thinning and turning to gray. He had a look of arrogance and satisfaction on his face. "That should hold her," he said.

"I hope she was worth it," the third man said as he released her. He was dressed as a soldier, in chainmail. There was blood on one arm and shoulder.

At the sight of the blood, memories rushed over Mary: the battle, Roman falling, the Juggernaut withdrawing his sword, and Gregory's charge. Her fingers went to the tightness at her throat. They had placed a choker necklace around her neck, with a large stone.

"Don't bother," the heavier of the two standing men said. "It won't come off. It's a control collar. You can't jump."

"I am not sure she ever could," the slimmer man commented dryly. "Why would she have traveled here in such a roundabout fashion?"

"She's hidden talents before," the first man snapped. Turning his attention back to Mary, he went on, "In fact, you can't go more than a mile from me, or else." He withdrew a necklace from under his shirt and caressed the stone. Mary felt the choker tighten on her neck. She gasped, unable to breathe. The choker loosened. "Disobey me," the man said and again the choker tightened. "I think you get where this is going. This necklace is tuned to me. If something should happen to me . . ." Again the tug.

"Are you sure she can't undo it with her magic?" the soldier asked.

"No, no," the man said, "to break the enchantment without my consent would take a complex spell. That would be almost impossible for even the most powerful of mages."

"This is a bad idea," the thin man voiced to no one in particular. "To guess what a soft mage can or cannot do."

"This has been made necessary by your own failings, Gavin," the heavy man replied sharply.

"Circular logic, Shamus," The other man, Gavin, chided him in a none-too-pleasant tone of voice. "If you had not sent the men to capture her, none of this would have happened. Besides, we do not yet know if she can, or will, do what you ask."

"She will," Shamus answered. "And if she's half as powerful as her reputation, she can."

"I'd not be too sure," Gavin said.

"She must," the soldier said, helping Mary to her feet. He seemed to think this was all that needed to be said.

Mary's limbs coursed with a hot energy. It was a healing potion they had forced down her throat, but not like any she had made or sampled before. A potion of bitter herbs and harsh magics, its effectiveness was undeniable.

"What is it you think I must do?" she asked the soldier, hoping she appeared haughty and unafraid, but fearing she sounded as small and helpless as she really felt.

"One of our men is injured," Shamus said. "You must heal him. Come." He strode off. The soldier, grabbing her elbow, led her after.

"It has been a huge battle," Mary said to the soldier, confused. "Surely far more than one of your men is injured."

"Not those men," the soldier replied dismissively. "One of *our* men. Our sergeant."

"Injured is a rather optimistic assessment," Gavin said at the back of the line. They were being led through the camp toward a large, white pavilion. Two guards armed with crossbows held the entrance. "I would say he is more dead than injured," Gavin finished.

"He yet breathes," Shamus snapped. "'Tis plain to see."

In the middle of the pavilion, lying on a low cot, was the lead Juggernaut. His armor had been stripped from him. The many small cuts that ran the length of both arms paled in comparison to the gaping hole left in his right chest wall by Gregory's lance. His mouth worked slowly, and his body heaved as he gasped for air. His eyes were open but rolled back in his head.

"It's agonal breathing," Gavin said. "He's not getting any air. He is dead; his body just hasn't figured that out yet."

He's a healer of some sort, Mary realized. Looking at the Juggernaut she had to agree with Gavin's assessment, for the most part. With her magic, she could sense a life force still within him, but he was far closer to dead than alive.

"He is not dead yet," Shamus continued to insist. Looking at Mary, he said. "You are a mage, and your primary gift is healing. We know this. You will heal him. Now." He had the tone of man who was accustomed to getting his way.

"And if I do not?" she inquired. She hated to see a man die, but this war had taught her the cold hard fact of triage. She could save countless lives if she let this one go. Under that was the still too-fresh image of this man pulling his sword out of Roman's chest and of Gregory going down in a pile of fighting men.

"Guards," Shamus said casually, "if she does not heal him, kill her."

The guards raised their crossbows.

"You must do this," the soldier said again.

"I am not afraid of death," Mary said. Gavin gave Shamus a look that said *I told you so.*

"Good," Shamus replied undeterred, "because I am not afraid of killing."

Mary looked down at the Juggernaut. Something stirred within her. She was not afraid of death. But faced with its imminence, she found there was too much life within her. *I choose to live,* she told herself. *It is not that I am afraid to die.* She wasn't entirely sure why the distinction mattered to her, but it did.

Besides . . . this is what she had come here for, wasn't it? Now she would see the Juggernaut as close up as was possible.

"His wounds are great," she said. "I agree with Gavin. He's more dead than alive." She held her hand over his chest, sensing. "Should I fail?"

"Then you are worthless to us," Shamus replied, "and we kill you."

"He's a great motivator, that Shamus," Gavin remarked.

Mary had held men alive that were near death, while other healers worked on them. She had worked on men while others held their lives. To perform both tasks simultaneously was going to require her to push herself further than she had ever done before. Her right hand, curling into a mudra, tapped and came to rest on the heaving chest. Her left hand traced intricate circles over the wound. Her mind was falling into a deep trance.

***

Martin ran madly down the long, narrow hall of the boy's bunk room. Finding his bed, he flopped to the floor and slithered underneath. Once there, he fought to master his breathing. His heart hammered in his chest. How many times had he hidden himself here? How many times had he run from the bullies to spend his free afternoons lying under the bed, dreaming of a better life he had no hope of living?

Mary, lost deep in a trance, tried vainly to sort out this memory. It was real and vivid, the emotions raw. But there was something wrong too, something about the memory bothered her. She couldn't place it.

Boots sounded on the hard, wooden floor. Martin held his breath and waited. They came slowly forward, echoing with each step. There was a mere inch of light shining in from under the blanket, but through this tiny slit, Martin watched a pair of boots patrol up the bunk room. They stopped at his bed, and he stared at the greenish shine of dragon hide.

The bed was rising up, his cover blown. Martin rolled on his back as the bed was overturned. He stared up at the man. He wore dragon-hide boots, brown leather pants, and a crisp white shirt with gold cuffs. He was a trim and muscular man with short, gray hair and a severe face. Looking up in fear at the face, Mary realized this was not her memory.

***

Mary woke with a start. She was kneeling over the Juggernaut, both hands collapsed on his chest. Lifting her left hand, she found his wound gone, nothing but a small scar to mark where it had been. His chest rose and fell rhythmically. As she looked up, his eyes fluttered and opened. He regarded her.

Behind her, she heard a collective gasp. "She's done it!" Shamus whooped.

"Well, I'll be," Gavin muttered.

She laid her head on the man's chest, a deep

exhaustion coming over her. He reached up and touched her cheek. It was a tender, almost intimate gesture.

Then she remembered who this man was and pushed herself weakly to her feet. "He is weak," she said to Gavin, "but he will live. He should rest, several days at least." She was swaying, fighting to stay upright.

"Excellent," Shamus said. "You are quite the healer. Yes, you'll make a great asset, worth every drop of blood we sacrificed to get you, don't you think, Gavin?"

"I am impressed," Gavin said, "but I remain all the more skeptical of this endeavor, especially given her power."

"I think she'll make a great asset," Shamus ignored Gavin's remarks, "once she's been broken in a bit. You think the rest of the boys are up to a little fun?" This was directed at the soldier.

Mary went cold as the implication swept over her. "But, I just . . ." she stammered out.

"Helped us a great deal, yes," Shamus said. "And you will help us even more, once you've learned your place."

She looked around for any help. The soldier was regarding her appraisingly. He was obviously seriously thinking over Shamus's proposal.

The closest thing she got to support was from Gavin. "Gang rape?" he muttered in disapproval. "Your knowledge of women's minds and how to control them is really exceedingly poor." Without looking back, he walked out of the tent.

Mary's insides grew cold. The thought of being raped paled beside her other, deeper fear. Despite what she had done, she would not survive long. The day she had come to the healers, the day that Martin, the boy, had cut himself and became Mary, the girl, the healers had done all they could. What they could do was a lot, but not enough. They had understood somehow the motivation the boy had for cutting where he did. As they healed him/her, they had crafted carefully the appearance of female organs.

A healer cannot hurt. It was one of the first rules of healing that Mary learned. She later learned to bend even this rule, but for her personally, that one rule would haunt her life. The healers could not give her the internal organs of a female, nor could they give her sufficient depth.

She had never been large enough to accommodate a full-grown man sexually. As soon as one of these men tried, they would know she was not a natural-born woman. And they would kill her. She knew what most men, soldiers more so than most, thought of men who lay with each other. She knew that no amount of explaining or begging would bring mercy.

A form rose softly behind her, and she felt the Juggernauts sergeant's arms go around her protectively. "She is mine," he said.

They all looked up at him. Shamus opened his mouth to protest and then thinking better of it, shut it again.

"I have the right of conquest: to claim the first of any loot obtained," he said mildly. "And I claim this as mine."

I am not loot, to be claimed by another, she thought fiercely. Before she could voice this thought, his hands went around her waist, and she was lifted like a small child, her breath leaving her.

"You need rest. She herself said so," Shamus protested.

"Aye," the man agreed, "and I shall take a rest then." His arms were rock steady, but Mary could tell by his breathing that this was taxing him. She craned her head around to see his face. It was impassive and mild.

He walked through the entrance of the pavilion, Mary catching a last glance of Shamus' startled face as they left. They did not go far, entering another pavilion within the same semi-circle as the large one they had left.

This pavilion was smaller, with a cot on one side and a small chest on another. A wooden dummy stood in one corner, and Mary knew from her experience with Gregory's knights that armor typically hung on it when not being worn. The center pole had a small mirror and a basin for water nailed to it.

Mary was dumped shakily to her feet in front of the cot. Woozy, she sank down on it. He took her chin and raised it until their eyes met. "What you did back there . . ." he said slowly, as if searching for the words. "You were here," he tapped his chest, "inside me?"

Mary nodded. Even after years of practice, she had no real way to explain the kind of sharing that went with such a deep healing.

"You are mine," he said simply, "and I won't ever share."

She looked away. The tenderness in his voice would be gone soon enough. "Scoot," he commanded, and she slid wordlessly across the cot.

He flopped down heavily. "You were not kidding. I am as weak as lamb," he said with a yawn. He lay down and reached for her, pulling her tight against him. His eyes closed, and she heard him mutter one more time, sleepily, "Mine."

She squirmed in his grasp until she could see his face. His breathing was deep and rhythmic. He was asleep.

She stared hard at the sleeping face, trying to grasp at all the contradictions that tore at her. That this Juggernaut, this vicious killing machine, should be so mild mannered surprised her. But perhaps it should not. Was Roman the swordsman, or Gregory even, any different? They were polite honorable men off the battlefield, and vicious killers on it.

Should she feel gratitude that he had spared her from gang rape? She did. Should she feel angry that he had claimed her as though she were a thing? She felt that too. Her anger was tempered only slightly by the endearing reason he had for wanting her.

But most of all, she could not seem to reconcile the powerful fighting man that lay in front of her to the scared little boy that hid himself under his bunk. Surely that had been his memory she had experienced.

The mental and physical exhaustion of the day was claiming her. Her eyes drifted shut, opened and shut again. Her last thought, as she drifted off to sleep beside him was, *I don't even know his name*.

2 THE AFTERMATH

"Jordan!" The name cut through Mary's sleep. The Juggernaut, *Jordan apparently,* rolled over and sat up on one elbow to look at the speaker.

He was not as tall as Jordan, but tall. He had broad shoulders and blond hair. *The golden boy,* she thought.

"Hunter told me the whole story, how the mage healed you," the man went on cheerily. "When we pulled you from the field of battle, I was sure you were a goner. It's a miracle."

"Colton," Jordan said to the man, "how fares the battle?" Mary started. She had forgotten that the battle had not been decided when last she knew.

"Oh, it's a disaster," Colton said with the same cheerfulness. "These men are worthless without us."

"Did you fight?" Jordan asked.

"Nay, I did some guard work," Colton grimaced. "After the losses we took and your injuries, Shamus would not allow us to the front again."

"The battle is more important than any one soldier," Jordan said, sitting up.

"Not to Shamus," Colton replied. "We won, of course. But it was the not the win it should have been. We created a rout. They could not capitalize on it. The general is in a right state. He's here; that's why I came."

Colton caught sight of Mary suddenly. "Aah, company, I did not mean to intrude."

"This is the mage Mary. She is . . ." Jordan paused, considering. "Mine," he concluded.

Mary felt anger at the presumed ownership, but stopped short, realizing something else was being conveyed as well, something about her status and relationship to others. He was, in some roundabout way, protecting her, making it clear how she should be treated.

Jordan rose and stripped his shirt off. Colton gasped. "Damn, but she does do the trick, eh?" he said, very casually reaching out and touching Jordan's chest. "How do you feel?"

"Remember when we ran the length of the Isle of Numer?"

"Six days in full chainmail?" Colton responded. "Even with all the potions they gave us, I was dead on my feet. I could not forget if I wished it."

"Aye," Jordan agreed. "Exhausted but whole. That is how I feel."

"For one who was nearly dead, that's pretty good," Colton replied.

"Aye," Jordan agreed. He dropped his pants and, naked except for his undershorts, went to the chest and began to search through it. He came up with another identical set of clothes. "You will let the men know," he remarked casually as he dressed, "that she is mine. And have one of the camp followers find her more suitable clothing."

Mary sat on the edge of the cot. She toyed with the hem of the healer's robe, feeling small, dirty, and insignificant. Colton nodded and disappeared.

Jordan grabbed Mary roughly and pulled her to her feet. She looked up, frightened at this sudden change. He stared at her intently, fear in his eyes. "You are mine," he said. "You understand?"

What is he afraid of? That I might reject him? It hit her in a flash. *He was supposed to rape me. They cannot expect that a man barely back from the brink of death would be up to sex, let alone violent rape.* Yet as she looked into his eyes she knew it was true. If the men found out he hadn't forced himself on her, taking her against her will, they would think him weak. She nodded. "Of course, I am yours."

He let her go and relaxed. "Come," he said. Wordless, she followed him out of the pavilion.

It was only a short walk back to the large pavilion. The cot had been removed from the center of the space. Instead a number of wooden chairs had been arrayed in a circle around the edge. Two of these wooden chairs were taken up by Shamus and Gavin. Next to them sat a small man with dark hair and mustache. He was finely dressed with a number of medals on his chest. He radiated arrogance and irritation.

"You won the battle," Shamus was saying. "I hardly see how that counts as a disaster."

"There is food," Jordan said, pointing. Mary almost said she was not hungry when she realized it had not been an offer or a request. She spooned a thick porridge into a bowl.

Jordan had taken up one of the empty seats near the small man. Mary brought him the bowl. "Serve yourself," he said as he took the bowl. He did not spare her a second glance as she went to get a bowl for herself.

"We broke their lines and drove the baron's men from the field of battle," Colton said from his seat. There was a general murmur of approval. "That your men were not capable of capitalizing on the rout and did not, in fact, destroy his army is not our fault."

"My men suffered heavy casualties," the general huffed. "Besides, we do not have the cavalry."

"And we do?" Shamus asked.

"Of course not," the general amended, "but it remains that my men were devastated in the battle. My losses—"

"Your losses!" Shamus snapped. "Your losses!"

"My losses!" the general snapped back. "I lost over a thousand men, nearly a quarter of my strength, and we're still counting. Are you suggesting three can even begin to compare?"

"Let me explain," Shamus growled. "When I came to this accursed piece of soil I had twenty-one Juggernauts, twenty-one men like no other. Unique! Do you understand that word, General Klinefelter? Unique. You lose a thousand men-at-arms, and at a word, the duke replaces them with a thousand more. These men cannot be replaced."

Mary felt a flush of pride from around the room, and she knew that every man in the room believed what Shamus was saying and believed it implicitly. They were unique, special, distinct. Others simply didn't matter to them.

"Last year when Isole fell to a lance," Shamus went on, "you assured me it was an accident, a fluke. *These things happen in any war*," he mimicked the general, who scowled. "Now three of my men are dead, three precious and unique creations, gone."

"Look what we gave you," Jordan added, "we crushed their line. Their master swordman, dead. The mage, ours."

"The paladin?" the general asked.

"Fell to our blades," Colton answered. "As we have already reported."

"Dead?" the general asked.

"Fell," Colton repeated.

"His body has not been found," the general asserted. Mary started.

Colton shrugged. "We left the field of battle with our sergeant injured and our objective complete. Since we were not sent back onto the battlefield, I couldn't say what became of the body."

"Once before we have been told this paladin was dead," Shamus said.

"Indeed," the general muttered. There was an uncomfortable silence.

After some time, Jordan said. "The battle? What fared after I fell?"

"They were in full retreat and chaos when we left the battlefield," Colton replied.

"I amassed my forces," the general groused, "to overrun their camp and destroy them utterly. Three times a small group of knights charged us, held us back while the foot soldiers broke and ran. By the time the knights left the field, my men were too exhausted and had taken too many casualties. They could not pursue the chase."

Jordan chuckled dryly. "This paladin taunts you from the grave," he said. "A true warrior, he has trained his men well. They do not lose their discipline even when he is gone."

"Where are the baron's forces now?" Colton asked.

"They have regrouped at a nearby village. They have more wounded than fit to fight. We must send a force to destroy them immediately, before they can recover," the general said.

"Then send a force," Shamus said. "But don't think for a moment it will be this one. The Juggernauts need rest, time to regroup. And we must mourn our losses."

"We will do what we are ordered to do," Jordan contradicted. The general nodded.

"And those orders come from me," Shamus replied. "My orders are that you will rest until Gavin says you are fit enough to fight. Gavin?"

"I say they should rest, two or three days at least." Gavin began. "And I agree that with a man like the paladin, I would not count him dead unless I saw a body. However," he gave an angry glance in Mary's direction, "I would *n o t* agree to discuss strategy further with the mage in the room, no matter how tame you think her." He stood and walked out.

Mary looked down, unwilling to meet the awkward stares of the men. She wondered just how tame she was. Seeing that his task was pointless, the general let out a "bah" of exasperation and swept from the tent as well.

Shamus left shortly after the general. The Juggernauts, being left alone, began to talk of more mundane things. Mary waited until the conversation had taken a natural rhythm and she was essentially forgotten.

She toyed with the wooden cup in her hands, swirling the final remains of the herbal tea at the bottom. It was a simple magic, foolishly simple. *Even the weakest of hedge wizards turned their noses up at reading tea leaves.*

It was, Mary knew, only a means to an end. And she needed to know as much as she could about what had happened. So she swirled the leaves, stared at the patterns, and let the trance take her.

***

Mary was in the rear command tent. She recognized it instantly. Placing whose mind she was in, however, took a few minutes longer. He was broad, his hair dark. He was sitting at a crude desk, reading and writing dispatches. As the news grew more worrisome, he was filled with regret—regret that he was not out there fighting. He moved and his right leg twinged.

Mary knew who it was. It was Justin, one of the Gregory's best knights. He had received a large cut in one of the small engagements about a week before this battle. Mary and Shurya healed him but the cut had been nearly to the bone. Gregory decided Justin couldn't risk the wound being split open in the battle, and he needed a trusted man at the rear anyway. Justin had been bitterly disappointed, but he understood his duty.

A runner came up to the desk. He did not hold out a dispatch but rather spoke his report. "The line has been overrun," he blurted out. "Gregory is trying to establish a rear guard, and Roman is pulling the men back. Or was," the man choked. "I saw him go down, and I ran to bring you this report."

Justin turned to the small crowd of petty officers, aides, and squires who made up the rear command. Fearful, nervous faces met his gaze. They were good men, men with potential, but untried. *They will get a test by fire today,* he thought.

"Get the horses!" he barked at a pale faced squire, a boy of fourteen. The squire nodded and disappeared. Justin limped toward the flap of the pavilion ignoring the pain in his thigh. Aides, squires, and petty officers parted in front of him.

Mary, riding his mind and memory, felt the disappointment of not being able to fight give way to a fierce determination. The battle, the campaign, and the lives of many men hung in the balance. He would do everything he could to save them, damn his wound and his own life.

"We are lost. The lines are overrun," another runner cried as Justin threw open the flaps of the command tent.

"We know," Justin replied tersely. "There is a non-combatant group in Shilo. Go. Let them know we are falling back, fast and hard. They must ready."

The runner nodded and disappeared.

A knight rode up, weary and bloody. "Alas, Gregory has fallen." There was a gasp from the aides. Justin steeled himself.

"Where is Roman?" he asked.

"Dead," was the flat reply.

"And Gregory? Fallen or dead?"

"He breathed when they pulled him from battle and last I saw him. Now? I know not," the knight said.

"You must send Mary to him." Justin said.

"She is taken. Gregory was riding to her defense when he fell. She was seen being carried off by the Juggernauts as they left the field."

Pain shot through Justin.

"Then Shurya," he said.

"Dead as well." This time a twin pain, Justin and Mary's, pierced Mary's mind. She clung stubbornly to the trance state.

"Then find whatever healer is left us and send her," Justin barked to one of the aides. The squire came back, leading four horses. Justin took the reins of one. He grabbed the squire's collar with his free hand and pulled him close. "I need you to be brave, John can you be brave?" The squire nodded, determination showing through the fear. "You must go," Justin waved his hand back and forth in front of the squire, "everywhere. Tell the foot soldiers to regroup at Shilo. Send the knights to that knoll over there, to me. Do you understand?" The squire nodded.

Around them men were fleeing on foot or horseback. Teamsters were struggling to get pack animals moving through the camp, some packing what could be easily taken, others fleeing with nothing but the animals themselves. Here and there, enemy soldiers were already amongst the camp. Scattered groups were fighting, but there was no concerted effort being made to stop them.

Grimacing at the pain, Justin threw himself into the saddle. He looked down at the clump of aides and petty officers. "Clemens!" he barked at one of them, "Go to Shilo. Begin to organize the men as they arrive. We must have a line to fall back to. Now go!" The aide named Clemens took one of the horses and disappeared. "Harold, get the teamsters moving! John, get a reserve line of whatever spearmen you can find. Everyone, go!"

A shield was handed up to Justin, and a spear. There was no time for armor now. He turned to the knight and said, "Remember yourself! We are Gregory's men!"

The knight nodded.

The memories blurred as Justin rode through the camp and into the chaotic mess that the battle had become. He screamed at knights on horseback to remember themselves and their training. He screamed at the men to head for Shilo. The last clear memory Mary got was Justin riding up a shallow knoll. Sherry, one of the healers, was holding the reins of a mule-drawn wagon as the teamster helped three foot soldiers lift Gregory's inert form into the back of the wagon. Justin spared him one painful glance. A group of maybe thirty knights on horseback milled around the knoll and the cart.

His voice hoarse from shouting, Justin rode up to the knights and began to yell again. "If this be Gregory's last day," he shouted, "then let him die knowing what manner of men he led!"

The knights cheered and followed Justin down and into the battle again.

**

Mary jolted out of the trance with a shudder. She looked around the tent. She could not tell how long she had been in the trance, but the men were still talking quietly about military things that Mary did not understand, and no one seemed to notice her, so she assumed it hadn't been as long as it felt.

She looked at Jordan and saw his eyes were shut.

"You were as near to death yesterday as a man can be and yet live," she said to him. "You must rest today."

He nodded his assent and climbed to his feet. "Indeed, it as the healer says," he announced, and the men nodded.

They returned to his tent, and he lay down. Mary found a spare blanket and arrayed it on the bare ground toward the back of the tent.

"You do not wish to join me?" he said. He sounded hurt.

"I must meditate. Yesterday's healing was hard on me too, but in a different way."

He seemed to accept this excuse, and his breath was soon deep and even. Mary settled herself into wisdom pose and slipped into a deep meditative state.

What do I do now? In her mind she could hear Ashe's typical reply: *wait, expect nothing.* It was impossible in the midst of cataclysmic changes to see the underlying continuity, the underlying obviousness of what was happening. Those insights would come later perhaps. Right now she had to trust that whatever happened, the reason for it, and the next step for Mary would eventually come to her.

Mary hated self-pity—a weakness. But lying in the enemy's tent, a captive to the Juggernaut, with so many friendships and connections torn from her, she wept. Roman was dead; she saw it happened with her own eyes. Shurya, if the vision was to be believed, was also dead. Gregory's life was in the balance; he might be alive or dead. Spirits only knew how many other people she had come to know and care for now lay dead or beyond her reach. Overwhelmed at the thought, she wept until she felt empty and drained.

Colton interrupted them—her crying and Jordan's

nap. He had three women in tow, the camp followers whom Jordan had requested. Only one seemed to fit the bill of the prostitute that Mary had come to associate with the term 'camp follower.' One was far too old and the other a small, dirty, rotund halfling girl. She carried a parchment-wrapped package that she presented to Jordan with downcast eyes. He took the package without comment and tossed a copper coin at the girl. She caught it deftly and disappeared.

The other two women descended upon Mary. They had bolts of cloth and a small handful of skirts and tops that were loosely fitted. It was a much more basic and crude fitting than she had experienced at the baron's manor, but it followed much the same pattern. She was given three sets of outfits, all composed of separate skirts and tunics. One was made of fairly good quality cloth for dress occasions, the other two were more basic for day-to-day wear.

Jordan inspected the dresswear and nodded his approval. A piece of silver was tossed toward the elder of the two, and they headed for the door. Jordan snatched Mary's healer's robes, the bottom half of which was encrusted with dried blood stains. He tossed them at the women. "Commend those to the flames," he said.

The parchment package had contained a freshly laundered white dress shirt with elaborate embroidery work on the neck line and the cuffs. A pair of stiff, brown leather pants were there as well.

"There is a dress occasion?" Mary asked.

A look of pain and sorrow crossed Jordan's face.

"We mourn our dead tonight," Colton said.

It was late afternoon already as they made their way back to the main pavilion. The Juggernauts, she was learning, had their own semi-private encampment within the army's camp. Their main pavilion was filling up. Over a dozen Juggernauts were already there, lounging on wooden chairs and talking quietly to each other. They were all wearing the same dress uniform as Jordan. Shamus and Gavin came in a short time later. Shamus's dress uniform was slightly more elaborate, with medals on his chest. Gavin wore his usual black trousers and white shirt. He had exchanged his vest for another that was richly embroidered with various magical symbols.

Mary did not recognize most of the symbols, but she recognized enough. "He's our chirugeon," Colton confirmed. "Best in the business too. If it weren't for what happened yesterday, I'd reckon him every bit the healer you are."

A chirugeon, Mary thought. That made sense. Chirugeons were part surgeon, part alchemist, and part magician. She thought of the bitter healing potion she had taken yesterday, part bitter herbs and part magic.

She looked again at Shamus, the medals on his chest no less mysterious to her than the magic symbols would have been to the average person. Seeing his arrogant stance, she couldn't help but wonder how many of those medals were honorably earned and how many fake. Shamus was their leader, Gavin their healer. Jordan was the sergeant, the leader in battle. Outside of this, there seemed to be no rank and little formality.

Looking around the room, there were four other women, all of them dressed in finery, and all of them clinging closely to one man or another. One or two met her gaze defiantly, but none approached her.

"Company!" Jordan called out and led the men outside. The men lined up six long and three deep. "Women over there," he said to Mary. The four women had gathered to one side.

Mary made to join them and saw one step back with a look of anger. As Jordan's woman, she would outrank the other four, and they did not enjoy the competition.

Before Mary had taken two steps, a hand caught her elbow. Gavin gestured toward a spot next to him. Jordan gave him a look that he returned evenly. Then Jordan turned away.

"Everything in this army, nay, this world, is about status," Gavin said without looking at Mary. "You must learn this if you are to survive. Everyone has a place and everyone must keep their place. You can be anything, but you cannot be nothing. Ambiguity is not allowed. You can be his whore," he gave a dismissive wave towards Jordan, "or you can be a healer."

"I am a healer," she said with a fierce pride.

"Good," he replied. "I do not care what goes on in his tent, but outside it, you are not a whore. Because if you blend those lines in any way, shape or form, you cast doubts on my status. If you are a whore and a healer, then what am I? A whore as well? This will lead to problems for you and me. Understand?"

Mary nodded briefly.

They turned on Shamus's orders, now three wide and six deep, and began to march through the camp, the two healers side by side. As they marched, she caught Jordan's eye, and he gave her a small nod, as though pleased. She blushed and looked away.

Her status reflected on him as well. She burned at the thought, angry that she had to play such a petty game. She was angrier still to find herself looking to him to begin with, as though she valued his approval.

On the edge of the camp, a small crowd had gathered. Two companies stood at attention, their dress uniforms wrinkled from months of being locked in trunks. They stood at attention, their faces impassive.

It did not take much of Mary's empathic skills to see what emotions lay behind those sculpted expressions. The army had lost over a thousand men, nearly a quarter of its strength. Most of those were men-at-arms from poor holdings throughout the duke's domain. They would be buried in a shallow communal grave. A few rich officers would be buried in the nearest village cemetery, and even fewer had families who had already paid in advance to have the body returned home in event of death.

Only these three Juggernauts would have the full fanfare of a military funeral. For these three, two companies would stand at attention for the wake. Countless petty officers and nobles would bring a feast, give eulogies, and award posthumous honors. They were Juggernauts, set aside, feared, and revered at the same time. They brought death wherever they went, but they brought victory too. Their deaths would be felt more keenly than that of any lesser man.

As the company halted in front of three tall wooden pyres, a horn blew. Of the three dead, one wore his dress uniform. He looked pale and ghastly, a line of thread where they had crudely stitched his cheek back together clearly visible. The other two were wrapped in shrouds. What injuries they must have sustained in order to be deemed unsuited for public viewing made Mary shudder.

The funeral was long and incongruent. Officers offered praises and honors with thinly-veiled contempt for the men who stole their thunder. Several of the Juggernauts spoke, speaking of their comrades in glowing terms, calling them peaceful and gentle souls while describing what to Mary seemed to be horrific acts of barbarism. Finally, after the afternoon had given way to evening and then dark, the fires were lit.

She turned and watched the Juggernauts as the bodies slowly burned. She was hit forcefully by the chaotic emotions of the men, sorrows they could barely express, seething angers, and irrationally, a sense of joy radiating from a few of the men. None of them betrayed even the slightest hint on their faces. Jordan's face was long and sorrowful. A single tear coursed down Colton's cheek. Other than these small signs, the men were impassive and stoic.

Finally the horns sounded again. It was over.

3 KLINEFELTER'S DILEMMA

Mary was already awake the next morning when Colton called them to breakfast. Between lingering weakness and the long toasts to fallen comrades, Jordan had passed out almost as soon as they reached the tent and was still snoring heavily as Colton laughed and shook him.

Two nights she had slept with Jordan without having to perform any sexual favors. She was grateful for this, but the fear of what would come still haunted her. She could not avoid the harsh realities of her situation forever. She should be spending her time trying to find a way to escape.

She knew that Shamus had not lied. The choker about her neck was indeed a high-grade magic, and she could not break its enchantment easily. To simply flee in the night would not work. If she could only find a way to convince Gavin to take her on as a healer, and to convince Jordan to relinquish any sexual interest in her.

Breakfast that morning was far more informal. Neither the general, Shamus, or Gavin joined them. The conversation was relaxed.

"Poor Klinefelter," Colton joked. "Such a dilemma."

"What fares now?" Jordan asked, sparing Mary from having to appear curious.

"He has gathered a small force on the north end of camp, about a thousand men strong," Colton explained. "All who are battle worthy in this army. But he can't decide where to send them."

"Send them against the baron's men," one of the Juggernauts said. "They are still weakened. Even a thousand should be enough to take them."

"Aye," Colton agreed. "They are holed up in a village just a couple of miles away. Their wounded are more numerous than the whole, and they won't abandon them. They are frantically gathering what carts they have and cutting saplings for stretchers, to bear so many. Even when they can move, they will not move quickly."

"Still, every day they grow stronger," Jordan said. "Every day they will have a few more fighting men, a few more who can walk or carry another. The general must move quickly against them, or risk them regrouping."

"He must, and a thousand seems more than enough," Colton agreed, "but runners have been sent to Hogsleg. They know of the loss here, and the siege has been broken. Those men are rushing back."

"That is good news, is it not?" Mary asked.

"It is not," Colton said. "Three hundred men, men who have sat siege for months, rested and whole. Now they hurry to get past us and regroup with their main army. If they make it, whatever knight now runs the baron's campaign will have a formidable force again."

"So the general must stop them," a Juggernaut said.

"Hence the dilemma," Colton replied. "Move against the main force or the retreating smaller force? If he can catch the smaller force while it's still in the foothills, he can trap them and destroy them. If they reach the plains, they gain freedom of movement, and it could be a long cat-and-mouse chase."

"Crush the main force, and the smaller force is left far from friendly lands." That was the opinion of another man.

"I agree," Jordan said. "But the general is not bold enough. He's scared the knights will pull off another victory, and his situation could become dire again."

"I would think you too should be a little more cautious of the knights," Gavin's voice remarked from the tent's entrance. "And I thought I made my opinion clear about talking strategy in front of the mage."

"Bah," Colton said. "We do not have the general's ear. She gets no better or worse gossip than she would from a foot soldier."

Gavin entered, followed by two men carrying a large wooden box. The box had retractable legs and was quickly unfolded into a small table. It opened outward to reveal a small workbench, the sides covered in rows of shelves holding numerous small bottles and equipment of various sorts.

"Anyway," Gavin said changing the subject, "you all know what day it is."

There was a grumble of assent as the men made a

line behind Jordan at the bench. Gavin produced a small bottle of some greenish liquid. He poured a small measure of the liquid into a tiny glass and handed it to Jordan, who made a sour face as he drank it in one swallow.

"Over the teeth and across the gums," Colton joked cheerfully as he held his glass aloft, "watch out tummy, here it comes." He too made a sour face.

A fool does not listen to his own advice, Eli once told Mary. She smiled at the thought now. *Gavin is a clever fool, but a fool nonetheless. He complains that they talk of military strategy, which means nothing to me, in my presence. Then he gives them a magical potion.*

Mary watched through lidded eyes as the lines of power spread through the men's bodies. Their distaste for the potion went deeper than physical. They squirmed and shook themselves as the magic flowed and pooled and integrated itself throughout their bodies, seeping into bones and forming vague glowing orbs around joints.

"Practice time," Jordan called. "We must not lose our edge."

In the small courtyard of their encampment, they gathered. Someone brought out wooden practice swords and blunt spears. The men suited in leather armor and began to line up. Two by two, they took the field and fought.

Mary had witnessed many practice sessions with Roman and Gregory's men. She heard many of Roman's lectures about wooden practice swords. They can be, he reminded his students over and over, every bit as dangerous as a real sword. A hard blow can kill, break bones, and cause incredible damage. One must be constantly be careful and vigilant to protect one's training partners.

These men clearly had not heard, nor would have listened, to Roman's lecture. They went at each other with a speed and abandon that could only be compared to real fighting. On the rare occasions that one landed a solid hard blow, the recipient was told to "walk it off." And he did.

Their speed was enhanced by the potion, but they were far faster than any one potion should have made them. Their bones were strengthened . . . but again one potion should not have made them this strong. Gavin's comment, "You know what day it is," passed through Mary's mind. Obviously, they were given potions regularly. Could they have some sort of cumulative effect?

***

They practiced again the next day, though no potion was given to them. Gavin did stop by and watch the practice for some time. Mary busied herself the best she could in the circumstances. She watched the men practice in a partial meditative state so she could watch the lines of power. Their swordplay was brilliant, but the more Mary watched, the more she could pick out which parts were the results of magical enhancements and which were the results of training. It was remarkable how much simply came down to training.

Each night, Jordan would pull Mary into the cot next to him. He would kiss her with exaggerated tenderness on her cheek or the back of her neck. Then he would quickly fall asleep. She knew he would invariably want more one night, and she dreaded that moment, but for now she felt almost safe, protected in his arms. She too fell asleep quickly and slept more soundly than she had since the journey's beginning. It was frightening to Mary how easily she accepted her captivity. *Fool,* she thought to herself, *you know full well what is going on. Professional healers are schooled to maintain a distance from ex-patients. The deepest healings had a tendency to create an incredible sense of intimacy. Many healers ended up married to former patients. In places like Tomlin City, it was a relatively mild hazard. Now, in defiance of that training, she was being forced to spend practically every waking moment with this man, whom she had healed more deeply than she had ever done . . . a man she shouldn't be having these feelings for under any circumstances.* But the quiet voice in her mind kept telling her, *watch and wait. Blend with this. Do not fight it. The way will be revealed in time.*

In the evenings, he asked her questions about her life before she came here, simple mundane things mostly. Had she been a healer long? Where had she learned? What sort of training had she gone through? He spoke, in turn, about the places he had been, the sights he had seen. Two topics were consistently avoided: he never asked about her current mission or commented on his. Also, and it was with a start she realized this, they had neither exchanged one word about families.

On the morning of the second day after the funeral, they arrived at breakfast to find Shamus and Gavin waiting for them. Once everyone had assembled, Shamus announced, "Well, Gavin tells me that after yesterday's practice, you seem to be fit for fighting duty again. Predictably, the general wants us to try to catch up with his men before they engage the enemy in the foothills."

"The foothills?" Colton asked.

"Yes, apparently his men have some of the baron's men—who were setting siege to Hogsleg—trapped in some steep valley, but they are unable to press their advantage without us." He stood and clapped his hands. "Horses will be brought," he said, "and we will leave forthwith."

Gavin gave Mary a sidelong glance. "Are the healers going?" she asked.

Shamus gave her a sharp look. Jordan looked pleased. Gavin, though a twinkle in his eyes told her she had made the right move, was the one to voice the objection. "It will be a hard ride, with few rests. Can you ride?"

"Of course," she replied with a note of irritation. *They do not need to know how recently I learned.*

"Will she be safe?" Jordan asked. Mary flushed.

"You never ask that about me," Gavin joked as he walked out of the tent.

"It will be your duty to keep the enemy far enough from our lines that she will be," Shamus said.

Outside it appeared that the news of their departure had already spread. Four women, camp followers who were either permanently or temporarily attached to one of the Juggernauts, had gathered in the open space. Behind them, squires were busily packing and moving trunks onto a wagon. The men made for their tents to don their chainmail armor.

Mary followed Jordan to their tent. He shrugged into his chainmail hauberk. A squire assisted him to tie the leather stays down both sides and into the bracers at his elbows and knees.

"Is there anything you require?" Jordan asked. Mary shrugged and shook her head. "It must be nice to be a magic healer," he said, smiling. "We take near a half an hour to suit up for battle. Gavin requires two men to carry his stuff. At a nod, you are ready to go."

It took less than the predicted half hour for Jordan and his men to be suited and ready.

"We travel with the baggage train," one of the women informed her stiffly as horses were brought up for the men.

Just as she spoke, a squire approached the two of them with a young stallion that tossed its head and pulled at the reins. The woman's mouth dropped in amazement as the reins were handed to Mary, who would have enjoyed the scene more if it weren't for the horse's wildness.

Another test, she thought. She reached out for the stallion with her mind as he reared against the reins. *Peace,* she said into the horse's mind. Seeing the beast wanted nothing to do with peace, she changed tactics, telling it how tall and beautiful it looked, how proud Mary would feel to be riding on its back, how the rest of the horses would envy them. It stopped and stood regally over her, vainly giving its assent to carry her.

She swung herself into the saddle and rode over to Gavin. Shamus was regarding her covertly, and she could guess whose test this was.

Shamus led them out of the camp. He rode like a man used to the saddle, without much grace but with long hours of practice. Behind him was Jordan and Gavin, side by side. They both rode with an easy grace. Mary followed behind Gavin, and Colton behind Jordan. Colton, too, seemed to have a natural grace that translated into the saddle, but the rest of the men were indifferent riders at best. It was no wonder they did not fight on horseback. They lacked the control and grace of Gregory's knights.

The arrangement suited Mary well enough. Of all the Juggernauts, Colton seemed the most open and easygoing. In fact, it was hard to reconcile his casual mannerism, or Jordan's tenderness, with the vicious fighting force they belonged to.

Jordan would turn in his saddle from time to time to check on Mary, ask a question, or make a comment. "You are quite a rider," he said. "You must ride a lot at home."

Mary shook her head. "Truthfully? No. I have a way with animals, it would seem. Of course, such a proud and beautiful beast such as this makes it easy." She mentally sent the same message to the horse, who tossed his head in assent.

"And your family?" Colton asked. "Are they wealthy? Of noble blood?"

She shook her head no. "I am an orphan."

She could see Jordan's back tense and then relax.

"I am sorry," Colton said quickly. "I did not mean to pry."

"It's okay," she said.

"An orphan?" Gavin said. "Where in this empire do orphans get sent for magical training?"

"Nowhere," Mary said, and she paused trying to decide how to explain her past to these men. "I was . . . injured as a child," she began. "I was taken to the hospital. While they were healing me, they saw a deep magical potential. They let me stay at the hospital. I was practically raised by the healers."

"At a public hospital?" Colton mused. "I've heard of such places, but I can't imagine living in one."

"I stayed in the dorms with the apprentice healers," she told them. "I had my own room, because of my age and the nature of my injuries. They were slow to heal. After the orphanage, I thought it was heaven."

"Do hospitals in your area normally have mage-level healers?" Gavin asked, probing her story.

"No," she said, "how I came upon that is another story."

"Do tell," Colton prompted. "Your life seems utterly fascinating."

So she told him the story of how she met Ashe. She left out his name—she feared Gavin might know that name and connect her presence here with the Council of Mages. Gavin clearly knew far more of the inner worlds than the others did, and she was not supposed to reveal herself to those behind whatever plot was going on.

She said only, "There was a mage in my town. We met some years ago,"

"Years?" the man behind her wondered aloud. "You can't be more than twenty."

"I am old enough to be your mother," she shot back.

This made Jordan chuckle. "Doubtful," he said. She started to reply then stopped herself. They clearly had numerous magic enhancements; their appearance could no more be trusted to show their age than hers.

She kept her thoughts to herself and told them the story of how a building had collapsed and she met the mage while rescuing people. By this time she had learned, through trial and error, that she could bend many of the basic rules of healing. The mage recognized this for a deeper, more powerful magic and offered her an apprenticeship.

"And then you decided to take a break from the routine and travel to the most distant part of the empire for some rest and relaxation, I suppose?" Gavin said at the end of her story.

"And I suppose Shamus there just happened to be an old friend of the duke's?" she replied curtly. Colton chuckled, and nothing else was said for some time.

They rode, as Shamus had warned, long and hard. They rode well into the night before they stopped. Colton gathered the offered reins and hobbled the horses together in a small thicket. The men pulled blankets off the backs of the horses and arrayed them out on a bare hilltop. One of the Juggernauts named Humlin passed out small loaves of hard bread and a wineskin each.

When Mary's turn came, Jordan said to her, "It's all we have."

"If she thinks to ride with us," Shamus snapped, "she'll learn to bear the hardships of the road."

"In my training," Mary said, "I have often had to fast for days on end. It is more than sufficient."

After they ate, the men settled themselves onto their blankets. Mary laid hers close to Jordan, and he quietly scooped her, bedroll and all, into his arms. No one commented.

Mary rose after the men had drifted off and sat in the lotus pose, her legs wrapped underneath her. She drifted in deep meditation the rest of the night, but the spirits still gave the same answer: *wait, expect nothing.*

She came out of the meditation just as the earliest rays of dawn were breaking over the horizon. She found the men already rising. Shamus was sitting nearby, watching her closely and fingering his necklace, the one that controlled hers.

"It is a meditation, a mental exercise to calm my mind and rejuvenate my body," she told him. "Nothing more."

"All the men are awake and accounted for, sir." Jordan said with a hint of reproach.

Shamus dropped the necklace with a shrug. "Can't be too careful," he muttered as he went to the thicket.

The horses were brought forth, and they quickly disembarked again. By noon, they rode into the general's camp. It was on the far side of a heavy wooden bridge. A deep, fast-moving river flowed to their left and a huge outcropping of rock rose up to their right. Ahead, maybe two hundred yards in front of the camp, enemy pickets could be seen.

"We have them trapped, sir," a lieutenant explained. "We engaged them yesterday, but were repulsed and took numerous casualties. After that, the captain thought we should await your arrival."

Shamus snorted.

Mary rode up to him. "Let me do what I can for the wounded," she said.

He looked at her blankly.

"I am a healer, first and foremost. I told the baron, I do not fight on one side or another in this war. I give humanitarian aid as I see fit. I will aid your wounded, if you will let me. But I will aid theirs too, if they come before me. You must realize that."

"They," he replied with a nod towards the enemy's pickets, "will not need your help today. If you wish to see to this captain's wounded, that is not my concern. Just see that it does not interfere with *our wounded*." He turned and ushered his men forward. "Let's not dwaddle about this battle," he said.

Mary dismounted and followed the lieutenant into

the command pavilion. Gavin, too, dismounted but made no move to follow her. He, apparently, felt no need to offer his services to the captain.

The captain himself had taken an arrow wound in the fighting. It was not serious, but he had one arm wrapped in a heavy bandage and insisted she start with him.

As she was led to a small side tent, she saw that Shamus had returned and was sitting and talking with Gavin. Already she could hear the cries of men as the first charge was beginning. The two men, however, did not seem concerned in the slightest about the battle taking place a few hundred yards away.

Mary could not shut herself down from the sounds of men fighting and dying. Nor could she shake a sudden fear for Jordan, the man who had somehow become a tiny and tenuous piece of safety in an otherwise hostile world.

She was thankful for the healing work, which helped to take her mind off the battle and her own fears. She could not help but notice that those wounded who were brought to her did not include any from the enemy's side, and almost all were petty officers or higher.

With only a couple of exceptions, their wounds were not serious. They certainly lacked the gruesome depth and severity that she had come to associate with frontline fighters. There were no eviscerations, no severed limbs or to-the-bone gashes. The first injury she saw was a petty officer who had fallen in the first charge, six arrows protruding from various parts of his body. With no helpers, that healing alone had taken nearly two hours, and the battle was more than halfway over.

She caught snatches of what was going on from the aides who brought her wounded and frequently from the wounded themselves. The reports made her blood run cold.

The Juggernauts, aided by a company of the duke's men, had overrun the first picket lines before the men farther back could be assembled. The archers had gotten off a single volley before their lines were broken. During the wild melee that followed, the captain managed to bring most of his men into the fray. Hopelessly outnumbered, the enemy scattered. Trapped in a small canyon, they had few places to go.

A small group of bowmen had made a desperate stand at the lower end of the valley. They held off the duke's soldiers until the captain brought up archers of his own. Hidden behind a shield wall, they had slowly advanced, raining death down upon the duke's men.

Another small group of spearmen made a stand on a ledge, which gave them some advantage of high ground. They had managed to inflict the only other serious wound that Mary saw, a deep stab wound in the side of the petty officer who led the charge against them.

Two of the Juggernauts had scaled the canyon wall a little ways away and come down on that group from above, scattering them into the waiting arms of fellow Juggernauts.

Before the chuckwagon sounded the dinner bell, the battle was over. It had been as vicious as it was short. They had asked no quarter nor was any given. It had been, in the words of one aide, a complete massacre.

Shamus had been right, she thought bitterly. *Not one of the baron's men needed her help that day.*

4 KLINEFELTER'S DILEMMA PART TWO

As Mary left the tent, she saw the Juggernauts. They were standing together in a semicircle around two men who were kneeling.

There could be no doubt who their leader was. He was easily a head taller than the others. He stood with a wide stance. Three arrows stuck in his shield. His entire sword arm and sword were red and dripping with blood. He still wore his helmet, thought his eyes were lost and his mouth grim. She knew who he was, but could not reconcile this image with the mild-mannered man he had been the last few days.

At first she thought the two men kneeling in the center were prisoners. Then she saw Gavin tending one and realized they, too, were Juggernauts. One had an arrow protruding from his right shoulder. Gavin inspected the rent in the armor where it went in. He pulled the arrow out and said, "Let's get this hauberk off and stitch that up." A couple of aides pushed their way through the circle and went to Gavin's aid.

Mary walked into the circle and approached the other man. He looked at her impassively at first and then cocked his head. It seemed an odd gesture at first, then she noticed a line of fresh blood. She bent and inspected the gash that ran along the side of his neck.

"The sword bounced off your collar," she said. "An inch higher and even I would be of no help to you." He nodded.

"Take your helmet off," she commanded. He did as he was told and then gestured questioningly at his iron collar. "Its fine," she told him as she laid her open palm on his neck.

Mary almost started out of the healing trance at what she felt. She had grown used to the mix of emotions that soldiers often went through in battle: the intense fear, the excitement, the pain, and even the way they shut their minds down to the damage they were inflicting on each other. Each soldier she healed had his own unique ways of dealing with the stresses of battle.

She often caught flashes of old memories. They were shockingly mundane and minor. Faced with his own imminent demise, one soldier worried how his mother was faring with her goats. While driving his spear through an enemy's gut, one would sing an old folk song he had heard as a kid. There were a million ways the mind could hide from the cruelty of the moment.

What she felt from this Juggernaut was something she had never experienced before. It was an almost ecstatic joy, wrapped in rage. He didn't hide from the pain he was inflicting on his foe . . . he relished it.

Everything about his enemies—their

incompetence with their weapons, their poor armor, their weakness—was all proof that they deserved to be hurt, to be killed. The world was a place of hurt and pain. Every moment he was inflicting pain upon another was a moment that they were not inflicting it upon him.

She pulled her hand away, her heart racing with what she had experienced. A thin, red scar was all that was left of his cut.

He looked at her blankly for a moment. "It doesn't hurt," he said. He sounded disappointed.

"I have healed it," she said. "The pain should be gone."

"If you don't hurt, how do you know you're alive?" he asked. She had no clue how to respond.

"Juggernauts!" Shamus shouted coming into their midst. The men stood at attention. "You have won another battle!" Shamus cried. "You are released."

The tallest Juggernaut, the one she knew was Jordan, stabbed his sword in the soft earth so it stood on its own. He dropped his shield. An aide began to untie the stays on his hauberk as he removed his helmet. Two aides worked on him, removing bracers and helping him out of his hauberk. When they were finished, he removed his shirt as well. He stood bare-chested. His eyes were distant and unfocused. He turned slowly and walked toward the river.

***

When the men returned from bathing in the river, Jordan seemed himself again. He thanked her solemnly for assisting in the healing of one of his men. They were led as a group to an empty tent and served a hot meal. They sat on blankets on the ground, and by the light of a brazier, they ate their meal. They spoke in subdued tones, comparing this battle to others.

They had fought many others, in many places. This was the first time one let slip that he had been in the field for an extended period, but it was not his first war.

They asked Mary, too, what her experience had been. She told them she had little experience with battles before recently, but with the baron's army, she had helpers, both lesser healers and men to do triage work. They had served the entire army as well.

"We would never share Gavin," one of the men said.

"Mary is a great healer," Jordan said in her defense. "She worked all day on their men and still had the power to heal one of us."

They rode out the next morning. The army marched with them, and they rode at a slower pace. A small detail was left behind to bury the duke's dead. The baron's men would be left for the ravens to deal with.

It took them two and a half days to reach the camp again. They found it in complete chaos. Hoping to deliver the final blow to the baron's forces, the general planned on moving against the men camped at Shilo as soon as he had reunited his forces.

Mary was sent to Jordan's tent that afternoon while the men were debriefed about the upcoming battle. She saw him again briefly as he came to be suited in his armor. The army would move at night, he told her, in as much secrecy as possible. The general hoped to make a surprise attack at the first light of dawn. He paused in suiting up long enough to kiss her on the cheek, and then he was gone.

Mary spent the night alone in a state of nervous anticipation. She thought more than once about attempting to contact Gregory's knight and presumably now leader of his army, Justin, in trance. However, she did not know if the choker she wore would reveal or prevent such an act, and she did not know if Justin had enough magical awareness to receive such a message anyway.

At the darkest part of the night, there was a noise at her tent flap and Gavin appeared, lantern in one hand. "We ride in five minutes," he said.

"The battle?" she asked.

"We will arrive in Shilo as the beginning," he replied. "We will be safely out of the way, but nearby if we are needed."

Mary nodded and rose to follow. It was her, Gavin, Shamus, General Klinefelter, and a small team of his aides who rode together through the crisp morning fog.

As the fog deepened around them, Mary noticed something odd. After a long, restless night, she was becoming calmer. Outside of her own anxiety, the earth was still. There was neither the sense of an impending battle, nor the sounds of one commencing.

Then a figure loomed up out of the fog. He had his helmet off, and she could see it was Colton. He carried a scarecrow of sorts, clothed in armor and a metal helm, on a long wooden stake.

"Aargh!" he cried as he approached. He was jovial, almost drunkenly so. "Beware! 'Tis the most fearsome foe we have yet to face." He shook the scarecrow at them menacingly.

A lieutenant on horseback materialized out of the

fog. The general scowled at Shamus and then at the lieutenant. "What news is there?" he growled. "Has the attack been launched?"

"Launched and finished," the lieutenant replied. "There was nothing."

"Nothing?"

"The entire enemy camp turned out to be less than half a battalion of hobblers and these things." He gestured at the scarecrow. "The hobblers broke and fled as soon as we approached."

"It was a ruse," Gavin supplied, "to cover their retreat." He snorted. "If you had sent men against them sooner, you might have discovered that." He turned to Shamus, "Come, let us see if we can at least determine how long they've been gone." He rode off into the mist.

The village of Shilo was set upon a hill and the fog was already starting to dissipate from the hilltop. Mary rode through the town and soon spotted Jordan. His helmet was off, though he still wore his chainmail. He was sitting on a low rock wall sharing a loaf of hard bread with a young child, maybe seven. Mary rode up and dismounted. She looked from the tall warrior to the young girl and back again.

"She's an orphan too," he said, seeming proud of himself. "Like you, like—" he broke off.

"You are an orphan?" she asked him.

He looked away and flushed. For a long time, he didn't answer. "Maybe," he said, "maybe I had a mother and father somewhere. They never told us about our families."

"Did you never ask?"

"It is not allowed," he said quietly. "Anyway," he went on, "Erika and I are sitting upon a field of nonbattle and enjoying a bite of bread," he said, nodding gravely at the young child, "and celebrating the fact that grandpa isn't dying right now."

The child nodded gravely and continued to eat in tiny, mouse-like bites.

Mary sat on the wall next to him and smiled. "I am glad," she said.

"Glad?" Jordan asked.

"Glad Erika's grandpa is not dying," she said, "but glad, too, that a warrior such as yourself can celebrate that fact."

"I am a soldier," Jordan replied with a hint of reproach. "I don't enjoy killing, I just," he shrugged, "do it."

They sat on the rock wall, ate, and watched the sun rise. After some time, the girl climbed down and stood in front of Mary.

"You are very beautiful," she told Mary.

"The child does not lie," Jordan said.

"Hush, both of you," she protested.

The child took a deep breath as if gathering her courage and then said suddenly, "You are Mary."

Mary looked at her sharply. "You know me?"

"Everyone does," the child affirmed. "You heal people."

She nodded.

"I had a dream about you," the girl went on. "An old man said I would meet you. He told me I should give you a present. I didn't believe him, but when I woke up this was on my pillow." She held out an acorn.

Mary took it. "I wish I had something to give you in return," she said.

"It's okay," Erika replied. "You help people. That's

enough."

"No, no," Jordan said. "That will never do." He pulled a small scrap of cloth from under his belt. It was embroidered with a highly stylized bird of prey. "Here, take this," he said handing it to the girl. With a squeal of joy, she dashed off.

"Thank you," Mary said.

"It's nothing," Jordan replied. "It's a good luck charm. Colton buys them everywhere we go. No clue why. They're bunk, and he knows it."

She took his hand in hers. "There is good in you," she said.

He blushed and looked away.

***

"Are you not coming to bed?" Jordan asked as he settled on the cot.

"I will," she promised him and then she reached out, took his hand, and kissed it. It was a dangerous gesture. She could not afford to encourage him. That she had escaped any sexual advance so far was nothing short of a miracle. Nor could she afford any tenderness towards this man, this kind and gentle creature that could turn, on an order, into a ruthless killer. Yet she kissed his knuckles gently as she replied, "I promise. But first I must meditate."

He pulled his hand away. "I suppose, as I must practice my craft, so must you. Be quick, I will be scared without you," he joked.

Still smiling, she turned away and settled into lotus pose again. She placed the acorn in her lap and closed her eyes.

Her eyes opened, and she was sitting in a grove of Rowan trees. Harrod sat opposite her, his eyes open.

"I cannot come to you now," he said. "It is too

dangerous. The two men from the inner worlds watch you like a hawk. Are you being hurt? Are they treating you well?"

She paused and considered Shamus's threat, not forgotten, and her own precarious position with Jordan. "I am okay, for the moment," she replied.

He nodded. "And what do you intend to do?"

She thought again. "Wait."

"For what?"

"The right moment."

"The right moment to do what?"

"The right thing."

He closed his eyes and muttered, "Soft mages." But he nodded knowingly. "I see."

"And you?" she inquired. "What are you doing?"

"I stand with the peasants."

"Do you think they have hope?"

"Slim," he replied. "But the hopes of a peasant are always slim. Perhaps you have not yet seen that clearly enough. The paladin tempered his tyranny with honor. If you have not seen what these men you now travel with are like, you soon will."

"Surely peace is best hope for the peasants, for everyone," Mary persisted.

"No," he replied emphatically. "Peace is not hope, not in this land, not under this tyranny. Better perhaps for them to die free."

"I find that hard to believe."

"In time, you will see this for yourself," he said. "And then perhaps we will have a different discussion. Until then I remain," he paused and considered, "not your enemy. I will contact you again if I can, and help you if you wish."

She nodded. "I thank you for that."

***

Mary came out of the trance and stood, considering how to find a space on the cot next to the slumbering form of Jordan. He left little room on either side. This was an aspect of coming to bed late that she had not considered.

She thought briefly about making her own bed on the floor of the tent somewhere. She did not know how he would react if he woke and found she had not fulfilled her promise to come to him. Besides, she found that she wanted to. He was warm, and she felt oddly safe within his arms.

She was spared from this dilemma by a sound at the tent flap, and then a voice calling Jordan's name. Jordan's eyes opened and he sat up.

Colton's head came through the flap, illuminated by the lantern he carried. "Jordan, you must come at once," he said. "They are drunk. Again."

Jordan rose, pulled a shirt over his chest, and made to follow Colton. Mary followed the two men. If they noticed her presence, they did not object.

Colton led them out of the private encampment and through the maze of the general encampment. "Some soldiers invited our men to their encampment for ale. They played at dice. There was some sort of disagreement. It was Hammond. It got out of control."

Jordan snorted.

Ahead, three soldiers wearing leather armor and bearing wooden cudgels stood with a petty officer. Just beyond them was a large fire in the middle of a circle of tents. Four men Mary recognized as Juggernauts were gathered in a tight knot. The one called Hammond was being held by two of the others, though he was not struggling. The fourth was bent over, puking beside one of the tents.

About a half dozen of the leather-wearing soldiers, some sort of internal guard, were swarming over the campfire area. Several soldiers in rough-spun shirts and woolen pants clustered opposite the Juggernauts, watching them suspiciously. Mary spied two of the guards covering a man with a sheet.

"Hammond!" Jordan snapped angrily. "What happened?"

Hammond jerked out of the Juggernauts's arms and stood wobbling in front of Jordan. "Said I cheated, they did," he slurred. "I don't cheat, Sarge, I don't."

"So!" Jordan replied. "So you killed him for that?"

"No," one of the others protested. "It didn't happen like that at all. Hammond tried to walk away, but they wouldn't let him."

"Took us for half a month's wages," a voice muttered from the far side of the fire.

"It's true, Sarge, I tried to walk away. They wouldn't let me."

"One of them shoved me," another Juggernaut said. "So I shoved back. Didn't hurt him none though. Then one went and hit Hammond. Hammond hit him back, just a tap, nothing serious, but then the guy goes for his knife. What was he supposed to do? He hit for real."

"Didn't know it'd kill him, though," Hammond threw in. "Still, what was I supposed to do? Let him knife me?"

"You were supposed to stay in our camp!" Jordan replied. "And you were supposed to stop playing dice with outsiders!"

"I didn't cheat," he responded.

"No, you don't, do you?" Colton said. "You just happen to have three times the skill of a normal person."

"Isn't cheating," Hammond insisted.

"Isn't fair either," Colton said.

"Enough!" Jordan roared. "Whatever it is, it won't happen again, right?" He glared at Hammond.

Like a father, Mary thought. *Jordan was yelling at the Juggernaut like a father lecturing his child. That's what they feel: Jordan is their surrogate father.* Shamus and Gavin arrived. Shamus talked quietly to the petty officer while Gavin lifted the sheet and inspected the body dispassionately.

Shamus turned to the men and said, "You are confined to our encampment until further notice."

"Come on then," Jordan said with a nod, and they all made their way back toward the encampment.

This is all wrong, Mary thought as she followed them back. Her other experiences with military discipline had seemed to her far too strict. Harsh punishments and in some cases even executions were meted out for what she saw as accidents or fairly petty crimes. Now a man lay dead, the killer had admitted the act, and their solution was to confine him to his tent? It seemed absurd.

5 TREACHERY'S BEGINNING

The men seemed hardly affected by their punishment. A few grumbled at Hammond for bringing it on them, and a few grumbled about Shamus, who they saw as inflicting it.

Jordan pushed them hard in the morning training sessions. He lectured Hammond and the others for their "irresponsibility" and their drinking. Once again, Mary thought he sounded like a father lecturing ill-behaved boys.

The only one who actually seemed to be suffering from their confinement was the gregarious Colton. He was in a foul mood most of the morning and grumbled over lunch that the men were piss-poor company.

While the men took a long afternoon siesta in the main pavilion, Mary opted instead to sit outside in the sun. The men could be surprisingly juvenile in their talk and in their humor. It grated on her.

She wasn't sure what first caught her eye when the

clump of riders passed her, but a second glance confirmed that she knew at least one of the riders. He was flanked on either side by petty officers and behind by a local, who, from his dress, must have been a minor noble. But there was no mistaking Shanron. She scowled, wondering what he was doing here.

"You do not care for the good Bishop Shanron?" Colton's voice asked. There was a hint of coldness in the way he said the name that told her Colton's opinion.

"I do not," she conceded. "Is he a Bishop? I had heard merely a priest and a rebel to boot."

"Both," Colton agreed, "but soon perhaps he will be neither, and instead, a bishop."

"He sought to parlay with Gregory," Mary said, "and got nowhere."

Colton shrugged. "He's come to parlay twice now. Perhaps he's had better luck with the general."

Mary shivered at the thought.

***

"You do not wish to stay with the men?" Mary asked hesitantly as they entered the tent.

"I prefer the company here," Jordan laughed and pulled her close. He kissed her cheek lightly. She blushed and looked away. Then he kissed her cheek again, and she started to tremble. His grip on her tightened. "You are mine," he said. "I could have had you anytime I wanted."

Mary nodded.

"It's what men do, you know?" he said. In his world, perhaps. In Mary's world, no.

"I . . ." Mary began, but words failed.

"Other women would be proud to be with me," he

said. She nodded, knowing it was true. "I would prefer you come to me willingly," he said. There was an edge to his voice, a mixture of anger and fear. "But you are mine."

She grabbed his shirt and held him close, trying to convey with her body what she could not say. She would go to him willingly, she found suddenly, if she could. But she could not. Her body simply wouldn't accommodate, and when he found this out, he would surely guess the reason. The moment she had feared since he first uttered the word "mine" had finally come.

His gripped relaxed. "You are afraid," he said, relieved. *He is afraid, too*, she realized with a start. "Do not be. I would not be rough with a woman."

He lifted her easily and set her on the cot. He pulled his shirt off and stripped off his pants. In only his undershorts, he sat next to her on the cot. There was an awkward pause. Mary was still unsure how to begin explaining her problem. Jordan looked terrified suddenly. With a sudden motion, he stripped off the undershorts. He looked away and would not meet Mary's eye. He radiated tension.

Mary looked down and saw it. It wasn't deformed, exactly. It looked for all the world like an ordinary penis in shape. It was just . . . small. The dispassionate healer within her looked at it and wondered if it was a defect or merely the smallest end of the normal spectrum? Given the size of his body, it was likely a birth defect of sorts.

The rest of Mary's mind was filling with relief. She nearly laughed but caught herself quickly. In his current mental state he would surely misread any sign of humor. She ran her hand along his arm, to put him at ease but also to gauge if he was likely to lash out. He seemed close. As she touched him, her mind filled with memories, his memories: being teased as a child; as an adult, by women, prostitutes mostly, eyebrows arched and smirks on their faces. Moving carefully, so as not to provoke him, she lifted herself into his lap and straddled him.

All her life, she was careful of male lovers. She could not reveal her true heritage to most men for fear of their reaction. Then there was the act itself. Larsa had taught her positions that prevented a man from penetrating deeply. It was a passable compromise, but it always felt stilted and unnatural to her. With some men, she had learned, she could allow them to penetrate her anally. It could be pleasurable, if they were gentle.

Mary placed her hand on his cheek and spoke in half truths. "As an orphan in the streets of Draadustin, there was never enough of anything. After my injuries, the healers did all they could, but parts of me never grew up, never became what they should." Slowly he raised his eyes and met hers. "Always with a man it has been hard, painful for me. I did not mean to imply that you would be rough." She moved her hips slowly as she spoke, and she could feel him grow hard beneath her. Even hard, he could not have been more than three inches.

He growled and buried his face in her hair. She lifted herself enough to slide her skirt up and then sank her bare hips down upon him. Even as small as he was, it was a tight fit. Fully penetrated, his penis bumped, not unpleasantly, against the uppermost end of her vagina.

She spoke softly in his ear one thing that was

completely true. "I have always prayed that someday the spirits would send me someone who fit me perfectly."

With a mischievous smile, he scooped her up and laid her upon the bed. She feared momentarily that his weight would crush her, but he held himself up on his knees and elbows. "Far be it for me to deny the spirits," he replied, biting her ear playfully.

Mary wrapped her legs around his waist, and for the first time in her long life, she fully gave herself over to the experience of sex.

***

Breakfast the next morning was the usual thick oatmeal and a bowl of dried fruits. As Mary handed the bowl and platter to Jordan, he swung his arm around her waist and pulled her onto his lap. She did not resist. She felt like a small child, her feet dangling. She felt happy, too, as he began to feed her bits of dried apricots.

Colton smiled at the two of them. None of the others reacted or even seemed to notice.

Shamus stuck his head in and said. "Parade formation, no dress uniform. Ten minutes."

The men began to rise. "What's that mean?" Mary asked as she got up so Jordan could rise. He shrugged.

"Formation," Colton explained, "means someone is coming. Parade formation means it's someone friendly. And no dress uniforms means it's not someone important."

"Most importantly," one of the other men added, "being put in formation means they've forgotten that we are confined to our encampment."

Mary wondered how accurate that observation was

while she followed the men out. She saw one of the women sitting in the doorway of another Juggernaut's tent. She assumed that meant the women were not invited to whatever "parade formation" was. Then she had to laugh at the image of all the camp followers standing in formation: a whore's brigade.

She spied Gavin and made for him. She assumed her status as a healer required a presence of some sort. He barely gave her a second glance but did not countermand her. She followed him and

Shamus, and they walked in a leisurely stroll alongside the Juggernauts, who marched in a strict formation.

It was not just the Juggernauts who were being called into formation. Most of the army was slowly filtering out of the camp and onto a wide-open field outside of the village of Shilo. They stood, not exactly at attention, but not exactly at ease. A small team of noncombatant aides rolled several barrels out and put planks across them, making a makeshift bandstand for the general.

No sooner had they set a chair on the bandstand and the general had mounted it, than a long line of men crossed the horizon and came toward them. In the lead was an officer in a long, black, leather trench coat. He had a rank insignia and several medals on his chest.

Just behind him rode a dozen aides in a clump. Behind them was a long line of soldiers on horseback. They wore chainmail armor. They had long broadswords at one side, and each carried a shield. Mary guessed, by the fact that they did not carry lances or long spears, that they were likely hobblers. They rode two abreast along the narrow dirt road. There were so many that the column had dipped to the bottom of the hill and was rising toward the waiting army before the soldiers on horseback gave way to footmen.

The first of these were pikemen, each armed with a long, spear-like weapon with an axe head fixed to its top. They wore chainmail with pieces of metal plate over it. They marched four abreast and were not half as numerous as the horsemen. Behind them there were men-at-arms in chainmail with broadswords and shields, and behind them a veritable sea of spear-wielding men with little or no armor that Mary could see.

The officer came to a halt and called out to the general that he was Captain Marshell and was reporting with reinforcements and dispatches from the duke himself. The general accepted the report with a sour nod and gestured for his aid to help him down from the bandstand.

A hum of conversation broke out as the general disappeared. The new reinforcements dismounted and began to mill around. The ranks broke, some men making back for the encampment and others tentatively moving toward the new men, looking for gossip.

Gavin gave a quick look toward Shamus, who nodded back toward their encampment.

"The general seems in a bad mood today," Mary commented. Gavin snorted but did not reply.

"No cavalry," Shamus said from ahead of Gavin. "And not half the men he requested. I'd say he's in a bad mood."

"I don't understand," Mary said. "Didn't you defeat Gregory and his men? Hasn't he won?"

"The baron's men are defeated," Shamus said, "but not driven from the field. If they are allowed to regroup, or make it back to one of their strongholds, like Germain, or get reinforcements from the baron, then we will have to repeat the entire pointless exercise of that battle."

"Then there is the peasant rabble to contend with," Shamus went on as they reentered their encampment. "A single brigade could defeat them in an open battle, if we could get them in one place. It wouldn't be a full afternoon's practice for my Juggernauts. But they won't oblige us by staying in one place. To pacify the entire valley floor will take hundreds of men, and fast horses, to out-maneuver that rabble."

Mary found it hard to believe that it would take so many men to defeat the ragtag remnants of Gregory's army or the even more ramshackle bands of peasants.

***

The next morning Mary woke early to the sound of bugle calls. She threw a shirt over her head and slid into a skirt. As she left the tent, Jordan was only beginning his more elaborate dress in armor.

Their private encampment was swarming with aides and attendants. Looking beyond the borders of their encampment, it seemed the entire place was in chaos. The army was about to move.

She snagged a light, cold breakfast of bread and dried fruit from a chuckwagon and returned to the camp. Jordan had his chainmail on and was standing dutifully as the attendant tied the stays on the sides and attached his bracers.

He gestured to her, and she fed him bits of dried fruit as he stood there.

"Is it battle?" she asked.

He shook his head. "We will ride point guard, close to the front. If problems come, we will be ready. But no battle is expected."

"To where do we ride?" she asked.

He shrugged. "I don't have the general's ear. I presume we make haste after the baron's men now that we have more numbers."

Two teamsters stalked through, ignoring all of them, and hoisted Jordan's trunk. They exited without any comment.

As they left the tent, she saw Gavin approach, holding two horses by the reins. The stallion bucked and twisted, but as soon as it saw Mary, it stopped and began to prance. Gavin gave it, then Mary, a quizzical look.

"I have a way with animals," she said, taking the reins and making soft noises to the horse.

They arrived on the open field on the edge of town in time to watch the last of the hobblers disappear over the hillside to the northeast. The general, and his band of aides and bodyguards, watched them leave silently. Then the general turned toward the now assembled Juggernauts. He nodded and took off in the opposite direction.

It was apparent from the little gossip Mary was able to pick up during the first day's march that they were not heading in the direction anyone had expected. They were traveling down what was little more than a dirt strip through rolling plains of barley and oats, called Thrain's Road.

Thrain's Road, the cook at the chuckwagon was telling someone as he served hard bread for lunch, was nowhere anyone would want to be. Thrain's Road bisected the valley from east to west. To the north and the west lay the town of Germain and the road into the baron's land. To the south, in a broad sweep, lay four river towns of strategic importance that were all in revolt at the moment. No one seemed to have any clue what lay along this road that would attract the general's interest, or require the majority of his army.

6 WHY PEASANTS FIGHT

They ended their march by midafternoon on the outskirts of another nameless village. A sizable apple orchard lay on the edge of the village, and three nervous village elders greeted them there.

The general spoke with the elders briefly. They stated in anxious voices that they were peaceful and grateful that the duke had at last chosen to liberate them.

The general told the elders magnanimously that the army meant them no harm and would see that their village was safe from both the baron's tyranny and the dangerous peasant rabble that was loose. The general hinted he was interested in any information about that "mindless rabble" nearby, but said those who "had risen up justly, if too quickly" against the baron's dominion might entreat for peace. He hinted broadly, that the duke might have lands set aside for such people.

The general dismissed the elders and sent aides

back to organize the camp. The Juggernauts made a quick sweep of the village to confirm there were indeed no enemy forces within, then they too were dismissed.

Several fallow fields were already being commandeered by the teamsters and camp was being set. Mary followed Gavin and the Juggernaut to their tents. By nightfall the camp had been set, the fires lit, and supper was being served. The villagers had gifted the general with several sheep, and the Juggernauts were invited to a feast of mutton stew.

Their feast was interrupted by the arrival of an aide leading a procession of some nine peasants. A small pile of short swords, hunting bows, and knives were laid at the general's feet.

The lead peasant explained, in a rough, halting voice, that they were tired of fighting and, hoping they had not heard falsely: that there were indeed lands somewhere set aside for them if they came in peacefully. The general did not speak but nodded toward another petty officer, who led the men away. The feast resumed as if nothing had happened.

Mary thought of Shanron's presence in their camp days ago and of this mysterious march to nowhere. Perhaps the general had made some sort of deal with the priest. As much as she personally disliked the two men, this deal could perhaps be the beginnings of the peace she wanted. The peasants could be moved to the lands the duke had set aside. For better or worse, the war would be over.

***

Mary woke before sunrise the next morning. Unsure what impulse had awakened her, she rose and made her way through the still-sleeping camp. In the space between the army's camp and the village, any hope Mary had of a peaceful end to this struggle died.

The apple orchard had been razed to the ground, only bare stumps remained. All except for nine trees. Those nine trees had been shorn of all limbs, leaving only solitary trunks rising from the earth. Tied to the top of each of these was a body, lashed to the trunk, suspended above the ground and disemboweled.

A young girl knelt on the edge of the orchard, staring up at one of the bodies. Mary went to her.

"Did you know him?" she asked.

"It's my father," the girl replied, her voice flat.

They sat in silence, Mary having no idea what to say to that. After a long time, the girl added, "What I don't understand is Grandma says he's lucky. How is that lucky?"

Mary rose and looked around. She thought of the orchard, the "gift" of the sheep, the army camping on the fields. *They will starve,* she thought. To the girl, she said, "Tell your grandma to plant again. Hope has not failed completely." She walked back into the camp.

As they rode out that morning, Mary glanced around once to confirm the girl was gone, but she would not raise her eyes to the peasants' bodies again. She saw the blank downtrodden faces of the villagers as they rode out. She willed them to know she had not been involved in what had occurred. She felt guilt for it nonetheless.

"Fools," Gavin muttered as they rode past. If Jordan or the other Juggernauts had any feelings on the subject, they kept it to themselves.

Around midmorning, Gavin reined in his horse and brought it back even with Mary. Without introduction or preamble, he said, "What do you know of the druids?"

The question startled Mary, though she tried to not let it show. "Why do you ask?" she said.

"We are both magicians," he replied, "in our own rights. Surely you've heard of them."

"Of course," she replied, wondering where this conversation was going. "They are an ancient order, soft magicians who seek the wisdom of the woods and glades, all the wild places of the earth."

"They have great powers, or so I've heard," he said.

"Each to his own measure," Mary replied, "like most soft magics."

Gavin snorted. "Give me an incantation any day. I like to know what I am going to get as a result. Still, the druids were powerful once, that is clear. They were feared by many. It is said they have a glade on the imperial world itself."

"Their teaching is as old as the empire itself," Mary said. "Why the sudden interest?"

To her surprise, Gavin answered frankly. "There is a rumor that these peasants are aided by a mysterious man, a wise man with many magic powers. At first I wrote it off as superstition. This Shanron has been reported to perform miracles as well. You've met the man. Any glimmer of magic about him?"

Mary shook her head.

"Then again, I discounted most of what they said about you, until you healed a man I would have counted dead," he replied. "Still, this mysterious helper, I thought him some charlatan, but he attracted my curiosity nonetheless. I did some investigating."

"And what have you found?" Mary asked.

"Mostly the standard fare of random good fortune." He leaned in closer. "But he is said to travel this way and that at great speeds. Some claim he can walk into a tree and out another miles away."

Mary thought of the first time she had seen Harrod in the baron's orchard. "And do you give credit to those reports?" she asked.

"A man of very similar description has been spotted coming and going in the valley," Gavin said. "I've spoken with several scouts who have seen him. I am certain it is the same man. But the reports are often from opposite ends of the valley, but at nearly similar times. Now there are mages that can jump from place to place. But yet another mage in this valley? That I find unlikely."

He paused and considered her. "Of course," he went on, "your presence here hasn't been explained to my satisfaction yet."

"Perhaps I have been sneaking out at night," she said, "and changing my form to that of an old man."

"Bah," he replied, "the necklace would prevent that. Your healing is top notch, I'll give you that, but I've yet to see any reason to believe you have much in the way of other powers."

"Have you ever met a druid?" Mary asked to change the subject.

"No," he conceded, "but passing through a tree and coming out miles away? Only druids do that sort of magic."

"That's true," she said.

"You've met one?" he asked.

"I have," she replied.

"But what would one be doing here, involved in this?" he pondered. "Druids are guardians of peace and goodness."

Mary thought of her talk with Harrod. "Oh no, Gavin," she said. "Druids are guardians of balance not goodness, and of the wild, not peace."

He looked at her, eyebrows arched. When she did not go on, he muttered, "If only I could convince Shamus. This project gets more complicated with each passing day. We should quit this place and damn the duke and his men." He rode forward and did not speak to her again that day.

***

An eight-year-old Jordan sat on the hard wooden bench and stared at the double doors in front of him. His feet touched the wooden floor, more than could be said for most eight year olds. He looked around the hallway.

Next to him a baby-faced Colton sat. His legs swung nervously, and his lower lip quivered. A single tear slid down one cheek.

Despite the anxiety he felt, Jordan put his arms around Colton. "It's going to be all right, buddy," he said. Colton looked at him but didn't answer.

At eight, Jordan was already taller and bigger than any of the others. They already looked up to him, saw him as their leader. The responsibility lay heavy on his young shoulders.

"We survived last time, right?" he said, looking up and down the hall at the other Juggernauts.

Mary, riding in his mind, could recognize quite a few of the younger Juggernauts from their adult appearances. Others, she assumed, were among the departed she never met in life.

"Papa says these treatments make us stronger, so nobody can hurt us," Jordan said, trying to boost their spirits.

"The treatments hurt," one of the boys protested. "How's that protecting us?"

Jordan didn't have an answer. "Tomorrow we get a rest day," he said, "and a special dinner."

"Will it be Papa or Uncle Shamus?" one wondered.

There was a creak as the door opened. Knowing he had to do it to calm the others, knowing he had to do it to set an example, Jordan rose and went to the door. "Me first, please."

Inside, the room was dark around the edges and lighted in the middle. The middle contained a single reclining chair. Three white-robed magicians stood in a semicircle in front of it. Somewhere in the background, just out of the corner of his eye, Mary caught sight of Gavin. He had his back turned to them and was working at a small bench.

This was a memory and not hers. She could not will the head to turn to see what he was doing. She had only a glimpse of his profile, but it seemed he looked exactly the same as he did now.

Jordan approached the chair and lay back upon it. Overhead, strange instruments descended towards them. Neither Mary nor Jordan could guess their names or purposes. They were golden and shaped into mysterious magical symbols.

To the consternation of both the boy and the mage reliving the experience, the instruments had needles poking out at odd angles. Hands came then, followed by leather straps to hold him in place. The needles slid painfully through the skin. He tensed and wanted to flee but could not. The needles came to rest at the bone, and the magicians began chanting, sending energy through the instruments and incorporating it directly into Jordan's bones and core structure.

Mary woke with a start. Jordan still slumbered next to her. He gave the tiniest whimper in his sleep, and she knew they had shared that dream. She reached for his head and pulled it close. With a sigh, he fell into a deeper, more peaceful slumber.

What had been done to them? Mary was at last beginning to see. The sour potion that Gavin doled out weekly was not the primary magical enhancement: that had been woven into their bodies at a young age, through repeated "treatments." The potion merely sustained the effect.

There was no doubt about its effectiveness. Their bones were tough as metal, the muscles stronger, nerves faster, even their metabolism was souped up so they could heal in a fraction of the a normal man's time. It had taken a knight on horseback at a full gallop to strike a blow with enough force to kill one of these men.

She saw firsthand what they had achieved. The bigger question in her mind was, what had it cost?

***

The peasants, mostly old men and women, moved slowly through the desolate field of stumps. They planted apple seeds. They planted them mostly without hope. They had removed the bodies and buried them in the small cemetery on the far side of the village. It was overcrowded of late.

When the funeral for the nine men was done, they replanted their fields because maybe, if the summer held long enough, they would see enough of a harvest for some to survive the coming winter.

They replanted the orchard, not because they had

any hope that they would live to see another apple harvest, but because they had been told to. A young girl of the village told them Mary, the coppery-haired woman that some said could perform miracles, said not to give up hope. So, slim though it was, they would hope. What did they have to lose?

R. J. Eliason

7 NEWS FROM THE SOUTH

They marched hard for the next two days. Of course, a hard march for the foot soldiers and teamsters was little more than half a day's ride for the men on horseback. None of the Juggernauts, nor by default, Mary, had any responsibilities in the setting up or tear down of the camp.

Mary recalled her days with Gregory's army. As chief healer, she always had something that needed her attention: from berating the teamster to take extra caution with the wounded, to establishing the healers' camp, to seeing to the minor injuries of the day. She rose early and went to bed late. She found, somewhat to her surprise, she missed it.

The Juggernauts had no other experience, so they treated it as normal. Men that she knew had been conditioned to incredible hardships, they still managed to whine about small things, like being saddle sore and bored.

Toward the end of the second day, riders appeared

in the camp. Shortly after that, word spread around the camp that they would not march on the following day. The order carried no word of explanation. From two known facts—that riders had appeared and that they had come from the south—a wealth of rumors sprang. Mary discounted them. She was learning that men, soldiers in particular, were no more immune to gossip then women, and not one of the men present had any true knowledge.

The next day, around midmorning, they were once again called into parade formation. Again there were no dress uniforms. It was not somebody important coming.

They came from the south. The captain and four aides were the only ones on horseback. The men with him could not have numbered more than fifty. They did not even bother to march in formation; swordmen, pikemen, and many spearmen walked in a desolate clump.

The captain stopped in front of the general and gave a weary salute.

"This is all the men you bring?" the general demanded.

"Sire," the captain began, "these rabble have made pacts with the river bandits and with mercenaries, no doubt paid by the baron. We were spread too thin, trying to protect all four cities at once. Three fell without a word. I was lucky to escape Targill with my life and the few men you see here."

"Lucky!" the general raged. "You bring me word that all four cities have fallen to the enemy, and you come bearing a ragtag remainder of the men I left in your command, and you call this lucky?"

"Sir, I only meant—" he began.

"Don't tell me what you meant," the general interrupted. "I have no further use for your words. Be gone!" He turned back to the assembled men. "Tomorrow we march again."

A horn sounded the "at ease," and the formation split. As they were walking away, Mary saw the general gesturing at his aides and the ragtag men who had joined them.

It was still early in the day as they returned to their tents, and the army treated the news that they would march tomorrow as a vacation today. Mary followed Jordan to his tent.

"I must find something in here that amuses and pleases my lady," he joked.

She looked around the tent. "Hmmm," she said and then grabbed at his shirt, "here, here is something that pleases me very much." She pulled him close and kissed him lightly on the cheek. He bent and nuzzled her neck. She was thrilled at his touch, but frightened by how easily she had come to accept him as her lover. It was not like her. She had a mission—a mission to understand and then stop these Juggernauts. She was not here to play silly games or act like a lovesick maiden for their leader.

He lifted her and laid her on their cot. Their cot— that too had come all too easily. This was their cot, in their tent. But it wasn't their cot. It was his cot. More accurately, it was the cot the general had assigned to Jordan, and she was his possession. He was a professional soldier and cold-blooded killer. She was a captive, little more than a slave.

And yet she knew if her chance to escape came right now, she would find some excuse, any excuse, to put it off another day. He slid her tunic up, kissing his way up her belly toward her tiny breasts. All thought paused as she savored the impression of each kiss. Whatever problems she had to solve, whatever conflicts surrounded them, it would all have to wait until this afternoon passed.

And the afternoon passed quickly. After a short supper, he pulled her playful and willing back to the tent and they made love again through the evening. As the evening grew dark and cool about them, they finally fell back spent. Jordan pulled a heavy blanket over the two of them, and Mary closed her eyes and fell almost instantly asleep.

***

"Run! Run for your lives!" Jordan was yelling as Mary's eyes popped open. At first she was disoriented: she couldn't grasp where she was or what was going on.

Mary/Jordan was pulling a wet, bedraggled Colton out of a creek bed. Around them it was dark. The mustiness of old-growth forest was thick, mingling with another musky scent Mary could not identify.

The Colton that was before her, fighting for balance in the mud, was an adult, but much younger than the one she knew while awake.

All of the Juggernauts crowded around the bank, listening intently. They were wearing cloth, not armor, and each carried a single long dagger.

"There!" Jordan commanded. "Go!"

As a team, they tore up the bank and into the forest. A sound so faint it was barely audible followed in their wake.

The fear that permeated Jordan's mind faded as he became solely focused on dodging trees and branches in his way. A form, wolf-like but huge, appeared in the corner of his eye. It made almost no sound as it ran.

The first sound above a whisper was Hammond's scream as the beast snatched him. Without thinking, Jordan drew his dagger and stabbed the beast in the side.

The tiny weapon was unable to penetrate far enough to seriously injure the beast, but it dropped Hammon with a yelp. Hammond hit the ground rolling and was back on his feet running in a split second.

A dagger was simply not enough to kill the beasts that stalked them. This was a test. Another in a long series of tests. They couldn't fight; they had to flee for hours with the beasts in pursuit. Sometime around dawn, they would break out of the forest and come to a castle. There, huntsmen would handle the beasts and the Juggernauts would earn a rest day.

Until then it was mud, fear, adrenalin, and pain. Mary woke with a start beside the still slumbering form of Jordan. She lay there a long time, far from sleep. How could she ever reconcile the cold-blooded killer, the mild-mannered man, and the scared kid? How did he?

In the end, she rose. Her lack of sleep served yet another purpose—she had an unfulfilled promise to herself. She found a spot on the floor of the tent and settled into a meditative pose.

***

It was dark in the orchard, so dark that the stumps shone like little moons and the ground was an inky black sea. Mary could not see her own feet as she walked. Then again Mary wasn't really there, so who knew if she would have seen her feet anyway.

Harrod was seated at the edge of the orchard. He

315

appeared more solid than Mary. Maybe that was his earth magic or maybe he was actually physically present. Mary wasn't familiar enough with spirit-walking to tell.

Behind them the village was quiet, every door and every window shut and barred. The peasants had a hundred real and imagined reasons to fear the dark, and no one ventured out.

Mary noted, as she approached Harrod, that the villagers had taken down the bodies and cut down the trunks. She was glad. She did not need the reminder, nor did they.

As if on cue, Harrod open his eyes and spoke, "Have you see enough, Mary?"

Mary shrugged.

"They would not treat their cattle so," he said bitterly.

"But to meet this violence with more violence, without hope, how is that the solution?" she replied.

"If there is another way," he said, "I would be happy to listen."

"I yet wait," she admitted.

"In the meantime, Shanron builds an army for himself. He has gathered the revolts under one banner, in the west of the valley. He assured them that with his power, they are unstoppable."

Mary thought of their march, and Shanron's appearance in their camp. "He means to betray them," she said.

"So I have feared," Harrod replied. He sighed. "Well, I must act, even if you do not. Or have you something to do?"

"Something," she said, "not what I am waiting on, but something." She held her left arm out over the field.

"It was foolish to tell them to plant. It takes ten years for an apple tree to bear fruit," he said.

Mary closed her eyes and reached down into the earth. The earth pulsed, a single deep boom that she felt more than heard. She felt the seedlings' small lives. "Give me ten years," she asked of them. Not one refused her.

There was another big pulse, and then the life force flowed up from somewhere deep within. She heard Harrod gasp as the seedlings sprouted up from the damp earth. The night was filled with crinkling and crackling as the trunks and branches grew.

When she stopped and opened her eyes, the trees were not large, but each was of fruit-bearing age and many already had blossoms. "Mage indeed," Harrod said. "I should not have doubted. What do you wish of me?"

"Spare what lives you can," she said. "Beyond that, I ask nothing."

"You will find a way to fix all of this," he said. "I can see that now."

I hope so, Mary thought as she let the trance fade. *I hope so.*

8 TO CATCH A REBELLION

The army marched on another three days. The steep foothills of the mountains were gone, giving way to wide, rolling plains and low mounds. The road they traveled remained a thin, dirt line with only the occasional side branch. The villages they saw along the road remained small and mostly forgettable.

On the third day, scouts were seen intersecting the line around midday. They were led straight to the general, and their report was top secret; yet by the time camp was set for the night and supper prepared, the news was everywhere.

A large army of peasants mixed with a few mercenaries was coming from the south and the west. They would cross the army's path in a matter of days. Already a fair-sized band of peasants waited along this very road. They had been gathering from the north and from the nearby lands for several weeks now. A few individuals seemed to see this all as an incredible coincidence. Most were starting to see and suspect the general's plans. Many, though not all, of the men in the camp knew who Shanron was and that he had been in the camp to parlay.

Some thought the general had made some sort of agreement, and they would parlay for the surrender of the rebels and for peace. "The war is nearly over," one hopeful cook told Mary when she arrived for her supper.

Most were not being that optimistic. Shanron had amassed a large army, they theorized, and thought he could defeat the general in open battle, bringing the last two years' worth of guerrilla warfare to a conclusion.

When it was pointed out that the peasants stood almost no chance against the better-armed soldiers of the duke, and even less against the Juggernauts, some countered by saying "When will they have a better chance?" Their cause would only grow more desperate as time went on. With the baron's forces out of the fray, the duke could slowly send more and more reinforcements into the region until he had complete control.

No one doubted that Gregory's men were effectively out of service. The general had sent his hobblers after them. They were not a large enough fighting force to destroy the remnants of Gregory's army, but they could harass them all the way back to Germain and hold them pinned down there until the general had the time and leisure to go and destroy them. Riders came from that direction from time to time with reports. On those days the general was in a good mood, so it was assumed that campaign, at least, was going as planned.

Nobody voiced the one idea that had grown in Mary's mind to become a fact. Shanron was going to betray the peasants. He had come to parlay with the general. He left to gather all of the rebels under one banner. He would lead them into an open battle with the general, promising them they had the strength to win the day. Then he would walk away, and the Juggernauts would massacre them. It would be like the battle in the valley all over again: the tall, dark man in the chainmail and helmet, blood dripping from his sword. And Mary would somehow have to reconcile this man with Jordan . . . and somehow find a way to make it up to the peasants' families.

"Whatever happens," Hammond was saying over supper, "it will be a big battle."

"Not if they parlay for peace," Colton said.

"The general will not parlay with peasants," Hammond insisted.

"We will drink the blood of these peasants," a man called Formist said. "We will destroy them, then rape their women."

Mary looked away. Jordan scowled.

"Not Jordan though," Hammond threw in. "He's practically got himself a wife."

"You have a problem with that?" Colton shot back. Hammond said nothing. Laughing, Colton said, "Mary shall be mother to us all now." She had sensed that they all saw Jordan as a father figure of sorts, but this was the first time anyone had made any direct allusion to it.

"Jordan has never entered into those sorts of games anyway," another man said, "nor Colton." It was a sharp barb.

"Why should I?" Colton replied lightly, but there was an undertone in his voice, "I am handsome enough. I don't have to force myself on women. They come willingly to hand."

"Willing, but not often," a sour-faced Traimon muttered.

"You are saying?" Jordan said sharply. Traimon did not answer.

"You ugly bastards," Colton spat back, "may have to force your company upon others. But I do not."

"I am afraid you are all to be disappointed," someone said in an effort to change the subject. "The peasants don't bring their women to war with them. Not even camp followers."

"They have no whores," Formist said with a crude laugh, "'cause they have no money."

"I guess they must play the sissy for each other," Hammond laughed crudely. Formist began to caper around the pavilion, play-acting as a peasant, trying to get the others to "play the sissy" for him.

   ***

Jordan stood at attention in Mr. Manlin's office. The gray-haired soldier paced the wooden floor. Growing accustomed to these dream memories that leaked into her sleep, Mary quickly pinpointed this particular Jordan. He was thirteen. They were at the manor house where the troop had been raised and trained.

This Jordan had only recently learned that the chief trainer they had called papa most of their lives, and "Sir" to his face, was in fact one Horton Manlin the Third. Seeking to assert some sense of independence and adulthood, the thirteen-year-old Jordan licked his lips and said, "Mr. Manlin, Sir?"

Mr. Manlin raised his eyebrow but did not comment on the name. "Yes, Jordan?"

"What is to be Formist's punishment, Sir?"

"He damaged a very valuable piece of property. The principals won't be happy about that," Mr. Manning said. Mary's mind provided the details: by property he meant one Jordan's brothers, the principals were a mysterious group to whom the trainers answered. The principals were never seen in person but referred to constantly. Words like slavery or even indentured servant were carefully avoided, but it was made clear to the boys that everything in the program, themselves included, belonged to the principals.

"It was an accident, Sir," Jordan ventured. And it had been. A silly game of dares, heightened by the incredible stamina the Juggernauts, even at that age, had.

"It doesn't matter. One boy's leg is broken. It will cost weeks in training. He must be punished." Mr. Manning snapped the leather crop.

Jordan quailed, thinking of the beatings he had endured. He steeled himself for what he felt he needed to do.

"Sir?" he said quickly so he wouldn't lose his nerve. "I am the leader. I should not have let the game go so far. It's partly my fault."

"Leader?" Mr. Manning's voice was low, filled with a malicious joy. "You wish to be the leader? A leader takes responsibility for what his men do. Do you understand?"

Jordan did. Knowing he would have to take the beating meant for Formist, he closed his eyes and whispered, "Yes, Sir."

***

Mary woke, her back sore from the memory of the lashing Jordan had taken. She groped in the bed and found it empty. She opened her eyes and saw Jordan standing on the far side of the tent, bathed in the light of a lantern. His chainmail was on, and two attendants were tying on the knee bracers. He turned as he heard her stir.

"I was hoping we wouldn't wake you."

"It's okay," she replied. "What is going on?"

"I am not sure," he said, "but orders came. I have heard what *was* to be the battle plan, but things are uncertain."

Not sure she wanted to know, she asked. "And what was the plan?"

"Shanron was supposed to come, with a few hand-selected men," he said. "They would lead us to where the peasants were camped. We would surprise them at dawn. But Shanron did not show last night. The general is growing nervous. He will send us in as scouts first, bringing his men after. He fears he has been betrayed."

Mary snorted. "Men who deal in betrayal often have that problem. What would you have of me?"

"It is not I who would say, being but a soldier. Gavin will come by in a couple of hours, I presume, and you will ride as a healer, like always."

"Of course."

He put his helmet on, and again she had the image of him standing on the field of battle, blood dripping from his sword. Could she truly love such a thing?

9 TREACHERY'S END

It was foggy. A local had told her the fog was common this time of year in the early morning. Gavin came, as predicted, within a couple hours of Jordan's departure. Mary had spent the time in meditation, trying to keep her emotions straight.

They spoke little as they rode. The moon, which was nearly full, was just setting on one horizon as the first reddish-orange light of the sun shone over the other. In between was a wide dark sea of oats and barley. To their left, a small forest, maybe a mile wide and twice that deep, stood out like a craggy shoreline.

"It seems thick," Gavin said, "but scouts inform us, once inside, it's mostly open glade. Our reports placed the main branch of the peasants' army inside the woods." It was the first he had spoken since they started this ride.

As they approached the forest, Mary saw armed men standing sentry around the outskirts. There was no sound coming from within.

They turned off the main road and followed another that wound into the forest. At the very entrance to the forest was a clump of soldiers surrounding the general. They had torches, but the growing light was rapidly making the need for them moot.

From a large tree at the very entrance to the forest a body was hung, spread eagle. It was naked with the throat cut so that blood ran down and coated most of the flesh in dark red. Its head had been tied up so that it did not slump forward. Whoever did this wanted to make sure everyone could identify the body easily.

"So ends the life of Shanron," Gavin commented thoughtfully. "And he didn't even get to be bishop, more's the pity."

Gavin spurred his horse into the woods, and Mary followed. In the growing light of dawn she could see more bodies, some strapped to trees, but most lying out on the ground. In the center of the copse, several of the Juggernauts were gathered. Hammond had his helmet off and was drinking from a flask. When Gavin rode past, Hammond gave a sheepish shrug and said, "Wasn't us. We found them like this."

There was a crunch of boots in the forest duff, and Mary turned. Regular soldiers were now making their way cautiously through the small glade. They were wary and had their weapons out, but it rapidly became clear to them that nothing living remained.

"Some sort of internal dispute, I would guess," Colton was saying to some of the soldiers as they walked past. Colton, too, had his helmet off and sword sheathed.

"How do the peasants expect to fight us when they keep killing each other?" the soldier wondered.

"Don't be a fool," Colton warned. "For all this bloodshed, there can't be even a hundred men. That's not a fraction of the peasant's full strength."

The general and Shamus rode up as Mary sat in the copse, trying to absorb what had happened. Looking at the bodies, there had obviously been a bloody fight, but the peasants wore nothing to distinguish one side from the other. There was no way to know who was a conspirator and who had discovered and waylaid them.

"Mary!" Gavin's voice called. "Get over here."

Shamus and the general exchanged arched looks. All three made for Gavin's voice.

He was still in the saddle, at the top of a low rise. In front of him, another group of bodies lay in a small clearing.

The bodies had not fallen naturally, but at first Mary could not quite make out the pattern.

"What do you make of this?" Gavin asked.

Mary got down off her horse and found a stick. She looked at the bodies dispassionately and then tried to sketch the pattern in which they lay. When she was done she had drawn a crude circle, with a stylized three pronged spiral within, an ancient druidic symbol.

She remounted her horse. Gavin gave her a look. Before riding off, she said, "I think Shanron should not have tried to betray a druid."

Mary found Jordan and the other Juggernauts assembled on the edge of the road opposite the woods. Aides were busy cutting down Shanron's body.

They found a low stone wall on the far side of the road, where they sat and watched the proceedings. Aides on horseback galloped off with orders. The regular foot soldiers quickly confirmed what the Juggernauts had already found: the conspirators had been slaughtered to a man.

Soon scouts came running to the copse and were sent out in various directions to try to ascertain where the main body of the peasant army lay. The bulk of the general's army was moved up, and by midafternoon the fields behind them had been transformed into an encampment and the woods across had been razed back a hundred feet or so for firewood.

Once the tents had been set, the band went in search of their semi-private encampment. They unsuited and gathered in the main pavilion for a late lunch. Gavin and Shamus joined them there.

"Well, it appears that the peasants have disbanded and scattered," Shamus said with a sigh.

"Is that not good news?" Mary asked. "You don't have to fight them."

Shamus shook his head. "No, that's bad news, very bad news. It means they are returning to their old tried and true strategy, insurgency. It means instead of one big battle, there will be dozens of little ones— over the course of a year or more, at this rate."

"This campaign is a mess," Gavin groused. "The cities of the south are in full revolt. The north is still held by the remnants of the baron's forces. The general's little purge at the beginning of this march was no doubt a tool: send the peasants a message that there will be no quarter, drive them into Shanron's arms. Now that's backfired too, and those peasants going north may well treat with the baron again. Bah, to be done with it all!"

"I have spoken with our principles," Shamus said.

There was instant quiet. Even Gavin's attention was fully grasped. "They want us to continue."

"You can tell our principles," Colton joked, "that we now know the difference between a battle and war. In a battle, you take a town and that's that. In a war, you take a town, turn your back for one minute, and then have to take it all over again." There was a smattering of laughter.

"Our principles," Shamus went on, "want me to remind you that the purpose of this whole mission is to see how you hold up on a long campaign. Your losses so far, the setbacks we have faced, are all too common in a state of full-blown war. They want us to see this to the end."

There has not been a full-blown war within the empire for over three hundred years, Mary thought. *Why test them for that possibility?* Unless, of course, the principals were either expecting a war, or planning one.

"The general relies on us too much," Jordan said. "We can win him battles, but he must find a strategy to win the war."

"We would have won last year," one of the men groused, "if not for that stupid paladin."

"Do not become overconfident," Shamus replied. "The situation on the ground is always more complicated than people would like to believe. There will always be men like the paladin or these peasants, things to disrupt the cogs of any campaign."

"Expect nothing," Jordan said in a quiet, dream-like voice.

The next day, they were visited by the general. He seemed to share Gavin's dismal view of the most recent turn of events. "I just don't have the kind of manpower to hold hostile countryside," he complained. "And now I must divide my forces to fight on two fronts."

The northern front was now Germain. The remnants of Gregory's men had made it there and were holing up. The general's hobblers held the major roads in and out, but they were not a large enough force to take the city or even to siege it properly.

Riders had escaped back into the baron's domain with news. Spies reported that the baron had opened his treasury and was practically pouring out gold, hiring as many mercenaries as he could find. After two straight years of defeat, he was being forced to pay handsomely. Even then, he had few takers. It was uncertain what sort of force he might be able to send, or when.

The southern front consisted of the four river cities and the river itself. The duke still felt that if the river trade could be captured, one of the baron's main sources of income could be diverted and his coffers would empty, forcing him to accept defeat. The duke insisted the cities be recaptured as quickly as possible.

The general decided to divide his army. He planned to send most of the light units—spearmen with little armor—north. They would rendezvous with the hobblers; hopefully, their sheer numbers would allow them to encircle and siege the town of Germain.

Meanwhile, the more heavily-armored troops—swordmen with shields and chainmail, and pikemen in plate armor—would head south. The Juggernauts would go with them. They would have to recapture each town in close hand-to-hand fighting. The lighter units would have likely been ineffective in this situation, but the swordmen with the Juggernauts as a spearhead would cut through the town's defenses quickly.

The general hoped to have the towns back under his control and be able to turn his force northward before the summer's end. To move an army through the winter was a tactical headache he hoped to avoid.

The large swath of farmland that made up the bulk of the valley's floor was to be left a no man's land. None of the peasant bands were large enough to pose a threat to either army. Once the towns were under control, the peasants would eventually have to recognize the duke's dominion. If not, there would be time later for a village-by-village purge.

The general ended his visit abruptly, telling them that indecision had cost him much already. They should expect to march in the morning, to the south.

***

Jordan's eyes were open, and he stared up into a cloudless blue sky. He gasped, his breath painful. An old wound, one that should have killed him, had been reopened.

Mary could not place his age in this memory, nor the location. He felt old and worn, like he had experienced too much. He must be close to the age he was now.

All thoughts of what was going on, all feelings, were lost in the haze of pain. It all came down to this pain. It was cleansing him, a final punishment that would remove all his sins.

He was not aware that he had closed his eyes, but when he opened them again he was looking up at a small, coppery-haired maiden that Mary had never seen in his dreams before.

He tried to reach for the maiden, but his arms

wouldn't obey. He tried convey to her how much he loved her, how much good she had brought into his life.

The maiden looked down at him, her face filled with sorrow and understanding. With a start, Mary recognized the face as her own.

10 THE MANY USES OF A CAMP FOLLOWER

They set out on a side road, moving south at daybreak the next day. The pikemen marched in front with swordmen following them. A small detachment of archers came next, then the Juggernauts on horseback, the general and his aides, followed by the teamsters and the wagon train.

Mary rode with Juggernauts. They were not in formation. She and Jordan rode side by side with Gavin in front of them and Colton just behind. Mary felt irritable and on edge. Last night's dream had unsettled her.

A couple miles south of the forest, the road dipped down between two low hills. The long line was halfway through the valley when a horn blared. There was a twanging sound, and the air was full of arrows raining down on the pikemen and swordmen.

There was a hoarse cry as peasants rose up out of the tall grass on either hillside and charged down toward the men. They were armed with an assortment of weapons, most of them farm implements. They had flails, sickle knives, daggers, wooden staves, and numerous other items Mary could not name. None had armor of any kind. Their strategy struck Mary as nothing short of suicidal madness. Indeed, as the first wave crashed into the waiting pikemen, an almost sickening number went down in spurts of blood and gore.

Then the survivors were in the lines, and the advantage changed. The shorter makeshift weapons created havoc. The pikemen did not have room for a second swing, and even the swordmen were having trouble finding enough arm room to swing properly.

Some discarded their pikes and attempted to hold off the peasant's assault with a combination of fisticuffs and wrestling. Others were using the butt end of their weapon to hold them at bay. Many had already fallen in a bitter onslaught of blades and cudgels.

The air filled with the screams of wounded and dying men. Yet another set of loud voices pulled her attention closer to home. Shamus and Jordan were yelling at each other. Shamus said something about getting the men into battle. Jordan said something about "getting her to safety."

Something was pushing on Mary. It was a gentle but persistent sensation, mid-chest, much like a line of force but without the force. It was the ghost of an attack, an intention. Somewhere far down this line was a small, hard diamond—an intention translated into an action. That diamond was flying in her direction.

Allowing herself to perceive this and react intuitively, she felt her hand come up, directly under this line. She paused and followed the diamond with her mind. As it passed her hand, making for her chest, she closed her fingers together. She felt the rough wooden circle of the arrow slide against her palm, and the forward force stop suddenly.

She looked at the arrow. It was short with a metal hunting tip and a crude, feathered end. She turned it over in her hands.

"The mage," she heard Gavin's voice interject between the two men's argument, "can take care of herself."

They paused and looked at her. Acting on instinct, she reached out and snatched another arrow from the air, inches before it struck Shamus in the head. He started back and looked at her in astonishment.

"Nonetheless," Gavin went on, "we will take her back amongst the teamsters where it might be a tad safer for the rest of us. You do your job."

Jordan nodded, and the Juggernauts dismounted to join the fray. At a gesture, she followed Gavin through the chaos toward the back of the battle scene.

The battle was pitched and bloody, but thankfully short. The peasants did not have the discipline, training or weaponry for a long, open battle. Within a few minutes of the first charge, they were sounding the retreat.

The peasants simply scattered, running this way and that. There was no order, nor a central destination. The Juggernauts and a few other units who had held up in the fray gave chase but were quickly called back. The general did not want to risk losing scattered units in another ambush.

It was quickly apparent that the peasants had

miscalculated. If they had managed to ambush the lighter, less-armored units that went north, they could have devastated their enemy's numbers and seriously affected the general's whole campaign. However, many of the more heavily-armored men that had fallen under the peasants' assault were merely battered, bruised, or injured rather than dead.

The peasants, on the other hand, had left a large portion of their force dead on the edge of the road. The right-hand side of the road, where the Juggernauts had torn into them right before the retreat was sounded, was noticeably thicker with bodies. Mary and Gavin rode on that side, bypassing the throngs that crowded the road: men tending their own wounds or their buddies' . . . or just milling around waiting for orders.

The Juggernauts sat in a group, part way up one of the hillsides. While the battle had been a victory in terms of the number of dead, it was a bloody one, and the Juggernauts were not spared injury. The small weapons the peasants carried were wicked at close range.

Jordan was holding his left arm, trying to staunch the flow of blood. A sickle knife had caught him just below the elbow bracer and torn a wide rent in his chainmail.

He waved Gavin off as the healer dismounted and indicated instead that Mary should come. Gavin gave her a sour look but stood aside.

With a mild sense of trepidation, she laid her hand on his arm and called the magic to her.

She saw him leap into the fray of battle. His sword dipped in a precise arch and one of the peasants pitched backward, blood spraying from a huge gash across his face. Mary watched the spray dispassionately but Jordan had already moved on, turning his attention to the next fighter in line. His sword thrust forward, catching that one just under the chin and decapitating him completely.

A third fighter slammed into his side full force. The blow shook Jordan but did not knock him down. He was turning, the edge of his sword sliding against this new assailant.

There was something surreal about the battle as experienced through Jordan's eyes. It lacked any visceral feel. Instead there was a calm peaceful feeling, like when Mary meditated. Even when the sickle knife's point pierced the chainmail and slid into his flesh, Jordan's mind merely recorded the sensation but did not react to it.

It was over in an instant. Mary looked at the thin, red line on his arm and could trace countless other scars. "It's healed but not whole," she said. "You must be careful not to bust it open over the next couple of days."

She assisted Gavin in inspecting and healing the other men as well. She healed small injuries on two other Juggernauts. She glimpsed, briefly, the adrenalin, rage, joy and other visceral emotions that flowed through them in battle, so unlike Jordan's reaction.

Making their way back toward the main camp, they walked alongside the rows of men. Slowly, order was beginning to be restored, but there were still many wounds to tend to.

"Well, this fellow's got a wicked-looking cut," Colton joked. The man in question did indeed have a wicked-looking cut running across his forehead. He held a bloody rag to it and grimaced up at them. Blood oozed from around the rag, and the man seemed in danger of passing out. "Best be getting a camp follower for you," Colton went on. To one of the man's comrades, he said, "Mabel, I should think. Go on now."

"I could," Mary began, drawing the energy.

"No, you cannot," Gavin commanded.

"You are our healer," Jordan said possessively.

"I have already healed you," she said to Jordan.

"No," Colton threw in, "we can't have our special healer looking after just anyone. A camp follower will do." She turned to protest and caught a look of fear in his eyes. It made her pause.

Mabel was not an old woman by any stretch of the imagination, but she was definitely past her prime for the whoring business. Her tits sagged and her belly protruded. She had thick, curly, red hair that stuck out in places and a pale moon face. When she opened her mouth, it contained about half the usual number of teeth.

The girl with her seemed too young for the whoring business, but Mary knew she did it anyway. She was thin, pale, and blonde. Her face was hollow and haunted.

"Well, that's a right fine scratch there," Mabel said, pulling the rag back to look. "Give me my kit," she said to the pale-faced girl. When the girl handed over a small, cloth kit with needle and thread, she slapped the girl, not hard, but hard enough. "Pay attention now, girlie," she admonished her. "You won't be young forever."

The end of a leather belt was placed in the soldier's mouth for him to bite down on. She poured a measure of something alcoholic over the wound and then set to sewing the wound tight. When she was done, it was crudely but effectively sealed. His natural healing process would take over from there.

"Now you come see me in a week or so," she said. "I'll take them stitches out, and maybe we'll have a roll if you're up to it." She cackled playfully at her own joke.

"I ain't had no injuries," one of his comrades said, laughing. "Maybe I'll come for a roll tonight."

11 CAT AND MOUSE

By midafternoon, the army had regrouped sufficiently to continue on its way. They marched with weapons out and with scouts running on both sides to forewarn of another ambush.

Scouts were flying to and fro, and a constant stream of reports were coming in: the peasants continued to scatter. The scouts spotted smaller and smaller groups heading this way and that. One small group of maybe a dozen were seen entering a nearby village. With a nod, the general veered the entire column toward the village. It stood as if empty before them.

The general sent a crier in, calling the elders to come forth. Timidly, one elderly man made an appearance.

"My Lord," he said to the general.

"A band of brigands was seen entering this village," the general said. "They will be brought forth at once and dealt with."

"My Lord," the elder protested, "I know nothing of this."

The general did not even hear him out. He nodded and two soldiers seized and bound the man. With another nod, the Juggernauts and another squad of swordmen headed into the village. They went house by house. If doors were not opened for them, they kicked them in.

Slowly a group of men were dragged into an empty circle in front of the general. Four were found in a barn; two had injuries and all had blood on them.

Three more were pulled out of the inn, along with an old woman. One of the three had a long gash across his chest, and it was partially sewn shut. The old woman wailed as they dragged her along, pleading for mercy and crying that they had forced her to help them.

These men were obviously part of the rebellion. Others were dragged out too, but gave Mary far more doubt. Some seemed too young, or too old. Many had no marks on their clothes to indicate they had fought in a battle only hours before.

Toward the end of the search, a group of five men hiding in a root cellar tried to fight their way through. Screams rent the air, along with the clash of metal. It lasted only a few minutes. When the report came back, it was that all five were dead.

In the end, they gathered close to two dozen men and three women. Without bothering to ask a single question or interrogate a single suspect, the general ordered them all executed.

Mary turned to ride away, unwilling to witness an execution, even of a guilty man. Bitter tears and anger threatened to overwhelm her.

She found her way blocked by Gavin.

"You want the war to end?" he said. "This is how it ends." With that he moved aside and she rode out of the village.

***

"You are angry at me?" Jordan inquired stiffly as he entered the tent.

Mary was sitting in a meditative pose, but she was having trouble staying calm enough to meditate. In what she knew was a petty display of anger, she sat down facing the back of the tent. The men had returned some time ago, and supper had come and gone.

Now as dark was setting, he had finally dared to enter his own tent.

"May I ask what I did?" He sounded hurt.

"You must ask?" she replied sharply.

"Apparently, I must."

"I will not be party to executions."

He made a dismissive noise. "They were the enemy. This morning, they tried to kill us."

"When people die in the heat of battle, I don't like it, but I can accept it," Mary said. "When you drag them from a building by their feet, kicking and screaming, then kill them in cold blood, that's another thing."

"Do you think I like it?" he shot back. "I have no beef with these men. I do not hate them. They come at me with swords and knives, and I kill them. If it were up to me, I would leave it at that. But they won't leave it. If we let them go, they'll only attack us again later. It's never ending."

"I hate that too," she replied. "I would not be a soldier for my life. But not everyone who died today was an enemy. Many of those men were not involved. The women certainly were not, or the village elder. Why must they die?"

He sighed and sank on the cot. "That," he said heavily, "was most distasteful."

"Distasteful?" Mary said. "It was wrong."

He shrugged. "I am not the one who decides. Be mad at the general."

"I am," Mary said. "But how can you be party to that . . . that butchery?"

"How can I not? I am a soldier. I don't know how it is with healers, but soldiers do not get a say. We do not get to pick and choose what orders to obey. We do what we must. That is the way it is. If I find it distasteful, so what? I must do it."

She sank down in front of him, her anger spent. "I know. I just don't know how you bear it." Laying her head on his lap, she whispered, "I hate this war."

He lifted her into his arms and sat her on his lap. "I know you do," he cooed in her ears. "You are so sweet, so good. How could you not? You'd never make it as a soldier, but that's why I love you so."

***

The march south continued in the same fashion for the better part of two weeks. The peasant army had disbanded and most of the men were making for their home territory, but a sizable portion of them were from the south. They traveled in groups numbering from a couple dozen down to two or three single men.

The general pursued whatever groups who crossed their path with a vengeance. The army zig-zagged back and forth across the main road leading south. They raided copses in the night. They surrounded hollows. Any groups of peasants camping out that did not have sheep, cattle, or some other obvious reason for being out were summarily executed. Villages were entered and searched. The inhabitants were interrogated as were newly arrived strangers. Anyone with fresh injuries, suggesting they may have been involved in the recent battles, were executed.

The general stated his case to one village elder quite clearly. "You peasants must understand," he said, "if you rebel, you die. If you aid rebels, you die. If you consort with rebels, you die. If you talk about rebellion, you die. If you so much as think of rebellion, you die. Only when the entire countryside has learned complete obedience will the killing stop."

The men, both Juggernauts and the duke's soldiers alike, were forced to play the role of inquisitors and policemen. They detested it but soon became hardened. They vented their frustration on the peasants. They saw every attempt to evade capture, fight back, or beg for mercy as a sign of duplicity, or a sign that they deserved their fate. They dehumanized them and reviled them.

Jordan, Mary knew, hated the role worst of all. But he had no choice: he was sworn to obey orders. It turned his mood sour as the campaign progressed. He knew how Mary felt about the situation. She increasingly rode toward the back of the line and avoided the general and the Juggernauts until camp was set. He tried to shield her from what they did during the day. He did it partially to protect her feelings, but mostly to protect himself from another fight with her.

The men turned to making crude jokes about the peasants and their pointless attempts to avoid the inevitable. Some, she knew, were upset and handling it the only way they could. Others reveled in this new task. They had been hurt so many times themselves that they delighted in making someone else feel pain now.

Jordan tried to silence them when he could. He knew it was an even deeper sore spot with Mary. When one of the men would begin some story about their day—some anecdote that involved blood, pain, or killing—he would shoot them a dark look. If that didn't stop them, and often it did not, he would yell at them.

Mary took to spending more and more of her time in their tent, away from the others. He would find her sitting in one of her meditative poses, and often she had been crying. He, too, took to excusing himself early, leaving the men to their stories and jokes.

Mary and Jordan rarely spoke of these things. They either spoke of nothing or made love. There was a wide gulf between arguing about what was happening and the mad, passionate lovemaking, and neither could bear to stay in between for long.

Slowly, other members of Juggernauts were disappearing as well. Their confinement had never been lifted, but it was being ignored. Colton was the first to go. Always social, and decidedly the most stable of the men, he easily made friends among the regulars. With each passing evening, it was more likely to find him out drinking with another unit than at home.

Hammond, Formist, and a hulking hairy brute by the unlikely name of Deirdre began to hang out with one of the general's more elite sword units. They were hardened cruel men who drank heavily. It was a good fit.

One night they were all ordered to stay in. Mary hoped that someone had noticed they were not staying in confinement and would rein them in—not that she missed the three men much. That would not be the case.

Shamus informed them that they were within a day's march of the town of Koll. The general meant to set out early the next day, in full battle garb. They would march long and hard, hitting the city by late afternoon and hopefully taking it by surprise. As they returned to their tent for a short night's sleep, Jordan released a deep sigh of relief.

"What?" Mary asked.

"I know you don't like battle," he said, "but I can't help it. After all this," he waved his hands about to show what *this* was, "I can't wait to get back to an honest battle."

An honest battle? His victims would have weapons and would fight back. But they had no more chosen to be in this war than the villagers who had been massacred almost daily. And they would have no more hope either. But she was tired: tired of arguing, and tired of holding the one person in this camp that she cared for at bay. She closed her eyes and slid into his arms.

R. J. Eliason

12 THE CITY OF KOLL

In light of the battle that was to take place at the end of the day's march, Mary had little choice but to ride with Gavin and Shamus. Gavin was a curiously neutral figure in her mind. They could speak of intellectual things, bits of magical lore they shared, books they had read or other mundane trivialities of their lives back home, and it seemed almost normal. If they had met in other circumstances, they could be friends. But there was a coldness about him. He rarely betrayed any emotion and did not seem bothered in the least by what he referred to as "the necessities of the campaign." He could stitch a wound on one of the soldiers with absolute precision and seemingly no compassion. He looked after the men the same way he dressed, with a meticulousness that bordered on insanity.

It was much the same in the memories she shared with Jordan. Gavin appeared frequently throughout the training the boys—who eventually became men— had received. He was present at most of the treatments, but he was never the one who inflicted the pain. As a healer, he was a welcome sight after a battle or test. He could be friendly and sometimes helpful, but they all understood he was not their friend.

Shamus, on the other hand, Mary detested. He was pretentious and arrogant. He was callous. People were little more than tools to him: something to be used to achieve an end. The men saw him as weak and insipid. "Papa" Manlin had terrified them, but they also respected him. He gave them pride in their strength and their ability. He had recently left the project after suffering some sort of heart ailment. The men were angry that they had to obey Shamus, and they rebelled in little ways. But they were far too disciplined to disobey him directly.

It was late in the afternoon when she saw the lines slowly spreading out in front of her. "We are close?" she asked Gavin.

"Just over the rise," he replied. "When we took this city last time, it was a bitter fight. Thinking to hold it, the general commissioned a team of engineers to rebuild the wall afterward, better than before. Now we get to fight our own defenses. No wonder he hopes to take the town by surprise."

"Do you think we will?" she asked.

"Yes and no. Surely they know we are coming and will have troops ready. But hopefully they think they have a few more days before the hammer falls. A trading town, they can't afford to be too clammed up. One open gate and we're inside. It'll be a tough battle, hand to hand and doorway to doorway, but that's what the boys do best."

The men were cresting the hill in a wave, charging

down toward the city. As Mary rode past the general, it was clear from his scowl that they had not achieved the complete surprise he had hoped for.

Over the hill, she saw a wide, lazy river at the bottom of a long, steep slope. The town of Koll lay in the middle of wide basin at the bottom of the hill and was surrounded by a thick wooden wall some ten feet high. Whatever had once been in the basin by way of fields and buildings had been cleared of everything but a few foundation stones, forcing the army to charge across a wide-open field to reach the walls.

The men stopped at the bottom of the hill while archers were set and the general made plans to either scale or destroy the wall. Mary saw a small group of archers heading along the edge of the basin toward the river.

Looking at the river, she saw a line of barges leaving the city, crowded with people. Squinting, Mary could barely see the people on the barges, but they appeared to be mostly women and children.

"Refugees," Shamus spat.

Mary's eyes narrowed suspiciously. "What are the archers doing?" she asked. Already they were lining up on the bank. A cask had been rolled down with them and was being cracked open. The archers dipped the end of their arrows in the oil. A man stood nearby with a torch and would light the arrows before they were shot toward one of the barges. The refugees huddled as far from the archers as they could, but they were not the targets. Already one barge was ablaze.

"They are just civilians, fleeing the battle!" Mary raged.

"They are citizens of Koll," Shamus said, "and they must not be allowed to escape. They are the enemy."

"They are women and children," Mary retorted.

"Women," Gavin said as though discussing the weather, "that have brothers and uncles living on the far side of the river. Brothers and uncles who may well use those barges to come back and seek revenge."

The wind changed direction suddenly. An arrow in midflight was caught and dropped down into the water. It stayed alight, a fire floating slowly downstream. The barges were on the edge of range by now anyway, and with the wind against them, the archers were not able to reach them.

Mary felt a sudden tightness at her throat. She had almost forgotten the choker.

Shamus was facing her, his face suspicious and hateful. "This is your doing."

It wasn't a question, so Mary did not deny it. She met his gaze steadily. Trying to speak as calmly as she could and hoping that she wasn't showing how hard he was choking her, she managed to spit out, "I will tolerate this incessant war and these never-ending battles, but you will not kill innocent refugees while I stand by and watch."

"I could kill you in an instant!" he hissed.

"Then do it," she spat back, fighting to get some air, fighting just as hard not to show it. "Then go explain to Jordan why you did it."

She saw fear in his eyes. He wasn't sure he could control the Juggernauts without Jordan. *And he is not sure he can control Jordan without me.*

"Bah!" he exclaimed. The tightness let up, and

Mary took a long, shuddering breath. Shamus spurred his horse and rode off. Gavin sat there impassively. Mary could not tell if he was angry at her defiance or proud at her success.

The general had limited siege gear. A few archers rushed forward and fired flaming arrows at the wall. But the engineers had purposely used green wood that wouldn't easily catch.

Scouts soon came back carrying two driftwood logs of fairly decent size that might work as battering rams. The general had no ladders, but he did have a small unit of pikemen that carried grappling hooks and rope. The wall was not tall, and they could likely scale it. After that, all they needed to do was open one gate to let the swordmen and the Juggernauts in.

So again the archers rushed forward, this time all of them, and fired a volley at the wall. Most of the defenders ducked and hid. Under that cover, the men were able to cross most of the distance safely.

A scattered volley answered back, some arrows heading for the archers and some for the charging men. Mary saw a few bodies drop. The men threw themselves tight against the wall. The swordmen and pikemen huddled together beneath the swordmen's shields. The defenders would lean out to fire arrows down at them, but doing so left them vulnerable to the long pikes. Still, the pikemen could not get their grappling hooks up and scale the wall without exposing themselves.

The men at the gate seemed to be faring slightly better, but ramming down the thick gates was going to be time consuming. Some of the swordmen had daggers out and were hacking at the wall as though they could carve a path through. It was a pointless gesture.

Mary's attention was attracted to a small group of aides gathered around one of their own. He had an arrow protruding from his chest. One of his fellows was trying to extract it, but as he pulled, he nearly lifted the man off the ground.

Mary spurred her horse toward the men.

"Stop!" Mary screamed as she rode up. The men paused, looking at her uncertainly. "You'll kill him."

The general rode up. "What's going on?" he demanded.

"It won't come out," one of the men said. "It's . . ." he trailed off.

"What new devilry is this?" the general groused.

Mary dismounted quickly and pushed her way through the men. They parted reluctantly for her.

"Roll him on his side," she commanded, and they did as they were told. She broke the feathered end off the arrow. Grasping the shaft firmly she pushed, forcing the arrow through his chest and out the other side. There was a gasp from the men.

She held up the barbed tip. "It's a fishing arrow," she said. "They use them back home, too. If you pull it back you'll only tear the flesh and do even worse damage. You must push them through."

The general made a noise and rode off. Mary reached out to one of the aides. "You must send runners to all the units. They must know this, or many will die." She saw him nod quietly and disappeared.

She closed her eyes and set to healing the man.

When she was done with her healing, Mary remounted and rode halfway up the hill, where the command center had been established. Shamus and Gavin were seated on the hill watching the battle dispassionately. Having nowhere else to go and nothing to do, she joined them.

"Barbed arrows," Gavin commented to Shamus. "You see, she's far more useful alive."

Shamus scowled but didn't comment.

They were spared further conversation by a loud shout. "A breach, a breach!" One of the gates had given away, and there as a knot of fighting men around it.

"Now the fun begins," Shamus said.

A horn blew. The archers dashed forward again and shot a volley high. They dare not shoot directly at the wall and risk hitting their own soldiers underneath, but it still had the intended effect of forcing most of the defenders to take cover.

Under that cover, a second wave of men rushed the field: swordmen in a tight line led by the Juggernauts. They forced the knot of fighting men through the gate. The line, after only a short pause, disappeared into the city. The men trapped along the wall inched their way toward the open gate. Soon they, too, were gone and inside the city. From that point on, the battle was heard but not seen.

As the walls began to clear of defenders, aides rushed up and established a forward camp at the gate. Occasionally, one would rush in or back out, but there was little for them to do. Inside, the city was no doubt in chaos. The general sat in the command center and read from dispatches. This was not the kind of battle that could be directed anyway.

For Mary, this was worse in ways. She could hear the occasional clash of metal or the screams of a dying man. Smoke rose from portions of the town as fires were started, though whether by defenders, attackers, or accident was anyone's guess. The only reports coming out of the city stated that the battle "seemed to be going well."

In Mary's mind, she could see the Juggernauts, fearsome in their armor, tearing through the defenders like a wolves through a herd of sheep. She could see defenders and innocent civilians alike falling before their blood lust. The image of Jordan in chainmail, blood dripping from his sword, swam through her mind.

A shout brought her attention to present. In the evening light, she saw a familiar figure on the wall. He leaped lightly, falling the ten feet and landing almost cat-like. It was Harrod, the druid. Without pausing, he took off across the no man's land, heading toward a clump of trees on the northern edge of the basin.

Another figure, this one in chainmail, appeared on the wall and leaped as well. He landed heavily, falling to his knees. He, too, was back on his feet in the blink of an eye. It was Hammond.

"They are truly marvelous creations in action," Gavin said.

Hammond was pounding after the druid, sword raised. The druid was ahead, but Hammond was gaining fast. There seemed to be no way the druid could escape. Then he stumbled and went down. A cheer went up from the men as Hammond was on him, sword coming down fast.

Only Mary, it seemed, noticed that the fall was too precise, too graceful to be an accident. The druid rolled fluidly, his scimitar flashing as it slid from the scarab.

The scimitar came up ahead of him, deflecting the downward blow of Hammond's sword. Three flecks of dust flew into the air, flecks that Mary would later discover were Hammond's fingers.

Coming up in a crouch, the druid spun gracefully. The second spin of the scimitar rolled across Hammond's armpit, slicing deeply through the tendons and nerves. Mary had only a split second to wonder how she would heal such deep damage before the third spin of the scimitar landed with incredible precision in the gap between the iron collar and the helmet, severing the Juggernaut's head.

The druid had sheathed his scimitar and was already turning away toward the trees before the head hit the ground. Archers were running toward him, notching arrows. But it was too late.

The clump of trees was no more than four, but it was enough. His form entered, disappeared behind a willow, and was gone. Aides were gathering and shouting, beckoning men to surround the trees. Archers fired flaming arrows within.

"Fools," Gavin spat, echoing Mary's feelings. "The druid is gone."

13 SCREW THEM!

"I am going to hunt down and kill that druid if it's the last thing I do!" Formist spat out.

"You will not make such a vow," Shamus said reproachfully.

"I know you are angry," Jordan said, trying to keep the peace between them, "but there is still a war to fight."

"Screw the war!" another of the men yelled.

"We have orders, and we will follow them!" Shamus retorted.

"He's right," Jordan said. "We are soldiers. We will do what we must."

But the men were not ready or willing to leave it at that. "We have done nothing but follow their orders since we got here!" Deirdre protested. "We fight their enemies for them. Now, we have an enemy, and they say, 'Turn your backs, let him be.'"

"Not true," Shamus said. "The general will send men against him, he's promised. He wants the druid as badly as you. His men have been killed as well."

"Bah! They will not succeed. If we do not go, the druid will escape," another said.

"Hammond was one of us. Our companion," Formist said. "He must be avenged."

"He was one of us, at least," Colton muttered. Someone near him nodded agreement.

Jordan grabbed Formist by his shoulders. "In time, my brother, in time. We will see this through. But the general needs us to win this war. He needs us to go with him downriver. There will be time later for personal vengeance."

"He'll be long gone by the time this blasted war is over. If we don't set out at once on his tail, we will never catch the druid again. You know that," someone put in.

"What makes you think you can catch him anyway?" Gavin posed thoughtfully. The men ignored him.

"I say screw the general and screw orders! We go hunt the druid by ourselves," Formist insisted, pulling away from Jordan's grasp. It was the first time she had seen them openly defy either Shamus or Jordan. There were muttered comments and dark looks all around the pavilion. Hands were straying toward swords. Mutiny seemed a realistic possibility.

"They call it the principles," Mary said. "The training the druids undergo, their martial art . . . it's called the principles."

"You know it?" someone asked.

She shook her head, but went on. "They call it that because they believe that there are underlying principles behind every aspect of life, basic rules like the laws of nature. If you can understand these rules, victory becomes as inevitable as gravity. Nobody is exempt from the basic principles."

"You can teach us how to defeat him?"

She shook her head "no" again. She stood directly in front of Formist and said, "You will not go seek vengeance against this druid."

"Who are you to tell us this?" he demanded. "What do you know about anything?"

"Little of nothing," she shot back, "as I am constantly reminded. I know nothing about war or being soldier, less about being a Juggernaut. But I know this: when you go into battle, you lay aside all responsibility for what you do. You say, 'He raised his sword against me, so I killed him.' You say, 'I was given an order, so I killed him.' You say, 'He choose to be a soldier and fight, so it's not my fault that he dies on the end of my blade.'"

She came nose to nose with Formist, a cold anger burning through her. "You may be the best of the best, you may be unique in all the empire, but let me assure of you of this: you are not exempt. When Hammond raised his sword to the druid, he took his risk, just as certainly as the peasants and soldiers you kill every day take theirs when they raise a weapon to you.

"Go mourn your brother. Spirits know, it's your one redeeming feature that you can show sorrow. But don't think for one second that you have any right to be angry at a man who did no more than you have done a hundred times over."

Anger spent, she turned and stalked out of the tent. The conversation started up behind her, but it was more subdued, and there was no further talk of mutiny.

***

The next day, Shamus and the general entered the city to inspect the damage. Mary had no interest in going with them. The one good thing about the way the battle had played out was that she had not been forced to see the Juggernauts in action; she did not have to again witness the image of Jordan with blood dripping from his blade.

The Juggernauts avoided the town as well. They were making preparations for another funeral. For men who saw death almost daily, they had little clue how to deal with it. They had been trained to believe they were special, unstoppable. To learn they could die, or as Mary had said, that they were not exempt from this basic reality, was hard for them.

The funeral was much like the last one. They burned the body on the banks of the river. Again, Mary experienced the powerful rush of emotions that streamed off the men. However, they were having a harder time maintaining the disciplined mask over them. Formist and Deirdre, Hammond's closest friends, were already drunk and wept openly. Colton scowled at them in disgust and disappeared as soon as the funeral was officially over. They did not see him until they made ready to march, two days later. Jordan maintained his composure until they returned to camp. Then he pulled Mary back to their tent and broke down as well. She held him, awkwardly given how much bigger he was, until he had cried himself to sleep.

She woke to the sound of an aide at their tent flap. She turned to Jordan's sleeping form and was about to wake him when the aide spoke, "Mary?"

She rose and went to him.

"Please, come with me," he said. She nodded and followed him.

They left the semi-private encampment. It felt almost rebellious, almost like freedom. She had spent the last month constantly in the company of the one of the Juggernauts or one their keepers. To be moving amongst the camp without them was a novel experience.

The aide led her to the edge of the camp. She wondered for a moment if she was about to be offered her freedom. Then she saw the men and understood.

There were about a dozen of them, all slender but muscular men, accustomed to being out of doors. They wore brown wool and leather too light to be counted as armor. They were armed with longbows. Mary was not sure if the blades at their waist counted as long daggers or short swords.

She walked into the center of their circle and sat down. A middle-aged man with salt and pepper hair and a three-day growth of beard sat opposite of her.

"So we understand you know of druids, possibly this druid in particular."

"I do," she replied.

"What can you tell us?" he asked bluntly.

She paused, considering. Would this be betraying Harrod? She didn't know, but what she had said to Formist the day before applied to Harrod as well: he had chosen his course. These men had not chosen to seek him on their own. For them to stumble onto him blind to their own danger would be its own injustice.

"I am sorry to tell you that I know little that can be of use," she said. "I know their fighting style is called the principles, but I am not skilled in it. I know they train with curved swords and staffs. I can tell you little else."

"What of their magic?" the leader persisted.

"It's soft magic," she said, knowing the distinction meant nothing to them, "which makes it hard to predict."

"When he went into the clump of trees, he disappeared," another scout said. "Where did he go?"

Mary shrugged. "Anywhere there are trees."

"Damn," the leader said. "Seriously? Anywhere?"

"Pretty much. I've met this druid twice, miles apart. For all I know, he could be miles away, or even worlds away."

"Awesome," one of the scouts said, sarcasm heavy in his tone.

"Does he have other powers we should be aware of?" the leader asked.

"Honestly, I am not sure." Mary responded. She feared she might betray herself if this conversation got back, but she added anyway, "He has means of communicating through dreams. As a druid, he will likely know some healing and be knowledgeable about herbs, both healing and poisonous. He might be able to bend the will of animals to him, though I have not seen this particular druid do such a thing."

"I have heard tell that mages can shoot flaming arrows out of their fingers, or make lightning strike, or even shoot balls of flame or turn you into things . . . unnatural," one of scouts rambled out.

"Combat magic," Mary said, "is mostly hard magic. Druids don't deal in that. And I know this druid is not mage level, though he is powerful nonetheless. I don't know how much power he has or what he can do with it. Know this though: druids are cunning and wise. They serve the greater balance of all things. You shouldn't assume to understand what that means, to expect him to be good or evil, honorable or dishonorable. You see him as the enemy, but how he sees you, I cannot say. They don't face force with force if they can help it. It will not be easy to track or find this druid. If it is easy, it's surely a trap. Be cautious."

"What an excellent mission," the younger scout commented again. The leader on the other hand nodded knowingly.

"We will be careful," he said. "Thank you for being frank with us. I hope we have not asked you to betray a friend."

"Friend or no," Mary said, "to send you against him unprepared would be," she paused and considered, "cruel."

The scouts rose and made for the hillside. As they left, Mary caught the younger scout by the hand. "I do not think you take this mission seriously enough," she warned him.

He merely winked at her. "To chase a man who can travel by magic, doesn't want to be caught, and is cunning about hiding? In this war, I think we've the best assignment of all."

"Alfred!" the leader barked, but as he turned back towards the hill, Mary had a sense of just how hard the scouts were going to be looking for their prey. She felt better knowing that not everyone in the general's army was so willing to play the bloodthirsty killer.

***

They followed the road, a wide path paved in river gravel, alongside the river itself. The army moved toward the next town at a leisurely pace. Amongst the barges of refugees fleeing the other day had been several canoes with scouts and messengers being sent downriver.

There was no way the army could move as fast, so now every city in turn would be aware of their progress. The general had little choice but to abandon the element of surprise. Making sure they were not attacked unexpectedly was a higher priority now, and that meant marching in full battle gear and moving slowly.

The villages they encountered surrendered without a fight. The general, either sated by his purge or perhaps desiring cooperation, mostly left them in peace.

***

"We have a serious problem," Gavin said without preamble as he entered their tent one afternoon. "We need both of you, now!"

Mary and Jordan quickly untangled themselves from the cot and rose. She straightened her skirt while he put his shirt on. Gavin gave them an exasperated look and turned away. Mary blushed, feeling like a maid caught in the act.

There was no time to dwell on that. As soon as Jordan's shirt was on, Gavin was striding off, forcing them to run to catch up. He strode through the camp without looking back and into the village where they had made camp for the day.

They walked down the main strip of the village. On the far end, two guards stood stiffly at the gate of a farmhouse. Gavin turned in at the gate. Just outside of the house, Shamus stood next to one of the Juggernauts. He looked up at them as they approached. "He's just went crazy or something," he said with a shrug. "I have no clue what to do."

Just then there was a feeble scream from inside and a groan of frustration. Mary followed Gavin inside.

"Arrgh, tell me what I want to know," Deirdre was saying in exasperation. "Can't you see it's useless, what you are doing?"

A peasant was hanging from the mantle, bloody daggers through both hands and into the dark wood. He slumped, his eyes glazed in pain. His chest was bare, and there were dark burns all along his right side. Deirdre was holding a torch in one hand.

"What are you doing, Deirdre?" Jordan demanded loudly from behind Mary.

Deirdre turned at the sound, but his eyes were empty and vacant. Jordan crossed the short distance in a matter of seconds and shook Deirdre. It seemed to capture his attention. "Jordan?" he asked, staring into Jordan's face.

"What are you doing?" Jordan repeated.

"I have him," Deirdre gestured at the peasant.

"Have who?" Jordan asked.

"Him, the druid," he repeated, "but he won't tell me."

"That's not the druid," Jordan said.

"Yes, the druid," Deirdre insisted.

"Won't tell you what, Deirdre?" Mary asked quietly, edging toward the peasant. "What won't he tell you?"

"Where Hammond is," Deirdre said.

"He's gone mad," Gavin remarked.

Jordan shook Deirdre hard. "Hammond is dead. And this is not the druid."

A look of rage crossed Deirdre's face, and he lashed out with the torch, hitting Jordan upside the head and knocking him down. He turned back and stuck the torch into the peasant's side again. The man screamed.

"Tell me!" Deirdre raged.

Jordan regained his feet quickly. He snatched a chair from a nearby table and crushed it over Deirdre's head. The Juggernaut crumpled to the floor. Mary snatched the torch and fed it into the fire place.

Jordan crouched over Deirdre and checked his pulse. "He is merely out. What do we do?"

Mary turned to Gavin. "Give him a sedative and have them carry him back to the camp. You'll have to keep him sedated." She turned to Jordan and added, "Your men will have to guard him constantly, just in case. To heal a body is nothing; to heal a mind is another thing entirely."

"You can do this?" Jordan asked.

"Perhaps," she replied, pulling one of the blades out of the peasant's hands. He slumped forward into her. She noticed a woman and a child crouched mutely in the corner, bearing witness to everything. "Get his other side," she commanded. Jordan glanced down at Deirdre. "The guards can handle him now," Mary barked. "Help me." Wordlessly, Jordan rose and removed the other blade.

"To the table," she commanded, and they laid the peasant out. Mary knelt and felt over his head and chest. Much of his chest was severely burnt. The pulse was weak and the life force fleeting.

She lifted her eyes and met Gavin's. "I cannot do this alone," she said. He regarded her with his usual impassive manner. "At home we work in teams: one holds the life force and supports the vital processes while the other heals the damage."

"You want me to help," he said slowly, "heal a peasant?"

She turned on Jordan. "Deirdre did this, one of your men. This man did not raise a finger against you. You cannot shirk this."

Jordan nodded. "You will be paid whatever your services are worth," he said to Gavin.

"My services do not come cheap," Gavin replied.

"I would be in your debt," Mary said. She watched Gavin's expression as he calculated what a favor from a mage might be worth.

"Then hold his life force," he said brusquely. His two personal aides appeared. He turned to them. "You . . . the blue bottle is a sedative, carry that one," he pointed at the fallen Juggernaut, "back to his tent. If he so much as whimpers, two sips from the bottle. Understood?" The man nodded and gestured for the guards to come. "You," he said to the other, "set my case up, there." He turned to the woman in the corner and said, "From you I will require a piglet, the youngest you have. Now." The woman scampered away.

Mary laid her hands on either side of the peasant's head and reached out to his life force. "Hold on," she whispered to him.

When the woman returned with the piglet, which could not have been more than a week old, Gavin inspected it and nodded his approval. He took it from her and held it by its hind leg. It began to whine helplessly. Gavin inspected the crude rock wall, then took a string from his case and lashed the piglet's leg to a lantern stay on the wall, hanging it upside down.

Its whines turned more plaintive.

Gavin inspected the man's burns. "Deep, very deep," he said, "and very large." He looked up at Jordan and shrugged, "Never pass up a challenge, eh?"

He turned his back on them and removed a razor from his case. He sat to sharpening it on a strop. When it was sharp enough, he took one last look at the peasant and then began to skin the piglet alive.

Mary fought down a wave of nausea as the piglet's screams and pain washed over her. It took every ounce of will she had to keep her mind focused on holding the man's life force. She wanted to scream at Gavin but held her tongue.

Only when he was done skinning the beast did he quickly dispatch it by slitting its throat. Holding the bloody skin in one hand he turned towards the peasant and began to chant softly. He sat the razor down and placed his free hand over the burn.

Pain shot through the peasant and into Mary as the wound was scourged clean. Gavin continued to chant and pass his free hand slowly down the man's side. Wherever the hand passed the dead, burned tissue turned to dust and was stripped away.

When the entire wound was cleaned down to bare flesh, he inspected it again and then laid the pigskin over it. Mary glanced at the now dead piglet, the ragged patch of flesh missing from its side, then at the man's long wound. *A perfect fit,* she thought. *He is as much a master in his own right, whatever I think of his methods.*

Gavin ignored everything. He extracted a long, curved needle and a piece of fine thread. He set to stitching the pigskin in place, both along the edges and in the middle, like he was quilting. He chanted softly the entire time, blending the pigskin into the man's being. When he was done, the new skin was a pale match for the man's real skin and only the lines of tiny stitches showed where the burn had been.

The man was conscious, his eyes open. He felt weak, but Mary sensed little pain. The stitches hurt worse now than the burn.

"The younger the pig, the closer the skin matches," Gavin said to Mary in a matter-of-fact tone. Seeing the man had his eyes open, he said, "Well, we've undone the damage of this unfortunate little incident," as if this were apology enough for the fact that a soldier had broken in his door and tortured him to edge of death for no reason. Gavin turned to the woman and said, "He should drink plenty of water and broth. Best food you have. Have him take it easy for a week or so, and next moon, cut out the stitches. Any questions?"

With that he turned, washed his hands with water from an ewer his aide provided, and began to pack up his case. Within minutes and without a backward glance, he was gone.

"I am sorry," Mary said quietly to the woman.

"Thank you," she replied. "The others would not have helped."

***

When Mary came to the tent that night, she was exhausted. Her face was lined with tears but she was empty of emotions. She stumbled in through the darkness and collapsed in a heap on the ground.

"Are you okay?" Jordan asked in a whisper.

She shook her head. "But I shall be."

"I have never seen you like this from healing. You

say it gives you power too," he said.

"To heal a mind . . ." she broke off.

"Is he? I mean, did you?"

She shrugged. "It is too soon to tell. He's rational now, but I don't know if it will last." She paused and then spat out, "The things they did to you!"

He did not have to ask what she meant, who she meant. "They wanted us to be strong. Better soldiers."

"You were not soldiers, you were children!" she raged. "You didn't need to be strong; you needed to be cared for."

"We needed to be strong," he insisted, "to be safe."

"They were the only threat," she continued.

"They made us special. They made us great." he said.

Tired, not wanting to fight, she said. "You are great. But you are human too. They can't take the humanity out. They can't train the heart to stop feeling."

He reached down and scooped her into his lap. "When this war is done," he said, "I am going to talk to the principles. I am going to insist on some changes. I won't cooperate unless they agree. I am going to tell them they made mistakes. I am going to tell them I want my own manor, my own place: *our* own place. We can have children there, and we can love them as much as children deserve."

It won't happen, Mary thought, *because you are going to die on a field of battle, and I am going to stand over you, crying.*

"Just think on it. They'll be fast and strong like me and my brothers. They'll have your magic and your beauty. And they'll have our love. They'll be unstoppable."

She clung to him, wishing that future could be true, wishing it could be as easy as he said. Then, because he was so kind in that moment, she said, "Jordan, honey?"

"Yes?"

"You weren't an orphan." It was in his mind, bits and pieces from before. "You, all of you, came from the same area. Your parents were poor; they told them you would have a better life."

"I have parents?" he asked.

"Yes."

"And they cared about me?"

"Yes."

14 THE LOOTING OF TARGILL

Two days later, they reached the city of Targill. Deirdre marched with the men and spoke rationally to them. The crazed look had faded from his eyes but was not entirely gone. The men treated him casually enough. Only Mary with her empathy could see how nervous they were around him and how shaky his hold on reality was.

If she were home, she would have recommended a long vacation at the very least, or a stay at a sanitarium, or even a stay in a monastery for a time. Anything to get him out of the stress for a while and away from what was driving him mad. Here, however, in this time and place, Mary's voice counted for little and this was not how things were done. He was ordered into battle formation with the other Juggernauts as they approached the city.

On the wide field in front of the city, they found a medium-sized force of men standing in formation. In front of these men was a much smaller clump of men, kneeling. Their hands had been bound behind them. Beyond them, the crude defenses of the city were empty, and its gates were wide open.

Two merchants, with a body guard of three pikemen, marched toward the approaching army carrying the duke's flag.

A halt was called and the general, surrounded by a much larger bodyguard of aides, rode toward the men. Shamus and Gavin rode after them. More curious than afraid, Mary followed.

The merchants bowed deeply as the general stopped in front of them. The older and heavier of two spoke as he rose. "Your Grace, General Winthrop Klinefelter, you cannot imagine how glad we are to see you, Sire."

"What is going on here?" the general demanded.

"Hearing that you were again in the region and establishing order as you went," the merchant said, "those loyal to you rose up and overthrew the traitorous scum, the mercenaries who brought rebellion to this land and subjugated our city to their cause."

A ridiculous lie, Mary thought.

The general merely nodded and said, "Of course, of course."

"We have the traitors here, awaiting your punishment," the merchant continued.

Mary looked at the bound men. They bore little sign of having struggled. *There is more than one way to be a hero,* she thought to herself, *more than one way to give your life for your city.*

"These few held your city ransom all this time?" the general inquired.

"It has been hard to rally men with help so far

from hand," the younger merchant pointed out. The older of the two shushed him angrily.

"Many, we have slain ourselves," the elder merchant said smoothly, "and others had fled, no doubt to towns farther downriver."

The general made a soft thoughtful noise. "Of course," he said again. "You are to be commended. Truly."

The merchants relaxed slightly.

"You won't be needing such weapons anymore," the general said looking over at the men in formation, who were mostly spearmen with no armor.

"Of course not, not with you here to protect us," the merchant said quickly. "But when you leave?"

The general shot him a look. "I will see to your defense before then," he replied tersely.

The merchants nodded, though they seemed less happy. As Mary looked over the ragtag militia, she felt they should be happy with any deal they could get. They would not have lasted long against even the weakest of the general's men.

The general turned to his aide. "You and you, see to disarming the militia. You, take the men and march to the town square. We will take control of the city from there." He paused and turned to a final aide. "Have the traitors executed."

A sigh went through the small crowd. From the merchants, it was resigned, and from the aides content. They would take the city peacefully.

Mary stayed close to the general as he entered the city, as much to avoid seeing the executions as anything. The courage of their sacrifice and the helpless pain of the militia men who would watch it was too much for her. But she was relieved there would be no battle today.

The general rode to the town square, cautious and alert, as though he didn't fully believe the merchant's offer of peace. From there, he sent the Juggernauts and several other sword units out across the town. Only after all the units had returned and given the all-clear did he relax.

He stood on the edge of a small fountain at the center of the square and called the men to him. Jordan and his men removed their helmets and sheathed their swords. Deirdre still had a dazed and out-of-touch look on his face. Formist and a few of the other Juggernauts looked disappointed, but most of the men in the square looked relieved.

"Men," the general began in a booming voice, "we have taken the city!"

A cheer went up from the men.

He continued, "You have come here through much hardship and tribulation." Mary looked around the crowd, unsure what was about to happen. "You came expecting to be met with swords and with death. Thankfully, you have been spared that. You came also expecting that if you were one of the lucky that survived, one of the victors, you would be rewarded. I would be remiss in my duty if I were to deprive you of your rewards. Until dawn tomorrow, the town is yours."

Another cheer went up from the crowd, and they began to rapidly disperse. Mary struggled to find Jordan. She had a pretty good idea what was going on and did not want any part of it.

There was a crash as a door was broken open, and a cheer from a small group of men gathered around the door. One by one, they disappeared inside. In the distance, there were other crashes, other cheers, and occasionally a scream from the occupants within.

She found Jordan sitting on a bench at the edge of the square. The sign above him marked this building as a bakery. He watched her approach, impassive.

"Well, no battle today," he said.

She shook her head no. He reached for her, pulling her onto his lap. She let him.

Colton appeared in the doorway holding a wineskin and a loaf of bread. He tossed the bread to Mary and took a long pull from the wineskin.

"I had to help myself," he said lightly, handing the wineskin to Jordan. "The baker's wife was busy entertaining some men."

Mary closed her eyes, feeling pale.

"It is what men do when they take a town," Jordan said reproachfully. Mary couldn't tell if the reproach was meant for the men or for her.

"You do not," she answered, wondering if it was true. Wondering how Jordan had behaved in the months and years before she came along. She had not seen one memory of that, but that didn't mean it hadn't happened.

"To be third or fourth in line," Colton said disgustedly, "for a middle-aged peasant woman, bah!" He spat on the ground and found a seat on the far side of the door.

"Colton need but ask," Jordan said proudly, "and more than half of the camp followers would roll him for free."

Mary was stony, trying not to hear the noises that came through the open door.

"They live," Jordan said suddenly. "No battle, no killing. The entire town will live to see tomorrow."

"It's as bad as battle," Mary replied.

"But they live," Jordan insisted.

"Their homes looted, every scrap of wealth gone, the women raped; perhaps it would be better to be dead," she insisted.

"Of course not," Colton said. "They can rebuild. They can move on. Dead is dead."

She shook her head, feeling pale and weak. "I don't care. I do not wish to witness it all the same." She stood woozily.

Jordan stood quickly and held her. "Of course. You say the word, and we are gone. They will be setting camp at the edge of town. I have no need of this either." He tossed the wineskin and bread to Colton. "Enjoy," he said.

"Jordan need not stay," Colton joked, "he's found his loot already."

"And a greater treasure she is than anything this town holds," Jordan shot back.

Mary felt anger flare within her. She hated both of them for reminding her that she was Jordan's property, that even though she had gone to his bed willingly, she was not here by choice. She hated them for their casual acceptance of what was going on, the way they shrugged it off as what happens when you take a town. She should hate the other men, the ones out committing the acts of desecration, but she found she couldn't. She could only hate these two who she thought were better.

At the edge of the square, they retrieved Mary's horse. Jordan threw himself up behind her, dwarfing her in the saddle. They rode with her nestled deep within his arms.

From that vantage, she saw Gavin ride past. He

too had a woman, barely more than a girl really, nestled in front of him. Her eyes darted from side to side, terrified of what was going on.

He was talking to her quietly. "Really, this is much better," he was saying. "We'll get you back to the tent, get you a bath," his nose wrinkled as he said it, "and a nice meal. You'll see, it will be a pleasant evening, really."

Mary watched the pale, mousy blonde in revulsion, knowing all too well the choice the woman had made. It made her angry. It made her sit up straighter in her saddle, forcing herself more forward so she was not so obviously in Jordan's arms. He tensed but let go when she pulled the reins from his hands.

***

"We have a problem," the voice said. Mary groaned wearily. It was becoming an all too common way of being woken up. The sun had risen, and the camp was beginning to stir.

She rose from the bed, angry and disgusted with herself for having shared it with Jordan. She wanted to push him away, to assert her independence, if only to show that she could. But she clung to him; he was her only safety net.

He rose too, and if he had any internal conflicts about their relationship, he did not show them. They both dressed quickly and followed the aide. She wondered vaguely who had gotten too drunk and what they had done. She also wondered why it wasn't Colton who had come for them.

She soon found out the answer to her second question. The aide led them into town. It was quiet. Here and there a few drunken soldiers slept in heaps or in doorways. The militiamen had been released back into town with the dawn, and she saw a few hollow, hateful eyes looking out of busted doors.

In a small cul-de-sac between an inn and a smithy, they found Gavin and a couple of sentries gathered. At their feet, Colton was passed out. Even from the entrance of the cul-de-sac, Mary could smell the sour scent of wine and piss.

Colton was passed out with his arms wrapped around another man. A man, who from the look of it, had been dead for several hours. Mary bent and inspected the man. He was a soldier. He had a long, thin, mostly healed scar running the length of his forehead. He looked familiar, and Mary realized with a start this was the same man she had watched the camp follower stitch up after the peasant's ambush.

"Did he kill the man?" Jordan asked. He nudged Colton with his boot. Colton protested sleepily and rolled over.

"That was our question," a petty officer said as he joined them. "Any ideas?"

Gavin squatted by the dead body. "I'd say no," he said casually. "For one thing there's not near enough blood here. The man must have been killed somewhere else then brought here. And look at these wounds, see they're long and narrow." He stood, reached over and drew a knife from the sentry's belt. "Like this," he said pointing at the tip. "Our unit carries much thinner daggers."

"That blade is standard issue," The officer groused. "Could have been anyone in the entire damn army."

"Best be looking then," Gavin said with a smirk.

Mary was leaning against the rough wall of the inn, fighting the visions that wanted to claim her. She saw

Colton, the day of the peasants' ambush, the look of fear on his face when she offered to heal the soldier. He couldn't let her, or anyone, see that this one man mattered in the slightest, couldn't let anyone know he was important. Because then they would know.

She could see them, the men from the dead soldier's own unit. In her mind, they were cornering the man, in a far corner of the town, knives out. She heard the accusations they flung, about him and Colton. She saw Colton arrive, too late. She saw him fleeing with the body, finding a quiet place and then, because there was nothing else he could do, drowning himself in drink.

A sentry returned with a bucket of water. Jordan took it and threw it on Colton's face. He jerked awake with a start and stumbled to his feet.

He looked down at the body, and for a split second, the entire story played across his face. Then his face became a mask. When he looked up, he was Colton again. He gave an impish grin. "Well, I don't think one of us has ever gotten so drunk they woke up with a corpse before," he said with a laugh, "and I'll bet you thought Hammond or Formist would break that record."

Gavin turned away in disgust. Jordan said, "I am disappointed, Colton."

Colton swallowed. "I am sorry, Sir."

To the officer, Jordan said, "Is my man a suspect in this death?"

The officer shrugged. "I guess not."

"Then with your permission, we will return to camp," he said.

***

After they had taken Colton back to his own tent

and threw him on his cot to sleep off the remains of his binge, they returned to their tent. As soon as they were alone, Mary pulled Jordan aside. "There is something we must discuss," she said.

"What?" he asked.

"Colton," she said. "Colton and this man."

"You think he killed him?"

"No," she said.

He turned and went to the trunk, began digging within for a clean outfit.

"They were lovers," she said.

He stiffened. For a long time, he did not answer. She waited patiently. Slowly he turned to her, his eyes flashing. "Careful what you say of my friend."

"I mean no insult," she shot back, "it is just the way some men are. I think no less of him."

"Then why make such an accusation?"

"It's not an accusation. I thought you needed to know."

"To know what? That you think my friend is a sissy?"

"Gay," she replied. "Not a sissy. Not all are. I am not trying to accuse him of anything, nor do I think less of him. But you have to understand this death is not like the others. It's not just some soldier. This death will affect him."

"Colton is not gay," Jordan said defiantly. "I've known him my whole life. You will not say that about him."

"I am not trying—" she broke off. "I am just worried about how he's going to handle this."

Jordan glared at her. "You think I don't know why?" he said sharply. "Why this is so important to you? Since you healed me, since you walked inside me, our dreams mingle. You think I don't know? I dream of him too." His voice dropped to a whisper. "Martin."

Mary froze.

"I know what you are." His voice was quiet, ragged. "I know what it makes us. And I bear it, because . . . because I love you." He rose and shook his hands in the air. "It is different anyway, you and me. You are as like to a woman as one could be. To suggest Colton would . . . with some hairy soldier . . . do not say such a thing to me again."

With that, he turned and stormed out of the tent. Mary broke into tears.

15 RAGE AND DENIAL

Mary and Jordan did not speak on the subject again. When he returned a long time later, he shushed her with a warning look, and then when he spoke it was of everyday things.

That night at supper, Colton was awake and looking no different than ever. He joked about his binge and waking with a corpse. The others laughed crudely and teased him most of the evening.

The entire camp had a sated feel to it. They had not only avoided battle, they had been given the spoils. How the townspeople felt, Mary couldn't guess, nor did she wish to find out. As they marched through the center of town the next morning, Mary caught haunted, resigned looks. Colton had been right; at least they were alive.

The army marched downriver for several days. Jordan explained, in one of the many superficial conversations they had, that this was one of the longest stretches between towns. They passed a couple of small villages: one surrendered without a fight, and the other was completely abandoned. Mary felt, rather than saw, eyes watching from the far bank.

During the day, Colton was glib and superficial, seeming very much his usual self. Mary tried to talk to him several times over the course of many days. But how did one even start such a conversation? When she tried to ask him if anything was bothering him, he merely shrugged her off. When she tried to bring up that night, he laughed it off as a drunk.

Everyone else seemed as willing to accept his assurances as he was to give them. She tried one other time to talk to Jordan, but he did not want to listen. She asked Gavin, in a very circumspect way, if he saw anything different about Colton, but it appeared he did not.

How could he not? He was one of the least emotional and least empathic individuals she had ever met, but he was a sharp observer. And it didn't take a magician to see the look of pain that crossed Colton's face when he thought nobody was watching or the looks of malevolence he gave the regular soldiers.

He no longer disappeared into the main camp after supper, but he did not sit in the pavilion with the other Juggernauts either. Instead, he would disappear early into his tent and not be seen until the next morning's march.

Mary's relationship with Jordan had changed in some imperceptible manner with the revelation that Jordan knew Mary's past. *Just when I thought my feelings could not be more conflicted*, she thought while trying to meditate. She felt angry, angry that after everything she had done, after all the years and magic, she was still seen as she always had been: a boy in a dress. She was angry, too, that he saw their relationship as shameful as a result.

But at the same time, he was still here. He loved her. He loved her so much that he did not care about her past. There was an intimacy that came from knowing everything about each other, and now they had a chance at that level of intimacy. If they could survive this war.

*∗∗

Mary woke, unsure what had disturbed her sleep. She slid out of Jordan's sleeping embrace and pulled a dress over her frame. In the middle of their private encampment, a small fire burned in a brazier. By the flickering light, she saw a form moving from tent to tent, hesitantly.

She—for Mary could now see it was a woman—bent at Colton's tent flap and whispered "Mary?"

"I am here." Mary said, not loud, but loud enough to cause the woman to start. She turned and approached Mary.

It was Mabel, the camp follower. She bent in an awkward attempt at a formal bow. "M'lady."

"There is no need of formality." Mary said gesturing her to rise. "You seek me?"

"I come to beg your mercy, M'lady," she said, her face still downcast.

This made Mary angry. "You do not need to beg from me," she said more sharply than intended. "Tell me plainly what you wish."

Mabel nodded. "There is a case that is beyond me. Truthfully ma'am, many cases are beyond my help. I do what I can, because there is no one else for such as us. I . . . I value this one. I cannot ask the general for a doctor, nor could I approach the men's healer, though many say he is skilled. But you are a woman. I hoped I could appeal to you as a woman."

Mary nodded. "Take me at once."

A rebellious satisfaction filled her as they departed the private camp and made their way through the quiet labyrinth of tents. While they walked, Mabel spoke. "Her name is Schill, but most call her Squirrel because she is so small, so happy-go-lucky. For a time, she was one of the most popular. She went into labor last night. This morning, we bribed a teamster to let her ride instead of walk." Mary did not need to ask who had bribed him or how. "Now it is well past a day, and she has not progressed. I am worried the child will die, or it will kill her."

A clump of women were gathered outside a tent that was braced up against a wagon. They looked up as Mabel returned with Mary. They watched her cautiously, not sure how to behave around her.

Inside the tent was a low cot with a child in labor. *A child*, Mary thought. *Squirrel could not be more than thirteen.* Four women gathered around the cot. One was wetting a cloth and dabbing her forehead. Another held her hand. In the corner of the tent, the teamster sat on a low stool. So plain was the sadness on his face that Mary softened her criticism of the man.

"The father, he was large," Mary said. They gave her a blank look, as to say 'how would we know?' "Her hips are too small. This child cannot pass. In a few years, her hips will be wider, but right now, there is no way."

"There is no hope then?" one of the women asked.

"It is said," the teamster said slowly, pain in his

voice, "that in some cases the child can be cut from the belly and yet live."

"She would not live," Mabel said. "Must we choose, baby or mother?"

Anger flared in Mary, fiercer than she had ever experienced before. "I will not deal in these choices any longer!" she raged. The energy came upon her fast and furious. It rushed into her palms so fast that they glowed, causing the teamster to gasp. She clapped her palms together and stared down at the child.

She bent, scooped her palms down into Squirrel's belly. She wrapped her hands around the baby and lifted it out.

"Holy shit," one of the women muttered as she stared from the infant in Mary's arms to Squirrel's uninjured belly. Squirrel groaned and moaned, "It's coming."

"It's the afterbirth only," Mary said. "Your baby is here." As if on cue the baby, reacting to the cold, began to wail loudly.

One of the women held out a ragged blanket, and Mary sat the child on Squirrel's chest and wrapped it in the blanket. Looking at the ragged edges, she thought, *welcome to a life of poverty.*

She laid her hands on Squirrel's stomach again and closed her eyes. She felt the belly spasm as it expelled the afterbirth. Squirrel lay back exhausted. "I have told your womb to sleep," Mary told her, touching her cheek gently. "Just for a couple of years. So next time you will be wider, more able to give birth." Squirrel nodded.

"I can't ever repay you," Mabel said as Mary rose.

Mary took her hands and said. "You were right to

come to me. We are women first and always. Let the men stand on rank and status; we must stick together. As long as I am here, I will help any of you." As they went back outside into the larger group, Mary turned to them. "While I am here, you may come to me when you need. After I am gone, there is a man, an older man, tall with gray hair and beard." She heard a snort. Many men could match such a description. "He wears brown robes, and he carries a curved sword at times. He wears a symbol like this." She drew the druid's symbol in the dirt. There was a muttering, and she knew she had everyone's attention. "He is . . ." she paused and considered what to say next. "He is an enemy to the duke, but not to the people and certainly not to women. His name is Harrod. He knows many herbs—herbs to heal, herbs to aid in childbirth, even herbs to make the womb sleep for a time so you cannot conceive. If you meet him, beg his mercy, use my name if you wish."

Halfway back to the camp Mary found her way blocked by a group of sentries. Their leader was a tall man with shaggy, blond hair. He smelled of sweat and dirt.

"What's a girl doing out this late at night?" he asked, a malicious undertone in his voice.

"She's the Juggernaut's woman," one of the soldiers said fearfully. "The one they say has magic."

The leader's gloved hand grabbed her chin, holding her head up. "Indeed she is," he said. "Not as curvy as I would like, but a pretty morsel nonetheless. Perhaps we should have some fun with her before taking her back."

"She is their leader's," a soldier whispered nervously in his ear. "They say he's really possessive."

The leader paused, considering.

He grabbed Mary by the throat. "Do you know what we think of those . . . those monsters? Beasts bred to kill." He spat. "I should have you in my tent, and each of my men after me. Then deliver you back to your precious freaks. See how they feel…" He pushed her back roughly. "But it's not worth my life."

Again, rage flared through Mary, that she should be treated so, that her only protection was a man who had claimed her as a prize, as little more than a slave: a man she both loved and hated. She thought of the camp followers and the peasants, all the people forced to endure treatment like this their whole lives. A scream of frustration rose up within her. It escaped in a short staccato burst. It hit the man like a physical blow, lifting him off his feet and throwing him into a chuckwagon.

It was then that Gavin appeared. He stepped over the man, who had crumpled to ground at the base of wagon. He walked casually into the midst of the sentries. Mary stood still, shaking with rage.

Turning to the men, Gavin said lightly, "Afraid of the Juggernauts? You should be. But perhaps you should fear the mage as well, in her own right. She has powers you don't want to trifle with. Mary come, we must get back to the camp." He walked off without turning to see if she followed.

Jordan was awake when they arrived back at the encampment. He had woken to find her gone and roused Gavin to look for her.

"Where were you?" he asked, worried.

"There was healing I had to do," she replied.

"You should not be about on your own at night," Gavin said in reproach.

"I go where I am needed and do what I must."

"If you are to be our healer . . ."

Mary cut him off. "When a woman comes to beg my mercy, it will not be your decision if I stay or go."

With that, the argument was over. Jordan turned away, dismissing the matter completely. Gavin merely asked, in a casual tone, what the issue had been.

"A hard birth," she replied thrown off by this turn of events.

"In some cases the child may be cut out," he said as though discussing a theoretical case. "And if the woman is bound quickly enough, she too can be saved. I've never done such a thing. There's little cause in this operation."

Dawn was slowly coming over the horizon, and there seemed little point in going back to bed. One of the Juggernauts's women, a face Mary had seen at Squirrel's tent, muttered a quiet thank you at breakfast.

That evening, another camp follower appeared at the edge of the camp bearing a child that coughed weakly. "You'd best see to it," Jordan nodded, and to Shamus he said, "A woman thing."

Mary had inadvertently discovered a loophole in the army's logic. Women were not just a different rank or status, but a completely different world to these men. They objected to her healing common soldiers or peasants. They objected to her even fraternizing with people they saw as below their caste, and by default, hers. But when presented with a "woman's problem," they had no clue where that ranked and frankly didn't want to think about it more than necessary.

***

Mary's eyes popped open. In the dim light, she could see Jordan was awake too. "Something is wrong," he whispered.

They lay still a moment, unsure what impulse had woken them, but they both felt it. In the distance there was a muffled sound that might have been a cry.

"Stay here," Jordan commanded, rolling out of bed. Crouched low, he fished his sword out from beside the trunk and disappeared outside.

The edge of the tent felt unsafe, and Mary rolled out of bed. She found a spot in the center of the tent and sat there, alert. She could see Jordan's form moving silently across the center of their encampment.

Another figure detached itself from the shadows. Before Mary could draw her breath to shout a warning, Jordan wheeled on the figure. There was the sound of metal on metal, a gasp, and the figure slid to the ground.

"Juggernauts!" Jordan cried. It was unnecessary, the metal on metal had woken almost every one of them, and they came alert instantly. They appeared at tent flaps, swords already drawn.

"It's an ambush!" Jordan called. "To me!"

Across the camp, there were sounds of fighting. The Juggernauts came to Jordan, gathering around him, peering into the darkness for other forms.

Mary sensed, as much as heard, the knife slice through the canvas back wall of the tent, the assassin then entering through the gaping slit. He was surprised to find her kneeling on the ground, rather than in the cot, and his attack was clumsy. She evaded it easily and ran out of the tent.

She had taken only a couple of steps when she

heard the man behind her cry out. She turned and saw, out of the corner of her eye, Colton dispatch him with a dagger. Armed with a dagger in each hand, Colton gave her one haunted look and disappeared.

The rest of the Juggernauts were still clumped together, peering into shadows trying to spot their attackers. "Some light?" Mary said, calling up her magic. The brazier burst in a bright flame, illuminating two leather-clad men armed with long, wicked-looking daggers. Deirdre was among them in the blink of an eye, followed by Formist.

From the shadows, they heard Colton's voice, tinged with a hint of manic glee. "There's knife work afoot, brothers."

In the distance, a horn started blaring wildly.

"Torches," Jordan commanded with a gesture. One by one, the Juggernauts took a cold torch from the pile by the main pavilion and lit them at Mary's fire. Torches in one hand, swords in the other, they spread out through the camp. Jordan was last to go. "Stay here, be safe," he commanded.

"I can defend myself at need," she replied sharply. He nodded and was gone. The sounds of fighting spread throughout the camp as men were roused to find the enemy already in their midst.

"What the blazes?" Shamus said as he stumbled into the firelight, followed closely by Gavin.

"It's an ambush," she said. "I don't know how they got past the sentries."

"The men?"

"Already set to work," she said.

He nodded. "Best we stay here, then."

Mary snorted coldly.

They stood in the light of Mary's blaze, Shamus

adding logs occasionally to keep it from dying back down.

Only one enemy showed himself in the light of their fire. In a quick, almost negligent flick of his wrist, Gavin drew and threw a small sharp dagger that dropped the man were he stood.

Lights from fires and torches slowly grew around the camp, as the soldiers tried to root out the ambushers. A couple of times, men wearing the duke's insignia crossed the circle of light and inquired if they were okay.

Then the Juggernauts were back, hooting gleefully. "He's a wild man," Formist laughed. "Drove them back to the river and dang near across it."

Jordan was carrying a struggling form. He threw Colton, sopping wet and smelling like river water, at Mary's feet. Colton instantly sprang to his feet, screaming. A white hot, animal rage exuded from him.

Formist closed the distance in a second, wrapping Colton in a bear hug. "Brother!" he cried, wrestling Colton back down. "Battle's over, Brother." Someone came with a bucket of water and threw it on the two men. Colton stopped struggling but continued to pant heavily and glare about him.

"They came across on small boats, drifting downstream so they didn't have to row and make noise. Swimmers came first and took out the few sentries posted on that side. They were in the camp before anyone knew. More than a few of the duke's men were killed in their sleep before the alarm was raised," Jordan told her.

"It would have been a disaster if we hadn't been here," one of the Juggernauts said.

"We drove them back to river," Jordan confirmed, "and roused the duke's men. Colton went berserk—left a bloody trail behind and tried to jump on their boats."

"*Did* jump on their boats," Formist corrected.

"That was a sight!" One of the men hooted. "Him jumping from boat to boat. The boatmen were saying 'oh bloody hell!'"

To Mary, Jordan said, "He eventually missed a jump and crashed in the river. Luckily we managed to retrieve him before he drowned. He has some minor injuries. If you could?" She nodded, not sure she really wanted to touch Colton in this state, but not willing to refuse either.

By morning it had become clear that, thanks to the Juggernauts, the battle had been an uneven disaster. Less than one hundred of the duke's men were buried in a shallow communal grave at the river's edge. Close to three hundred rivermen, peasants, and mercenaries in light leather armor were piled on the shore of the river for the ravens to care for.

They marched past the grisly pile as they made their way downriver. Mary's eyes were drawn to a mass of coppery-red hair. The body it belonged to wasn't much more than a boy: a pale, drawn face and slender shoulders and arms sticking out from under another corpse. The eyes were partially opened, and the expression was resigned and bitter. It could have been Martin, had Martin survived long enough to be full grown. Mary looked away, but there on her other side was Jordan—Jordan, who could have been this boy's killer.

It seemed a cruel trick of fate. This man was, in so many ways, perfect for her. He fit her, physically, in a way no other man could. He knew her, knew her past, and he was still here. Perfect, except for the fact he was a cold-blooded killer. Last night in the dark, she had been able to rationalize it so well. They were attackers, assassins that came in the night. He was a soldier. He did what he must to protect himself and his people; this was the easy morality of the battlefield.

In the daylight, seeing the corpses, it was different. They were poor, desperate peasants. They fought without hope. Against the duke's army they had scant hope. Against the Juggernauts, they had none.

The reason Jordan was perfect for her was because she, Mary, was imperfect. If she could heal herself fully she could accommodate any man. She knew that. If she could heal herself fully, she could be simply a woman, like all the other women. She could love without fear of her past.

Why couldn't she? They told her it was beyond their healing powers when she was young. But she grew beyond their teaching years ago. She had broken so many of the rules she had been taught. Why did this one elude her?

Here on this world, so unlike her own, she was confronted by the memories of him constantly. A thousand miles from home and she could no longer escape the truth: she was still bound by what Martin had done.

Everywhere around her countless peasants struggled in abject poverty with no hope. Countless orphans lived in cramped quarters and grew up to desperate futures. Jordan's family had sold him, as a young boy, into what amounted to slavery, on hopes that at least he would not starve. He had been tortured and turned into something both greater and lesser than human.

Out of so many horror stories, one boy had escaped. He fled the dry and dusty streets and into a world of magic. He became the girl he wished to be, become a healer and mage. Her life in Tomlin City had been a dream. Now confronted by the harsh realities of life in the empire, she was forced to confront another fact: Mary had survivor's guilt.

16 COLTON

They were well within a day's march of the city of Trent when word came back through the scouts that the city was in a state of revolt.

"According to sources fleeing the city," the general explained that night over supper, "the town council was divided. Having heard reports of what happened at Koll and to the river bandits that ambushed us, some think the only hope lies in surrender. Others thought to make a last stand." *No doubt having heard what happened at Targill,* Mary thought to herself.

"The vast majority of townsfolk," an aide added, "are fleeing the city entirely, seeking refuge wherever they can, though there's few enough places that will have them. Those with boats are crossing the river and chancing the long journey through wild country to the Marquis. Others are heading downriver towards Shanton, though that will be the next stop on our journey and they all know it. Many are heading northward, hoping some village will have them."

R. J. Eliason

"They do not matter," the general said. "The city is all that matters right now. Once it's under our control, they will come back. It's their life after all."

The council's indecision led to blows, and there was a civil war raging within Trent. The general thought it was best if a small number of men, led by the Juggernauts of course, were to hurry under the cover of darkness to reach the city. Those loyal to the duke, or seeking surrender to his general at least, were slowly losing the civil conflict, and the general hoped to arrive while they yet held one gate. If they could just get their swordmen within the city, it would fall quickly.

After supper, the men went to their tents to suit up for the night's march. Mary went to Gavin.

"You need to keep the men out of this battle," she said.

"How am I supposed to do that?"

"Go to Shamus and tell him they aren't fit to fight," she said. "He'll listen to you."

"And why am I doing this?"

"Because, they are not fit to fight."

"They seem whole enough to me," he replied, "quite healthy."

"You've seen the look in Deirdre's eyes, surely."

"I am to tell Shamus he's not fit to fight because he's got this look in his eye?"

"You've seen it too; I know you have," Mary said. "He's not all there, not all the way connected to reality. Think about what happened with the peasant. What if he went like that in the middle of battle? He could kill his own friends and not even know it."

Gavin shrugged. "He seems rational enough. And if we keep him out, he'll be shamed in front of the others."

"So keep them all out," Mary persisted. "Especially —"

"Especially Jordan?" he interrupted. "You're worried about your man?"

"No," she said. "I am worried about Colton."

"He distinguished himself in the ambush," Gavin said. "It was the best showing he's ever given."

And he's not yet lost the manic glint in his eyes, she thought. "I know. That's what I am worried about."

"What? That he'll be good?" he said.

"Do you know why he was so good?" she responded. "He's hoping someone will kill him."

Gavin raised one eyebrow but didn't comment.

"Formist is drinking." Gavin rolled his eyes but she continued, "More than usual. And Hunter and Traimon, they have been drinking too much as well. All of them are near to their breaking point."

"And then what happens?" Gavin asked.

Mary shook her head. "I don't know. But the middle of a battle is no place to find out."

"And you want them out of action for how long?"

Mary shook her head again. "It's hard to say. They need help and time to think things through, to react."

Gavin snorted. "You think Shamus will agree? You think I can walk into his tent and ask this? You must think I have a lot more pull than I do."

"Is there nothing you can do?"

He sighed. "No," he said. As she turned to go, he added, "For what it's worth, I do understand. If it were my choice, we would have left this cursed place months ago. Something is wrong. I can feel it in my bones."

Mary watched helplessly as the men lined up in

formation and marched out. Afterward, she returned to her tent and tried to meditate. She could not get her mind to settle. Then Gavin was there with her horse. They rode with the general's entourage through the night. It was dawn when they arrived, well after the Juggernauts and the swordmen, but well ahead of the main army.

The men had reached the gate in time and were already inside the city. There was the occasional scream or clash of metal. Smoke rolled up from several places around the city.

Mary was glad that she didn't have to watch the battle and glad to have heard that most of the townsfolk had fled. Still, she could not help but to think this was a bitter, bloody battle, made more bitter by the fact that the townsfolk had turned on each other only hours before.

In terms of lives lost, this was one of the better battles she had experienced, but in other ways, it was more destructive. Fires had raged unchecked for most of the night, and there seemed little chance that anyone would be attempting to control them today. One corner tower was ablaze, as was part of the wall. If the townsfolk returned, as the general believed, they may well find their houses destroyed.

By the time the army had arrived in force, they received word that the city was firmly in the duke's control. The Juggernauts left the city just as the first sentries swept in.

Mary went to them, heedless of the blood. Physically, they were all whole, with only minor scratches to show for their day's work. But it wasn't their bodies she was worried about. Colton paced on the edge of the group, a manic look in his eye and a fixed grin on his face. His hand kept straying to his sword. Deirdre had wide eyes and he seemed lost. Mary heard him ask a couple of times where Hammond was. Formist's hands shook. *Like an old alcoholic,* she thought, *though he can't have gone more than twelve hours without a drink.* But when Shamus called them to order, they all went obediently and stood perfectly still.

After a bath and a change of clothes, they had a long leisurely lunch. The men seemed jovial. The whole army was in good spirits. The majority of the men had arrived in time to participate in the final mop-up and looting, but had faced no serious threat. That was a fact worth celebrating.

"I've heard the fifth pike unit was putting out a warehouse fire," Formist said. "Burned to the ground." He paused. "It had a well-stocked wine cellar."

"That sounds wonderful," Colton said, the smile still fixed on his face.

Gavin gave her a look that said, "What were you worried about?"

She couldn't help but feel a vague sense of foreboding.

***

The pikemen passed the bottle. It was a good day: no battle, some light firefighting, and then this boon. The only problem was that everyone in the camp seemed to know about their good fortune, and it was draining away with each new visitor.

Even *they* knew. Three of them had shown up around dusk. The pikemen had no interest in drinking with them, especially after they found out about their fellow soldier Mark—him and that Colton and their unnatural relationship. Still, one couldn't just tell them no. Men had been killed.

So they drank a toast with them. Then they bribed a camp follower handsomely to take a wine cask and the three of them off somewhere, anywhere. It had cost a pretty coin at that. It was rumored that the dark-haired one was hard on the women when he lay with them, and the tall one had developed the sort of look in his eye that made no man want to be alone with him. There was no telling what was going on behind those wide, piercing stares. Still, the pikemen had several flasks left to divide between nearly fifty men in their camp, and maybe a dozen more friendlies. It was enough for everyone to get a decent buzz and enjoy the fine night.

A wave of silence swept across the campfire and the pikemen followed the dark, suspicious looks toward the edge of their encampment. *He* was standing there, looking at them and smiling. It was not a pleasant smile. It was Mark's friend. The one they had thought friendly once, until they found out he and Mark were more than friends.

He strode forward into their camp, his golden hair glinting in the firelight. He squatted down and regarded them levelly. He was the weakest, the least offensive of them, but he was still one of them. Once upon a time, they had thought these things were invincible, could not be killed. The paladin taught them otherwise—taught them that with enough holes, they too would fall bleeding to the ground.

With this thought in mind, a pikeman spoke. "You are not welcome here anymore, Colton." There was a grumbling of agreement.

"Oh," Colton laughed. "But all I wanted was to

play a game."

"We want none of your games," another voice said.

"There are fifty of us, one of you," said another. All around the fire, hands were reaching discreetly for weapons: sheathed swords, or bludgeons.

"Don't you even want to know what the game's called?" Colton said.

Wearily, the pikeman humored him. "What's it called then?"

Daggers appeared in both his hands. "Who wants to die?" he said.

***

"You must come now!" Gavin's voice shouted at their tent flap. "Hurry!"

"What now?" Jordan groused as he rose.

"Now!" Gavin's voice said again, his tone rising. As soon as he saw Jordan coming, he set off at a rapid clip into the encampment. Mary had to run to catch up to the men.

"What's happened?" Jordan demanded.

"Ask Mary," Gavin said. "Though perhaps it would have been better if we'd listened to her in the first place."

"Deirdre's snapped again?" Jordan said.

"Worse. Colton."

Jordan stopped in his tracks. "Colton? But he's—"

"Fine?" Gavin said. "Come see for yourself."

They way was blocked by a shield wall of swordmen with their weapons drawn. "Make way," Gavin said savagely, and the soldiers fell back to make a path for them. Further down the path was another unit of soldiers, and they, too, had shields up and swords out. Gavin, Jordan, and Mary stood unarmed in the middle.

"This way," Gavin said with a gesture. Between two wagons, a side path opened into a large semi-private encampment. A fire blazed in the middle. Around the fire, it looked like a battle had been fought. The field was littered with dead.

There was a sound from within the pavilion and two men ran out. One stumbled and fell, a dagger sticking out of his back. The other darted sideways and disappeared behind the tent. Colton stepped out of the tent and retrieved the dagger from the fallen body.

"Whoo!" he yelled. Catching sight of them, he smiled broadly. "What an awesome night, Jordan!"

"What have you done?" Jordan spat out.

"Man," he went on, ignoring Jordan's question, "have you ever just cut loose, just said 'fuck it man, let's see what these souped-up bodies of ours are really capable of?' By all the empire, it's a rush." He shook his blond hair playfully.

"Stand down, Colton," Jordan barked.

Colton's eyes flashed. "No."

"That's an order," Jordan barked again.

"I'm done taking orders," Colton threw back.

Several of the other Juggernauts had arrived by then, and they hung back with Mary and Gavin, watching the proceedings with mute horror.

"You will drop those knives and stand here," Jordan growled, pointing at a spot right before him, "or so help me—"

"Or what?" Colton demanded. "What do you think you have to take from me?"

Jordan knelt and retrieved a sword from a fallen soldier, "This ends. You either stand down this second or face me."

"You would kill me?" Colton's mouth spat the words out defiantly, but his eyes were pleading.

"Do not make me do this, Brother," Jordan said.

Colton growled and leaped.

They sparred briefly, Jordan fending off the two daggers easily. He broke Colton's defense and stepped in, hammering him with his left hand. The blow knocked Colton off his feet.

Jordan had only a split second to relax, to think he had stopped the fight, before Colton rolled and was back on his feet. They spared again and this time Jordan hit Colton heavily on his back with the pummel of the sword. It rocked Colton, but he spun and caught Jordan with a long, wicked cut across one arm.

He's not good enough to beat Jordan, Mary thought, *but he's too good to be disarmed or knocked unconscious.* Jordan seemed to realize this too. His face hardened. "Don't," he croaked.

Before he could get the rest out, Colton was on him again, knives flashing, almost too fast to see. Jordan fell back three measured steps, blocking the onslaught, and then he stopped.

Colton was standing stock still, staring at Jordan and down at the sword protruding from his chest. A look of relief spread across his face. "I didn't think you had it in you, Brother," he whispered. When he opened his mouth to speak again, blood came out. He fell to his knees.

Mary rushed forward, placing her hand on Jordan's and gently prying his grip off the sword. Colton hit the ground. Jordan's face was blank.

"Come," she said pulling him. He stood still.

"I must see to—" he began.

"No," she said softly, "let others take care of this, come."

He looked at Gavin and Shamus. "We've got it handled," Gavin said, "go."

He followed her meekly to their tent. Standing in the center, he shook his head and seemed to come to himself. "What did I do?" he asked.

"You did what you had to," she answered.

He fell to his knees and began to sob uncontrollably. "He was my brother, he was my brother."

Mary stood and held him, holding him close and brushing his hair with her fingers.

After what seemed like a long time, Gavin appeared. "It's been attended to," he said curtly. "Any idea why?"

Jordan stiffened in her arms.

"No, no idea," she answered quickly.

"Just a couple days ago—" Gavin began.

"A premonition," she replied, "instinct. I knew something was wrong."

He looked at her sharply then shrugged.

***

"Twenty-seven men!" The general was fuming when Mary entered the main pavilion the next morning. "Twenty-seven!"

"He went crazy or something," Shamus said trying to placate the general. "We had no idea that was even possible."

"It's like a battlefield in that camp," the general raged on. "There must be punishment."

"He's dead," Gavin said coolly, "is that not punishment enough?"

The general rounded on Shamus. "You're men are out of control! This has to stop. I am warning you!"

"My men," Shamus said stiffly, "have saved you far more than twenty-seven lives in each and every battle we have fought. Hell, Colton saved more lives than that at the ambush alone. He must have taken out fifty men by himself. Your army would have been butchered that night if we hadn't been there." He puffed his chest out. Mary thought about how he had looked that night, clinging close by the fire, far away from the fighting.

"They are valiant in battle," the general said. "I'll give them that, but they're terrors off the field. My men can't stand them: can't stand marching with them or having them walk the camps at night. They're terrified. And what am I supposed to tell them? Don't worry? Should I tell them, 'they've saved lives in battle, so if they kill a few of you off the field, it's okay'?"

"Tell them whatever you wish," Shamus said.

"You must take some responsibility as well," the general fumed. "I will not have this in my command."

"Then perhaps we should leave all together," Gavin put in, "as I've been advocating for some time. You've enough men at your command to finish this war on your own, and you won't have to deal with us anymore."

For a moment, Mary thought Shamus and the general were considering Gavin's words. She could imagine returning to the manor with Jordan, and him demanding his freedom. A long, slow recovery: a chance to heal the psychic wounds, a chance for them to be together. A chance for him to be a human and not an unstoppable killing machine.

"Your contract stipulates—" the general began.

"We stay until the end of the conflict," Shamus finished, "of course. We are not breaking our contract." To Mary, he said, "How is Jordan this morning?"

"He sleeps yet," Mary said, "I was going to get breakfast before I woke him. It was a long night."

Shamus sighed and betrayed a solitary look of grief. "Aye," he agreed, "it was."

17 CALLED NORTH

Colton did not have a military funeral like the others. This was a small private affair between the Juggernauts. In fact, while they were on the beach burning the body, the rest of the army had a much larger funeral for their fallen comrades.

Everywhere, there were looks of hostility and anger. If it were not for the fear that the Juggernauts inspired, it may have gone beyond looks. They stuck close together and no one left the private encampment. Even the aides and servants who worked for the Juggernauts, who had no choice in the matter, were being harassed.

The general sent an aide to tell them they would march in the morning. He felt it was best for all that they leave this place as quickly as possible. Besides, the end was now in sight. They would march on the last city and then turn north where the hobblers still had the remnants of the baron's men under siege at the city of Germain.

In the morning, no teamsters arrived to tear down camp nor did any order to march come. A few of the men, made jumpy and paranoid by the events of the last few days, suggested the army meant to desert them. Gavin pointed out that the rest of the army had not moved either.

It was Mary who got the gossip first this time. One of the camp followers told her a rider had come in the night. The general had sent away his usual companion and ordered most of his petty officers woken. They had spent the rest of the night in consultation.

It was near to nightfall that they finally were given direct word of what was going on. An aide arrived, the general making a point by his absence, to tell them they would now march on the next morning.

"Word has come," the aide told them, "that Gregory yet lives. He is well enough to travel and fight, but he commands only a small force. They have thrice tested the roads, and we have held them back, keeping them in Germain." The men started and made angry noises at the mention of Gregory's name.

"It's his fault," one of the Juggernauts hissed. "Before him we were whole, we had not lost a one. But for him, none of this would have happened."

"Worse still," the aide continued, "the baron has raised a new force, mostly mercenaries. It's small. They are demanding high wages to serve the baron these days, and he has little choice but to agree. This force is no threat to us, even without the Juggernauts."

"Then why concern yourselves at all?"

"Because, if this force manages to reach Gregory and his remaining knights, they will combine to have a force that *can* threaten us. It has become imperative that Gregory be defeated and killed before this happen."

"So now we must change direction and march north?" Shamus said.

"Indeed, we will taking the northern road, marching hard. We leave by sun up tomorrow."

"This is fate," Jordan said as the aide left. "This is fate."

"What is fate?" Mary asked.

"Before we faced the paladin, we had never lost a man," he said.

There were nods of approval from around the room. "Last year he killed one of ours. Then three more. Since then what has become of us?"

"Hammond," Formist said, "dead."

"Colton," Jordan said, "fairest of us all, dead."

"This will not end," Deirdre said, "till we face him again, and kill him."

There were nods and muttered agreement.

Gavin rolled his eyes. "Superstitious nonsense," he said. "The paladin got lucky last year."

"And this year?" someone asked. "How do you explain that? Was that luck too?"

"Luck favors the quick witted," Gavin said. "He got lucky last year, and we underestimated him. He saw what he did by chance, and repeated it on purpose. We," he shot a disapproving look at Shamus as he said it, "should have seen what Traimon's death revealed, as the paladin did. We should have been more wary of men on horseback."

"And Hammond? Was that an oversight too?" Shamus asked archly.

"Perhaps," Gavin said coolly. "Perhaps the druids'

fighting style needs to be incorporated in the training regime, if we can find a teacher."

"What of Colton? Was that not ill fate?" someone asked.

"Colton should not have gone crazy," Gavin snapped and stormed out of the room.

***

"Jordan, we need you." Shamus's voice was flat, holding no hint of urgency.

Jordan rose obediently and followed him, Mary on his tail. The sky was still black, but red lit the eastern horizon. She saw teamsters stumbling wearily from tents. Soon they would be breaking camp while the men began their march northward.

They moved quietly through the bustle of rising men and made their way to the southernmost edge of the camp. There they came to a grove of trees by the river.

"What am I to be seeing?" Jordan inquired.

Mutely, Mary touched his elbow and pointed.

It was Hunter, the first Juggernaut she had healed, what seemed like an eternity ago now. The one that delighted in hurting, because the world had hurt him. She hadn't understood then.

They watched the body sway in the breeze, silent. Finally, Shamus spoke, "Any idea why?"

Jordan shook his head. "He said nothing to me."

"Maybe he said something to one of the men," Shamus said.

"I will ask, but I think they would have come to me, or to Gavin."

"He said nothing," Mary said.

"How can you be sure?" Shamus said.

"Because he did it," she replied. "Those that talk,

want to be stopped. Those that are serious, don't talk."

"So what do we do about the body?" Shamus asked. "I don't think the general will brook any delays."

"We leave it," Jordan said.

"But," Mary said.

"This is a dishonorable thing," Jordan said, interrupting her. "We cannot honor it." He turned and stalked off before she could say anything more.

"He's right," Shamus commented and left.

Mary turned to look at the body one last time. She saw a piece of parchment tied to a nearby tree limb. It fluttered in the breeze. She held it still and read. "I am sorry, Colton." She let it go and turned back toward the camp.

***

The march north passed quickly. It was now the third time Mary had crisscrossed the valley, and she was starting to recognize sights.

The first four days, the general took a huge gamble and had the armor and most of the weapons put on carts and hauled. It meant the men marched unarmed in crude flax garments, but it also meant they could cover nearly twice as many miles.

After that, the fear of an ambush outweighed that option. He still pushed the army hard. They passed Thrain's Road early on the fifth day. Mary saw her orchard in the distance.

"Your doing? Or the druids?" Gavin commented casually as they passed. Mary did not answer.

She spoke little throughout the trip. She felt surrounded by so much sorrow, and so little of it could be expressed. Jordan seemed possessed by it too, and when they were alone together, they hardly spoke. She could not reconcile the gentle man he was when they were together with the killer he was on the battlefield. She knew she would never be able to reconcile that those two men were one and the same, and she knew the one she loved would be ripped from her all too quickly.

The rest of the Juggernauts were barely holding it together. They were surly and tense. Someone had to be assigned to watch over Deirdre because his behavior was becoming more erratic and irrational. Mary worried constantly that Jordan would be forced to kill him one day, and she didn't think he could bear it. Formist was almost constantly drunk.

They had all become convinced that if they could face down and kill Gregory once and for all, things would return to normal for them. They muttered about it over meals and swore solemn oaths to see it fulfilled over drinks.

It drove Gavin nuts. Shamus encouraged the idea, thinking it was drawing the men together, helping them become a unified fighting force once again. He and Gavin fought about it frequently.

"You must put a stop to this madness," Gavin raged one evening.

"Must I?" Shamus retorted.

"A man on foot cannot match a man on horse, not one to one, not in a charge," Gavin said, "No matter who that man is."

"So?"

"So," Gavin went on, "they must use strategy. We must lure the paladin and his knights into a charge, then retreat behind the pike line. That's the only way to bring them down."

"And we shall bring them down," Shamus said.

"Not if they have it in their heads that this is some sort of personal vendetta," Gavin yelled. "They'll lose their heads and try to stand a charge. And we will lose men again."

"They will not. They will follow orders exactly. And this time, the general is listening to our strategy. We will not fail again."

Indeed, the general was listening. After only a couple of days of sending aides and petty officers in his stead, it became too cumbersome. Regardless of what message it sent, the general once again began coming in person to their camp almost every night. Shamus and he poured over reports and maps, plotting strategies for the upcoming battle.

**

The army came to a halt at the base of a long, rolling hill about five miles from the city of Germain. Camp itself was set on the southern base of the hill, but the command center was established at the top of the hill. The general believed that Gregory would have no choice but to ride out and meet them. It was his only chance to use his knights with any effectiveness against the Juggernauts.

The Juggernauts and a contingent of swordmen would be the bait, luring the knights into attack. The balance of the general's men, particularly the pike and spearmen, would be hidden behind the hill, to roll out in a pincer movement against the knights. Shamus and the general played the plan out over and over in their heads and on maps.

They had not camped a day when word came that Gregory was, indeed, on the move, with a far larger force than anticipated.

"The peasants have sided with him," the general spat. "And they have traveled off the roads, by secret ways. We were not aware they had encamped in his city."

"They are peasants," Shamus replied lightly. "Once we have dispatched the paladin, we will set the Juggernauts to work on them. They will not stand long against my men."

Mary turned away and fled toward the tent she shared with Jordan.

"You are upset?" Jordan asked as he followed her in.

"Yes," she admitted. "We must go. We must sneak out tonight and flee this place. Please."

He grabbed her and thumbed her necklace. "You cannot go, my love," he said softly. "Nor can I."

"You do not understand," she said again. "We must."

"I do understand," he replied sharply. "But we cannot. I dare not speak directly to Shamus, but I have spoken to Gavin. I swore him first to secrecy and I made him swear."

"Swear what?"

"That when I am gone, he should use every drop of money owed to me to secure your release. If he can pay off Shamus, so be it. If not, there are counter charms, for a price," Jordan said. "You will be safe. If there's anything left after that, it's yours."

"What are you talking about?" she said.

"Don't play coy," he said. "I have shared your dreams often enough. I know this field of battle." She had seen through his eyes, him looking up at her as he lay dying on a field of battle. And he had seen it too.

"It doesn't have to be," she whispered, "if we leave

now . . ."

"I cannot leave now," he said. "Our contract."

"Damn your contract."

"And my brothers," he said, "shall I damn them too?"

"No," she whispered.

"Besides, I am soldier. What am I to do? I have seen enough of your life in Tomlin to know I have no place there, no matter how much you might want me there."

"You can learn a trade," she said. "Become something other than a soldier."

"Can I wipe the stains of blood from my hands?" he said. "It's not as easy as you might think, Mary." He stopped and wrapped his arms around her. "Please, let's not spoil this night with fighting."

She nodded wordlessly.

***

This was the third major battle Mary was to witness, the third long, sleepless night of nerves. It was by far the worst. When Jordan was awake, they clung to each other, desperate in their lovemaking. When he slept—and it was astonishing to her that he could sleep—she paced the tent. She was not able to settle into meditation, no matter how she tried.

And she needed to. She needed to solve the puzzle of her necklace. She had grown complacent. She should have spent every night since her capture trying to find a way to break that enchantment and free herself. If she could, they could leave. She could help the entire group, if that's what Jordan wanted. She could take them somewhere safe, help them heal.

But she couldn't break the charm. Even if she could, he would not leave, not without his men. And most of them didn't want to leave; they didn't want to give up the killing, or being better than everyone else around them. They would go right on killing until they either went crazy or got themselves killed.

At times, her anxiety became so intense it was physically painful. She would fall to the ground and heave huge, racking sobs. She feared she was going mad.

18 THE FINAL BATTLE

Mary felt surprisingly calm when the aides arrived to help Jordan into his chainmail. He stood passively while they tied the stays and attached the bracers and knee guards. When he was fully suited, he asked the aides to leave.

"I would say I love you," he said, "but you already know that. I would say I'm sorry, but I hope you know that too. I don't know what I can tell you, so I'll tell you the truth."

"Yes?"

"I knew about Colton." He shrugged. "How could I not? We were twenty-one boys living in this giant manor by ourselves. As kids, we did stuff. Kid stuff."

"You and Colton?"

"Most of us, at one time or another. Nothing serious: pleasing each other or touching. But Colton was always there, at the center of it. You knew if those sorts of games were going on, you'd find him."

"As we grew older and as they grew aware of what

we did, they added women to our little world." He sighed. "For the rest, it was the easiest lesson learned. Only Colton never grew out of it. I wish it was like you said: that it was just the way some are born and no fault to them. In my world, it's not so. For that too, I am sorry." With that, he was gone.

Mary headed for the flap, intent on finding Gavin and seeing where they would watch this battle. She was met by Shamus, flanked by two guards carrying crossbows. She backed into the tent.

"I have grown increasingly concerned about you, Mary," he said, "and about my men."

"I will be okay after this battle," she said.

"I think you misunderstand my concern," he growled. "You have divided the loyalties of my men. You have, on more than one occasion that I am aware of, performed magic without my approval. And I cannot help but to think that I will find you at the root of many of the problems we have had on this campaign."

"But I—" Mary started.

"Deny it all you want," Shamus said. "But the more you heal my men, the more you work your insidious magic around them, the more unstable they become. Tell me this is a coincidence."

She stopped and sat on the bed. It was true, she realized with a jolt, but not in the way he implied. She understood why the principles and the mages who had conceived this experiment used Gavin as their healer. His methods were effective but mechanical. He healed the men, but kept them in the soldier's mindset. Mary's healing was more holistic—the magic tried to heal both their bodies and spirits. The men could not reconcile their role as an elite killing squad and their base humanity any more than she could.

"It can't work," she said suddenly. "It just can't. Don't you see it? You can't turn boys, men, into machines. Sooner or later, they have to reconcile who they are, what they do. These Juggernauts will never be able to do that successfully. In the end they'll all either go mad or give in, like Hunter did. It wouldn't matter if I were here or not."

"It can work. It does work. We've trained this group successfully for many years. It was working," he said.

"No, it wasn't," she replied. "It was falling apart before I got here. You just hadn't seen the results yet."

He slapped her, a stinging slap that knocked her down on the bed. "I don't believe you," he snarled. "I believe you are screwing with my men. I don't dare kill you, as much as I would love to, because Jordan would have a fit. But you will stay out of the way this time. And we will see. We will see my men win this battle. And then I'll have my proof. Then even he'll have to see.

"Guards," he said, "watch her. If she so much as blinks, kill her." He stormed out.

Tears welled up in her eyes. Jordan was out there, going to die, and she couldn't see him, couldn't intervene. If by some miracle he survived, it would be proof in Shamus's mind of Mary's treachery, and she would die. And suddenly ever miscarriage of justice, every brutality and every sorrow she had witnessed was rushing on her. She saw the cross-dressed refugee. She saw a dirty peasant girl staring up at the body of her father, his quick death kinder than the starvation she must face. She saw Colton on the end of Jordan's sword. She saw the boy that looked like Martin, empty eyes staring up at nothing.

The first moan left her in a high-pitched whine. She took a deep breath and let go into the madness that was overwhelming her. Then came the scream, a deep, whole-body noise with no rationality behind it. Somewhere in the middle of that scream, she felt a tightness at her throat snap and give way.

***

Jordan stood with his men in the front line, waiting for the horns to signal the first charge. He drew his sword and began to beat on his shield rhythmically.

Something was wrong. He was afraid. He'd never been afraid before.

He wasn't afraid of the men gathered opposite him, nor was he afraid of death. If years of practice and numerous battles hadn't taught him that these soldiers were no threat to him, he had only to think of Colton. Colton, who had tried to kill himself by picking a fight with over fifty men. Colton, who had failed, because even in suicide his instincts were too sharp for him to be killed so easily. It had taken a fellow Juggernaut to do that.

Nor was he afraid of death. He had inflicted it on hundreds of men . . . why should he be any different? *But he had never* felt *it before.*

That was what had him unnerved, a feeling. He had learned, long ago, before they had even been in battles, back in the treatment room as a boy, not to feel. He had learned that when the pain started, the adrenaline flowed and the action began, he could shut it off. He could escape somewhere in his mind and feel nothing. A calm sense of peace would descend over him about now, and he would see the whole battle as though someone else were living it. His training and his instincts carried him easily through.

Then she came, the one who walked in his heart. He loved her. That had been his downfall, if only he had realized it sooner. He loved her, and love was a feeling. It was an all or nothing thing. You had feelings or you did not have feelings. There was no in between, no picking and choosing.

So he loved her. And loving her, he would go into battle with feelings. In a few moments, he would rush into battle. He would smash his sword into another man's head, and he would *feel* it give way. He would *feel* the blood splatter against his helmet and shield. How would he return from that and look her in the face? Could he bear it?

He shook his head. It was pointless to wonder because he knew, deep down inside, that he was not going back. Even if she had not had a premonition, this battle had a weird sense of finality to it. *So let it end,* he thought.

"This is it, men!" he screamed. "Today we redeem ourselves." The men cheered. As the horns blared and the charge began, Jordan added to himself, "For Colton."

They were not halfway across the space when the enemy line halted. Jordan could feel the tramp of hooves.

"We can take them!" Formist was screaming. "We can take them!"

"And we shall," Jordan replied.

***

"What the hell am I supposed to do now?" The general was shouting, jumping up and down.

"They seem to be getting their sea legs, as it were,"

Shamus commented.

"Indeed," Gavin said. "They've lost only one man, Jerad, I think. And they've repelled the knights twice so far."

"I don't care," the general raged. "This is not according to the battle plan."

Horns blew, and Gregory's spearmen charged. "Now what is he up to?" Shamus groused. "He's got to know they'll tear through them like nothing."

Gregory did. The Juggernauts cut easily through the line. Behind the lines, and away from support, Gregory's cavalry crashed into them. Several went down, and two did not rise.

"Damn it," Shamus growled. "They must be more careful."

"We've another problem," an aide squawked nearby, pointing. The horns were blowing the retreat from both sides, and a gap was widening between the armies. In the middle, a tall chainmailed figure was running, attacking friend and foe alike.

"Deirdre," Gavin said. The rest of the Juggernauts were still caught up in the melee as the enemy, too, tried to recross the line to their own side. They seemed unaware that Deirdre had defected.

"He's attacking my men!" the general raged. "What are we going to do?"

"I have told you many times, these Juggernauts are far more valuable than any of your—" Shamus started irritably.

Gavin cut him off, "He's gone mad again. Kill him."

Both men looked at the healer sharply.

"He's a lost cause. It was nothing short of a miracle that Mary brought him back last time. He's dangerously insane now. Kill him, and quickly."

Shamus's face went beet red, and he sputtered at Gavin, who met his gaze evenly. The general merely gave a curt nod to one of the aides.

"An unfortunate part of my job as healer," Gavin was saying, "is to recognize when an injury is too severe and to end the life humanely." Shamus didn't answer.

On the field, archers were gathering. The aide waved a flag and a volley of arrows fell into the widening gap, catching the figure on his unprotected right side.

Deirdre wheeled, three arrows protruding from him at odd angles and began to stalk toward the archers. Four petty officers armed with crossbows stood in his path.

Two bolts buried themselves in Deirdre's shield ineffectually and one went wide. The fourth shattered the brace on his thigh and buried itself in his knee. He staggered but didn't fall. When he began his march again, it was slower, with a decided limp. Pikemen were circling him, using their pikes to keep him at bay. He disappeared into a circle of blades.

Horns blared again as Gregory's knights took to the field. Only the Juggernauts remained to face them down.

"Now!" the general screamed. "Now, we have them! Signal the reserves, bring them around." Aides were waving signal flags and shouting orders. The general stared expectantly.

"I think we have a much bigger problem," Gavin said from behind him.

"Where are the reserves?" the general sputtered. When no one answered, he tore his eyes from the field of battle. Looking back over the hill at what remained of his camp, the clash as the knights and the Juggernauts hit was driven from his mind.

It looked as though several small tornadoes had ripped through the camp, uprooting tents and carts. Directly beneath them, a group of teamsters brawled, their faces filled with blind rage. On his right, the pikemen of an entire regiment had dropped their weapons and were standing arm in arm, swaying slightly, as their captain led them in a song. The regiment on left had fled.

"What madness is this?" he asked.

As if in answer, something came flying out of the camp. Gavin reached out a hand and caught it deftly. He opened his palm. It was Mary's necklace.

"Uh-oh," Shamus said quietly.

19 PEACE

The three men picked their way through the remains of the camp. The general had left only one quick order, "Hold the line the best you can."

Each section of the camp had been affected differently. In some areas, it was mostly physical: tents upbraided, carts overturned. In many areas, it was the people who were affected; in one area, they raged at each other incoherently. In some places, they gathered around fires, oblivious to the battle, drank, and clung to each other. In other places, they hid, quaking with unnamed fears.

The Juggernauts' private encampment was the eye of the storm and complete peace reigned within. The guards now stood in front of Jordan's tent, holding their crossbows like they were religious relics rather than weapons. Their eyes were closed and their faces serene.

"Has she gone mad?" the general wondered.

"There are two kinds of madness," one of the

guards intoned.

"There is the madness that breaks you apart," the other said.

"And the madness that breaks you open," the first replied.

Timidly the men entered the tent.

Mary was seated on Jordan's trunk like it was a dais. Her hands were held up in a sign of blessing and her form glowed faintly.

"Mary?" Gavin started hesitantly. "Jordan's in trouble. I can't save him without your help."

Mary's eyes came open. "Sorrow leads to compassion," she said, her eyes distant, as though she didn't see them. "Compassion for all living beings." Then her eyes sharpened and darted toward the three of them. "Except you," she snarled.

She made a motion, as if flicking a fly. The general was thrown in the air as if tossed like a rag doll. He flew end over end, out of sight.

The remaining two men shared a nervous glance, and Shamus licked his dry lips. "Mary, we need you to save Jordan. He'll die if we don't stop this battle somehow."

She focused her eyes on them. Shamus winced. Then she vanished.

***

Jordan rose and shook himself heavily. His shield was shattered beyond usefulness, and he tossed it aside. He inspected his sword briefly. The tip was broken and blood ran down the length of it, but it was still long enough to be an effective weapon.

His men were rising, gathering around him in an ever smaller clump. There were maybe six of them left on their feet. Five cavalry charges they had faced down, knocked off their feet and overrun, while the rest of the army fought a purely defensive battle.

Ahead of him, another group of knights was preparing for a charge.

"To me!" Jordan cried hoarsely holding his sword aloft. "For Colton!" He raged and ran at the knights.

***

Justin hefted his lance as he watched the men rise and regroup. Even after all he had heard and seen of these Juggernauts, it was incredible to see them in action. Between his group of knights and Gregory's, they had run them over five times. They had literally run them over, several hundred pounds of man and warhorse hitting them full speed. And time and again, they rose. Unless they managed to drive a lance or spear directly into a vital organ, these men rose and kept fighting.

So be it, he thought. *I'll just have to hit squarely.*

The horn blared, and he spurred his horse forward, aiming for the leader of Juggernauts. He hit the man square in the chest and drove him to the ground. He was nearly unseated by the force as his lance bent and snapped beneath him.

He dropped the broken lance and grabbed for the pummel, willing himself to stay in the saddle. A squire broke ranks and rode out holding a new lance. At the end of his run, he took the lance and turned, looking back at the battlefield. A few footmen still fought here and there, but for the most part, both armies had stopped and were watching the drama unfold between them.

One lone Juggernaut was on his feet, and Justin could see it was not the leader. He scanned the ground for the fallen form. Suddenly, Mary was there.

He would recognize her slight form and coppery-red hair anywhere. He shook his head. He had not seen her approach, nor did she seem to be moving. It was as though she had just appeared there.

His eyes sought the far end of the battlefield. He could see Gregory and his men. The paladin raised a hand, indicating they should pause.

***

Mary was filled with a sense of deja vu as she stared down at Jordan. The lance had struck almost exactly on his scar, the wound that Mary had once healed. It had been driven through his body, pinning him to the ground.

He looked up at her, his mouth making ineffectual movements. The look on his face was not of pain or fear; it was relief. His eyes began to go unfocused. She looked at the bodies arrayed around him. How many years had he protected them? How many years had he held the band together, always the leader, always the responsible one? It must have been a heavy burden.

She saw, with eyes and senses that filled rapidly with new powers, that she could reach out and draw his life force back. She could heal even this—bring him back from the dead. A selfish part of her mind said, *do it*.

She could not. He had found relief: freedom from the pain they had inflicted on him, release from the responsibilities he had voluntarily taken, and some sort of insane redemption for the killing. She could not take those things from him. Tears filled her eyes.

She looked up. On either side, knights in armor sat on horseback, waiting for the command to charge. Behind her, groups of foot soldiers still fought.

"This will stop now!" she yelled. Her voice,

magically amplified, carried to every corner of the field. The men stopped and stared.

The one remaining Juggernaut, Formist, glared at her. "You will not order this," he said. "You cannot tell me what to do." He raised his sword.

He froze and was lifted off the ground. He hung suspended in midair. Mary regarded him coolly, looking at the shattered remnants of his mind. "I am sorry, Brother," she said quietly, but somehow everyone could hear it. "You are damaged beyond anyone's ability to repair." She reached out with her mind and snapped his neck. He fell to the ground and crumpled in front of her.

She turned toward the rest of the men, now frozen. "I said this will stop." Obediently, they began to back away from each other. Justin moved forward, his gait slow and his lance high. He would bring Mary home, away from her captors. But as suddenly as she had appeared, she vanished again. He stopped short and stared at the place she had been.

***

Three trunks lay open in the tent. Gavin was going through one, throwing clothes and other items behind him. Shamus sat on the cot and watched anxiously. "It's gotta be there," Shamus said distractedly.

Gavin growled, "If you kept your stuff better organized . . ."

"I didn't think we'd need it in a hurry."

"You didn't think, period," Gavin snapped.

"It's in there somewhere, I swear," Shamus said.

More clothes went flying as Gavin completely emptied the trunk. He overturned it and then kicked it savagely. "Well, it's not in this one. Why don't you start on that one, while I work over here," he suggested.

"Looking for something?" Mary inquired quietly. The men jumped.

She was standing at the back of the tent. Shamus's eyes glanced toward the entrance and back to Mary.

"Don't be a fool," Gavin groused. "She's learned to jump magically."

"When I first arrived," Mary said, ignoring Gavin's comment, "I discovered the locals had this odd superstition about a magic user needing his wand." She held a rod of wood in her hands. It was about a foot and half long. One end was a smooth handle, the other side was ringed in wooden gears carved with symbols, the gears could be moved like a combination lock to form different symbol sets. "At first, I wondered about that. Then I realized that would be true if the individual in question was not a true magic user, but merely had an enchanted object."

Gavin sighed and sat down on a trunk.

"This allows you to travel, right?" Mary said, holding out the wand. "It takes you back to your base? Different symbol sets take you different places?"

Gavin nodded.

"Remember, Mary," Shamus interjected desperately, his eyes darting around, "that when we captured you, we did not kill you."

"You put a choker on me," she snarled, "and threatened more than once to kill me. You would have had me gang raped by your men. Now you would beg for mercy?" He fell silent.

Shamus stiffened suddenly, grabbing at his throat. "Know this," she said. "I don't need a necklace to choke you. And I don't need an enchantment to track you down and kill you." He sank suddenly as the pressure was released. "But I do have a use for you, both of you, alive."

Gavin nodded and relaxed slightly. "What would you have us do?"

"For now? Find the highest ranking captain yet living and tell them to be prepared to parlay this evening. You two will be there as well."

When they looked up, she was gone.

***

"For my part, I would be glad to negotiate an end to hostilities," Captain Ivarice was saying from one side of the small wooden table, "but I simply do not have the authority to speak on the duke's behalf in this manner."

"As would I," Gregory said from the far end of the table, "but I too lack the authority to grant more than a short-term truce."

"I suggest then," Harrod said from where he sat behind Gregory, "that we await Mary's return."

"I agree," said Gavin from the far corner of the tent. Mary had appeared briefly in Gregory's camp to tell him he must set a tent in between the armies and to be prepared to parlay before disappearing again. She had not been seen the rest of the day. Now evening was fading into night, and there still had been no sign nor word from her.

***

Mary stood at the entrance to the tent. Next to her was a boy, maybe thirteen years old. He had brown hair, cut short, and he wore a simple tunic and leggings. She looked down and put an arm on the boy's shoulder. He looked scared and uncertain.

"What just happened?" he said.

She couldn't explain what she had done to come here, only that she did it. She closed her eyes, visualized who or what she wanted, and she was there. "We have traveled many miles by magic," she said. "Come, it is time."

They entered the tent together. Justin saw her first and dropped into a deep bow. "Mary, welcome," he said. "I am overjoyed to find you safe."

"As am I," Gregory said, bowing as well.

Mary regarded them. She had always liked Justin, but she could not quite forget that he had delivered the killing blow to Jordan. Gregory too was a good man, but a career soldier who had killed countless people in his day. Mary was tired of making accommodations for men such as him.

So she didn't. She waved Gregory away from his seat, and he obediently stepped aside. With a gesture, she made the boy sit. With another gesture, she unseated Captain Ivarice and took his place. She sat the wooden rod on the table.

"Shamus," she said. After a moment's hesitation, he came forward. "This boy," she told him, "is James. He is the youngest and only surviving son of the former sheriff of the valley. As such, he inherits the title, correct?"

"Yes, ma'am," Shamus replied promptly.

She handed the rod to Shamus. "You will take the boy into your care," she said. "You will take him to one of the central worlds. You will find the highest ranked, most petty and possessive noble you know, one who will not let even the smallest holding, no matter how distant, leave his grasp. You will take the boy to that noble and have him swear fealty. Do you understand?"

He smiled slyly. "Aye."

"For this service, I will grant you your life. When this service is rendered, you will return here with the boy. You will bring such gold and resources as needed to rebuild every city and every village this war has destroyed. For that service, I will grant you your freedom. Understood?"

"Aye," he said again.

"A clever solution," Captain Ivarice said. "Neither the duke nor the baron will dare challenge the boy's authority, if it comes from someone much higher than them."

Gregory stood, drew his sword and then laid it upon the table. "Still, there will be many things that will need seen to, and the boy is young. I offer my sword and service, till he reaches manhood."

Harrod laid his staff upon the table. "And I, my advice."

James looked at Mary, who nodded slightly. "I accept," he said, relief plain in his voice.

"Gavin," Mary said.

"Yes," Gavin replied.

"I have but one task for you, but it shall not be easy."

"I am ready," he said.

"You will go to the principles. You must make them see this experiment was a failure."

"That should not be hard," he said.

"They must understand why," she said sharply. "They must understand that men cannot be raised or treated this way. They must not think, if only we change this, or that, it will work. They must understand that the whole concept is flawed. People cannot be made into machines."

"The principles care little for ethics or emotions," he cautioned.

"Then you must use logic," she replied. "You must convince them that no matter what happened here, the experiment would have failed anyway."

"Yes," he said, "I can see that now. They would have gone mad, sooner or later. I will do all that I can."

Mary walked off into the darkening night. She left the men to discuss the boy's fate and the future of valley. She was tired and ready to go home.

On a nearby hilltop, they waited for her, as she knew they would. When she caught sight of them, she began to cry, and to run. She ran first for Ashe, whose arms opened to receive her.

After a time she turned and hugged Larsa as well.

"We are delighted to see you have come through your ordeal so well," Ashe said.

"Was it really necessary?" she said. "Must I know this? Must I deal with wars and killing?"

"Oh yes," Larsa replied sadly. "What happened here in this valley is but a taste of what is to come."

She looked at him sharply.

"You have time, Mary," he said. "These people's lives will come and go in peace, but *we* will live to see a time of great chaos."

"That time has been delayed, thanks to you." Ashe put in. "Those called the principles will not try to breed super soldiers again. Without them, they will not risk challenging the status quo. But there are other players and other plots."

"There will be time, though, for them?" she said looking out at the valley.

"You cannot save them all, Mary," Larsa chided.

"But I can save some," she replied. She reached out with her mind for the life force of the earth. It answered her with a single deep pulse. She turned back to them.

"I am ready to go," she said.

"What will you do now?" Larsa asked. "Now that you have come into your full power?"

"I will face my past," she replied. "Then, in time, I will let it go."

"Good answer," he said. They turned, and all three disappeared.

***

The locals called it the mage's autumn, when the weather stayed fine until late in the season and the fall crops grew so abundantly that it filled everyone's larder with enough for the winter and more. During the cool, clear nights that would accompany such seasons, they would tell stories of a coppery-headed girl that had walked the valley once, a girl with powers they could hardly imagine.

EPILOGUE

A child of maybe ten stood on the small hill at the edge of Draadustin, staring down at the low buildings of the city and across the river at the green town of Tomlin. The child wore burlap brown pants and a shapeless shirt with hair that had been butchered short as though sawed off with a knife. There was a quiet sound as someone approached, and the child turned quickly and stared at the woman standing there.

She wasn't much taller than the child. She had coppery-red hair worn long and loose. She wore a simple dress and sandals on her feet. She stared out at the city below them.

"It's beautiful," she said. The child snorted. Nobody described Draadustin as beautiful, unless they were mad. Perhaps she was; why else would she be out here on the desert's edge? It was said that there were bandits out there, though the child was beginning to suspect this was only a story told to keep kids from wandering too far. Bandits lived by stealing, and no one on this end of town had anything worth stealing.

"You are an orphan," the woman said turning her attention to the child, who shrugged. "You live in an abandoned building just there," she pointed, "and you look after four other kids, all younger than you."

The child watched her cautiously now. She could not know this. They were always careful of their surroundings, and they had not seen this woman watching them before. The child would have noticed.

"You do not wish to go to an orphanage?" she asked.

"And fight with a hundred other kids for scraps? No thanks," the child replied defiantly.

"Instead you fight with rats," she replied.

"If the rats wish to fight," the child gestured savagely with a stick, "Then that's a meal right there."

The woman chuckled. "You are brave and self-reliant."

"What of it?"

The woman looked away and then changed tactics. "Your grandmother was named Dryad." The child shrugged, curious how the woman knew that, yet afraid of anyone who knew so much. "Your father was named Martin, after a boy she took care of in the orphanage. And you," the child tensed, as though waiting for a blow. The woman, however, stopped, regarding the child with a look that said she everything. "It was a mistake," she said quietly. "The midwife didn't know, couldn't know, what was truly in your heart. She could only see your body."

The child looked up, wanting to believe the woman understood, but afraid.

"What do you wish to be called?" The woman asked.

Testing the woman's understanding, the child said, "Mark."

"Well, Mark," the woman said. "I am Mary."

"You want me to go to an orphanage?" Mark asked.

"No," Mary replied, "I want you to help me build one. But more than an orphanage. A place where kids are not just fed and housed, but educated. A place where they can learn to be anything."

"Anything?"

"Yes. Even that."

"That's not possible," Mark said.

Mary took the stick from his hands and drove it into the sandy soil of the hill. It began to sprout leaves and limbs, growing into a small tree. She reached up and pulled a fig from the branches and handed it to the child. "Do not tell me what's possible," Mary commanded. She gestured for him to sit.

Under the shade of the tree, she drew in the sand with her finger and at times pointed down the hill. "The tower will go here," she said. "The school here, and the dormitory here."

"What is it you want me to do?" he asked.

"You will be my right-hand man," she said. "You will convince the street kids, the ones who do not trust the other orphanages, to come in, to take a chance."

***

Chase Marlin stared across the conference table at the two people before him. He closed his eyes and wondered briefly if this was his secretary's idea of a joke. Why had she scheduled this meeting? And in the conference hall of all places? It was a ludicrous request.

He opened his eyes again and looked at the young, redheaded girl and the dirty, urchin boy. He looked down at the table. The table had been painted with a map of the entire city of Draadustin on it—his city. He didn't own it, but as city administrator, he good as did.

He decided if this was a joke, he had best play along for the time being. "As to the land on the city's edge, why certainly, assuming you can show the necessary assurances, prove you have the wealth to pay for it, it's yours. The city can always use a little revenue. But as to buying streets? Explain that part again."

"We want every other avenue from here to here," the woman said, pointing first at the river's edge and then back to the desert.

"Every other avenue running from the river's edge and back? And then?"

"And then every third avenue running parallel to the river from here to here," she said.

"But they'll still be available to the public?"

"We're going to dig trenches," the boy put in. "To the river to make canals. But there will be walkways on either side and bridges for traffic."

He almost laughed in their faces, but just then a door opened and another man entered. Chase stopped and stared. He had seen Kenneth Fornell at state functions in Tomlin City, but the man had never come to Chase's city. Kenneth was the second son of one of Tomlin's wealthiest families. His brother was one of the city's top healers, his sister was head librarian at the university, and Kenneth himself was a distinguished civil engineer.

He came down the steps quickly. "Mary," he said, "when Markus informed me you were back, I was overjoyed, overjoyed." He swept the redhead into a hug. "When he told me what you had in mind . . ."

He turned and slapped the table. "I am so excited!" he said to Chase. "We will begin the trench works here," he said pointing at the map, "and work our way forward. Just think! Fresh water in every section of the city. What's more, with the depth you want for the cross canals, in a matter of years they'll be teaming with fish. The poorest urchin will be able to drop a fishing pole in and come out with supper."

He turned back to Mary. "And this is only the beginning," he said with a smile. "Once we start on the tower, the school, the dorms and the orphanage, this will rival anything your master has done."

"Then it's a good thing her master is not so vain as to be jealous," a voice said at Chase's side, and Chase turned to find himself face to face with the mage, Ashley La Margin, himself.

Chase fell heavily in his chair. He watched in stunned silence as the room slowly filled with people. There was the Lady Sharlene pumping his hand and insisting that the High Street Ladies Society simply must be allowed to fund at least one bridge, with a plaque of course, for the project. Tomlin's rich and elite, the ones who usually thumbed their noses at him, were suddenly eager to have some part in this massive reengineering of his city.

The clomp of a pair of boots caught his attention: something about the regularity of the stride and the sure grace of the walker commanded respect. The boots were the best dragonhide. The man's pants were black, his shirt a brilliant white. He wore a black vest with detailed embroidery work on it. His face was pinched and narrow, his hair black and curly.

He carried a brown leather wallet, tied shut with a leather band. He stopped directly in front of the table. Nobody greeted him, and he did not glance at the growing crowd.

"It seems that I recently became the executor of a soldier's estate," he said throwing the wallet on the table. "His dying wish was that his resources be used to aid this woman." His curt nod toward Mary was the closest thing to recognition that he gave.

Chase opened the wallet. Inside was a stack of parchment pieces, each containing the official seal of the banking guild, each stating in cursive script full assurance, and each worth more gold than Chase had seen in his life. He let out a low whistle. "That must have been one heck of a soldier," he said.

"One of a kind," the man answered. He turned and walked away.

R. J. Eliason

ABOUT THE AUTHOR

R. J. Eliason loves lushly built worlds of both fantasy and science fiction. She grew up on classic science fiction and fantasy writers ranging from Ray Bradbury, Isaac Asimov, Arthur C. Clarke, Marion Zimmer-Bradley, Ursula K. Le Guin and many more.

R. J. Eliason can be found online at her website rjeliason.com and on many social media sites under her given name Rachel Eliason. She is active on Twitter, Google plus, and Goodreads. Subscribe to her newsletter to get the latest updates and many special offers.

She also writes YA under her given name Rachel Eliason.

www.ingramcontent.com/pod-product-compliance
Lightning Source LLC
Chambersburg PA
CBHW051432260626
47162CB00001B/51